UNSICKER ROAD

WRACK AND RUIN
BOOK 3

OTTO SCHAFER

SOUND EYE PRESS

Copyright © 2025 by Otto Schafer

All rights reserved.

No part of this book may be reproduced in any form or by any electronic or mechanical means, including information storage and retrieval systems, without written permission from the author, except for the use of brief quotations in a book review.

All characters and events in this publication are fictitious and any resemblance to real persons, living or dead, is purely coincidental.

Published in 2025

ISBN 979-8-9907050-4-3 (hardback)
ISBN 979-8-9907050-3-6 (paperback)
ISBN 979-8-9907050-2-9 (ebook)

Cover design and illustrations by Rafido @99Designs
Editing by The Blue Garret

Sound Eye Press
www.ottoschafer.com

I'd like to dedicate this book to my search history.
You've been through a lot.
You've seen things—terrible, disturbing things.
And yet... no one's kicked in my door. Not yet.

Despite searches like:
"Would a shotgun blast to the abdomen cause someone to drop their intestines?"
"How much force does it take to break open an adult skull?"
"What handguns will remove limbs at close range?"

Thanks for not flagging me to the authorities.
I swear it's all in the name of fiction.
(Well... mostly.)

CONTENT WARNING

This book contains scenes of zombie mayhem, brain munching, and apocalyptic chaos. Reader discretion is advised for those with an aversion to the undead, excessive gore, and characters who make questionable survival decisions. Side effects may include sleepless nights, sudden urges to stockpile canned goods, and an irrational fear of rain. Proceed with caution, and remember: it's the third book in the series, so you should know by now no one is safe! And for heaven's sake, don't forget your umbrella—it's not just for staying dry anymore!

Unsicker (*adj.*)
[Scottish]
Uncertain. Unsafe. Unstable.
The road where survival is a question, and every step forward is a gamble.

CONTENTS

PART ONE
PUZZLES

1.	The Farmhouse	3
2.	Side Mission	9
3.	Irish Coffee	16
4.	Well-Fed	29
5.	Spilt Coffee	35
6.	The Need to Feed	46
7.	Benson's Secrets	56
8.	Something in Between	68
9.	What's in the Barn	73
10.	Silhouette	80
11.	We're All Ghosts Now	88
12.	That Came from the House!	98
13.	The Big Bad Wolf	103
14.	Fallen	110
15.	The Amalgamation of Tommy	116

PART TWO
THREE STRANGERS

16.	The Escape	123
17.	Nine Minutes	132
18.	That's Two for Lance	141
19.	The Promise	147
20.	Cross that Bridge When We Get to It	159
21.	A Strange Resilience	172
22.	The Gas Station	185
23.	Dewormer	192
24.	Room Thirteen	203
25.	Unraveling the Thread	218
26.	Flaming Sausage	224

27. When It All Goes Horribly Wrong	232
28. Wakey Wakey, Eggs and Bakey	246

PART THREE
THE NEXUS OF DESTINY

29. Echoes	257
30. Inside the Lion's Den	266
31. A Fraction of a Chance	275
32. At the End of the Hall	288
33. The Promise	296
34. The Deadly Dance	299
35. Dissolution and Desperation	308
36. Betrayal and Redemption	318
37. Hope	327
Epilogue – The Letter	339
The Parasite Field Guide	350
Acknowledgments	353
About the Author	355
Also by Otto Schafer	357

PART ONE
PUZZLES

Every puzzle has a solution. The hardest aren't the ones missing pieces, but the ones where the pieces don't fit the way you expect.

ZOE MCCALLISTER

CHAPTER 1
THE FARMHOUSE

IT WAS good to be inside. Good to be away from the sky and the rain... and whatever other hell awaited them out there.

The entryway to Benson Meyer's farmhouse mansion was a portal to a world of rustic charm and timeless elegance. As Zoe stepped through the heavy wooden door, she was greeted by a spacious foyer adorned with intricate woodwork and polished stone floors.

"Whoa, Mr. Mayor!" Jurnee gasped, spinning in place as she took it all in, her saucer eyes lifting to the vaulted ceiling. "This place is huge!"

Oliver huffed a laugh, shaking his head, while Meyer just frowned.

Following her gaze skyward, Zoe couldn't help but notice a magnificent chandelier hanging from the vaulted ceiling, its crystals sparkling like stars in a night sky. The soft glow of its light was as surprising as the fixture itself, a stark contrast to the dim world she'd grown used to. It hadn't even been that long – just a couple weeks – but already she'd adjusted to the flickering glow of candlelight, the harsh beams of flashlights bouncing against dark walls. The idea of working light fixtures felt almost foreign, like a luxury from another lifetime.

She exhaled, reminding herself that the south side of the mansion's roof was covered in solar panels. As old as this place felt, there was a comforting modernness about it, a bridge between the past and whatever uncertain future awaited them.

Aaron, the autistic teen they'd met at the church, stood off to the side hugging himself as he too seemed to be taking it all in. Behind her, Oliver entered the foyer, stepped to the side, and placed a hand on her back. Beside her, Melissa stood on weak legs with her arm intertwined with Zoe's. Zoe did her best to support her; after all, the young woman had given birth less than two hours ago. She needed rest – real rest. Melissa's boyfriend, Adam, stood on her other side but he was holding baby Jonathan and wasn't able to offer much help.

Oliver slung Zoe's backpack over his shoulder and placed his arm under Melissa's. "Here, let me help."

"Thank you," the young woman said, smiling weakly.

To Zoe's left, a grand staircase ascended gracefully upward, its banister worn smooth by countless hands.

On her right, a cozy sitting area beckoned with plush armchairs arranged around a crackling fireplace. The warmth of the flames danced across the den, casting a soft glow on the paintings in the style of Van Gogh adorning the walls and the shelves lined with leather-bound books.

"Bathroom is through here," Meyer grumbled, pointing through a set of pocket doors leading into the heart of the mansion.

Jurnee hurried ahead with Louie on her heels.

"On your left! Your other left!" Meyer called after them.

Then the elderly man began to cough like he had outside. The cough was raw and harsh. He quickly pulled out his handkerchief and covered his mouth.

"That's a bad cough," Zoe said, hoping Meyer might offer some explanation to help her diagnose why he was coughing. It reminded her of a severe whooping cough, but the cause could be a number of things.

Meyer glanced back at her, his face void of expression – or, if there was one, she thought it might be annoyance. But maybe that was just how he always looked. Zoe couldn't be sure.

Now he was frowning... for sure he was frowning. He stuffed the handkerchief back in his pocket and stomped back past them, throwing the deadbolt on the door. "No wonder you folks had so much trouble at the church if no one bothers to lock the door behind them!" he snapped.

Oliver stepped forward. "Sorry I... I was about to when I saw—"

"That's the main room," Meyer said, pointing through an arched opening set between a pair of colonnades. "The kitchen is on the other side."

Through the archway she caught a glimpse of plush sofas and oversized ottomans arranged around a grand stone fireplace. Zoe could see herself sinking into the sofa and dozing off next to the warmth of a fire, her body finally giving in to the exhaustion pressing down on her like a weight. But she couldn't afford to let her guard down – not yet.

For now, they were inside. Sheltered. But for how long? Meyer had invited them in, reluctant as the invitation was, but trust was a fragile thing, and she knew better than to mistake hospitality for permanence. The house felt safe but so had the church. So had their home in Mackinaw. Safety was always an illusion, a fleeting thing that could be torn away in an instant.

Beyond the sofas, across the room was an opening revealing a kitchen and dining area. Marble countertops, tile floors, and cabinetry with clear glass doors stretched all the way up to the high ceilings. It was the kind of place that looked untouched by the horrors outside, frozen in time. A place meant for family dinners and lazy Sunday mornings.

A place meant for a world that didn't exist anymore.

Zoe swallowed hard, pushing the thought away. Right now, it didn't matter how long they had – only that they made the most of whatever time they were given.

"Upstairs there are several bedrooms. It doesn't make any difference to me which ones you settle into. Each one has its own bathroom. Towels are in the linen closet." His eyes settled on Zoe's blood-smeared clothes and hands. "Check the closet in the bedroom on the right at the end of the hall. I think you'll find some clothes in there that should fit you."

Zoe saw something behind Meyer's eyes – the pain of a memory passing through him like a cold chill. "Thank you, Mr. Meyer."

He cleared his throat and nodded. "You folks should head on up, pick a room, and get yourselves washed up. Get, um... What's your name again?" he asked, looking at Melissa.

Melissa blinked slowly. "Melissa," she managed.

Meyer nodded. "You should get Melissa settled in. The rest of you meet me in the kitchen, once you get cleaned up." He paused, his face serious. "Listen, before you go let's just get this out in the open. You can stay the night, a couple if you need to, but then you best be moving on. I don't have provisions to support you for any longer than that." With that, Meyer turned on his heels and headed for the kitchen.

Zoe stood in the slate-tiled shower watching pink water circle the drain. The tension she'd been holding in her shoulders slowly melted away. But she wasn't sure all the tension would ever be gone, not fully. If there was one thing the events since the asteroid had taught her, it was that everything can change in a split second. Even now, standing here naked and vulnerable, all she could think was hurry, get out, get dressed – be ready. She closed her eyes and there in the dark was that horrible image of the amalgamation – the monster made up of a hodgepodge of humans somehow congealed together and controlled by what she was sure could only be an alien parasite. Images of the monster and the horde of zombies attacking them at the church flashed through her mind. The whole thing was straight out of some hellish nightmare. Subconsciously, she knew the moment she drifted into sleep this creature would be there waiting for her in her nightmares.

She stepped out onto the heated slate floor and toweled off with a white terry bath sheet, wrapped it around herself, then used a smaller towel to wrap her braids.

Outside the bathroom Oliver sat in an overstuffed chair waiting patiently for his turn. She glanced around. "Have you checked on Jurnee?"

Oliver nodded. "She and Louie are in the little girl's bedroom across the hall."

They hadn't had a chance to ask Meyer about his own family, but clearly a little girl had lived or stayed here. "Okay, but have you checked on her?"

"Zo, you were only in the bathroom for like ten minutes." He stood and crossed the room, his arms loaded with clothes he'd found in one of the bedroom closets.

"Hey, before you shower let me get dressed first."

Oliver frowned. "Okay, I mean I don't mind watching you dress but..."

Zoe shook her head. "You're a pervert, you know that?"

"It was your idea. You're the one who wants me to watch you dress, so who's the perv?" Oliver grinned.

Zoe tried to smile back. She wanted to, she really did. But after the church, what that maniac Tommy had done, and the amalgamation, how was she supposed to smile? The events of the day had her anxiety at an all-time high. She felt like any minute the hammer would drop. Would it always be like this? She tossed her towel on the bed and pulled on a pair of black yoga pants, a sports bra, a tank top, and a cashmere sweater. Whoever they had belonged to, these clothes fit her almost like they were her own. "I... I know, I just don't like the idea of us not being prepared." She pulled on a pair of socks and slipped one foot into her boot and then the other. "I want to be ready just in case."

Oliver turned away from her and peered out the window. "It'll be dark soon but as far as I can see, the gate is closed and all is quiet."

"That doesn't mean anything, Oliver."

Oliver glanced back, his expression consoling. "I know, and when we head back downstairs, I'll talk to Mr. Meyer about making this place more secure. But there won't be much I can do in the dark. So, let's try and get through the night."

Right, just get through the night, she thought. Exhausted as she was, she knew she wouldn't be sleeping a wink.

CHAPTER 2
SIDE MISSION

TOMMY FORCED himself to jog down Unsicker Road, his stomach sloshing up and down, up and down. It was like trying to run on a belly full of milk and cereal. But his stomach wasn't full of cereal, it was full of something much tastier. Something he needed more of – *had* to have more of.

At least he no longer felt the pain of his ruptured stomach or the sting of his empty eye socket. He lifted his brain-crusted index finger, inserted it into his eye hole, and swirled it around. It didn't hurt at all. "You healed me, is that it?" He glanced down at his now blood-slicked finger. "No, not healed. I can't feel it because you took the pain away. Because you need me."

But there was pain. Ungodly pain. In the beginning he would have described it as an irresistible hunger pain, but this was so much more than hunger. He had never done heroin or crack cocaine, but he'd heard of people wanting the stuff so bad they would sell everything they owned to get their fix. That's how bad they needed it. But this – this

9

was worse, had to be worse. So much more than want and far, far beyond need. This... this was what he lived for.

"Live for," he moaned. As something caught his attention from the corner of his eye, Tommy stopped short and stood in the middle of Unsicker Road, peering across a cluttered yard strewn with old vehicles, piles of junk parts, and car tires. None of that interested him. It was the light. He'd seen it... was sure he had. Red mist collected on his bare shoulders and soaked his white wife-beater as he remained motionless, watching and waiting to see the light again.

A blue tarp covered a portion of the home's roof while moldy white siding did its best to cling to its walls, though much of it had come loose and now hung there like rotting strips of flesh coming loose from the bone.

In the back of his neck all the way into the center of his head, Tommy felt a wriggling squirminess – a sort of tickle. But what followed did not tickle. The jolt of pain ripped through Tommy's abdomen like a serrated knife through Jell-O, reminding him of his one true purpose. "I'm fucking trying!" he growled through a clenched jaw.

Chad was lucky. Chad was dead. Not infected, not undead, but dead. He'd done his son the ultimate favor and in return he'd filled his belly with Chad's brain. Chad and so many others. Jesus Christ, he was a hero. He'd sacrificed himself to save them all, liberated them from all their suffering. Isn't that what Jesus had done? Taken the burden onto himself. That's it. He was like Jesus.

Across the lawn a light flashed on from around the back of the house.

"There you are." Tommy smiled and jogged across the overgrown front yard to the side yard, his boots crunching against gravel as he crossed a once-manicured driveway, now weedy and rutted from neglect. The house loomed ahead, its back porch sagging with age, the wooden steps warped from time and neglect.

For a brief moment, he considered darting up to the porch for cover, but instinct told him to stay low. Instead, he veered toward the side yard, ducking down behind a rusted-out Jaguar with weeds growing up around it.

A gruff voice shouted, "I don't think I can reach the chicken coop again tonight. It's still misting out there."

"Well, then get back in before you get wet!" a woman's voice urged.

"I ain't gonna get wet! What do you think, I'm ignorant?" the man barked.

"I just want you to be careful! You fed the chickens once today. They'll be okay till morning," the woman said.

"I know, dammit. I just don't like it," the man shouted back, then muttered something under his breath.

Tommy bolted from behind the car and darted across the twenty yards to the side of the house. He slid to a stop and slapped his palms against the siding.

"Hey, did you hear that?" the man asked.

"Russ, please come inside. We have enough eggs for tonight! Let's just feed them in the morning, when the rain stops and we can collect more eggs!"

Tommy listened as footsteps crossed the porch. "No shit, Janie! I'm not talking about the damn chickens. Didn't you hear that? Sounded like something hit the house."

Tommy pressed himself against the wall. Russ would have to come off the porch to see around the side of the house and he wasn't about to do that in the rain.

The footsteps stopped just around the corner. Tommy sucked in a long breath, his eye rolling back in his head. He could smell the man's brains. And once he smelled them, he couldn't stop himself; all attempts at stealth were disregarded. He had to have him. He had to take it right now!

Tommy lunged around the corner.

The man, who had his back to him, was overweight, with graying hair. Tommy was within reach of the man in two strides. All that stood between them now was the porch railing.

Effortlessly, Tommy stepped up onto the edge of the porch, placed a hand on the rail, and jumped over, landing with a soft thump.

The man turned back toward him and startled. "Hey! What the fu—"

Wasting no time, Tommy swung his shotgun up and smashed the butt of the gun's stock into the bridge of the man's nose.

The big man staggered back, a fountain of blood spilling onto his soiled bib overalls. "Ahhh! Please!" the man moaned as he fell onto his ass.

"Russ!" a woman cried out.

Russ held his hands out defensively as Tommy towered over him. "No, please!" he babbled.

Such a pathetic waste! Tommy thought as he glared down at the man. "Don't worry, I'm going to give your life purpose." He rammed the shotgun's stock into the man's mouth, crushing his front teeth.

Russ fell onto his back, gagging on the ivory shards of his broken teeth, then coughed a spray of blood into the air like an erupting volcano.

The woman appeared in the doorway screaming. "Russ! Oh my god!"

Tommy spun the gun around and fired the twelve gauge into the woman's paunchy abdomen. In the movies a blast from a shotgun at this distance would blow a person off their feet, but in reality, and to his surprise, the fat bitch didn't fall back at all. She just stood there, her jaw working her mouth open and closed but saying nothing. Her blue eyes were stretched open. At first, she just stared at him but then she looked down. Tommy followed her gaze.

The angle of the buckshot blast must have been just perfect to open her right up because her shredded intestines had fallen out of her tattered T-shirt, and she was holding them in her hands.

"Janie! Oh! Oh... nooo!" the man moaned through a mouthful of blood.

Tommy turned his attention back to the man, bit his lower lip, and smashed the butt of the stock down into the man's face over and over until there was no resemblance of the man – no face at all. But Tommy didn't stop; he kept going, pushing the man's head to the side so he could have a go at breaking it open from a different angle.

From just beyond the door he heard another scream. "Mom!"

Oh good. There was more inside.

Somehow Janie was still standing – still holding her bowels in her hands doing that same ridiculous fish-out-of-water gasp. With his shotgun in one hand, Tommy stepped forward and snatched the woman by the throat with the other.

Janie's hands dropped, her bowels unspooling toward the floor like a tangle of rope tied to an anchor cast into the depths. Her mouth stretched open to scream, but no sound came out.

Tommy shoved her head back, banging it off the doorjamb once, then again. As the woman started to fall, he let go of her throat and snatched up a fistful of her hair, yanking her into him while at the same time spinning her to face the doorway.

A young man stood inside, his face horror stricken.

"Mom!" he shouted, lifting a rifle. "Let her go!" he demanded.

Tommy did not let her go; instead he held her there, his own personal shield. With his other hand he lifted the shotgun. Then, pressing his nose into the woman's ear, he snorted in a hard breath through his wrecked sinuses. And oh, the smell! That wonderful one-of-a-kind sweetness. Nothing could compare. Nothing could come close to this.

"I said let her—"

Tommy fired the shotgun.

The younger man dropped and began convulsing on the floor. The image reminded Tommy of when he was a kid. His father raised rabbits. As one of their chores, he and his brother took turns doing the butchering. He'd crack the rabbits over the head with a hammer and they'd get to flopping around just like this kid was doing now.

From deeper in the house, a girl screamed. Tommy laughed. "Damned if I didn't hit the jackpot!"

Janie slumped, dead in his arms.

"That's right. I'm here to save you. You're free now. You're all free." He let her collapse down to the porch. Squatting down next to her, he decided he'd start here.

As Tommy began smashing Janie's head in with the stock of his shotgun, he wished he had a hammer. But in the end, it didn't matter. The force broke her skull open nonetheless, revealing the prize inside. Pressing his fingers deep into the woman's pink blood-slicked brain felt like pushing them into a bowl of firm Jell-O. In the back of his head Tommy felt something slippery wriggle around. His mouth salivated. "Oh, you like this, don't you?" He licked his lips and shoved a handful of brains into his mouth, swallowing down the thick creaminess without bothering to chew. "Ohhh," he moaned, falling back onto his ass.

Sitting with his legs crisscrossed, he bent forward, scooping up another handful. Hastily, he picked out a shard of bone, discarded it, and stuffed his mouth full once more. There was no feeling on earth like what he was feeling right now. No pleasure to compare this to.

Moments later, Tommy pulled loose the last remaining chunk of bone from Janie's skull and licked it clean, making sure not to leave a drop before tossing it back down onto the porch. Once he finished sucking his fingers clean of every bit of brain matter, he would work his way through the other two and then he would explore the house to see how many others were hiding inside. Yes, that was a good plan. Eat what's right here fresh and warm. No need to hurry. No one left in that house was going anywhere. The rain would see to that.

Turned out tonight would be magical after all. As for tomorrow... Well, tomorrow was simply today's dream and as long as Tommy lived, his dream would lead to one place: Oliver and Zoe.

CHAPTER 3
IRISH COFFEE

OLIVER HEARD LAUGHING as he approached the kitchen. Giggling, to be specific. Curious, he paused to listen.

"This ice cream sure is good, Mr. Mayor!" Jurnee shouted as if she was yelling at someone across a busy highway. Maybe she thought the old man was half deaf. For that matter, maybe Benson Meyer *was* half deaf. But more likely Jurnee was shouting because, well, that's what six-year-olds do. "I haven't had chocolate ice cream in forever!" she continued to shout with excitement.

Benson laughed so hard he started coughing. When he finally caught his breath, he said, "I'm no mayor – how about we forget all this pomp and circumstance and you just call me Ben?"

"Pomp and what!?" Jurnee laughed. "You sure are funny, Mr. Mayor!"

Ben hacked hard, clearing his throat. "You... you think so, huh?"

"Yep!"

Oliver entered the kitchen to find Jurnee at the counter

sitting atop a barstool. She was hunched over a bowl of ice cream as big as her head.

"Oliver! Look!" Jurnee shifted onto her bottom and held out her feet. "I got new shoes!"

"Wow, you sure did!" he said, glancing curiously at Ben.

"My granddaughter's. I kept extra clothes for when she'd visit," Ben said, his face suddenly hollow. "Where's your wife and that other fella?"

"They'll be down soon. Zoe is checking on Melissa and the baby," Oliver said, pulling a chair back from the table.

Aaron appeared from the doorway and pushed his blond bangs back, tucking them behind his ear. "Of course, I haven't eaten in hours. May I have some ice cream as well?"

"Help yourself. Spoons are in the first drawer on the left," Ben said, eyeing Aaron with what Oliver interpreted as annoyance. The old man glanced back at Oliver and said, "Odd duck."

Oliver didn't want to announce Aaron was autistic with him standing right there, so instead he cleared his throat and changed the subject. "Mr. Meyer, I noticed you haven't boarded up your windows. Aren't you worried about an infected or zombie smashing its way inside? I'm honestly surprised it hasn't happened already. But Adam and I can help you get—"

"Don't need boards," Ben snapped.

"But aren't you—"

"You know who designed this house?" Ben interrupted with a flourish of his hand.

"Well, no. I suppose not."

The old man lifted his chin and hooked a thumb into his chest, giving it two good jabs. "I designed it. Granted, my Maggie put her own touch on the decor, but the security was my design. You see, son" – the way Ben said 'son' wasn't endearing but more like, *you're young and stupid and I am old and wise* – "my family was the most important thing to me. I was never naive to the fact my business practices made me... well, let's just say not a fan favorite in the local community. And I wasn't about to have some lowlife try and take what I've earned."

Oliver didn't understand what this had to do with the very real fact the windows were not covered and if Meyer was talking about some kind of alarm system, he didn't really see how that was going to help them now. "But the windows."

Zoe entered the kitchen and crossed over to the table.

"Don't worry about the windows, Oliver. In fact, don't worry about anyone getting in here that I don't want in." Meyer's attention fell to Zoe then and he nodded approvingly. "I see Ellie's clothes fit you perfectly."

Zoe glanced down at her clothes then back at Meyer. "Are they your daughter's?"

Meyer nodded. "Indeed. Maggie and I kept her room just as it was when she moved away. And then we set up a room for our granddaughter, Riley, a few years back."

Zoe sat down at the table next to Oliver. "Do they visit often?"

Meyer's face dropped. "No... No, they don't."

The silence grew into awkwardness as Oliver searched for the right thing to say or ask. In truth, he really just wanted to make a plan to get the windows covered and couldn't understand how this man thought they were safe sitting here exposed. Even with the gate and the fence, if something got past those barriers they were just sitting ducks.

Jurnee kicked out her legs. "Zoe, look at my new shoes! They're yellow! Did you know yellow is my favorite color?"

"Really? Wow! Those are cool shoes and they're your favorite color too? That makes them even better! Did you tell Mr. Meyer thank you?"

"Uh-huh, I sure did!" she said, loading another spoonful of ice cream into her mouth.

Aaron sat down at the table and began hurriedly shoveling ice cream into his mouth too.

Ben frowned. "What's wrong with you, son? You eat like someone is about to steal your lunch!"

Aaron froze, his spoon dripping over, halfway between his bowl and his mouth. Slowly, he started to rock back and forth, a pained grimace twisting his face.

Meyer's frown deepened with irritation. "Did you hear me? When an adult speaks you ought to answer. Now slow down. You're at a table, not a trough."

Aaron dropped the spoon and slammed backward into the chair.

Zoe's eyes went wide and, before Oliver could get any words out, Meyer said, "What in the hell is wrong with you? You some kind of re—"

"That's enough!" Zoe said, banging her palm down on the table. "Aaron, it's okay, you didn't do anything wrong."

Aaron gave the side of his head a hard slap. "Can we go back to the church?"

Zoe pushed her chair back and hurried around the table. "Aaron, it's okay," she said softly. "You're okay."

"Can we? Can we? Can we?" Aaron asked as he rocked harder now.

"What in the hell is wrong with—"

Zoe cut Ben a murder-sharp glare that instantly silenced the man.

"We can't go back. You know that, but we can go watch TV? Did you know that TV works here and that there's a DVD player?"

Jurnee pushed her palms down on the table and leaned forward. "Mr. Mayor, do you have Disney movies? Disney movies are my favorite!"

Aaron, still swaying back and forth, hand still held on his head, looked at Jurnee and his body slowed. "Of course, Disney movies are quite good. Though I prefer Marvel."

Jurnee scrunched up her nose, tilting her head. "I don't know what a Marvel is, but what's your favorite Disney movie?"

Aaron's eyes blinked rapidly, his words coming quick. "I suspect you're referring to animations due to your age of six years old. If this is true, I would say my favorite Disney animated movie is *The Sword in the Stone*, which I believe to be Excalibur though some say Arthur received it from the lady of the lake rather than pulling it from the stone. *The Sword in the Stone* was first released in 1963. However, if we cannot find that one there are many other Disney animations that include swords."

"Huh? Well, I don't know about that, but if Mr. Mayor has it, I'll watch it with you!" Jurnee said assuredly. "Do you have that one, Mr. Mayor?"

"It's just Ben, remember?"

"Sorry!" Jurnee said dramatically. "I mean Mr. Ben."

"In the basement there is a theater. One wall is covered in cases full of DVDs. My daughter also liked Disney movies and I'm sure you'll find plenty to choose from. If you're done with your ice cream, I bet I can get one started for you. But first you have to put that bowl in the sink." Ben pointed.

At the sound of Ben's voice, Aaron went back to slapping himself on top of the head with his palm. Thankfully, he wasn't hitting himself hard, but Oliver wondered if he would hurt himself if he became upset enough.

"It's okay, buddy," Oliver said, trying to replicate Zoe's soothing voice.

Aaron looked toward the basement door with longing. The boy clearly wanted to get away from Ben. "Of course, I am quite proficient in the operation of a DVD player."

"Alright then. Bottom of the stairs, first door on the left."

Aaron hurried out of the dining area with Jurnee on his heels.

"I will be right down to join you," Zoe said, turning her attention back to Ben. "What the hell is wrong with you?"

Oliver's eyes darted to Zoe.

"Excuse me?" Ben asked, pulling a sour face.

Oliver's eyes flicked over to Ben. All he could think was, *This is going to be bad... for Ben.*

Zoe placed her hands palm down on the table and leaned in, her voice low but stern. "Aaron is autistic, but even if he weren't your tone and words were completely out of line!"

"Um, guys," Oliver tried.

Ben pointed at Zoe. "You dare come into my home and take that tone with me? An hour ago your husband was standing in my driveway uninvited and begging to come inside!"

Zoe straightened and crossed her arms. "If this is how you speak to your guests, we will happily find somewhere else to go, right now!"

"Guys," Oliver tried again.

Ben narrowed his eyes as if the two were playing poker and he was trying to read her to see if she was bluffing.

"Really? It's dark out there and you're going to, what? Stomp off into the night?"

Zoe huffed. "You think we won't?"

Ben flushed. "You know where the door is!"

Oliver shouted. "Both of you stop!"

Both turned, frowning at him.

"Don't look at me like that! And we aren't leaving. Not in the night. That'd be suicide."

Ben smiled. "Finally, common sense wins the day."

Zoe lifted a finger. And Oliver knew she was about to lose her shit.

Oliver held up a hand. "And Ben, you need to apologize."

"What?" Ben snapped.

"You heard Zoe. Aaron is autistic – you can't talk to him like that. Even if he weren't, that was just rude."

"I didn't... I didn't know the boy was autistic!" Ben countered as a fit of sudden coughing overtook him. He scrambled for his handkerchief but couldn't get to it in time.

Hastily, he pulled his hand away from his mouth and began wiping it with the handkerchief, and that's when Oliver noticed the blood. His eyes darted to Zoe. The look on her face told him she noticed too.

Ben brought the cough under control and cleared his throat, doing his best to quickly conceal the hanky, stuffing it into his jeans pocket. "I already told you I didn't know he was autistic."

Adam appeared from the doorway looking from Zoe to Ben then Oliver. "Hey, guys."

Zoe shook her head. "I'm going to check on Aaron," she said, spinning on her heels and storming out of the kitchen.

"Did I miss something?" Adam asked, his brow furrowed.

Oliver sighed. "You call that an apology, Ben?"

Ben stared after Zoe, then turned to Oliver. "That wife of yours is something else."

Oliver thought he knew where this was going and turned in his seat to square up with Ben. "You were wrong."

Ben waved a dismissive hand. "I know that, son. Your Zoe reminds me of my Maggie. Yep, Maggie through and through. Can I offer you some advice?"

"No offense, but I'm not so sure I want your advice," Oliver said honestly.

Adam pulled out a chair and dropped down into it. "Oh, I definitely missed something."

"Hold on to that one. She's smart as a whip, tough as nails, and won't put up with any shit." The old man picked up his coffee cup and took a long pull. Leveling his eyes on Oliver, he said, "Women like her are not a dime a dozen. Long ago and far away I should have taken the advice I'm giving you now. Maybe if I had, Maggie wouldn't have left and my Ellie would have still come around. Maybe I would have gotten to know my granddaughter, but now I don't even know if she's still..." Ben started coughing again and this time it seemed to go on and on.

Oliver didn't know what to say so he asked, "Do you have any medicine for that cough?"

Still hacking, Ben pointed at a cabinet above the sink.

Oliver hurried over to the sink, opened the cabinet, and frowned. "It's just alcohol."

"The Irish whiskey," he croaked.

Oliver brought the half-empty bottle of Bushmills Single Malt Irish Whiskey over to the counter. "I was thinking maybe some real medicine like a cough suppressant."

"This is all the medicine I need. Now grab yourself a

shot glass or a coffee cup if you prefer it the way I drink it and let us men have... have a talk."

Oliver didn't care for alcohol but didn't want to be rude. Besides, after what he'd seen at the church, a drink might not be so bad. "Adam?"

Adam slapped a palm down on the table. "Hell yes. Count me in."

"Coffee cups are in the cupboard above the coffeepot."

Oliver retrieved the cups and filled the first one halfway up with coffee.

"No coffee for me, thanks. I'll just take mine straight." Adam rubbed a hand down his face.

"Not a coffee drinker?" Ben asked.

Adam's face fell. "No, I mean yeah, I... I'm just not in the mood for it."

The men sat and sipped. Ben caught his breath and for a few moments it was quiet. Internally, Oliver couldn't get his mind off the windows and the fact they were sitting ducks.

"What's troubling you, Oliver? Worried about your wife? Well, don't. She's mad at me, not you. You backed her up and told me to apologize, that will earn you some points."

Adam lifted his eyes from his cup, following the conversation.

Oliver said, "I'm not trying to earn points. I backed her up because you were out of line."

"Fair enough. What's on your mind?"

"Okay, it's the windows. You can't sit here in this house knowing what's out there and feel safe. Don't you get it?"

Adam lifted the bottle of whiskey off the table and poured another two or three shots into his coffee cup. "Oliver is right, Mr. Meyer. The thing Zoe calls an amalgamation came through the church wall. I'll be hearing those metal two-by-fours twisting and that thing croaking in my nightmares, assuming I ever sleep again."

Ben studied them both like he wanted to say something but wasn't sure he should.

Adam set the bottle down and picked up the cap.

"Just leave it off. That bottle will be empty soon enough." Ben drew in a deep breath. "I'm going to tell you both something. But before I do, I want to trust you are both men of your word and you won't get any ideas of taking this place for yourselves."

Oliver was about to take another sip from his coffee but froze. He placed the cup back on the counter. "Of course not. We would never—"

Ben held up a hand. "Just listen. Against my better judgment I let you in my home, but don't think for one second I'm not prepared to deal with you if I'm forced to."

Oliver glanced over at Adam, who appeared as confused as he felt.

"So can I trust you? And before you answer, do not make me regret this."

Oliver nodded. "You have my word."

Both men looked to Adam.

Adam's head bobbed up and down. "Honest, you can trust us, Mr. Meyer. I'm just appreciative you allowed us a safe place to stay the night. Melissa and the baby need rest."

"A simple yes would suffice."

"Ye... yes, one hundred percent."

Ben nodded solemnly. "Money has never been a problem for me, but I made some enemies acquiring it." He took a sip of coffee and pointed at the kitchen windows then the back patio door. "Every bit of glass you see is top of the line ballistic glass. You can throw a punch, a brick, or even fire a bullet. Makes no difference, we don't need boards. Far as the walls, you're in a brick home but that's only what you see. I also took liberties with the internal structure."

"Liberties?" Oliver asked.

"Let's just say there's more concrete and rebar in these walls than a parking deck. Now I'm telling you this so you stop asking about the goddamn windows and just maybe you can get a few good nights of sleep."

Adam pushed his chair back and crossed the kitchen to the patio doors. "Even this glass here?"

"I said all the glass, didn't I? Do you doubt me or are you just thick?"

Adam scrambled for words. "No. I don't doubt you."

"Thick then."

"No, Mr. Meyer, I just haven't ever seen a home with bulletproof glass. That's incredible." Adam placed a hand on the glass.

"No, not incredible, just expensive. And stop calling me Mr. Meyer."

Adam crossed back to the counter and sat down. "Sorry."

"There's more, but I'm not telling you and I likely won't. I know you see me as a sick old man, but it's what you don't see. I promise you men this, if you were to try something, well... I'm prepared."

Oliver looked Ben in the eyes and stared at him for a solid three count before he finally spoke. "You don't have to worry about us. I said it before you let us in and I'll say it now. We mean you no harm."

Ben stared back at Oliver almost like he was looking right through his very soul. "I do believe you. Now spend what time you have here resting and planning." He lifted the bottle, poured the remainder into his coffee cup and stood. "I'm off to bed."

As Ben moved down the hall, he was gripped by another fit of coughing. Slowly the coughing grew distant and then faded behind a closed door.

Adam leaned in and whispered, "What do you think he meant by there's more he's not telling us?"

Oliver shook his head. He had no idea what secrets Ben was keeping to himself. "I don't know, but ballistic glass? That's some next-level shit."

Adam raised his eyebrows. "Hey, maybe this house could withstand one of those zombie monsters."

"I hope we never have to find out." Oliver pushed his chair back. "I'm going to check on Zoe and make sure Aaron is okay."

"Yeah, and I better get back to Melissa and the little guy," Adam said, throwing back the remainder of his whiskey.

"Try and get some sleep and we'll figure out our next move in the morning."

Adam paused, his face stone serious. "I... I never told you but Jesse and I were going to start our own company. We were going to call it Brew Brothers Coffee Fusion. We'd spent months developing flavored coffee and alcohol fusions. We were so excited to quit our crap jobs, so close to going for it. I'd never seen Jesse more excited for the future."

"That's why you didn't want the coffee when Ben offered?"

Adam nodded, swallowing down the emotion as his eyes welled and threatened to spill. "Jesse was more than my best friend. He was like the brother I never had, Oliver. What Tommy did to Jesse... Fuck me. And after what we heard and saw, I don't know if I'll ever sleep again."

The words 'best friend' made Oliver's thoughts go to Sam, his own best friend, and the horror of what had happened to her. What Oliver already knew and Adam would learn soon enough was that when exhaustion outran emotion, sleep would find him, but so would the nightmares. Nightmares he didn't wish on anyone. Oliver pressed his lips into a tight line and placed a hand on Adam's shoulder and squeezed. "See you tomorrow, Adam."

"Right, tomorrow."

CHAPTER 4
WELL-FED

TOMMY STEPPED over a pile of dirty clothes as he entered the house and made his way through the laundry room. The house was a mess and it stunk. The people who'd lived here had cats and the whole place was cluttered and smelled like piss. Cat piss to be specific.

A cheap three-wick candle burned bright on the kitchen table, illuminating a sink and counter full of dirty dishes. The vanilla scent did nothing to mask the ammonia reek of the cats – if anything, it was making it worse. A calico cat jumped off the counter and two more lay in a tangle on the seat of a kitchen chair, their tails flicking lazily.

As he crossed the kitchen he felt the stickiness of the yellowed linoleum under his feet. The living room was worse. The beige carpet, stained and matted, stretched toward a wall stacked high with boxes, garbage bags bulging with clothes, and plastic bins spilling over with random junk – old shoes, tangled cords, crumpled magazines. An overstuffed recliner sat lopsided in the corner, its fabric shredded at the arms, stuffing poking through like exposed bone.

Tommy didn't give a shit about the mess or the smell. But it was making it hard to find the young girl hiding somewhere among all this crap.

As he maneuvered around a stack of boxes and more clothes, the seventh cat he'd seen so far stepped in his path, meowed, and rubbed against his leg, releasing a soft purr. It was a long-haired black-and-white Persian. Tommy reared his foot back and kicked the fleabag, making sure to dig the toe of his boot into the thing's ribs.

The cat screeched and went airborne, bouncing off the far wall. It tried to stand up but something had broken and all it could do was drag itself behind an armchair piled with junk.

Now the fucking thing was screeching something awful, and the noise was messing with his concentration. He pointed the shotgun at the base of the chair and fired.

The screeching stopped and the room fell silent again. Tommy closed his eye and drew a long breath through his nose. "There you are," he muttered. Crossing the room, he hurried through a door on the opposite side and into a hallway. To his right, the front door stood open.

Tommy stared out into the night. It was still raining and pretty good too. Somewhere beyond his vision a desperate moan broke through the pitter-patter of the rain. The familiar sound was one of endless hunger – a squeal of pain he knew too well. "No, no, no, no," he murmured. "She's mine. She's all mine." He pushed the door closed and locked it. The girl didn't go that way. She just wanted him to think she had.

The hallway was dark enough he could only make out the shapes of the door frames both on his left and right. The first door on his left was a bathroom, next a bedroom, then another bedroom across the hall. All a mess, but no smell of brains and no one hiding, not in the shower, not under the beds, and not in the closets. Finally he reached a set of stairs leading up to the second floor.

Tommy climbed up two steps and paused, sniffing at the air like a dog on a scent. His bloated stomach growled and a stabbing pain shot through his guts. "There she is," he murmured, then shouted up the stairs, "Come out, little one! I won't hurt you. I'm just here to free you from this miserable shitshow of a world!"

No answer, but it didn't matter. Even in the pitch black of night and the clutter and filth, even through the stench of animal feces and piss, she couldn't hide her delicious scent, not from him – not from the thing wriggling in the back of his skull.

He hurried up the stairs, allowing the sweetness of what she held to guide him. Another hall, but he didn't even pause as he passed another bedroom and another bathroom before reaching the last door on the right. He could smell her sweetness, the only thing in the world that smelled good to him now.

Tommy kicked the door so hard it splintered and came off the frame, her smell greeting him like the opening of an oven full of hot apple pie. The impatient bastard controlling his pain writhed, its tentacles doing whatever in the fuck they did to make him crave – to make him hurt for the prize. There was something different about this girl. It was the same as with the kids at the church. More excitement for the young brains. He wasn't sure why. But they smelled better... sweeter somehow. Like veal or a tender young deer. Back when that sort of thing sounded good.

Rushing forward he crossed the toy-cluttered room and ripped the closet door from its track.

The girl squatted, pressing herself into the corner. She let out a scream.

"Come here!" Tommy growled, groping for her in the darkness and grabbing a fistful of her hair as he jerked her out of the closet.

The girl bolted for the door, crying out as her hair was ripped from her scalp by the roots. She was quick but he was quicker, diving after her, his hands finding her throat as he drove her down to the messy floor. Something plastic collapsed and crunched beneath them as they landed in what felt like a pile of scattered toys and clothes.

There they tangled in the darkness, she kicking, screaming, and begging. He couldn't see her. Couldn't look her in the eyes as she screamed for her mom and dad. She must have been about Chad's age. Chad had tasted so good.

He squeezed her throat until she couldn't scream, then he squeezed harder.

Her little legs kicked wildly, futilely.

Tommy rolled atop her, pinning her down, squeezing harder still. "No one is here," he whispered. "You are alone and you are *mine!*"

Under the cover of darkness a moment of quiet desperation stretched out as the girl's tiny body bucked beneath him. But Tommy held fast, his bloated stomach pinning her to the floor. His hands gripped her little neck as if she were a chicken and he was trying to make her head pop off. That would have been fine with him – at least then he could simply carry her head to the kitchen. But her head didn't pop off. Instead, her fight slipped away and he felt her go slack beneath him.

Tommy sighed, lifting the girl's entire body and flopping it over his shoulder before retrieving his shotgun.

He made his way through the dark house and back to

the kitchen. The vanilla candle still burned bright on the overflowing kitchen table. It was a wonder this hellhole hadn't caught fire. Tommy pushed the candle to one end and swept his arm across the table, clearing enough space for the girl.

He flopped her off his shoulder and down onto the table, revealing a mess of sandy-blond hair. In the candlelight he could see she was indeed young. Twelve, he guessed, but no more than fourteen. She wore pink pajamas with unicorns. Oh, how good she was going to taste.

Mouth salivating, Tommy crossed the kitchen. Like a crackhead searching for a rock, he ripped drawer after drawer from the cabinets, frantically searching for a tool that would get him into her head. He picked up a meat tenderizer before dumping a junk drawer where he scored a screwdriver. He sat both on the table next to the girl and turned back, pulling the last drawer from the cabinet – the knife drawer. Among the blades he found a heavy meat cleaver. "Oh. Well, roger that." He smiled, licking his lips.

Something crashed behind him. Tommy spun in time to see a man rush into the room and crash into the table. For a split second, Tommy thought the man was trying to save the little girl but as he grabbed her, he didn't try to take her. Instead, he bent over her and bit the side of her head.

"Hey, fucko!" Tommy shouted, crossing the kitchen in a few strides.

The zombie, a shirtless, out-of-shape fat-ass, looked up and moaned.

The girl's eyes popped open, and she screamed.

"Get your own!" Tommy swung the cleaver, severing half the zombie's ear and planting the blade in the side of its head.

The zed blinked once and collapsed on the floor.

A strange pang of pain radiated through his head.

The girl, still screaming, scrambled off the table and bolted for the back door.

Tommy snatched the meat tenderizer off the counter and threw it, clocking the little shit in the back of the head just as she exited onto the porch.

Tommy blinked. The pain in his head faded, replaced by the now familiar unquenchable deprivation. "What was that? You don't like me killing your own?" he mumbled, heading for the porch. "Well, too damn bad. You made me this way and until I'm dead I get a say!"

Tommy snatched the girl by the hair and dragged her back into the kitchen, slamming her down onto the table. "Stay!" he ordered. But judging from all the blood leaking from her head he guessed she wouldn't be waking up this time. He closed the back door and locked it, retrieved the cleaver, and went to work. The little girl's skull was already cracked and getting in was easy enough.

Twenty minutes later Tommy sat in a wooden chair at the kitchen table, licking his fingers and feeling well fed. His eyes were heavy. The feeling of exhaustion consumed him. Maybe the undead didn't sleep or maybe they did, but either way, he wasn't dead yet and he sure as fuck felt like he could fall asleep standing up. "You satisfied now? I've stuffed it all down, every bit I could find." On the other side of the dead girl's empty skull, the vanilla candle sat in a puddle of bloody goo.

The chair creaked beneath him as Tommy pushed himself up and reached across the table, snuffing the life out of the tiny flame.

CHAPTER 5
SPILT COFFEE

ZOE WOKE WITH A START, bolting straight up, gasping for breath. In her sleep she was delivering a baby, a zombie baby. As the baby's head delivered and its face came into view, it bit her hand. In the nightmare the baby had a mouthful of shark teeth, and her hand started to turn black and rot.

She sat there taking a moment to breathe, catch her breath, and remember where she was.

Finally, she felt her pulse slow. She threw back the blanket and swung her legs off the bed.

When she had somehow dozed off, she'd been talking to Oliver. She glanced over to find he was still asleep with his back to her and one of Jurnee's arms flopped over his head. There was no way the little girl was sleeping on her own; besides, she felt better knowing they were all in the same room. She couldn't shake the feeling that at any minute they were going to have to run for their lives.

Crossing the room to the window, she pulled back the curtain and peered out. The sky had that pre-dawn glow, and she could just make out the shape of the gate on the opposite side of the front yard.

Glancing back at Oliver and Jurnee, she decided not to wake them.

She changed out of the pajamas she'd found in one of the closets, slung her backpack over her shoulder, and made her way to the kitchen. As soon as she stepped into the hallway, she could smell it – coffee!

In the kitchen, the only sign of life was the coffee percolating on the counter. No Meyer though. Maybe he had the coffeepot set up on a timer? She found a mug in the cabinet above the coffeemaker and poured herself a cup, retrieved the *Parasite Field Guide* from her pack, and sat down at the kitchen table. She couldn't stop thinking about the amalgamation in the church and something she had read in the field guide. She flipped through the pages until she got to the section on *Pristionchus pacificus,* also known as the roundworm. This specific microscopic parasite was the only one she knew of that amalgamated. Though she couldn't put her finger on why yet, this single fact could be important and she wanted to learn all she could. She traced her finger along the lines, scanning for the passage.

"In order to latch onto a passing beetle, the *P. pacificus* larvae will stand on their tails and wave back and forth. Scientists found that, in many instances, thousands of the quarter-of-a-millimeter-long larvae will group up and merge together to form a tower. These towers become so tall they can be seen with the naked eye and allow the larvae to gain enough height to reach the beetle."

Zoe wondered less about why they amalgamated than *how*.

She leaned over the page and kept reading. According

to the field guide, the towers, made up of thousands of worms, were incredibly strong. Scientists had even tried poking the towers with a steel wire and still they didn't break apart. Next, they tried placing the tower in water and the collective began to swim, but still, they held together. As they examined the substance binding the tower together, they discovered that the worms exuded a chemical over their skins. The chemical contained one of the longest fatty wax molecules found in any animal or plant. The scientist called it nematoil.

"Nematoil," she repeated, feeling her pulse quicken.

The back door opened. Zoe gasped and jumped, spilling her coffee. "Shit!"

"Ms. McCallister, I didn't mean to startle you," Ben said, pushing the door shut and locking it. He was dressed in a pair of dusty Wranglers and a T-shirt with a flannel over the top, his sleeves rolled up to just below the elbow, as if he'd been out there working. She noticed for the first time that Ben had a tattoo on his inner forearm, though she couldn't make it out.

Zoe moved the guide clear of the spill and hurried into the kitchen to grab some paper towels. "Sorry, I... I wasn't expecting anyone from outside."

"Well, despite the happenings, the farm needs to be tended to." Ben slid out of his boots and crossed the dining area into the kitchen, retrieving a mug and filling it. "These days I figure that when the sky is clear it's best to take advantage while you can. I see you found the coffee."

"I did. I... I hope you don't mind," she said, wiping the table.

"Not at all. Here, let me top you off," he said, lifting the pot.

Zoe gave the man a slight smile and nodded. In this moment, Benson Meyer seemed almost friendly. "Listen, about last night. I... Well, I didn't mean to snap at you like that. It had been a long day... We lost many of our friends..." Zoe choked on the words, feeling her eyes well at the memories.

"You don't have to apologize. I'm an old crusty asshole. That's no secret."

Zoe only nodded in response as she pulled out her chair to sit. She was hoping he might reciprocate and also apologize.

"Hold on." Ben nodded towards the den. "Listen, why don't we sit in there by the fire? It's a bit more comfortable."

"Sure." Coffee in hand, she picked up the field guide and joined Ben in the den, settling into an overstuffed leather chair. Zoe sat with her legs crisscrossed, her socked feet tucked beneath her thighs. Her boots were upstairs – she'd have to make a run for the stairs to get to them should something unexpected happen. She hadn't wanted to leave her boots by the front door in case she needed them in the night. But she had forgotten to bring them with her to the kitchen. This was her reality now – worrying about where her shoes were when they weren't on her feet.

"Is it a secret?" Ben asked.

"Huh? A secret?" Zoe's face twisted in confusion.

"I think maybe you were somewhere else for a moment, ruminating perhaps?" Ben asked.

Zoe flushed. "Yes, sorry."

Without warning, the older man pulled a pained face and started to cough.

"Are you okay? Can I get you something?"

Ben waved her off, clearing his throat. He pointed at the

field guide. "I was asking about the book. Curious what you're reading."

Zoe glanced down. "It's a book on parasites. I'm searching for similarities among known parasites to compare them against what's happening here with the zombies."

Ben took a sip of his coffee. "And what do you hope to achieve?"

"Achieve? Well, a better understanding would be a start. Maybe if I understood, I could find a way to treat the infected."

Ben looked dubious and now that she'd said it out loud she felt ridiculous. Like she and she alone could find a way to stop something like this. It sounded crazy even to her. She also wanted to find a way to stop the amalgamations, but after her first admission she wasn't about to say that out loud. Especially the way he was looking at her. But his next words weren't what she expected.

"I can see the determination in your eyes. You really think that book might hold the solution to this?" There was no mockery in his tone.

"I... I don't know, but it's a start." They sat there in the quiet house as another minute passed. In the fireplace a log shifted and settled, sparks sizzled, and the wood popped. "Can I ask you a question?"

Ben gave a reluctant nod.

"The tattoo on your forearm, what is it?"

Ben glanced down, turning his hand palm up. His fingers brushed absently over the ink as if the act of touching it might erase the memories tied to it. His expression shifted – just for a second – his usual intensity faltering into something quieter, something far away. Finally, he sighed through his nose. "Not what I expected you to ask."

Zoe caught a clearer view now. It was a striking design, bold black ink that had softened with time but remained vivid. A skull stared back at her, its hollow sockets framed by the edges of a scuba dive mask, rebreather tubes curling outward like the tendrils of some deep-sea monster. A frayed bandana was tied around its head, the fabric torn and weathered, as if it had seen one too many battles. Behind the skull, a dagger and an old flintlock pistol crossed in an X – past and present weapons bound together in eerie symmetry.

"What did you expect?" Zoe asked.

Ben smiled, as if to say, I'm not doing the work for you. "The tattoo is from another life. One in which a very young man with very little money decided the best way to see the world would be to join the military. And so he did, but as it turned out it wasn't the world he expected to see. You see when we're young, we think we know the meaning of it all, then we get old and realize we don't know shit. I think, young lady, that is the emptiness of youth and maybe why ignorance truly is bliss."

Zoe took a sip of her coffee. "Hmm, that's very poetic. What branch?"

"Army." His eyes were locked on the tattoo like the ink held secrets – horrible secrets.

"And what did you do in the military?"

"I was a clerk, but that was a long, long time ago."

"Bullshit," she said.

Ben smiled. "You are something, you know that? You really do remind me of my Maggie."

"You're trying to flatter me so you can change the subject, but okay. What happened to Maggie?" Zoe assumed the woman had passed and knew this might be especially sensitive.

"I wish I knew." Ben's gaze drifted over to the fire. "I wish to hell I knew."

Several more questions spun in Zoe's mind, but she didn't want to push her luck. So instead, she said, "Yesterday with Aaron, you should know that could have escalated. He is high functioning with intense interest in certain topics, but he's also socially awkward. Calling him out or calling him names will almost certainly result in an episode."

"An episode?" Ben asked.

"He might become agitated – you saw how he started to rock. If he becomes severely agitated or upset, the rocking could intensify. He might become inconsolable. He might scream or have a tantrum. He may even begin to hit himself – harder than he did. The point is, he could get hurt."

Ben released a heavy sigh. "I didn't realize... I... I am sorry for that. Other than those in my employment, I have been alone for some time and I... Well, when you're the boss you can pretty much say what you want but, regardless, I shouldn't have..." He trailed off, looking away again at the fire.

Zoe figured that was close enough to an apology. "Ben, it sounds like you were alone before this happened? What about your wife, daughter, and granddaughter?"

Ben's whole demeanor changed at the pointed questions about his family. "Jesus, you want to know my whole life story? My life is my own business, and you won't be around long enough to get to know the details." He stood. "Now, I don't have farmhands around here anymore and there's plenty I best be tending to. If you'll excuse—" The cough came abruptly this time, a harsh hack followed by bloody spittle down Ben's chin. The man's coffee cup slipped from his hand, smashing onto the hardwood as his eyes rolled back and he swayed on unsteady legs.

Zoe set her coffee on the end table and shot up and out of her chair. As Ben started to go down she supported him, guiding his fall backwards into the chair. "Ben! Ben, can you hear me?"

He was unresponsive.

"Ben!" She shook the man. "Come on, Ben! Wake up!" Zoe placed her ear by Ben's mouth to see if he was breathing. She wasn't sure. Damnit! She felt for a pulse on his neck, all the while calling his name. "Ben! Wake up, Ben!" Zoe opened his flannel, made a fist, and dug her knuckles into his sternum, rubbing vigorously. She'd used the sternal rub on unresponsive residents when she worked in the nursing home with some success. But if this didn't work, she'd need to get Ben on the floor where she could perform CPR. "Oliver!" she shouted, hoping he would hear her as she raked her knuckles across Ben's sternum again.

This time Ben's eyes popped open and he grabbed her wrist. "Son of a bitch!" he growled.

Zoe let out a relieved breath. "Ben, thank god."

Ben let go of Zoe's wrist and placed his hand over his heart as if he were about to pledge allegiance to the flag. "What the hell did you do, punch me in the chest? I thought you were a nurse."

Zoe made a pained face. "Yeah, sorry but you really left me no choice. It's called a sternal rub and it's designed to stimulate an unresponsive patient. The intent is to determine the patient's level of brain function. Thankfully in your case the pain woke you up."

Ben rubbed his chest. "So you didn't punch me? This wasn't payback for last night?"

Zoe laughed. "No, I didn't punch you."

"Alright then," Ben said, reaching up and touching his fingers to his mouth. He looked at the blood on his hand then back at Zoe. Clearly, he hadn't wanted her to see what he could no longer hide. Twisting in the chair, he reached into his back pocket and fished out his handkerchief.

Zoe knelt down next to the chair. "Ben, you're clearly not well. I think it's time you tell me what's going on."

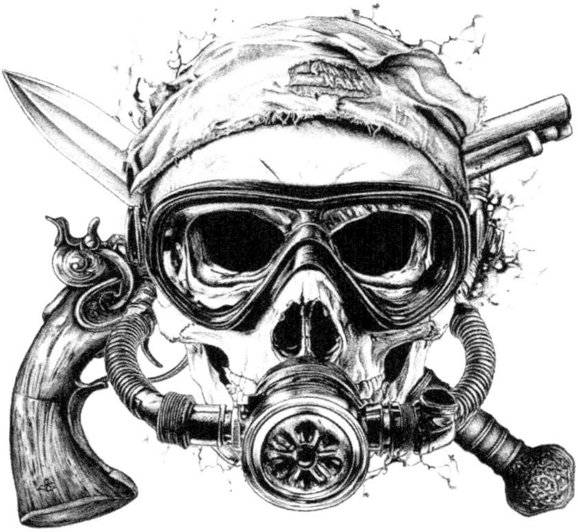

CHAPTER 6
THE NEED TO FEED

SLEEP, if you could call it that, didn't leave Tommy feeling rested at all. Pushing a gray cat off his legs, he sat up on the couch. His clothes were damp with sweat. *Where am I?* He pressed his face into a scowl, trying to remember how he'd gotten here. He licked his dry lips and tasted the blood and brain tissue crusting his mouth. *Oh, that's right, the tasty little girl.* Just the thought of her sent a wave of hunger pains through his stomach. Placing his hand on top of his belly, he expected to feel a massive lump but there was no lump. In fact, his stomach seemed to be sunken in... empty. He was starving, though he couldn't understand how that could be.

He ran a hand through his hair and down his neck. The lump on the back of his neck was as big as his fist. He held his hand over it, feeling it move beneath his fingers. He pushed himself up and onto his feet, remembering the nightmares. In his sleep he'd dreamed of slithering snakes squirming inside of him. Snakes filling his stomach, feasting on its contents. He knew it now – those tentacles could elongate, wriggling their way deep into his guts. That's how it grew so fast. It devoured what he devoured, consumed what he consumed.

In the morning light the place looked different than it had the night before. It was still a mess and still stunk of cat piss, though he smelled it less now. The walls were covered in yellow nicotine stains. Dirty dishes sat on the floor. He nudged a stack of them with his boot, revealing a swarm of cockroaches. The brown bastards scattered. Tommy couldn't have cared less. The only thought running through his mind was the pain and the need to relieve it. By now he knew there was only one way to do that but there was no food here – no brains. It was time to go. He had to find his next meal before the pain became too much to bear.

Suddenly his bowels had a different idea, cramping to the point he nearly dropped to his knees. "Guahh," he moaned, rushing for the bathroom. Like the rest of the place, the toilet looked like it hadn't been cleaned in years, but he wasted no time dropping trow and releasing an explosion of blood-soaked shit into the bowl.

Feeling at least a little better, Tommy picked up the shotgun and passed back through the kitchen, where the little girl's now headless corpse lay sprawled and pasty across the kitchen table. He picked up a piece of her broken skull by the tuft of dirty-blond hair still attached, flipped it over, and licked it, but there was nothing there.

Next to the girl, a cat sat lapping at a pool of coagulated blood, its perfectly white fur streaked in a smear of crimson. Tommy picked up the fur bag and held it in his arms. "What do you say? Will this work?"

The cat let out a disapproving hiss.

Tommy twisted the cat's neck until it popped, tossed it down onto the kitchen floor, and stomped on its head. Picking through the bone shards, he was only able to scoop a small amount of the cat's brain into his palm. He stared down at the pinkish-gray goo and then shrugged, throwing it back like a Jell-O shot.

"Ahh!" he shouted, spitting the mouthful onto the floor. It tasted exactly like you might expect a cat's raw brain to taste like, which was nothing like the sweet savory flavor of a human brain. He gagged and ran to the sink, turning on the tap. How could they be so different? How could one be the worst-tasting thing he'd ever put in his mouth and the other the most divine? The pain in his stomach intensified. He had to get the taste out of his mouth and water wasn't working. Without another thought he hurried back to the table, lifted the meat cleaver, and cut a chunk of flesh from the little girl's thigh. There was a thick layer of yellow fat over a hunk of fleshy pink meat. Shoving the whole wad into his mouth he chewed, moving the fatty chunk from one side of his mouth to the other before finally swallowing it down.

The raw flesh tasted good enough, but it did nothing to ease the pain in his belly. At least the foulness of the cat was mostly gone. "Okay, I get it." Tommy wiped his mouth across his sleeve. "Only human brains. Fine then. We best be moving on."

Tommy crossed the junkyard dump of a front lawn and stepped back onto Unsicker Road. The sky was clear and the air cool and crisp. He sniffed into the wind. No cat piss but no smell of sweets either. Glancing south, back towards the smoldering heap that used to be the church, he realized he hadn't made it far at all. There were two houses beyond the church further to the south but to the north the road stretched on for miles with several more farmhouses in that direction. Plus, Tommy knew for sure, Oliver, Zoe, and the others had gone north. And he was almost positive they had ended up at Old Man Meyer's place. The parasite inside him wanted brains and he wanted Oliver and Zoe. No reason not to have his cake and eat it too. "North it is." Gripping his shotgun in his right hand, Tommy settled into an easy jog along the shoulder of the road, gravel crunching rhythmically beneath his boots.

Through his one remaining eye, Tommy saw the world in a haze of red. The sky, the fields, the road – everything was bathed in the same bloody tint, as if the world itself had begun to rot from the inside out.

He knew he wasn't long for this world, not in the living sense anyway.

As he jogged along, those mortal thoughts were invading his mind, but they were pushed back by the pain forcing him to focus on the mission – find more, always find more.

His mind flickered, just for a moment, back to a different mission, a different road. Afghanistan. He had been part of a patrol of three light armored vehicles tasked with conducting curfew enforcement. As the patrol approached the border between the mountains and the city, the trail vehicle was hit by an improvised explosive device, followed by an ambush of rocket-propelled grenade, machine gun, and small arms fire. His team had quickly taken control of the situation, forcing the attackers to flee. The enemy had fled into the caves, thinking the mountains would protect them. They were wrong. Tommy's company had flushed them out, pinned them down, left their bodies cooling in the sand. That was the first time he'd killed another human. If he had felt anything at all, he sure didn't remember.

It was the same then as it was now – eyes forward, breath steady, boots hitting the pavement in perfect rhythm. But back then he didn't really care about the cause. He just wanted to get to kill someone. See what it was like to take another life. Now it was all different. Now he was focused like never before because now – now only one thing mattered.

He wondered though, when he did finally die, would he be called to a gathering? Would he be bonded to one of those monsters? Maybe so, but he wouldn't know it. He would be undead and gone, his body donated to their cause. That was fine with him. Let this pain end and they could do whatever they wanted with him. But not before he found that son of a bitch Oliver. And not before he feasted on Zoe and, even better, that little girl's brains.

A chuckle overcame Tommy as he thought about how he'd wanted to fuck Zoe. He'd risked it all to have her and now he couldn't care less about those mortal desires. There was only one need now. The need to feed.

Behind him a low hum built to the sound of an engine approaching.

Tommy spun on his heels just as a red sedan crested a small rise and sped toward him.

Tommy stepped into the road and raised the shotgun. A feral sneer stretched across his visage as he sighted down the barrel with his only eye.

Tires screeching, the car locked up its brakes.

At ten yards Tommy fired through the windshield.

The red Camry swerved just in time to avoid hitting him. The front end dipped low in the ditch, the front bumper biting into the embankment on the other side.

The driver was instantly ejected through the windshield, tumbling in a bone-breaking tangle of limbs before settling ungracefully in a twisted heap.

Inside the car a woman was screaming.

Slow and careful would have been the smartest way to

approach this situation, but the smell of sweet creaminess in the air was too much. The pain it elicited was too much! Tommy threw all caution to the wind as he rushed around the side of the car, unable to control his desire.

A young woman probably in her early thirties with long brown hair tied back in a ponytail sat twisted in the passenger seat. Judging by her wrongly bent arm and bloody face, she had sustained some injuries. The good news was – her head was intact.

Mouth salivating, Tommy jerked up on the door handle only to find it locked.

Lifting the shotgun, he flipped it around and slammed it into the side window. Glass showered the woman. And for the first time she turned to look at him. Her green eyes went wide – cartoonishly wide. Tommy chuckled. "That's right, bitch. You know why I'm here."

"No! Please! Help! Bobby! Bobby, please!" she screamed.

Tommy reached in and unlocked the door. "If that guy in the field is Bobby, I'd say you're fucked because he ain't getting up – ever." He pulled the Camry's door open as the single crack of a gunshot rang out. At first he couldn't understand where it had come from. He looked at the woman, but she didn't have a gun. Confused, he looked over at the man lying in the field, but he hadn't moved. Then he felt it. A sharp pain in his left shoulder. He'd been shot.

His left shoulder had been facing the car when he opened the door. Tommy stepped back and to the side, then squatted down. Whoever shot him must have been hiding in the back seat. "Fucker!" Tommy growled. Raising the shotgun above his head with both hands, he fired through the back passenger window of the Camry.

The gun bucked wildly in his hands as the glass

exploded. From the back seat a new scream emerged. It sounded like a kid.

Tommy stood just enough to peek over the door, then ducked back down. "Gotcha!" With the woman still screaming in the front seat, Tommy shuffled to the side and pulled open the back passenger door.

The gun fired at him again. *Pop! Pop!* The bullets bit harmlessly into the dirt. A moment passed.

"Please! Don't hurt him!" the green-eyed woman cried. "Don't hurt my baby boy!"

From the back seat something dropped onto the floorboard with a thump.

Tommy peeked in again. The boy, a teen of maybe fifteen or sixteen, sat slack in the back seat. He wore a Chicago Bears jersey and a matching cap that sat askew on his head. His chin lolled on his chest and the gun had fallen to the floor. His whole right side and face were peppered with buckshot. The boy was dead, and all Tommy could think was, *I hope I didn't ruin his brain.*

He stood up, reached into the back seat, and retrieved the .22 Ruger from the floorboard.

The woman stammered pathetically from the front seat. "Jimmy? Jimmy, are you okay? I... I can't see you. My back... Oh Jimmy, please answer me!"

"Jimmy is okay. I freed him just like I'm going to free you." Tommy pressed the barrel of the Ruger into the back of the passenger seat.

The woman cried hysterically as she struggled to move, to twist and see.

Tommy fired through the seat, once, twice, then again. Finally, the bitch shut up.

Tommy went to work cracking open and consuming the brains of the three passengers, starting with the man in the field. He found the man's skull had been crushed. On the upside, it was easy to get into, but on the downside, he had to eat slower, carefully picking out the bone shards as if he were removing bits of eggshell from scrambled eggs. And no one liked eggshells in their eggs.

By late morning he was finishing up with the teen, his stomach so bloated it was like a dead carcass in the summer sun ready to burst. *Time to go.* But before climbing out of the back seat, he loaded the Ruger's magazine with rounds from a box of shells he'd found on the floorboard. Ready to move on, Tommy climbed out of the Camry and tucked the Ruger into his waistband.

Something felt weird.

Tommy forced down a swallow as a sudden pressure constricted in his throat. He could feel the parasite's excitement. It was happy to feed and it rewarded him, lessening the pain in his stomach. The thing inside him was growing faster than he could have imagined. Its slippery tentacles slithered their way down and down, drawing up the brain matter like snakes swallowing mice.

He reached up and touched his neck. Near his jugular he could feel a ripple beneath his skin. His chest fluttered and his stomach swirled with what he could only describe as a strange tickle. "You're hungry. Go right on then."

The strangeness of it wasn't lost on him, but compared to the gnawing, insatiable pain of hunger, this was better. The parasite had eaten, at least for now. And as long as it was satisfied, so was he.

It was almost funny – this whole thing reminded him of when his wife had been pregnant. That was a fucking ordeal, listening to her go on and on about the baby "kicking" and how she could feel it moving inside her. She'd acted like she was some goddess of creation, while all she really did was get fat, puke all the time, and bitch about back pain.

Tommy grimaced. Giving birth was a joke. She had no idea what real pain was. Well, at least this thing inside him didn't whine. It didn't cry. It wasn't going to come out of him one day and ruin his life for the next eighteen years. No, it just wanted to be fed. And Tommy just needed to eat. Because the feeling of his insides coming alive was nothing compared to the hunger.

But for now the parasite seemed content and he'd take that any day of the week.

Grabbing the teen by the ankle, he pulled the dead boy from the back seat, letting the body flop into the ditch. Eating the three had been a laborious task and now with the thing feeding inside him he thought he'd just take a moment and rest.

Crawling into the back seat, Tommy closed his eye. He didn't sleep, but he used the momentary relief from the pain to sit and rest. The only time he could really focus on anything other than eating was after a full feeding.

But the moment was too short, and with no warning, pain seared through him like a hot poker to the stomach.

It was instant, unbearable – his muscles locked, his vision blurred. But inside the pain, there was a message, one that didn't need words:

"Get your worthless ass up and find more!"

The command hit him like a drill sergeant's scream in his ear. His body snapped to attention before his mind could even process it because this wasn't the first time he'd been treated like a disposable piece of shit.

Boot camp. The mud, the sweat, the heat so bad it felt like his skin was melting off his bones. He could still hear Staff Sergeant Holloway barking orders while Tommy clawed his way up a hill, his legs cramping so hard he thought he'd pass out.

"Move your ass, Thompson! You crawl slower than old people fuck!"

Tommy had collapsed face-first in the dirt – a mistake. Before he could suck in a breath, Holloway's boot slammed into his ribs, flipping him like a ragdoll.

"You wanna quit? You wanna be weak?"

And now, years later, that lesson had burrowed so deep inside him that he obeyed without thinking. The parasite wanted more. That was all that mattered.

He gritted his teeth, shoving himself upright.

"Get up. Move. Find more."

This time, there was no boot to his ribs – just the parasite, spurring him forward with its cruel, unrelenting hunger.

CHAPTER 7
BENSON'S SECRETS

"OLIVER? Oliver, I think I heard Zoe yelling for you!" came the little girl's voice through the bathroom door, followed by a bark and a wine.

Oliver dropped the towel and pulled on his jeans. "What? You sure?"

From the hall, Adam shouted, "Oliver! Did you hear that? It sounded like Zoe yelling for help!"

Oliver flung open the bathroom door and ran across the room.

"See! I told you!" Jurnee shouted after him.

As Oliver bolted barefoot and shirtless down the hall, he realized not only was he half-dressed and still dripping with water, but he didn't even have a gun. He hoped Zoe had her .357 on her hip and not in the nightstand back in the bedroom. As he approached the staircase he couldn't keep the bad thoughts away. Had a zombie broken in or were there other intruders? But how? What if the old man had become infected somehow? It was all he could do not to scream for Zoe – to shout that he was coming, to just hold on!

As he bounded down the stairs two at a time, he heard Adam and Louie on his heels. Why in the fuck did he decide to shower this morning? Why didn't he come straight down the stairs and check on his wife? Fucking stupid!

Through the colonnade he caught a glimpse of Zoe in the den. She was kneeling. His first thought was that she was hiding but as he rushed forward, he saw the old man sitting in the chair.

Louie barked, running full speed ahead into the room.

"It's okay, Louie," she said, giving his head a pat with her free hand.

Adam stopped next to him. "What happened?"

Her other hand held Ben's wrist. The man looked pale as a ghost. "It's okay, guys, I... I thought I might have to perform CPR."

"I'm fine," Ben grumbled, pulling his hand away.

Zoe narrowed her eyes at the old man. "That's bullshit. I never said you were fine. I would love to get a pulse oximetry on you. I'd bet money you're dangerously low." She frowned. "Ben, do you have oxygen for your condition?"

"My condition? I never said I had a condition. And what kind of bedside manners are those anyway? Is that what they're teaching doctors these days, to cuss at your patients?"

Zoe smirked, taking Ben's wrist again. "Given all those expletives you were spouting a few minutes ago, I didn't realize you were so sensitive to foul language – I'll clean it up for you. Now be still."

Ben rubbed his free hand over his heart. "I had a reason. You punched me in the chest."

Oliver shared a look with Adam. "You punched him, Zo?" he asked in disbelief.

Zoe gave him the side eye. "Of course I didn't punch him. But he did pass out. Now, Ben, I need you to tell me what's going on, so I know how to treat you. I can ask them to leave if you want it to just be us, but I can't help you if I don't understand."

"Treat me." Ben laughed but there was no humor in it. "You can't treat me."

"What is it, Ben?" Lowering her voice, she gave him a steady look. "Cancer?"

Ben drew in a wheezing breath that sounded loud in the silent room and gave what Oliver thought was a slight nod.

Jurnee burst into the room, breaking the silence. "Hi, Mr. Mayor – what are you guys doing? Did you have breakfast yet? Oh, I sure hope I didn't miss it. I'm sooo hungry! I feel like I haven't eaten in years!"

Aaron entered behind her dressed in blue jeans, a T-shirt, and a long khaki trench coat he must have found in the closet of the room he slept in. "Of course, with breakfast being the most important meal of the day, I would enjoy some eggs."

"Melissa and Baby Jonathan are still sleeping. If it's alright, I'll fix these guys something," Adam offered.

Ben cleared his throat. "I put some fresh eggs on the counter and there's some pancake mix in the pantry. Help yourself."

"You heard him, eggs and pancakes it is. Come on, you guys," Adam said, ushering Aaron and Jurnee into the kitchen.

"I like mine all scrambled up and no runny business!" Jurnee announced as she disappeared through the doorway.

Oliver turned to follow.

"You might as well stay." Ben frowned. "Your wife is going to tell you anyhow."

Zoe placed a hand on Ben's shoulder. "Hey, I respect patient-doctor confidentiality. I won't say a word to anyone, but Ben, I need to know everything."

Oliver didn't know if he should stay or go so he paused, awkwardly waiting to be told what to do.

Ben waved her off and Oliver took that as an invitation to stay.

"You can't save me. My cancer is terminal and it's spreading. The doctors didn't give me long."

"What about chemo?" Zoe asked.

"Tried that. Made me sick as hell but didn't stop the spread."

"Why are you home alone? Does your daughter know? And what about your wife?"

"They don't know. I haven't seen my daughter Ellie in two years, three months, and five days. It's been even longer since I've seen Maggie. Neither of them knows." Ben's eyes welled up.

Zoe looked at Oliver. He could see in her eyes what she wanted to ask and, when she bit the corner of her bottom lip, he knew she was contemplating it. Why was Ben here alone? Why hadn't he told his family?

Instead, she said, "You didn't answer my question earlier."

Ben's gray eyebrows scrunched up like two silver caterpillars about to wrestle each other.

"Oxygen? Were you prescribed any?"

Ben nodded. "Ran out days ago."

Zoe sighed. "And what about pain management?"

"I had a home healthcare nurse who managed that for me but the day this all happened she never showed up. I assume the worst." Ben pushed himself forward in the chair as if he were about to stand. "I have plenty of medicine and a whole cabinet full of whiskey. I'm making do."

"That's your plan?"

"You have a better one?" the man asked with annoyance.

"I'm working on it, but I'll tell you this – whatever I come up with will be better than the suicide cocktail you been taking."

Ben huffed. "Suicide? What's it matter? Dead is dead and I'm on my way."

Zoe smirked. "So that's your plan then?"

"Aren't you even going to ask me why my family is gone, why I didn't tell them about my condition?"

Finally, Oliver thought. He'd been wondering exactly that.

Zoe didn't answer right away, then finally she said, "No, but if you want to talk about it, I'm happy to listen."

"Well, I don't." Ben pushed himself up out of the chair.

"Hey, easy. Just go slow, okay?" Zoe said, steadying Ben as he stood up.

"I'm fine. Now, as long as the sky is clear I have chores that still need tending to."

Zoe nodded toward Oliver.

"Oh, right. Ben, let me grab a shirt and my shoes and I'll give you a hand with whatever you got going on."

His face skeptical, Ben asked, "Oh yeah? You ever worked on a farm before, son?"

"Well, no, but I'm no stranger to hard work."

Ben regarded him, thoughtfully. "Well, I could use some help with feeding the horses in the barn. As far as your worth, guess I'll be the judge of that. Meet me out back when you're decent."

"I'll come too," Zoe offered. "That way you can just supervise. Besides, I love horses."

"No!" Ben snapped.

Zoe frowned. "What? Why? Honestly, I don't mind getting my hands dirty."

"I... I just want some time alone with Oliver – man to man. But later, I'll take you out there myself." From the tone of his voice, it was clear the topic wasn't up for debate.

"Alright then. I'll check on Melissa and the baby, but later on I want to see those horses."

"Of course." Ben nodded at Oliver, then hooked a thumb over his shoulder toward the kitchen. "There's a black jacket hanging by the back door – it's cold out, so wear it." Steady now, Ben slowly walked toward the kitchen.

"Oliver," Zoe said, whispering into Oliver's ear, "keep an eye on him. If he faints, come and get me."

"Faints? Shit. Is that likely?"

"Yeah, it is. There's no way he should be going out there to do any sort of work."

"Why didn't you tell him that?"

"You think it would have mattered?" she asked, unclipping the holstered .357 from her hip. "He's stubborn as a mule, more stubborn even than you." She stood up on her tiptoes and gave him a peck on the cheek. "Just keep an eye on him and be careful. Don't go out there if there is even one single cloud in the sky."

"Okay, Mom." He smiled, giving her a peck on the forehead.

Zoe slapped his shoulder and passed him her gun. "You think you're so funny."

"I do alright," he said with a grin. "Will you be okay while I'm gone?"

Her face turned from worry to a deeper concern. "Yeah,

I'll check on Melissa, then I'm going to try and figure out what medical supplies I'm going to need for Ben."

Oliver raised an eyebrow. "Really? You think you can help him get better?"

She shook her head, sadness washing over her face. "Ollie, if what Ben said is true, he isn't going to get better, but maybe I can help him be more comfortable."

Outside, the sky was an ocean of blue with old big-yellow at his back, burning just as bright as it ever had. To his left, across the property's well-manicured lawn and fence, the sky bled into a forest of quiet trees, their leaves clinging like brittle scabs on dying limbs – still not ready to give up on summer's warmth and their once vibrant greens, now lost to a season past. Straight ahead, beyond the back privacy fence, a freshly harvested pumpkin field sat empty, preparing to hibernate for the winter. On the far side of the field was a water tower marking the edge of Groveland. In the far left corner of the pumpkin patch more timber met a cornfield. Oddly the small strip of cornfield was unharvested. Their dry stalks rattled in the breeze like old bones.

To Oliver's right was a large red pole barn, a chicken coop, and beyond that a cow pasture.

Having glanced around and taken in the vistas of forest and field, Oliver stepped forward to join Ben, who was standing next to a large inground swimming pool complete with a water slide and grotto. Even with the pool covered for the winter, he could tell it was an impressive size.

"Biggest waste of money ever. You know what they say?"

Oliver glanced over. "No, what do they say?"

"The two best days for a pool owner are the day they open it and the day they fill it in with dirt. My Ellie loves to swim. She's like a fish. You should have seen her face the day we opened this for the first time. Waste or not, I was all for it if it meant keeping her home more and giving her and her friends a place to hang out where we could keep an eye on them. When I tell you she couldn't get enough, I mean I had to force her to come in at dark and she'd be right back out here at the crack of dawn. All summer long. Couldn't get the kid out of bed on summer vacation for any other reason in the world but when that pool was open you'd bet your ass she was going to be in it every waking hour." Ben seemed to leave for a minute. Back to some old memory – a good memory, judging by his expression.

Oliver allowed himself a moment too. Not a memory but a daydream. He could see it now, a hot August day, Jurnee with those floaty wing things around her arms, giggling and jumping off the pool deck, as Zoe lay in a lounger, sunbathing on the tanning shelf. He'd be out there too in wet trunks, grilling some burgers.

Of course, he knew they'd likely be long gone by August and besides, he wasn't even sure that world existed anywhere but in a daydream, not anymore.

Oliver's moment of bliss was broken as the old man's face fell, his thoughts clearly turning sour as he suddenly looked much older, much... sicker. "Well, that was a long time ago. So, are you just gonna stand there, or are you coming?" Ben asked, rifle in hand as he started across the pool patio.

Oliver pressed his lips tight, his heart heavy as he struggled to find the right words. But in the end he couldn't, so he simply said, "Right behind you."

They made their way across the pool patio and onto a

stamped sidewalk weaving its way through a perfectly manicured lawn, finally ending at the door to the barn.

Ben reached for the latch on the barn door and paused, his expression suddenly troubled. "Oliver, I need to tell you something so that when I open this door you won't be... well, alarmed."

Oliver's ass clenched at the sudden turn from feeling sorry for the dying man to instantly wondering, *What in the unholy fuck is in that barn?* Remembering all too well what the owners of the last farm had kept in their basement and how Zoe had almost become food for the twins, Oliver did his best to stay calm and relax his ass cheeks. "Ben, what's in there?"

Ben turned to him, his expression grim. "When this whole mess started, I had several farmhands working the farm. Before I got sick, three men helped with the cattle and the horses, but several months back the day-to-day became too much for me, so I hired another hand, Randy. Honestly, he was the hardest-working man I'd ever hired."

Oliver didn't like where this was going.

"Randy was married to Annie and had a little girl, Katie, about your little girl's age – about my own granddaughter's age." Ben's voice broke and he started to cough.

Oliver hadn't expected the man to show this vulnerability, and in the moment he didn't know what to say or if he should say anything at all. Instead, he averted his eyes, taking the moment to check their surroundings. The tall fence enclosing the back yard connected to each side of the barn. Inside the safety of the fence all was quiet but he knew anything could be on the other side and it wasn't hard to imagine a mob of zombies crashing through the wooden fence or, worse, one of those zombie monsters like back at the church. Instinctively, he reached into his borrowed jacket pocket and touched the .357, its cold steel offering some comfort.

Ben wiped his mouth and swallowed dryly, his wet eyes glistening in the morning sun. "Randy and Annie had an older son too. Just barely in his teens. Name was Tobias but he went by Toby. The family was staying in my barn. Before you judge me, I know how that sounds. One old asshole and all this house forcing the help to sleep in the barn. I think by now you know there's some truth to the asshole part."

"Ben, I never said you were an—"

Ben waved him off. "Just stop. I know exactly what I am and how I have treated people over the years. I also know what you've heard about me. There's plenty of truth in that too. It's a fact I acquired my millions in part by buying up all the land as it became available. At first, I mortgaged one to get another but in time I was making so much off the farmland I'd acquired I was able to easily outbid everyone at every land auction within a hundred miles. Then I got greedier. Waiting for land to go up for auction wasn't enough. I needed more, so I started approaching landowners who weren't even selling, but you could tell just by looking at the unkempt properties they were struggling. And so I capitalized on their hardships. This... method of doing business earned me the reputation I deserve."

Ben glanced back at the barn door and licked his lips. "Far as Randy's family goes, the truth is the barn has a very nice studio style apartment in the upper loft. It isn't like I had them sleeping on piles of straw in the horse stalls. Believe it or not, I was trying to help them get on their feet and they were grateful. They provided me with hard work, and I provided a roof and decent pay. That was the deal."

The October breeze found its way down the back of

Oliver's neck, prickling his skin in goosebumps. He pulled the collar of his jacket up and shoved his hands deeper into his pockets as if he were imitating James Dean in *Rebel Without a Cause*. "It's cold. Can we finish this talk inside the barn?"

"Son, it's time for you and I to share some honest air."

Honest air? What the hell was the old man talking about? "I... I don't understand."

Ben tipped his head back, his eyes searching the sky for words he expected might be hanging there pinned to the canvas of blue like puffy white clouds. When he found them, he closed his eyes as if preparing himself. Finally, he lowered his head and opened his eyes, settling his gaze on Oliver. "I can't go in there again, Oliver... not after what I've done."

Oliver stepped back from the door, the hair on his neck coming to attention. Ass-clenching fear was quickly becoming his ready stance, and he didn't much care for it. "You didn't ask me out here to help you feed the horses, did you?"

Ben's lips became a tight line of determination.

"No, son. No, I indeed did not."

Realizing in that moment Benson Meyer was keeping some horrible secret in that barn, Oliver gripped the handle of the .357 in his pocket and looked directly at the old man. "I'm going to ask you again, what's in that fucking barn, Ben?"

Ben's eyes were suddenly grayer than their normal icy blue. The color of gray you might find choking the sky just before a heavy snowfall. The old man's jaw quivered as wet streams spilled down wrinkled cheeks peppered with silver stubble. A long second passed, then two, and finally in a voice almost too low to hear, Ben whispered, "I killed them."

CHAPTER 8
SOMETHING IN BETWEEN

ONCE AGAIN, Tommy stood on the shoulder of Unsicker Road, his single, bloodshot eye staring unblinking to the north. "You want more?" he growled through split lips, a twisted sneer forming on what remained of his face. His voice was thick, guttural, almost unrecognizable as human. "Of course you do, you motherfucker. You always do!"

He shifted slightly, his thick, swollen tongue slithering out to lick the dry, cracked corners of his mouth. His skin felt wrong – all of him felt wrong. His body had felt wrong since the infection took hold, since the parasite began digging its claws deeper into his flesh, but this... this was different. He could feel it, something stirring deep beneath the surface, like an itch in the marrow of his bones that he couldn't scratch. He'd been shot in the shoulder. His right eye had been punched out with the spike end of a throwing axe, leaving a gaping, pus-filled socket. On top of that, he was pretty sure he'd ruptured his stomach the first time he'd eaten so much. Shouldn't those wounds have killed him? Shouldn't they at least hurt? Well, they didn't.

It wasn't just the fact the only pain he felt was hunger pain, it was something more. It was like with every passing minute he was getting closer to... to what? The end? Was he dying and just couldn't feel it because the monster inside him blocked all that out? Maybe, but there was something else. Something more ominous than even death. He couldn't shake the feeling he was being prepared for whatever came next. Maybe. Or maybe he'd die soon and the monster inside him would answer the calling. Except, despite his misery, he didn't want to die, not yet. He was still hungry, and the tiny bit of humanity left in him longed for revenge.

Tommy shoved the .22 Ruger in his waistband and pumped another round into the shotgun. "Well, you bastard, I'm not ready to die yet. I'm still hungry and so are you! So let's go get it!"

He started walking again, his steps uneven but deliberate, his body swaying slightly with each step, like a man stitched together wrong, every movement held together by will alone.

As he reached the intersection of Queenwood and Unsicker Road, Tommy paused. Out of habit, he glanced both ways; the motion was almost reflexive – like he was just some guy waiting for a break in traffic. But there were no cars. No people. No life. Just silence.

The world he'd once known – the one that should have been here – was gone.

Something shifted inside him, something deep and unfamiliar, but he shoved it down, focusing instead on the only movement in sight.

Down the road, a lone undead wobbled into view, its sagging skin clinging to the bone like a wet sheet draped over a skeleton. Its clouded, empty eyes barely seemed to register its own existence. Its mouth hung open, waiting or maybe hoping for something to fall into it.

Tommy's lip curled in disgust. From here, he couldn't tell if the thing was male or female, but it didn't matter. It wasn't a threat, and more importantly, it wasn't food. Tommy neither waited nor hurried across the road. There was no need for fear anymore. Fear was for the living, and though his heart still pumped he was something else now – something in between dead and undead.

Ahead, a two-story white house loomed on his left, its boarded windows giving it an occupied look. He bet there were people holed up inside. As soon as he saw it, the familiar hunger roared inside him, twisting his gut with sharp, stabbing pains. The parasite surged, urging him to stop, to go inside, to feed. His stomach churned violently, and for a moment, Tommy thought he might give in again, the call of fresh brains almost too much to resist. But he firmed his resolve, clenched his jaw, and forced himself to keep walking, each step a battle of will against the monster inside him. "Benson Meyer's farmhouse is just up ahead, you gluttonous bastard," he hissed through gritted teeth. His voice trembled with strain as he fought to maintain control. "I know there's plenty there. They have a baby and a little girl – fresh and tender. I promise we'll come back if we have to but let me show you. Let me show you what's waiting up ahead."

As Tommy forced his way down the road, and the white farmhouse disappeared behind him, he felt the faintest flicker of control return. His mind, clouded and frayed as it was, latched on to that sliver of clarity like a drowning man grasping at a lifeline. His pace slowed, his ragged breath coming out in short, uneven bursts. For a brief moment, the pressure in his skull and the constant pulsing hunger gnawing at his insides seemed to ease. But he knew it wouldn't last long. The parasite was growing stronger, and soon, whatever control he had would be lost forever.

Ahead, the road narrowed slightly, a patch of dense timber creeping up on the left side. The dark silhouettes of the trees seemed to stretch taller in the light, their gnarled branches reaching across the road like skeletal fingers. Beyond them, the faint outline of a concrete bridge came into view, the structure standing out against the wilderness like a scar on the land. Tommy's gaze sharpened, his single remaining eye fixed on the bridge and what lay beyond.

The wrought iron gate stood sentinel, tall and imposing, its bars bent, twisted, and chained together, giving it a proven look, like an old battle-scarred soldier who you could tell had been in the shit but came out the other side.

His lips curled into a twisted grin, split and bleeding as they were, as two familiar vehicles came into view beyond the gate – a truck and a van. *Oliver.* The name, spoken only in his thoughts, carried with it a surge of dark satisfaction. He could almost see the man now, cautious as ever, thinking he could hide behind iron gates and a tall fence. But he should have known better.

"I knew it," Tommy rasped, his voice barely more than a growl. "You're too predictable, Oliver."

Tommy felt his stomach tighten, the pain flaring up again, twisting in his gut like a knife being driven into his intestines. He hunched forward slightly, gritting his teeth as the hunger surged, stronger this time. The parasite was growing impatient, pressing against his mind, pushing him toward the gate. *Feed. Feed now.*

"No," Tommy muttered, shaking his head as if trying to ward off the beast inside him. His hand twitched toward the Ruger in his waistband, the weight of the shotgun slung over his shoulder, a cold reminder of the violence he was capable of. But this wasn't about feeding. Not yet. This was about something else, something deeper than the hunger. Revenge. He needed to be smart.

He wiped the back of his hand across his face, dried blood flaking from around his mouth. His eye narrowed as he studied the gate and the house beyond, his mind already working through the possibilities. *Oliver thinks he's safe. He thinks these gates and walls will keep him hidden.*

Tommy's fingers twitched again, this time with anticipation. The thought of breaking through that gate, of ripping through whatever stood between him and Oliver, filled him with a twisted sense of purpose. It wasn't just the hunger driving him now – it was the need to settle a score. The last shred of humanity left in him screamed for revenge, even as the parasite whispered for brains.

"Let's go," Tommy growled under his breath, his voice barely human. His boots scuffed across the concrete as he stepped toward the gate, his mind already picturing what lay beyond – Oliver and the others, unsuspecting, unprepared. He could already taste their brains, feel the warm creaminess coating his mouth.

The parasite inside him sensed it too, pulsing with approval, urging him forward – and forward he went.

CHAPTER 9
WHAT'S IN THE BARN

THE WIND FELT SUDDENLY COLDER and the morning darker. Oliver felt his spine tingle as a chill ran down his back. It wasn't the cold, though – it was the way Ben shifted his weight, the pause before he began to explain what was in the barn. After everything Oliver had seen and done, what in the world could Ben be hiding that was so bad? Still there was something about the way the old man hesitated, reluctant to go on as they both stood breathing in the crisp air. It made Oliver's stomach churn. *He's stalling. Trying to keep it together,* Oliver thought. He knew that look well enough. A man on the edge of a story too heavy to tell but one he couldn't keep locked away anymore. "What happened, Ben?"

"Let me start at the beginning." Ben's voice cracked, but he took a deep breath and continued. "The day the rain started Jose, Raul, and Greg had already checked in and started their day. Jose had a fall crew of about a dozen men and women set to pick pumpkins in what we call the west forty." Ben pointed across a barren field to some distant place Oliver couldn't see. "Raul and Greg were set to harvest one of my smaller plots of corn I use for cattle feed. I never saw those two again. The rain..."

Ben lowered his voice, almost like he was telling a secret. "Jose came back, maybe forty-five minutes after it started. But he... he didn't come back the same. His car rammed through my front gate, cut across my yard, and smashed into the porch."

Oliver nodded, vaguely recalling that morning. "I passed by your place that very morning. I saw the wreck, the car in the flowerbed, your front gate smashed. My garbage truck was overheating, and the situation here didn't look good, so I moved on." The memory was foggy, as if it were part of someone else's life. So much had happened since then. He felt a pang of guilt for not stopping, but the world had been unraveling so quickly that day. His truck had been overheating. *What if I had stopped? What could I have done?*

"Small world, I guess. It's probably best you didn't stop here anyway, not on that day," Ben said, voice distant as he delved deeper into the memory. "I... I didn't have the front door locked, but with the weird rain and after the strange asteroid announcements on the news I'd had the foresight to have a gun handy. I was about to head out into the rain and check on Randy and the others. I wanted to make sure they could still get the job done despite the rain. Well, that's what I thought I'd tell them, but I can admit now what I really wanted to do was make sure Toby and Katie were okay."

Ben scrubbed a hand over his stubble, his face tight. "As I reached for the back door, I heard something out front. A loud metal-on-metal crash. A moment later a loud boom shook the house. I spun on my heels and darted through the kitchen and into the den just as the front door burst open. It was Jose, but he looked all wrong. His face was slicked with the red rain and his eyes – his eyes were wild and oozing blood. He had a tire iron in his hand. He charged at me screaming something... something crazy. It didn't make sense, none of it made any damn sense! I had to shoot! I had no choice!"

Ben's face and hands were shaking now.

"It's okay," Oliver reassured him, fearing what might happen if the ill man got too worked up. "I know you didn't have a choice. Believe me, I know."

"But you don't know. You don't know what I've done. That was just the beginning. After I shot Jose, it wasn't hard to put two and two together. I figured whatever had happened to him was caused by the red rain. I knew I couldn't go out to the barn until I was sure I could do it without getting wet. I retrieved my Special Ops drysuit and—"

"Wait, you were in the military? You never mentioned that."

Ben swallowed and coughed. "Oliver, I am an old and very sick man. What few advantages I have are only advantages if potential threats don't know about them."

Oliver nodded. The realization wasn't lost on him. Ben had looked at him and the others as threats. But now he wasn't only confessing some horrible thing to him, he was trusting him. "Go on," Oliver encouraged.

"A lifetime ago when I served, I was in the Special Forces Underwater Operations program. We specialized in combat operations involving the use of underwater infiltration methods. As life beyond the military moved forward, I still had a passion for scuba diving, and I had the finances to keep up on the latest and greatest gear. Hence the modern wetsuit. Call it a hobby."

Ben shrugged, then forced himself back to his story. "Like I was saying, I donned my wetsuit and mask, then switched out my rifle for a pistol and headed out into the rain. I didn't make it three steps out that back door before I heard Katie's screams." His voice faltered, and he placed his palm on the barn door, as if steadying himself. The way his fingers pressed into the wood, trembling slightly, made Oliver's gut twist. Ben was reliving it. Every moment.

"I ran across the yard and flung this very door open, charging forward. The first person I saw was little Katie. She ran right past me. I lunged for her, but she slipped through my gloved fingers. Jesus, I had her! She was right there, and I couldn't stop her! She ran right into the rain."

Oliver's heart raced as he listened, the macabre scene playing out almost as if he were there standing alongside the old man.

"Then I heard more screams," Ben said, barely above a whisper. "This time it sounded like Katie's mom, Annie. I forced my legs into a run and climbed the stairs. The door at the top of the stairs was standing wide open.

"That's when I saw Randy. He was coming at me in a full run. He had blood and... I don't know... chunks of... Oh god," Ben moaned. "It was smeared across his face. I screamed, pointed the gun, and shot him twice center mass. But he didn't die. You put a couple rounds in a man's chest, and he drops. I know, I've done it more times than I'd like to remember, but not Randy. I mean he went down and that should have been the end of it. But then he let out an awful screech and got right back up. I swear I shit myself right then and there. I'd never seen anything like it. Then I remembered I'd shot Jose in the head. I fired another round, and it flew true, but Randy was on his feet and running again.

"The man collided with me before falling dead. I nearly went backward down the stairs. I stood there for a moment panting and listening. Annie wasn't screaming anymore. I ran across the living room and through the kitchen to the back bedroom." A sob broke from Ben and a huge lump formed in Oliver's throat. "I found Annie. Toby had beat her to death with her own curling iron. Do you understand? He and his father had broken her head open! Little Toby was scooping out her fucking brains and eating them like he'd never eaten before.

"I must have screamed because I swear I will never forget the look when that boy's head snapped around. His bloody eyes were wide, impossibly wide – and those teeth. His lips stretched open, and I could see the skin and flesh in his teeth. He hissed like a fucking snake and sprang up. He didn't stand, he fucking jumped up into the air. I fired. Do you hear me?! I killed a thirteen-year-old kid with one to the head."

Oliver flashed back to a memory of his own. It was the first time he and Jurnee were at the church and he'd been forced to kill an undead teenager, but the difference was he had not known the kid in life. While he could empathize, he couldn't imagine how that must have felt. Oliver swallowed hard, his throat dry. "I'm sorry, Ben." The words were automatic and instinctual, but they didn't feel like enough.

Ben let out a heavy breath. "If the story ended there, maybe I could live with it. Once I got to the bottom of the stairs I heard Katie sobbing. I found her soaking wet, curled up in a ball in the corner of an empty stall. I promised her it was going to be okay, that I was going to take care of her. 'Katie, you have to get the rain washed off! We have to do it now!' I told her. I grabbed a water hose for the horses and doused her. She cried, not understanding. Once I was sure the rain was washed off, I went to work looking for some plastic to cover her with, to protect her from the rain. I wanted the fuck out of that barn! By the time I found some plastic, Katie was saying things that didn't make sense. No. No! I was screaming, begging god not to let whatever happened to the others happen to this little girl!"

Ben was crying now and Oliver felt his own eyes fill and blur.

"But her eyes were red as hot coals. She didn't even seem to care about what I'd done, what her father and brother had done. She kept saying she was starving and that she could smell it. Smell the sweetness. She said it hurt and she had to have it." Ben shook his head, unable to continue, his face twisted in a visage of pain.

Oliver felt his own chest tighten, his vision blurring with tears he tried so hard to hold back. What could he say? What could anyone say to this? A whole family – all of them lost to the rain, to the madness that followed. Oliver's mind flashed with images – little Katie's red eyes, her voice pleading for something she didn't even understand. Starving. Wanting something she couldn't resist.

"You did the right thing," Oliver forced out, knowing it wasn't enough. It would never be enough.

But Ben shook his head, his shoulders slumping as if the weight of the world had settled there. "No. You don't understand. I'm not ashamed of what had to be done. I know they're at peace now. It's what I failed to do."

Oliver blinked, confused. After everything, what could he have failed to do?

Then Ben said it. The words that hit Oliver like a punch to the gut.

"You have to finish it. You have to kill Katie."

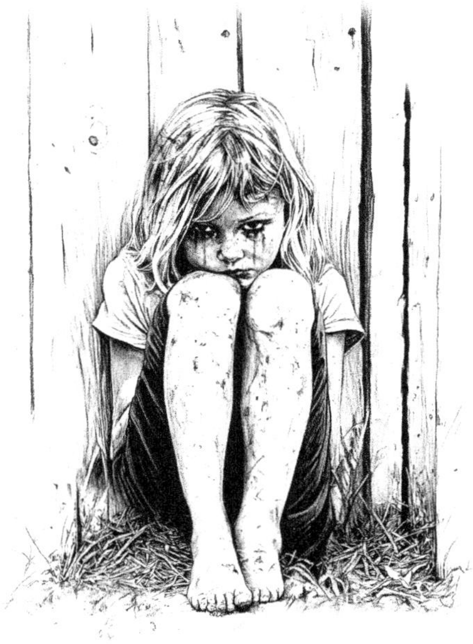

CHAPTER 10
SILHOUETTE

ZOE CLIMBED THE STAIRS, the wooden steps creaking slightly under her weight. The house was quiet, but there was an unsettling stillness in the air. She didn't like Oliver being outside. She didn't like him being out of her sight at all, but she knew she couldn't keep him next to her every second of the day. Plus, Ben was in no shape to be doing farm chores alone. At least the skies were clear, and the property was fenced in.

Telling herself for the dozenth time it would be okay, she took a deep breath, calming her nerves before she knocked gently on the door to Melissa's room. She really did want to check in on the new mom and besides, a visit to see Baby Jonathan might help her forget about the constant hum of anxiety in her chest.

Melissa was sitting up in bed, cradling her newborn in her arms. Her blue-streaked hair was pulled back in a ponytail and she wore fresh clothes that likely had belonged to Ben's daughter or perhaps his wife. The soft light from the window framed her in a gentle glow, and for a moment, Zoe felt a wave of calm wash over her. This room was safe, untouched by the chaos outside.

"How are you feeling?" Zoe asked quietly as she stepped inside, her voice soft so as not to disturb the baby.

Melissa smiled, though it didn't quite reach her eyes. "Tired, but we're okay. The hot shower was nice." She adjusted the baby, who stirred a little but didn't wake. "I think he's got his days and nights mixed up."

Zoe knelt beside the bed and checked the baby's pulse, gently touching his tiny hand. "That's normal," she said, smiling. "He looks good. You're doing great."

Melissa nodded but the tiredness in her face was undeniable. Zoe felt a pang of sympathy for her friend. Caring for a baby in normal circumstances was hard enough, but in this world? She couldn't imagine.

"Did you see Adam?" Melissa asked.

"Yep. He's down in the kitchen helping Jurnee and Aaron with breakfast. He's going to be a great dad."

Melissa's tired smile brightened. "He really is doing great with all this. But if he really wants to earn some good boyfriend points, he better bring me something to eat."

Zoe giggled. "Tell you what, I'll give him a gentle reminder when I head back down."

Melissa nodded her appreciation but then her expression turned serious, her face creasing with worry. "Zoe, we had been stocking up on baby supplies at the church but that's all gone. The baby needs diapers, some infant clothes, bottles, pacifiers – the list goes on." She let out a shaky breath. "What are we going to do? We have to have supplies."

Zoe reached over, squeezing her hand. "We'll figure it out. There's got to be places we can scavenge – stores, pharmacies, even houses if we have to. Don't worry, we'll get what you need."

Melissa swallowed hard, shifting the baby against her chest. "It's not just that." She hesitated, looking down at the small bundle in her arms. "He's nursing, but my milk hasn't fully come in yet."

Zoe softened. That was normal, but in a world like this, where formula might not be easy to come by, it could be a problem if Melissa's milk supply remained low.

"Are you getting enough to eat and drink?" Zoe asked.

Melissa let out a humorless laugh. "If Adam doesn't stop giving me snacks, I'm going to burst. And water – I mean, I'm trying, but I know I should be drinking more."

Zoe nodded. "Hydration's everything right now. And even if your milk's slow, colostrum is enough to get him through the first few days. But if you start feeling weak, or if he's not getting enough, we'll need a backup plan."

Melissa sighed, brushing her fingers over the baby's cheek. "Formula."

"Yeah. If we can find some, we need to take it. Just in case."

Melissa's shoulders slumped slightly, but she nodded. "I just hope we can find some."

Zoe squeezed her hand again. "One thing at a time. He's here, he's nursing, and you're doing everything right. We'll get what we need."

Melissa gave her a tired smile. "I hope so."

Zoe didn't let on she was also worried about supplies for baby Jonathan. But the new mother was right, and the worry had already crossed Zoe's mind. Regardless of how long Ben let them stay, at some point very soon someone would need to make a supply run.

After a few more quiet reassurances, Zoe headed back

downstairs. The sound of faint giggles greeted her as she entered the kitchen, where Jurnee and Aaron sat at the table finishing breakfast. Zoe smiled softly at the sight of the two of them – Jurnee's bright eyes full of mischief, and Aaron's calm demeanor a steadying presence. Aaron was a bit of a mystery to her, but she'd learned over the past couple weeks that he had a sharp mind and an even sharper focus when he was interested in something.

"Zoe!" Jurnee announced through a mouthful of syrup-soaked pancakes.

Aaron glanced up, revealing a shy smile. "Good... good morning, Zoe," the boy said.

"Good morning," she replied, noticing Aaron's eyes flick toward the basement door.

She frowned curiously. "What?"

"Well, last night after the movie, I saw something down there," he said, his voice quieter than usual as he pushed his bangs back from his eyes. "A padlocked room."

Zoe paused, glancing toward the basement door, then over to Adam, who was standing with his back to her at the stove, stirring eggs. He glanced back, his expression just as curious as hers. A padlocked room? She hadn't paid much attention to the basement, even when she was down there last night, but Aaron's curiosity had a way of uncovering things others missed.

"Of course, I don't know what could be inside," Aaron continued, his eyes darting away as if hesitant to guess. "Can we look at the solar power system? I want to see how it's all connected. And maybe... maybe later we could ask what's behind the locked door."

Zoe's brow furrowed slightly. Aaron's fascination with swords and now the solar system was harmless enough, but something about a padlocked door in a house like this, owned by a man like Benson Meyer, set her on edge. But it wasn't only that. The simple mention of a padlocked room in a basement triggered Zoe on a whole different level. Images of being drugged and nearly fed to the twins flooded her mind. She felt her pulse quicken to the point of near panic. *This isn't that place*, she told herself, then forced a smile. "Oh really? I hadn't even noticed when we were down there but sure, we can ask about it later, okay?" she said, trying to keep her voice light.

Aaron nodded. *"The world is full of obvious things which nobody by any chance ever observes* – of course, that's from Sherlock Holmes, *The Hound of the Baskervilles*, by author Arthur Conan Doyle. It was originally published in *The Strand Magazine* from August 1901 to April 1902—"

"Wow, Aaron," Jurnee interrupted. "You sure do know lots of stuff."

Aaron gave another shy smile, but his gaze lingered on the basement door, as if whatever was down there behind the locked door was calling to him.

"Right, okay then," Zoe said briskly. "I'll ask Ben later but for now no snooping around down there. Ben said we could use the movie room and the rooms upstairs. Let's stick to those."

"Hungry, Zoe?" Adam asked as he dumped a pile of eggs onto a plate.

"Actually, I just left Melissa and the baby. She's really hoping you'll bring her some breakfast."

"I'm all over it. Whipping her up some eggs, bacon, and pancakes right now, but there's plenty left over here for you and Oliver. I made enough for that grouchy ass Ben too," he said, grinning.

Jurnee giggled at that.

"Thanks," Zoe said, "but I'll stick with coffee for now. I

want to do a little more reading. And when the guys get back inside, we need to group up and talk about next steps. Baby Jonathan needs supplies."

Adam's smile slipped into concern. "Yeah, good call. Washing cloth diapers is the worst."

Jurnee pulled a face and pinched her nose. "PU! That's gross!"

"You ain't kidding, PU," Adam agreed. "You wouldn't think that much awful could come out of a thing so tiny and cute."

Zoe topped off her coffee and moved toward the den, but something caught her attention. Frowning, she stepped into the room and froze. At the base of the chair where Ben had gone unresponsive, the edge of the area rug was scrunched up and folded over, revealing what sure as hell looked like a dark bloody stain.

Her heart skipped a beat as she crouched down to examine it. It was old, dried, but unmistakably blood. She touched it gingerly, her mind racing.

She had been sitting here this very morning warming by the fire as she read and conversed with Ben. She stood up, and a sense of unease settled over her. *What the hell happened here?*

Aaron's words echoed in her mind. *'The world is full of obvious things which nobody by any chance ever observes.'* She scanned the room as if for the first time. Had there been a fight? An injury that no one talked about? And if so, why had Ben not mentioned it? She bit her lip, pushing down the rising tide of anxiety. Something wasn't right in this house.

The sound of a low growl snapped her attention to the front door. Louie stood at the vertical window alongside the door, his hackles raised, a deep rumble coming from his throat. Zoe's chest tightened as she moved quickly to the den window, her heart pounding in her ears.

Outside, just beyond the gate, a figure stood. The silhouette was barely visible through the wrought iron bars, but it was tall and broad-shouldered. Her first thought was of Tommy and for a moment, Zoe's heart leaped into her throat. No. That was crazy. Tommy was dead. Tommy was definitely dead. Still, whoever that was could only be trouble.

"Louie, quiet," she whispered, her hand trembling as she reached for the dog's collar, giving him a scratch behind his ears.

She turned and rushed back to the kitchen to find Adam. He was at the sink cleaning up, his face drawn with the same exhaustion that clung to all of them.

Adam glanced back as she entered. "Don't worry, doc. Mel is up there right now devouring that plate of eggs and bacon, plus I took her a whole..." He must have read Zoe's fear because he trailed off, his face draining of color. "What? What is it?"

"Adam," Zoe said, her voice urgent, "there's someone outside by the gate. He looks just like Tommy."

Adam's eyes widened, and without a word, he followed her back to the front door and peered out the sidelight window. But when they arrived, the figure was gone. The gate was still chained closed, the road beyond it empty.

Zoe's heart was still pounding in her chest. "He was there," she insisted, feeling a cold sweat on the back of her neck. "I swear, I saw him."

Adam frowned. "Zoe, Tommy's dead. You saw Oliver kill him. You've said so yourself."

"I know," she acknowledged, biting at her thumbnail.

"Of course it wasn't him. But damn – the way he stood, his silhouette."

Adam nodded, his gaze still fixed on the empty yard and vacant front gate. "Stay here," he said, his voice firm. "I'll go out on the front steps where I can see better and check it out." He reached for the deadbolt, turning it with a soft click.

The sound of distant gunshots cracked through the air.

Adam stopped, his hand on the door handle. "That came from out back!"

Zoe's blood ran cold. "Oliver and Ben," she breathed, already moving toward the back door.

Adam followed, his expression grim.

The two of them ran through the house, sprinting toward the sound of gunfire.

Her mind raced as they ran, a thousand questions spiraling through her thoughts. What was happening? Had something – or someone – attacked? And what had happened inside this house that Ben wasn't talking about?

They rushed outside, the cold wind biting at their faces. Zoe's heart pounded as she scanned the darkening late-morning landscape for any sign of Oliver or Ben. Overhead, thick red clouds dotted the sky, periodically swallowing the sunlight and casting an eerie dimness over the world. The gunshots had stopped, but the air felt charged, tense, as if the morning itself was holding its breath, waiting for the next moment to strike.

CHAPTER 11
WE'RE ALL GHOSTS NOW

OLIVER FELT the weight of Ben's words sink like an anchor into his chest. *Kill Katie. Finish what Ben couldn't.*

His mind whirled, fighting to grasp the enormity of what Ben was asking. He had seen death. He had killed before – his aching joints and bruised face were reminders he'd killed just yesterday as he fought his way out of the Farm and Feed and then the church. But this? Ben wanted him to kill a little girl no older than Jurnee. A child who'd been innocent before the world turned upside down. Oliver's throat tightened.

The stillness that followed made the world around them feel smaller, quieter. Oliver's hands instinctively curled into fists in his jacket pockets, fingernails digging into his palms, while he wrestled with the gravity of Ben's confession and the request that came with it. "Ben, I—"

Ben held up a hand. "Before you say no, listen to me, son. I may yet live for weeks or maybe even months. I was fixed on sending you folks on your way tomorrow at the latest. But if you do this for me, you can all stay and once I'm gone the house and everything in it is yours for as long as you want it. All I ask is that when I die you drop me in a hole next to Katie and her family."

Ben's face was a map of exhaustion and grief, every wrinkle a marker of how far he'd come, how much he'd lost. Oliver studied the man's hands – once steady, now shaking. He was holding on to whatever scraps of control he could muster, but it was clear he was close to the edge. His eyes were the worst of it, though. There was something hollow there, something gone, as if whatever spark had once fueled the man had long since been snuffed out by the horrors of that day.

"Why me?" Oliver asked.

"I know I've only known you since yesterday, but I know enough. You saved that little girl from the rain when I couldn't save Katie. I know your wife is a special woman. You're good people and honestly, I got no one else. I can't just set the damn barn on fire. Believe me, I've considered it. But my horses are in there. I have been feeding them through the stall windows. Besides, a fire would almost assuredly end up catching the house ablaze." There was a dire helplessness that dripped from every word Ben spoke. "Do this for me, Oliver. Do this and you and your family can stay here."

Oliver's mind circled back to Katie. A little girl. Jesus, a little girl the same age as Jurnee. He swallowed hard, forcing back the lump in his throat. The image of her – small, scared, broken by the same madness that had consumed her family – lodged itself in his brain. He couldn't let it go, couldn't stop the gut-wrenching empathy he felt. He knew what Ben was asking, and the weight of it pressed down on him like a physical thing.

Ben wasn't just asking him to clean up. He was asking him to end what little was left of the girl. To kill her. *But she's not a little girl anymore,* Oliver reminded himself, trying to harden his resolve. She's not Katie. Not anymore.

He blinked hard, forcing his thoughts back into focus. Ben had trusted him with this, laid bare his soul in a way Oliver wasn't sure he deserved. But there was no turning back now. Not for Ben. Not for Katie. Not for any of them.

Oliver took a deep breath, letting the brisk air fill his lungs. His mind churned over what Ben had said about the Special Forces, the equipment, the plan. All of it seemed so distant now, like it belonged to another life. Yet here he was, standing on the edge of another nightmare.

"Alright," Oliver said finally, his voice steadier than he felt. "I'll do it. But... Ben, you know this is going to haunt you. It's already haunting you." As the words left his mouth, he wasn't sure if they were meant for Ben or himself.

Ben didn't answer at first, just looked down at the ground as if searching for something he'd lost. When he finally spoke, his voice was soft and determined. "I've been haunted for a long time, Oliver. This... this is just another ghost."

Oliver nodded, unable to argue. *We're all ghosts now*, he thought bitterly, as he shifted his weight and prepared himself for what had to come next.

Oliver reached for the door and lifted the latch.

"Wait. I... I can't come in there with you. Not until it's done. Once you finish this, come get me. I'll pull the backhoe out the other side and dig the hole, but I don't want to see her. Make sure she's covered. I can't see her. And Oliver, don't use your gun. If you fire a shot, Zoe and Adam will come running. They don't know about this and I'd like to keep it that way."

"But Zoe is my wife. You can't expect me to keep this

from her." The truth was, he hated to think what Zoe would say if she knew what he was about to do.

Ben's face was pleading. "Just until I'm gone, okay? Then tell whoever you want. Besides, we don't want to draw undead to the barn from the other side. We'll be noisy enough with the backhoe – we don't need gunshots announcing what we are about to do."

"What am I supposed to use?" Oliver asked, feeling more and more nauseous as the seconds passed.

"Look to your left when you go through the door. You'll have options. I'd rather not know how you do it, just please, get it done... for Katie."

Oliver nodded, took a deep breath, and pulled the barn door open. It creaked, the sound piercing the heavy silence that had settled over Meyer's farm. The stale smell of earthy decay washed over him. Dust swirled in the pale light, filtering through cracks in the weathered wood. He hesitated at the threshold, the weight of the task ahead pressing down on him like an invisible hand squeezing his chest.

Behind him, Ben started to push the door closed.

"Hey, what the hell?" he called.

"Just in case. When it's done just knock. I'll be here." With that Ben gave him one last look before the door closed.

He wasn't sure he had the strength to go through with this, but the thought of leaving that little girl in there – trapped, suffering – was worse. *This is the right thing to do – the humane thing*, he told himself.

His fingers brushed over the handle of the .357 in his pocket, the metal cold against his skin. Despite what Ben had said about not using the gun, at least he had it if he needed it.

In the dim space all he could hear was the pulse in his ears, a steady drumbeat that echoed in the stillness. The barn felt too quiet, like a predator waiting for him to make the first move. *One foot in front of the other*, he reminded himself, but his body resisted, his legs heavy with the knowledge of what he was about to do.

Oliver's shoes scuffed across the dirt floor, each step deliberate, careful, as though any sudden movement might set off something he couldn't control. He could hear the rustle of hay somewhere deeper inside, and the faintest sound – like horses breathing.

On the wall to his left hung an array of farm tools. First, he looked at a sledgehammer. *Too heavy to wield*, he thought. Then a scoop shovel, but he decided it was too awkward. Next to the shovel hung a hay hook. He'd have to get close and aim carefully if he used that. Finally, he saw a pitchfork. He swallowed hard, lifting the tool from the hook and weighing it in his hand like Poseidon preparing to throw his trident.

The horse stalls lined both sides of the shadowed corridor. His eyes adjusted slowly, finding shapes in the dim light, but there was nothing that looked like a little girl. *Come on, where the hell is she?*

His heart thudded louder, and then he heard it – beneath the shuffling hoofs – small, shallow breaths, uneven, coming from the far corner of the barn. He couldn't see her yet, but he knew she was there. He took a deep breath. *Katie*, he thought again, as if repeating her name would somehow bring her back from wherever she was lost.

Moving toward the sound, he passed one stall, then another. His hand tightened around the pitchfork, each step feeling like it took an eternity. Near the back of the barn was a tack room used to equip horses for riding. As Oliver rounded the corner of the last stall and peered into the tack room, he saw her, huddled in the shadows. A small figure, curled up against the rough wooden wall, her knees drawn to her chest. Her blond hair was matted and streaked with dirt.

"Katie," he whispered, the name slipping out before he could stop himself.

She didn't move at first, just sat there, her thin body trembling. Her head was bowed, and for a split second, she looked like a helpless little girl.

But then she lifted her head, and what light there was caught her face. Her eyes were red as the devil's, bloodshot and wild, staring through him like he wasn't even there. Her lips were cracked, her skin pale, but it was the look in her eyes that sent a chill down his spine – hungry, feral, like an animal cornered and desperate.

"I'm... I'm so hungry," she whispered, her voice barely a rasp. "It hurts."

Oliver tried to steady himself. For some reason he'd been stupid enough to think he was coming in here to kill an undead girl. But Katie wasn't undead. She was very much alive – warped by the parasite infecting her, but alive.

This isn't her, he had to keep reminding himself. *This isn't Katie*. But it was. It was her voice, her face, her small hands clutching the hem of her shirt as though she were just a scared little girl again.

Except she wasn't.

"Katie," he said again, trying to keep his voice steady. "I'm sorry... I have to do this."

She blinked slowly, and for a fleeting moment, her expression softened. Her brow furrowed, and she tilted her head, as if trying to understand what he was saying. But then the hunger twisted her features again, and her mouth opened, revealing teeth that were stained with blood – her own, maybe, or someone else's.

"I can smell it," she said, her voice growing hoarser. "I can smell the sweetness. Did you bring Ben, too? Oh, oh, how I'd like that." Katie started to sob. "He left me. He locked me in and left me to starve!"

She moved then, quick and jerky, her small frame shifting with unnatural speed as she pushed herself to her feet. The air between them crackled with tension. Oliver raised the pitchfork, the only thing between him and the little girl. His hands trembled, but he held fast. *You can do this.* But as he prepared to lunge forward, his vision blurred, the figure of Katie flickering between the little girl before him and Jurnee. How could he do this? Because this wasn't Jurnee and it wasn't Katie, not anymore.

From one of the stalls a horse neighed.

"I'm sorry," he whispered again, his throat tight with grief. He didn't even know if he was saying it for her, for Ben, or for himself. "You don't have to be alone anymore."

Katie's lips pulled back into a twisted smile, her blood-red eyes locking on to him. Her movements were erratic, fast, like she couldn't control her own body anymore. Her small fingers twitched, and her head snapped to the side, the motion unnatural, jarring. Her eyes blinked as if in slow motion. "I'm not alone, silly. But I am hungry, so hungry."

Oliver didn't understand but it didn't matter. He had to act now. He reared back and lunged forward with the pitchfork, intent on driving the tines through the girl's head. But as he thrust in, something hit him in the center of his back – he heard a grunt and then the crack of teeth from a snapping jaw.

As Oliver fell forward, the pitchfork dipped low, plunging into Katie's little chest.

Through the handle Oliver felt her rib bones breaking as his body shoved into hers.

Oliver landed in a tangle of limbs, quickly rolling off Katie as her teeth bit, snapping-turtle quick, at his neck.

"Muaaah!" a voice moaned deep as an ocean, filling the barn.

A man he was sure could only be Randy fell onto all fours, grabbing hold of Oliver's ankles. The man's long greasy bangs fell over his dead eyes – eyes so pale it was like he'd bled out all the color, leaving behind only cloudy sacks of smoke. A sharp line of open flesh started at the man's cheekbone and traced a blood-crusted wound around the left side of his head, where a chunk of ear dangled by a bit of decaying flesh. No doubt the result of a bullet that had missed its mark.

"You're supposed to be dead!" Oliver plunged a hand into his pocket and tried to pull out the gun. It caught on the fabric of his jacket pocket, refusing to budge. "Fuck me!" he shouted.

Next to him, Katie had fallen onto her back. She let out a final gasp and died.

Oliver kicked at the man's face, knocking him back while at the same time pushing himself away with one hand as he struggled to free the gun.

His back hit the wall, stopping him from retreating further.

"Reeeaaa!" Katie let out an awful cry as she came back to life, now an undead.

The man pulled Oliver towards him as Katie grabbed his arm.

"Fuck!" Oliver shouted again, abandoning his attempt to free the gun. Instead he simply pointed it forward from inside the pocket and pulled the trigger, fabric from his jacket blowing outward.

The sound of the gunshot echoed through the barn,

deafening in the confined space. The bullet ripped into the undead man's shoulder.

Katie bit down on his arm.

"Guah!" Oliver shouted.

The man yanked his feet, pulling him away from the wall and onto his back.

Oliver fired twice more from his awkward position. Bullets tore through his jacket pocket, one missing completely and the other hitting its mark and blowing out the back side of the zombie's head.

Zombie Katie's body jerked and twitched as she threw her arms around his shoulder and pulled herself towards his neck.

Oliver planted his left palm against the girl's forehead like a running back stiff-arming a tackler. The motion forced her head to twist up and back. Katie's teeth gnashed and clacked at the air.

From this position he couldn't twist the pocketed gun into a position to fire without potentially shooting himself.

"Get... off me!" Oliver growled through gritted teeth.

Katie answered with another low "Reeehaaa!" as if she were gargling olive oil.

With his other hand, Oliver pulled with all he had and then gave a desperate jerk of the gun. The jacket pocket tore open, freeing the .357.

Pushing the gun's barrel into Katie's right eye, Oliver closed his eyes and pulled the trigger.

The report was ear-splitting.

Katie collapsed instantly to the barn floor as Oliver pushed himself away from her and sat up. His breath came out in ragged gasps, his hands shaking uncontrollably as he lowered the pistol. He stared at her small, still form, his vision swimming with unshed tears. She didn't move again.

For a long moment, all he could hear was the pounding of his heart and the rush of blood in his ears. The barn was silent once more, but it felt different now. Heavy. Suffocating.

He stood – his legs were weak beneath him, barely able to hold him up. His arm throbbed with pain. Glancing down he was relieved to find the jacket's fabric had prevented Katie's teeth from puncturing his flesh. He leaned against the wall, his head falling back against the wood, and let out a long, shaky breath. He'd done what Ben couldn't. What needed to be done.

But it didn't feel like a victory. It felt like another piece of his soul had been chipped away.

As he stood there, the weight of it all pressing down on him, Oliver realized something he hadn't before. They weren't just fighting to survive – they were losing parts of themselves with every step, with every shot. And he wondered how much of himself he had left to lose.

CHAPTER 12
THAT CAME FROM THE HOUSE!

THE COLD AIR stung Zoe's lungs as she and Adam sprinted toward the barn.

Adam pointed. "That's Ben! But where's Oliver!"

"Come on," she gasped, her feet crunching through frost-glazed grass as they neared the barn. The structure loomed ahead, red and imposing against the soft blue morning sky.

Adam was right behind her, his breath ragged but determined. The distant shots had stopped, leaving a soul-shaking silence in their wake – a silence that unnerved Zoe more than the gunfire. Something was wrong. She could feel it in the pit of her stomach, a sense of dread that gnawed at her like a persistent whisper in the back of her mind. Whatever she had seen out front had come back here to the barn!

As they reached the barn, they found Ben standing just outside the door.

"Ben!" Zoe called out, rushing up to him. "What happened? Where's Oliver?"

Ben opened his mouth, but no words came out at first.

His lips quivered, and he stammered, trying to form a coherent sentence. His face was streaked with sweat, his eyes wild with panic.

"I- I..." Ben's voice was barely a whisper, his hands trembling violently now. "It was... Katie... the girl... and Oliver... in the barn."

Zoe didn't wait for him to finish. Her heart hammered in her chest as she shoved past him, fear gripping her as she rushed into the barn. The smell hit her first – dirt, hay, blood. The air was thick with it. Horses neighed and kicked at the stalls, frightened by whatever events had transpired.

"Oliver!" she screamed, her voice cracking as she ran deeper into the barn. The space seemed endless, dark corners and horse stalls blurring together as she searched frantically for any sign of him.

She could hear Adam behind her, his heavy breathing as frantic as her own, but she barely registered him. Her focus was singular – finding Oliver, making sure he was alive, making sure that whatever nightmare had unfolded in this place hadn't taken him too. "Oliver!"

"Here!" a faint voice called from the back of the barn.

Zoe sprinted to the other end of the barn, reaching the tack room, her heart in her throat. The door was partially open, the hinges creaking as she pushed it wide. And then she froze.

Oliver stood leaning against the wall, holding his left arm. Relief flooded her for a split second before her eyes took in the rest of the scene.

Adam appeared in the doorway behind her, his eyes wide. "Jesus Christ," he muttered, stepping carefully around the bodies.

At Oliver's left was the body of a young girl. She was small, her blonde hair matted with dirt and blood. Her remaining eye was lifeless, staring at the ceiling in eerie stillness. Thick black blood oozed from the bullet hole through her eye socket, and Zoe's stomach lurched at the sight.

At Oliver's feet lay another body – a man, his features twisted in death, a bullet hole in the center of his forehead, the back of his head smeared across the wall of the tack room. Blood pooled beneath him, the metallic scent of it filling the room.

Zoe rushed forward and Oliver threw his right arm around her, pulling her into him. "Zo!" he whispered as he started to slide down the wall onto his ass. She let herself be pulled with him, dropping to her knees beside him.

"Oliver, are you hurt? What's wrong with your arm? What the hell happened here?" she begged, scanning his body, checking for any serious wounds. His jacket was sticky with blood, but it wasn't his.

"Zoe," he whispered again, his voice hoarse. "I... I had to. There was no other way..."

Tears stung her eyes as she shook her head, trying to stay focused. "What happened?"

His gaze drifted to the girl's body. "She was already gone," he whispered, his voice trembling. "She wasn't human anymore."

Zoe's throat tightened as she looked at the lifeless girl again, her small body twisted unnaturally on the floor.

Glancing up, she found Ben standing next to Adam, his eyes wet with grief. "Oh, sweet Katie. You did it, Oliver."

A wave of anger flushed through Zoe's chest. "You sent him in here to do this?!"

Ben nodded solemnly, pressed his lips tight, and then said, "It's true. I did ask him to do this for me."

"You could've gotten him killed! And you!" She

snapped her head around to glare at Oliver. "You went along with this? What the hell were you thinking?"

"Zoe, I thought the only one in here would be Katie."

Ben pointed at the dead man. "That's Randy, Katie's dad. I shot him in the head, I swear I did. I don't know how he could still be alive."

"It's alright, Ben. I know you didn't know. The bullet didn't penetrate – it wrapped around his face and ripped off his ear. The impact probably knocked him unconscious. See for yourself."

Ben stepped closer, clearly doing his best to avoid looking at Katie.

Oliver pulled off his jacket and covered the girl.

"Thank you for that. Thank you for everything, Oliver. And rest assured I'm a man of my word," Ben said, wiping his eyes on his coat sleeve as he examined Randy's body.

"It's alright, Ben. It's over."

"Alright? None of this is alright, Oliver McCallister. You could have..." Zoe trailed off, a terrifying thought occurring to her.

"What is it?" Oliver asked.

"The gunshots weren't you fighting Tommy," Zoe whispered, her voice barely audible.

"Tommy? Why would you think that?"

"She thought she saw a zombie that looked like Tommy standing at the front gate, then he disappeared and we thought maybe he came around back when we heard the shots."

"Well, I can assure you this barn has been locked up tight for a couple weeks now," Ben said.

Oliver held up a hand. "Hold on. So whoever you saw at the front gate, where is he right now?"

Zoe's eyes went wide.

Before any of them could say anything more, the sharp sound of another gunshot answered with a crack from somewhere close by.

Zoe's relief for Oliver was quickly replaced with heart-stopping fear as dread settled back in.

"That came from the house!" Zoe gasped, rising to her feet and rushing out of the barn.

When she and the others broke from the barn in a dead run, the sky above was thick with clouds of crimson, blocking out the sun. Suddenly the day was colder and darker, and Zoe knew, deep down, that the nightmare was far from over.

CHAPTER 13
THE BIG BAD WOLF

IN THE END, the urge to feed overwhelmed Tommy. His resistance crumbled the moment he stumbled away from Meyer's gate, the relentless hunger ripping through him, consuming every last scrap of restraint. He could feel the parasite pulsing, demanding, the pain it inflicted like a knife twisting in his guts. He had a sudden urge to shit himself and it was all he could do to not let loose right there. Despite that, it felt like his intestines were being wrung like a dirty dishrag. Somehow, he clenched and held it in – most of it at least.

"Bastard!" he moaned, instinctively placing a hand on the back of his neck, where the parasite had grown thick and bulbous beneath skin that was rice-paper thin. The giant slug-shaped lump throbbed, rippling like a snake coiled beneath his flesh.

The sensation sent a shiver down his spine.

His fingers traced it down the length of his neck. It was the size of a softball now and already seemed close to breaking through his skin. How much larger could it get? How much hungrier?

To the left of the massive gate he spotted a small game trail that followed the fence line deeper into the woods. He wanted to take his time and approach carefully, to scope things out, but his body had other plans. Without hesitation, he clambered over the fence, driven forward as if the parasite itself were pushing him. Planning was out of the question. It was time to feed.

As soon as his boots landed in the grass, Tommy broke into a run, his eyes fixed on Meyer's front door. His mouth was already watering, imagining the sound of cracking skulls, the warmth, the taste of fresh brains. He gripped the Ruger tightly, lifting it as he neared the house. He lined up his aim with the narrow side window by the door, hoping to shatter it and reach through the broken glass. With that, he'd have entry and could take them by surprise.

From ten feet out, he fired.

The shot shattered the silence, echoing off the walls of the house and the fence around the yard. But the glass didn't break. Instead, the bullet left a small chip, barely scratching the surface.

"What the fuck?" Tommy growled, his frustration bubbling over as he fired again, only to be met with the same unyielding glass. His jaw clenched, the parasite thrumming with fury at the delay. He couldn't afford to waste time like this; he only had a few precious seconds before they'd realize he was here.

Tommy raced up the steps and onto the porch. The whole advantage was the element of surprise. Rush the house, gain entry, and start shooting. Kill them all before they knew what hit them. No playing games; no hesitation.

But now that plan was fucked! He'd just have to risk losing the element of surprise and use the shotgun to blow the fucking door off the hinges.

Instinctually, he reached for the door, knowing it would most assuredly be locked. But to his surprise, when he turned the knob, his hand twisted and the door gave way, swinging open freely.

How fucking stupid could they be? He nearly laughed out loud as he rushed across the threshold. The first thing he noticed was the smell. Not the smell of a stranger's house or recently cooked food, but the sweet smell of a little girl's brains. She was close. Very close. "Oh, Little Red Riding Hood," Tommy whispered, sniffing at the air like the wolf he was. "The big bad wolf has come a knockin'. Don't you want to see what big teeth I have? The better to eat—"

Something lunged at him from the darkness of a doorway. Tommy barely had time to react before a blur of muscle and teeth barreled into his chest, the impact sending him stumbling backwards over the threshold and back onto the porch. Louie, Zoe's pit bull, was on him, growling and snapping as his teeth sank into Tommy's shoulder.

Feet tangling, Tommy tipped backward off the porch, falling and at the same time lifting his arm as he tried to hold the dog at bay.

The concrete sidewalk came fast and hard, Louie's weight pressing him down as the dog released his shoulder only to bite again, his jaws clamping Tommy's forearm like a toothy vise. From inside, he heard a little girl's scream – a high, piercing sound that cut through the fog of hunger clouding his mind. The thought of her only fueled him more, driving the parasite into a frenzy. He needed to get inside, needed to reach the girl, the others, but the damned dog wouldn't let go.

With a snarl, Tommy pushed his arm forward, but the pit bull was relentless, growling and barking furiously with each snap of his jaws. Louie's teeth tore into Tommy's flesh again, making a deep gash. Blood, dark and thick, oozed from his already wounded shoulder and arm, but Tommy barely felt it; his body had numbed to all but the pain of hunger.

"You can't beat me!" Tommy hissed.

Still, the mangy mutt wouldn't relent, his jaws locked around Tommy's arm.

Straining against Louie's grip, Tommy reached for the pistol.

The dog's growling grew louder, more frantic, as if he sensed what was coming.

With one swift motion, Tommy jammed the pistol against Louie's side and pulled the trigger.

The shot rang out, and Louie yelped, his jaws loosening and finally letting go as he staggered back, injured but still snarling with defiance.

From inside the house a girl screamed, "No!"

Louie tried to lunge in again but listed to the side like a sinking ship about to capsize.

"Bull's-eye, motherfucker!" Tommy sneered, though his voice was a rasp, barely a whisper of the triumph he felt. He scrambled to his feet, the hunger now a full-blown inferno inside him, consuming every thought, every hesitation. Even from here he could still smell the little girl.

Louie was injured, weakened, but the dog's spirit remained unbroken. Even as he fell onto his side, unable to stand and fight, his teeth were bared, his eyes blazing with fury.

Having no time to spare, Tommy ignored Louie's defiant growl, his own steps heavy as he raced up onto the porch once more.

The door stood wide open before him, inviting him

inside with the fragrance of the only thing that mattered in this whole shit-show of a world.

Stuffing the pistol in his waistband, Tommy unslung the shotgun. The parasite pulsed in time with his steps, each beat filling him with a single, driving mission: Consume. Devour. Feed.

Behind him the dog lay bleeding out on the sidewalk, whimpering pathetically. He was begging, but not for himself.

Tommy glanced back and smiled. "Not so tough now, are you? Well, beg all you want, mutt – you can't save them now."

He stepped inside, hunger his only guide as the house drew him in, promising him everything he desired. The little girl and a baby. He'd never eaten a newborn brain. The skull would be soft, the brain succulent. The thought sent warm pangs of pain through his stomach as his mouth began to salivate.

The house was quiet with nobody in sight. He thought they would at least try to face him but it seemed the cowards were all hiding. *Good. Make this easy as I take you one by one.* He sniffed at the air. "I can smell you, little one," Tommy whispered. "Come out, come out."

Suddenly, a distant door crashed open, slamming into a wall.

Voices shouted from the back of the massive house. First a familiar woman's voice – Zoe! "Jurnee! Aaron! Where are you?"

Then a man – Oliver. "We're coming!"

He could hear movement now, the shuffle of hurried footsteps, the frantic whispers, a bolt on a rifle locking into place. Well, it seemed they weren't hiding after all. They knew a predator had breached their sanctuary. But Tommy was beyond caring. He'd face them all – eat them all. He lifted the shotgun, ready to kill the first person who came through the door, but then something strange happened.

A powerful sensation tugged at his mind, like an invisible leash had been tethered to his will and viciously yanked. The urge to turn and flee was undeniable. "No! They're right there! I can handle it." But the urge didn't subside. As strong as the need to feed had been, the urge to run was suddenly stronger. Under no control of his own, Tommy backpedaled, stealing a final glance back as he exited the front door of the house.

He got only a glimpse of Zoe's silhouette as she rushed forward from the next room, but he knew it was her. He knew the uniqueness of every curve of her figure like a fingerprint.

As Tommy jumped off the porch, ran alongside the house, and ducked around the corner of the garage, he argued with the parasite controlling him – or maybe he was just arguing with himself. He had no way of knowing if it heard him or understood him if it did. "I had them! We could be feeding right now if you hadn't pulled me away! I had them! Let me turn around! Let me go back!" he begged.

But he couldn't go back. The invisible leash forced him toward the fence, up and over, and back into the woods.

He was safe now. He could wait here, regroup, and try again. But the urge to move further away didn't relinquish; it pulled harder, tugging at him to run deeper into the forest. "What's happening? Stop! Let me stop!"

The pain in his stomach was completely gone and he realized he no longer felt the need to eat. It was strange. This was the first time since becoming infected he didn't want to feed. "Oh god." A terrifying thought occurred to him as he pushed through a patch of brush. Was he being called? Is that what this was? Was he being called to join a mother parasite? Fear gripped him. He hadn't heard a scream but maybe the parasite controlling him had?

"Hey, I'm not dead yet! I'm still alive, you son of a bitch! You can't do this while I'm alive!" But could they? Did he need to be dead to be mashed into some other poor bastard? Shit! If that's what this was, he didn't want to be alive for it.

Tommy reached the center of the small forest and his legs froze up, fixing him in place. Frantically, he scanned the area, expecting to see a screamer, but no one was here. He couldn't see the fence behind him, the fields to his west, nor Unsicker Road to his east – no zed, no screamer, only trees.

Relieved, Tommy sucked in a calming breath. He didn't know what the fuck was going on but at least his worst fear hadn't manifested.

He tried to step forward, but he couldn't lift his feet. It was like they were rooted to the ground. "What the fuck!" he grunted through gritted teeth as he strained to move.

Then he felt something else.

A new impulse overtook him. His head tipped back, his vision set on the sky, and his mouth stretched wide – too wide! He couldn't control it, couldn't stop it.

And then, Tommy stretched his arms out to the side and screamed!

CHAPTER 14
FALLEN

JURNEE BARRELED into Oliver's arms, her small frame racked with sobs that tore through him. "Louie! Louie got shot, Oliver!" Her voice was high, breaking, every word a desperate cry.

Oliver's eyes darted between Jurnee and Aaron. "Shot! Shot by who?"

Aaron pointed at the open front door. "It happened so fast. We were in the kitchen when we heard shots and then we heard Louie attacking someone... or something."

Before he could process Aaron's words, Zoe was already bolting past him, flying out the front door and into God only knew what.

"Zoe, no! Wait!" Oliver shouted, voice tight with worry. He held Jurnee for a moment longer, trying to shield her from the view of Louie lying on the sidewalk bleeding.

Adam appeared next to him. "I got her. Go!" He took Jurnee into his arms and pulled her back from the open doorway.

Oliver turned, dread settling over him as he hurried out onto the porch. The air was thick, heavy with the smell of body odor, rot, and feces. Zoe was already on her knees beside Louie, her hands hovering over him, shaking.

"Please! Please, stay with us," Zoe whispered, her voice desperate, breaking as she pressed her hands around Louie's wound. Blood was pooling beneath him, dark and slick, staining the sidewalk. Louie's breaths were shallow, each one rattling with pain. His eyes found Zoe's, full of fear but trust, and it broke Oliver to see him like this.

His gaze shot around the yard, searching for whoever had done this. Who would shoot a dog? The yard was empty, silent, but his skin prickled with unease. They weren't safe. Maybe safe didn't exist at all but it certainly didn't exist here and now. "Zo, I need to bring him inside. We don't know who did this or if they're still out there watching us right now."

"Tommy did this!" She spat the words.

Oliver's heart somehow found a way to sink even deeper into the pit of his stomach. Had Zoe been so messed up by what happened at the church that she was seeing things? "Zoe, Tommy's dead."

She shook her head. "No. No, I saw him! I know it was him. Tommy did this. Oh, Lou. Oh, please be okay. Please. Please!"

"Bring your dog inside, quick!" Ben shouted from the house.

"I've got to lift him, Zo," Oliver said quietly, feeling the weight of the moment settle around them. "We're not safe out here."

He wrapped his arms around Louie's body.

Louie whimpered softly.

"It's okay, boy. I got you. You're going to be alright." He wanted the words to be true, but feeling the sticky warmth of the dog's blood seeping through his shirt made his heart sink even further.

As Oliver carefully adjusted his arms to cradle Louie, a scream ripped through the air, chilling him to the bone. It was high-pitched, unnatural, and unending.

The scream didn't stop – it just kept going, twisting into something shrill and horrifying.

"It's a screamer," Zoe whispered, fear lacing her words. "Over there!" She pointed to the woods beyond the fence. "It's a zombie calling for others." Her face, already tear streaked and pale, looked stricken, and Oliver could see the weight of her worry for Louie mingling with fear for them all.

"You folks best bring your dog and get back inside now," Ben said again, his voice reduced to an anxious whisper.

"He's right, Zo. Come on," he said, urgency tightening his voice. "We have to get inside."

Once inside, Ben bolted the door and motioned them to the kitchen, his face set in grim resolve.

"I have to go check on Melissa. She'll be freaking out," Adam said, scaling the stairs two at a time.

In the kitchen Ben cleared a space on the table with one swift motion. "Lay him down."

Oliver eased Louie onto the table, his hands lingering, as if letting go would somehow break the fragile thread of life tethering Louie to the world. Aaron and Jurnee followed them, their faces stricken with the same concern they all felt. But it was Jurnee who ran in between him and Zoe, her small hands gripping the table's edge as she peered over, her eyes pleading. "Is Louie going to be okay?" she whispered, the words thick with tears.

"I... I don't know," Zoe answered honestly, her voice wavering, barely holding steady. Oliver saw her trying to keep it together, fighting back her own tears, her hands pressing gently around Louie's wound as she assessed the damage. But he could see the fear in her eyes – the same fear that mirrored his own.

"I don't want Louie to die!" Jurnee cried, her voice breaking. She reached out, her tiny fingers brushing over Louie's fur. "Louie, please! You can't die! You can't!"

Louie let out a soft whine, a weak, almost apologetic sound, as if trying to answer her, to let her know he was still with them. His nub of a tail gave a feeble wag, just once, and the sight of it undid Oliver. He felt the tears he'd been holding back spill over, hot and silent, tracing down his cheeks. Louie's gaze shifted to him, a flicker of loyalty still shining through the pain. "You're a good boy, Lou," he whispered, placing a hand gently on the dog's shoulder.

In that moment, surrounded by the sobs of Jurnee, the quiet anguish in Zoe's expression, and Louie's barely there whine, Oliver felt the weight of the world crashing down on him. For all the times Louie had protected them, for all the times he'd stood between them and danger, now it was Oliver who felt helpless. "He's losing too much blood. What can we do?"

"We have to stop the bleeding!" Zoe said. "Aaron, pass me those paper towels."

"Of course," he said, hurrying to the counter and retrieving the paper towels.

"Then will he be okay?" Jurnee begged.

Zoe shook her head, her face as desperate as Jurnee's. "I... I don't know."

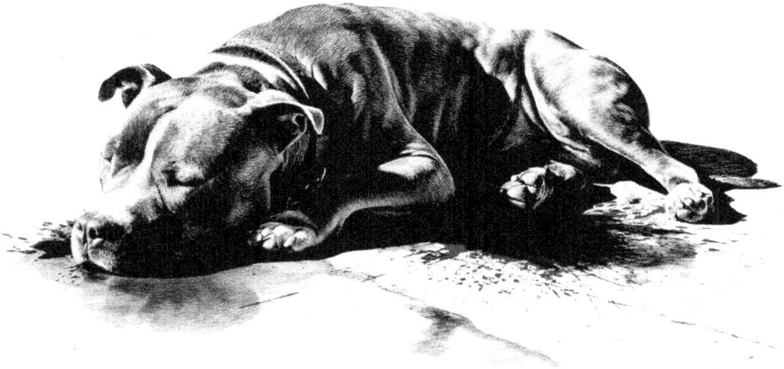

CHAPTER 15
THE AMALGAMATION OF TOMMY

TOMMY SCREAMED, an endless, guttural shriek that ripped through the woods. He had no control over the horrid sound – it poured from his throat, unstoppable, his mouth frozen wide open. His lungs strained, burning for air, but the scream went on, endless and involuntary. Panic flooded him, a raw, visceral terror that drowned his mind. *I can't breathe! Let me breathe!* But even as his body begged for oxygen, somehow he drew a breath – and yet the scream never stopped, never paused. How? How was it possible he could scream and breathe at the same time?

The immediate fear of suffocation faded, but a new horror replaced it. His jaw throbbed from the relentless strain, his throat burned as if coated in acid, and he could feel tears welling, searing his eye as he desperately tried to shut his mouth, to regain control of his own body. *Stop this! I'm still here! I'm alive!* His thoughts were frantic, but the parasite ignored him, or maybe it simply couldn't hear him. It cared only for that endless, unholy wail that sliced through the quiet woods. He was just a vessel now, held captive by his own body as the parasite twisted it to its will.

Seconds turned to minutes as he stood there, frozen in the midst of the trees, screaming, immobile. And then, in the agony of his forced stillness, came a grim realization: *I'm not being summoned by the mother parasite. I am the summoning – I am the calling!*

How long he'd been screaming, he couldn't tell. His sense of time had collapsed into the single, perpetual moment of his own terror. But finally, through the red haze of his own suffering, he heard something. The sound of bodies crashing through the underbrush – a tearing of twigs and branches, the soft thud of heavy footsteps closing in on him.

A figure appeared from his left. A zombie, sliding into view with the eager energy of an addict finding a fix. His eyes, beet-red and oozing blood, bulged from his face like two bulbous sea sponges being squeezed of all color. He was a middle-aged man, overweight, and moaning with delight as he stripped himself bare with a frantic urgency.

Free of his clothes, the zombie turned his attention to Tommy.

No! No, damn you. No! Tommy screamed inwardly, but his voice remained locked, his mouth still forced wide open as the parasite continued its summoning. The fat man approached, his bloody eyes fixated on Tommy, and began tearing away Tommy's clothes, his movements jerky, desperate. Tommy could feel the cold air on his bare skin, but all he could do was watch helplessly as his blood-soaked undershirt was torn away.

His fatigues slid down his legs, and as they did, his skin began to tingle. The cold was overtaken by a surge of heat that spread across his skin like a flame. He could feel his body begin to sweat profusely, but it felt wrong – sticky, and thick as oil. It poured out from his pores, down his sides, down his legs and his chest.

Another crash sounded to his right, and he knew another zombie was coming. This one was an old woman, frail, with a stained green nightgown torn open revealing her emaciated, bruised skin. She collapsed at his feet, her bloated stomach pressing into the dirt. The old woman's silver hair was matted, with bald patches where it had been torn away. She quickly found her feet, scrambled back up, and pressed her face into Tommy's bare chest.

The smell of rot, blood, and decay filled his senses, mingling with the sticky musk of sweat and shit.

More zombies arrived, pushing and shoving each other, ripping off their own clothes, their bodies slick and glistening. They surrounded him, pressing against him, each jostling for a chance to touch his skin, to merge with him. His own skin burned with their contact, an endless onslaught of sticky, oozing limbs, as if each was eager to become part of him.

As he watched – helpless to do anything but burn, sweat, and scream – the zombies closest to him began to change. Their mostly naked sweat-slicked forms took on an opaque sheen. Then the milky transparency solidified, like they had bathed in cream-colored motor oil.

Tommy's thoughts were a frantic mess. *I'm burning. God, I'm burning. Stop! Please stop!* But he could only think it.

Mercifully, his scream faded, his mouth falling open, slack, his jaw hanging in twisted relief. For a brief moment, he felt the rush of air again, the peace of silence, but he was still frozen, still trapped inside his own mind, locked away from control.

And then, the zombies began to press into him harder.

The fat man shoved his body against Tommy's side, their flesh melding where it touched. "Get off me!" Tommy tried to yell, but the words barely croaked out of his wrecked vocal cords. The man stuck to him like glue, their skin bonded and fused. Then the old woman dragged her face around his ribcage and climbed onto his back, her thin, bony arms wrapping around his neck, her sagging face pressing into his hair as her body melded with his. More followed – a young boy clung to his leg, his pale face expressionless as he adhered to Tommy's thigh.

They piled on, one by one, until Tommy could barely see past the mass of bodies pressing into him from all angles. Fleshy fat rubbed across his face, pressing into his slack lips, filling his mouth with secretions as thick as road tar. They were climbing over him, clinging to his arms, legs, back, wrapping him in a grotesque cocoon.

He felt each new touch like a hot brand, each added weight pinning him further in place. And all he could do was scream silently inside his own head as his body betrayed him, becoming part of something far beyond his control.

The daylight faded, but the horror continued. They kept coming, more zombies layering over him, melding to him, each one adding to the thickening, sticky coat that smeared his skin. He caught a glimpse of his own arm, cadaver white beneath the opaque film.

A large, hairy man gripped his wrist, pulling and yanking until the skin tore, until the shoulder socket popped with a sickening crunch. The pain was blunted, distant, like a tooth pulled before the anesthetic fully set in. The pain was minimal but the wrongness was unmistakable. His own arm was twisted back, glued to his spine by the viscous substance oozing from his skin. Like a fly pressed into flypaper. He couldn't tell where the flesh of the man who'd melded into his side began and Tommy ended. It was all the same fleshy white goo and blood – so much blood. Whose? His? Yes. Theirs? Yes.

More and more came, suffocating him with their flesh, until Tommy's sense of self began to fracture, each piece of him becoming buried beneath the writhing bodies pressing closer. Tommy had never been claustrophobic, but this? This was on another level, and it threatened to drive him mad.

The parasite inside him pulsed, and he felt his body begin to shift. He was reshaping, his skin, muscles, and bones being pulled, twisted, rearranged. It was an invasion, a violation beyond anything he could comprehend. He was being broken down, remade into something monstrous, something neither human nor fully alive.

As the sun dipped behind the trees, his body merged with those around him, their bones pressing into his flesh, their muscles fusing with his own, their features and limbs blending seamlessly into a single, monstrous mass.

As his mind shattered under the weight of it all, he could only cling to one desperate, final wish, a plea that would never be answered.

Please, let me die. Let me die!

But the parasite refused. It held him there, awake and aware, bound to the horror unfolding inside him, forcing him to endure every last second.

Tommy's consciousness clung on, unable to fade, trapped inside the nightmare as his body was remade into a vessel for something beyond himself – a creature that would know no mercy, no will, only the endless, insatiable drive to consume.

PART TWO
THREE STRANGERS

They say whatever doesn't kill you makes you stronger.

But I say it's what you don't see coming that kills you.

LANCE PAYNE

CHAPTER 16
THE ESCAPE

RIVER CITY COUNTY JAIL had once been a fortress, a place where men like Lance, Grady, and Slim were caged like animals, locked behind bars with no hope of freedom. But the world had changed. The sounds of the city that once hummed outside their concrete walls had fallen silent, replaced by a haunting symphony of moans and the shuffling of undead feet. Now, the jail was nothing but a tomb, filled with echoes of the dead and the smell of decay.

Lance knew all about the shitstorm beyond the cinderblock walls and steel bars. He'd heard about the rain, the insanity it caused, and the zombies. He'd heard the stories from the guards before they'd fled or turned. The first wave of infected had taken out half the city in a matter of hours. The fools who'd been dumb enough to stay behind to protect the jail had been slower to fall, but once one of them had become infected it was just a matter of time. Three days since he'd seen a guard. Two since he'd eaten the last of his stash. Hell, it had been nothing more than stupid luck their little corner of the cell block had been forgotten. They were the survivors – the last rats on a sinking ship.

Lance sat on his bunk, his back pressed against the cold concrete wall, listening to the distant growls and the occasional scream. There were no windows in this place and, without the guards calling for lights out, the days were starting to blur together. But there was one thing he knew for sure: They were going to die in here if they didn't get out soon.

In front of him, Grady paced the length of the six-by-nine cell, muttering under his breath. The big man was all muscle, his bald head glistening with sweat even in the cold air.

Lance glanced through the bars to an adjacent cell, where Slim sat perched on the edge of his own bunk like a coiled spring, his thin frame tense, his eyes darting around the room. Yesterday, at least he thought it was yesterday, Slim had strangled his cellmate. It was the damnedest thing seeing a guy as small as Slim scale a man two-and-a-half times his size, put him in a rear naked choke, and take him down in less than what? Five seconds? Once unconscious, Slim had stomped Teddy to death.

"This is bullshit," Grady snarled, slamming his fist against the bars. "Haven't eaten in three days! Those fucking guards playing it straight, not letting us out of here. They know the world's fucked out there and still they kept us locked up. Well, now what?! I'll tell you what. We're sitting ducks! What the fuck we supposed to do now?!"

"Plenty to eat over here, friend." Slim smiled.

Grady grabbed the bars in both hands and craned his neck. "Yeah, right, you fucking psycho. I know you're not actually eating Teddy."

Lance wasn't so sure about that. Nor was he sure how

long it would be before Grady got desperate enough to start thinking of him as dinner, but he had no intention of finding out. He leaned forward, eyes narrowing. "Shut up! Both of you. You hear that?" He gestured toward the hallway where the distant groans of zombies echoed, growing louder with each passing minute.

The guards had stopped bringing them food three days back. At first, he wondered if they'd finally said *fuck it* and abandoned them. Wouldn't have surprised him. Hell, if the tables were turned, he'd have been out of here the first break in the rain. But from the sounds beyond their hall, it was clear the guards had never gone anywhere – something had broke bad. "That one is getting closer. Closer than it has so far," he said quietly. "The smell of us is drawing them in. You better just hope it's a guard and not an undead county orange."

Slim let out a nervous laugh, his thin lips twisting into a crooked smile. "Great. Locked up in here while a bunch of walking corpses feast on what's left of the guards. Wouldn't that be poetic?"

Grady stopped pacing and pulled a face. "Why in the hell would we want it to be a guard and not one of our own?"

Lance pushed himself off the cot and stood in front of the giant of a man. "Because, you big idiot, the guard will have keys."

Grady's face flushed with anger.

Lance held up his hands in mock surrender. "Easy, big guy. I'm just saying, if we don't figure something out, we're going to end up like them – just another snack for the undead buffet. But if we can get a guard to come close enough..."

The idea seemed to register, lighting the big dumb

bastard's eyes like a ten-watt lightbulb flickering on. It was dim, but it was there.

From across the aisle, Slim laughed. "So what, we just ask the moaner to come on down like the price is right?"

"You got any better ideas, Slim?" Grady snapped, his eyes flashing with anger.

Lance's eyes flicked to the far end of the hallway. The metal door leading out of the cell block was slightly ajar. "In here, you dead puke! Come get some!"

"You crazy bastard!" Slim whisper-shouted. "What if it is another county orange?"

Lance shrugged. "Well, even if it isn't a guard, it isn't like it can get into our cells."

Beyond the door, they could hear the telltale shuffling of feet, the dragging sound of something heavy scraping against the floor. And then, they saw it – a shadow, moving closer.

"Here we go," Lance hissed, pointing a finger toward the door. "Look."

A zombie guard shuffled into view, its uniform torn, its face a mask of dried blood. One eye hung loosely from its socket, swinging like a pendulum as it staggered closer, sniffing at the air. It was missing a shoe and the bloody foot dragged limply across the floor, like its Achilles' had been severed. And there, dangling from its belt, were the keys. Lance's heart skipped a beat. *This is it. This is our chance.*

"The keys," Slim whispered, his voice filled with a mixture of hope and fear. "But how the hell are we gonna get them?"

Grady's fists clenched, knuckles cracking. "Simple. We take 'em. Hey! Come here!" the big man shouted.

The zombie twitched, its blood-crusted eyes stretching wide as it half limped, half ran down the hall toward them.

It reached Lance and Grady's cell first, pressing its decayed face against the bars, its teeth snapping uselessly as it tried to bite through the metal.

"Come on, you ugly bastard," Grady taunted, reaching through the bars. He grabbed a fistful of the zombie's uniform, yanking it hard against the metal. The creature let out a low growl, thrashing as Grady held it in place.

"Don't let him bite you!" Lance warned.

"I got him! Get the keys!" Grady grunted, straining against the weight of the zombie.

Lance darted forward, reaching through the bars to grab the keys. His fingers brushed against the cold metal, but the zombie jerked, pulling away just as he was about to snatch them.

"Hold it still!" Lance snapped, panic rising like bile in his throat. His pulse thundered in his ears, dread tightening his nut sack. This might be their only shot, and it was slipping away.

"I'm trying!" Grady snapped, tightening his grip. He jerked and slammed the thing's head against the bars, cracking its skull with a sickening thud. The zombie slumped, momentarily stunned.

Lanced lunged again, finally closing his fingers around the keys. "Got 'em!" Lance pulled the keys free, a surge of manic relief surging through him. Finally, they were getting the fuck out of here.

"Let me out!" Grady roared, still holding the now-limp zombie against the bars. He shoved it away, sending it sprawling onto the floor.

Lance wasted no time, jamming the key into the cell's lock and twisting it. The door swung open with a loud creak. Behind him, Grady stepped out, flexing his fists, a dark smile on his face. "I've been waiting for this," he growled, stomping down on the zombie's head, crushing it with a single, brutal strike. The moaning stopped abruptly, replaced by an eerie silence.

Slim stood on his tiptoes, his arm outstretched. "Come on, come on, come on! Get me out!"

"Leave him!" Grady said.

"No. That's not how this works. We're getting out together," Lance said, quickly crossing the aisle to free the man. As he slid the key into the lock, he glanced into the cell, where Teddy lay dead near the back wall, a large strip of flesh missing from his back.

Slim glanced back, following Lance's gaze. Then he turned back and narrowed his eyes. "You gonna let me out or what?"

Lance studied Slim's beady eyes and rat-faced features. He knew he was looking at a man that would kill without a second thought. A man capable of doing whatever it took to survive, even if surviving meant eating someone. Lance smiled, nodded, and turned the key. This was a man he could use.

Slim smiled and nodded back, a wordless agreement shared silently between the two men. Lance accepted what Slim was, and Slim acknowledged that this acceptance put Lance in charge. At least, that's how Lance read it.

The cell door swung wide.

"Alright, what's the plan?" Slim asked.

From down the hallway, they heard more groans – multiple voices, all in unison, growing louder. Shadows moved, and soon they could see them – dozens of zombies, guards and inmates alike, burst through the door, running toward them, filling the narrow hall.

"Shit," Lance breathed. "We've gotta move. Now."

The three of them bolted, sprinting for the door at the opposite end of C block.

Lance fumbled with the keys.

"Hurry the fuck up!" Grady shouted.

"What do you think I'm doing!" Lance growled as he threw the steel door open. The three men burst into the main corridor of the jail, the sound of the undead following close behind.

"This way!" Lance shouted, leading them toward the stairwell. They took the steps two at a time, Slim panting behind them, Grady charging ahead like a battering ram. Above, the dead filled the stairwell.

They reached the main floor, bursting into the lobby, where sunlight streamed through a spiderweb of fractured windows, casting long shadows across the blood-smeared floor. Bodies lay scattered everywhere – guards and prisoners, torn apart, their heads emptied, faces twisted in eternal screams.

"There's the exit!" Slim pointed across the lobby, but just as they made a break for it, a group of zombies burst into the room from a side hall, blocking their path.

Grady didn't hesitate. He grabbed a metal baton from the floor and swung it like a baseball bat, cracking the nearest zombie across the head. It went down, but another took its place, lunging at him with rotting hands outstretched.

Lance pulled a gun from a dead cop's waistband, firing twice. The bullets found their mark, dropping two more uniformed zombies, but there were too many. They kept coming, an unending tide of decaying flesh in a mix of county orange and bloodstained blues. Prisoners and guards no more. Now they were all the same — simply the hungry.

"We're surrounded!" Slim shouted, backing up until his shoulders hit the wall.

"Shut up and fight!" Grady barked, swinging the baton again and splitting open a zombie's skull. Blood sprayed across the window, but Grady didn't flinch. He was grinning, wild-eyed, reveling in the chaos.

Lance grabbed Slim's arm, pulling him toward the side door. "Grady, this way. We can't fight them all."

The three men shoved their way through the door, slamming it shut behind them.

They found themselves in an alley, the sun warm on their faces, the open sky a welcome sight after days spent in the cold, dark cells.

Grady shoved the baton through the door handle and wedged it.

From the other side came muffled moans and dull thumps.

"That should hold for a while," Grady said.

"We made it," Slim panted, doubling over to catch his breath.

"For now," Lance muttered, wiping the sweat from his brow. He looked back at the county jail, at the darkened windows and the sounds of the undead echoing inside.

Grady spat on the ground, wiping the sweat off his face. "But we're not out of this yet. We need a plan, a safe place to hole up while we figure out our next move."

"I know just the place," Lance said, a grin spreading across his lips. "There's a solar powered mansion on the outskirts of Libbyton. Belongs to this elderly rich bastard – Benson Meyer. I did some electrical work there a while back. The place is incredible and secluded."

Hands still on his knees, Slim glanced up. "Just one old man?"

Lance tucked the pistol in his waistband. "Yeah, and he's probably dead by now, but if he isn't, well... we'll take care of that."

"How far?" Grady asked.

"Only a twenty-minute drive. But it's perfect and when you see what he has in the basement, well... trust me, you'll shit yourself."

Grady's massive chest rippled beneath his orange regs as he nodded slowly, a grim smile tugging at his mouth. "That's good enough for me."

Slim pointed down the alley. "Well, boys, sounds like we've got a plan, now let's grab ourselves a new ride."

And with that, the three men took off down the alley, leaving the River City County Jail and all its horrors behind.

CHAPTER 17
NINE MINUTES

ZOE BENT OVER LOUIE, her hands slick with the dog's blood, her breath coming in short, panicked gasps. The paper towel she pressed over the bullet hole in his side was already soaked through, turning a deep crimson as the blood seeped out. She could feel his life slipping away, each shallow breath ragged and uneven, like the flutter of a heartbeat on a failing EKG, sputtering between erratic spikes and long, ominous pauses. It was the labored, shallow breathing she had seen in trauma patients just before they coded – a harbinger of a body on the brink, desperately fighting against the pull of shock.

"He's still bleeding," she muttered, more to herself than anyone else. The panic in her own voice startled her. She was a nurse – she was trained for this. But this was Louie. This was her baby.

"Stay with us, pal! Please, stay with us." Oliver's voice broke, raw with desperation as he knelt on the other side, his hands trembling as he stroked Louie's head.

Louie's eyes fluttered, half closed and unfocused.

Zoe pressed down harder, feeling the pulse beneath her

fingers weaken, the beat slowing to a dangerous rhythm. And then, his eyes rolled back, and his body went still.

"No!" she cried out, her voice cracking. "No, no, no, not like this!" Zoe's heart hammered in her chest, her own tears spilling down onto Louie's fur. She leaned in close, her ear hovering over his snout, listening for any sign of breath. But she couldn't hear anything.

Ben shuffled forward and bent over Louie, his hand steady as he pressed his ear against Louie's chest. He didn't say anything at first, his face a mask of concentration, his brow furrowed in deep lines. Then he moved to Louie's snout, feeling for a faint exhale, a hint of warmth against his skin.

"He's not gone," Ben whispered finally, looking up with a glint of hope. "He's still with us, but he's going into shock. Your dog's losing too much blood." He pointed down, and Zoe's stomach twisted as she saw the spreading red stain beneath Louie.

"We need to roll him over," Ben said, his voice firm now, taking charge.

Oliver didn't hesitate. He gently lifted Louie's body, rolling him onto his side.

Zoe sucked in a breath as she saw the exit wound, a gaping hole just behind his ribcage. The bullet had passed clean through. It was both a relief and a new terror – the wound was severe, but at least it hadn't shattered bone.

"We have to get these wounds cleaned and closed," Zoe said, her voice tight with the urgency of a doctor in crisis mode. "I need sutures, antiseptic – anything we can use."

Ben nodded sharply. "What with raising cattle and horses, you'll be surprised what I have on hand. Wound care kits, pain meds – hell, I've even got IVs." He placed a reassuring hand on Zoe's shoulder. "You can just slide that hand under him and keep pressure on the entry wound and, Oliver, you apply pressure to the exit wound. I'll be back in a few minutes." Without waiting for a response, Ben turned and started across the kitchen.

"Wait, Ben!" Oliver called after him, a sharp edge of fear in his voice. "It might not be safe out there."

Ben turned, his face grim but determined. "If we don't stop this bleeding, your pup doesn't have a chance," he said simply.

Oliver's next words hit Zoe like a punch in the gut. "Then let me go with you."

The old man's gaze softened as it locked with hers. In that moment, she realized how much she needed Oliver to stay. He was her anchor, the steady presence she relied on, and the thought of him stepping into danger made her chest tighten.

"No," Ben said firmly. "Stay with your wife." His lips pressed into a thin line, a quiet insistence in his voice.

"Ben, we don't know what's out there—"

Ben cut him off with a wave of his hand. "I'll be fine, to the barn and back. Three minutes tops." He gave Zoe a small, reassuring nod. It was a silent exchange, a look that said everything she couldn't put into words. Gratitude, trust, hope. And then he was gone, slipping out the back door into the cold, darkening yard.

Ben moved through the yard with quick, purposeful strides. The sky above him looked more like a rusted piece of sheet metal than a sky, the clouds churning with the promise of rain.

Beyond the south fence the otherworldly scream continued, strange and wrong. He did his best to ignore it, focusing instead on getting to the barn as fast as possible and hoping whoever had shot the McCallisters' dog wasn't watching him this very moment.

As Ben crossed the yard, no shots were fired and no bullets ripped through him. But rather than relief, an old fear pressed in. The barn loomed ahead, dark and foreboding, and the memory of what lay inside clawed at the edges of his mind. He'd failed once before in that place. The weight of it was like a stone in his chest, heavy and unforgiving. But he couldn't fail again. He wouldn't.

He pushed open the barn door, the creak of the hinges loud in the stillness. The air inside was thick with the smell of old hay and death. He forced himself to look into the tack room where they'd left the bodies – Randy and his little girl, Katie. Her small form was twisted on the floor, still and lifeless but covered with the jacket Oliver had mercifully placed over her. He swallowed hard, the taste of bile rising in his throat.

"I'm sorry, Katie," he whispered into the darkness, his voice breaking.

He didn't let himself linger. Moving quickly to the shelves, he grabbed rolls of gauze and vet wrap bandaging tape, antiseptic, a suture kit, an IV bag of saline solution, and all the IV gear he had. Hands shaking, he shoved everything into a paper sack and turned to leave. As he crossed the barn, a coughing fit seized him. He doubled over, clutching his chest as he struggled to breathe. The taste of blood filled his mouth, sharp and metallic. He pressed a fist to his lips, fighting to suppress the coughs, to stay upright.

You weak piece of shit! Don't you fail me! Just breathe. I need you to breathe. He forced himself to straighten, sucking in deep, ragged breaths. The sky rumbled overhead, a low, ominous growl that made the hair on the back of his neck stand up.

"Shit," he muttered, trying to force his legs into a run. He hurried past the empty swimming pool, up the stairs to the back patio. He had just reached the door when a single wet drop landed on his lip. He licked it away, tasting salt but also something else – something slippery. A drop of sweat, or something worse?

Ben glanced up at the sky, his heart pounding in his chest. That wasn't rain, he told himself as he reached for the door. He almost believed it, but then he felt another drop hit his cheek, and then another. As the sky rumbled and let loose, a shower of red rain fell. "No!" Ben cried out, wrenching the doorknob and pushing.

"Thank god!" Zoe cried as Ben burst through the door. She looked up, her hands still pressed against Louie's side. "The bleeding has slowed, but we have to get these wounds closed now."

Ben shuffled forward and dropped the sack onto the table, his breath ragged.

She glanced up just as he hastily wiped a smear of blood from his chin.

She narrowed her eyes. "You okay, Ben?" she asked, her voice tinged with concern.

"I'm fine," he said, waving her off. "Just a coughing fit. I had to hurry to beat the rain but I'm alright." He began unloading the supplies, his hands moving with a practiced efficiency.

Zoe didn't press him, but then she caught a look from Oliver.

She frowned and narrowed her eyes, trying to ask the question without words. *What? What's wrong?*

Oliver tipped his head toward Ben, and she looked at him again, only then realizing what Oliver had already noticed. Ben's face, his clothes, the paper sack, all speckled with... rain.

Zoe's hand went to her mouth. "Oh, Ben! Oh no!"

"I'm fine," he reassured them. "Now focus on your pup."

But Ben wasn't fine and Zoe knew it. As her fingers went to work disinfecting the wounds, she glanced at the clock on the microwave. The display read 11:23. They had thirty minutes max before Ben would lose his mind and start craving brains.

She flushed the bullet hole with saline, then gently dabbed it dry with a clean cloth.

Louie flinched, lifted his head, and let out a sharp whine.

Quickly assessing Louie's condition, Zoe asked, "You have something we can sedate him with first to prevent him from thrashing around and worsening the injury?"

Ben rummaged through the supplies. "I have a topical, but it won't be enough by itself. This is acepromazine. It's for horses but if you only use a small amount, it might work."

"Or it might kill him," she said, making no attempt to hide her concern.

Ben readied a horse syringe. "I'm afraid that's a risk, but if you try to stitch him without a sedative, you're going to get bit. I don't care how much he loves you, he won't be able to help it. And if he fights us, we can't help him."

She knew Ben was right. "Yeah, let's do it."

Ben prepared a small dose as Zoe rubbed Louie's ear and whispered, "It's okay, boy. This will help you sleep."

As the sedative took effect, Louie's body relaxed, his breathing evening out.

"Here we go." She applied a topical antibiotic ointment to prevent infection.

Ben removed the cap from a small tube and handed it to Zoe. "Here, this is a lidocaine gel."

"What's that do?" Oliver asked.

Zoe pulled on a rubber glove and applied the cream. "It's a local anesthetic and should help numb the area around the wound."

They waited a few minutes for the numbing cream to take effect, each silent in their thoughts. Jurnee held Princess with one arm, her opposite hand patting Louie's paw. Aaron sat quietly at the other end of the table, rocking himself back and forth, like a metronome keeping time.

Time. Zoe glanced at the microwave. The display read 11:28.

"Oliver, hold him still," she ordered, her voice sharp with authority. She threaded a needle, her hands steady despite the chaos in her mind. She had to put Ben out of her mind and focus on the task in front of her. The sutures came next, small, precise stitches that pulled the ragged edges of flesh together.

Louie whimpered softly, his eyes half open, glazed with pain but still aware. He turned his head, nudging Jurnee's hand with his nose, as if trying to comfort her. The little girl let out a sob, burying her face against Oliver's leg.

"He's going to be okay, right?" Jurnee pleaded, her tear-streaked face lifted to Zoe.

Zoe forced a smile she didn't quite feel. She had never

lied to the little girl and she wasn't going to start now. "We're doing everything we can, sweetie."

They worked in silence, the only sounds the soft snip of scissors, the rustle of gauze, and Louie's labored breathing. When the last stitch was tied, Zoe sat back, wiping the sweat from her brow. The wound was closed on both sides, the bleeding finally stopped. "He lost so much blood. I think an IV would help stabilize his blood pressure and maybe keep him from going into shock."

Ben cleared his throat. "And we could use it to deliver more pain medicine later."

Zoe nodded. "That's true, but I've never administered an IV to a dog."

Ben took Louie's paw in his hand. "Neither have I, but I watched Dr. Bows do it plenty of times. He and I are old friends and he's been my vet for thirty years. You want to go into the cephalic vein on the front leg. I'll show you where, but you'll have to put it in."

Ben found the vein and Zoe successfully administered the IV.

"All we can do now is wait," Ben said quietly, lowering himself into a chair, his hand pressed against his own chest as he fought back another cough.

They gathered around Louie, who lay still on the dining table, his side rising and falling in shallow breaths. The room fell silent, heavy with a collective, unspoken prayer. Jurnee's small hand rested on Louie's paw, her lips moving in a whisper only she could hear.

Zoe wrapped her arm around Oliver's waist, leaning her head against his shoulder. She closed her eyes, wishing, hoping, willing Louie to fight. To make it through.

Ben sat in the chair, still as stone and quiet as a church mouse. The man appeared to be lost in thought.

Zoe moved towards the sink to wash her hands. The microwave clock displayed 11:43. Twenty minutes had passed since Ben came inside from the rain. She looked at Oliver, hoping he would look at her, hoping for a signal of what to do. But his eyes were fixed on Ben. They had to do something – to say something. Her eyes flicked back to the microwave. The display read 11:44.

Nine minutes to go.

CHAPTER 18
THAT'S TWO FOR LANCE

AS THEY STEPPED out of the alley and into the open, Lance's stomach twisted with a mix of excitement and unease. River City looked like something straight out of an apocalypse movie – the kind where everyone's dead before the credits even roll. A garbage truck lay on its side in the middle of the parking lot, like some giant mechanical beast gutted open, trash spilling out like entrails. Police cruisers were scattered around it, crumpled and tossed aside like empty beer cans.

Lance ran a hand over his short, dark hair, feeling the grit of sweat and dirt. "Well, that solves the mystery of the noise we heard a couple weeks back," he muttered, his eyes scanning the chaos. The air stank of decay and burnt plastic, and he could almost taste the coppery tang of blood on the back of his tongue.

"What in the unholy fuck?" Slim whispered, his voice thin and shaky. He took a step back, his skinny frame hunched like a nervous bird ready to take flight. The man was all nerves – twitching fingers, darting eyes, always fidgeting like he was waiting for the other shoe to drop. But despite the smaller man's unease, Lance knew the truth. Slim was as dangerous as a rattlesnake.

Grady, on the other hand, stood with his chest puffed out like he was about to wade into a bar fight. With Grady there was no mystery – you knew exactly what you were dealing with. He took in the destruction with a wolfish grin, the kind of smile that said he was already thinking about the chaos they could stir up next. "Hell of a mess," he said, cracking his knuckles one by one, each pop like a gunshot in the quiet.

Across the lot, what was once some sort of office building was now nothing more than a burned-out shell. As far as Lance could see, the streets were lined with wrecked cars, dead bodies, and debris.

Slim pointed above the burnt-out skyline of River City. "Speaking of unholy fucks, check out that sky." Above the horizon, clouds rolled in, dark and swollen, tinged with a sickly red hue. It looked like the sky itself was bleeding. "We better move, and quick. It looks like it's about to let loose some serious zombie-grade shit."

Lance gave the sky a cursory glance. "We need a car," he said, keeping his voice calm, almost bored. He'd found that calm unnerved the others, made them listen closer. He liked that feeling of control, like he was the only one who understood what needed to be done in a world gone mad.

Slim was already shaking his head, looking at the twisted wreckage around them. "Yeah, but where? These cars are trashed. We'll never find one that runs."

Lance's lips curled into a slow, calculating smile. "Maybe not all of them." He pointed across the lot. "But look at that."

The SWAT vehicle was a beast – all black and armored

to the teeth, sitting like a fortress on wheels amidst the chaos of wreckage.

Grady's face lit up with a grin as he followed Lance's finger. "Oh, hell yeah!"

Slim's face contorted with disbelief. "Come on! You know damn well that thing won't have keys in it. And it's probably locked. But even if it isn't, what do we do, hot-wire it? Does anyone know how because I sure as shit don't. I couldn't hot-wire a toaster, let alone an armored vehicle."

Lance clapped a hand on Slim's shoulder, squeezing hard enough to make him wince. "Doesn't hurt to look, does it?" He gave Slim a shove, urging him forward. "Quit your whining and let's move."

They jogged across the lot, the wind carrying the smell of rot and smoke. Lance kept his eyes darting, scanning every shadow, every crevice. He didn't trust this silence – it was the kind that came before a storm.

Grady reached the vehicle first, yanking open the back door. He barely had time to react before a SWAT officer in full gear leapt out, teeth snapping. The man's face was a nightmare – eyes bloodshot and wild, mouth smeared with blood.

"What the—" Grady roared, catching the zombie in midair by the throat. He lifted him like he was weightless, slamming the man's back onto the pavement with a bone-crunching thud. Grady's grin was manic, a sick kind of joy lighting up his eyes.

"Don't let the damn thing bite you," Lance warned.

He stepped back as the zombie scrambled onto all fours, hissing like a cornered animal.

Slim snatched the pistol from Lance's waistband, aiming for the zombie's head. But Lance was there, shoving his arm down. "Don't shoot!" he hissed, his voice cracking with rage. He pointed across the lot. "Look, you fucking moron, the noise is already drawing them in!"

Across the lot, shadows ran between cars.

Slim's jaw clenched, but he hesitated and held his fire.

Lance capitalized on the moment and snatched the gun away from him. His blood boiled and for a split second he contemplated putting a round in Slim's brain pan, yet somehow, probably the fact they were already drawing a crowd, he bit back the urge to shoot.

Grady kicked the SWAT zombie onto his back and started stomping his face, his boot coming down hard enough to cave in the helmet. Once, twice, three times, until the thing's head was nothing but a smashed pulp. He wiped his boot on the pavement, looking disgusted. "There, that ought to do it."

Behind them, the alley erupted with movement – more zombies, at least four of them, sprinting towards the noise like a pack of rabid dogs.

"Shit, they're coming. Get in!" Lance barked, shoving Slim toward the door. He motioned to the now dead zombie cop. "Grady, throw him inside and let's go!" Lance climbed into the back of the Humvee.

"Why are we bringing him?" Grady growled.

Lance didn't offer an explanation, and he didn't need to. He had a plan, even if the others didn't see it yet. Instead, Lance shot Grady a look that said do what you're told.

Grady, to his credit, obeyed and hauled the limp body up, tossing it in the back like a sack of potatoes.

Slim climbed in after them, slamming the door shut just as the first of the zombies hit the side of the armored car. The vehicle rocked under the impact, the windows rattling.

"We got a problem! No keys in the ignition," Grady announced.

"You asshole! I told you there wouldn't be keys," Slim said, panic filling his wild eyes. "I swear, if we don't get out of this, I'm feeding you to the zombies first!" The wiry man's clenched fists shook with rage. "We're so fucked!"

"Grady, check the cop!" Lance ordered, pushing his way to the front.

Grady's eyes went wide with realization. He knelt over the body, frisking the pockets with desperation. "Nothing in the pants – wait, here!" He pulled a set of keys from the man's tactical vest, holding them up like a trophy.

"You sure?" Lance asked, his voice a mocking drawl.

"Oh yeah," Grady said, sliding into the driver's seat. He jammed the key into the ignition, and the rig roared to life.

"Yes, thank god!" Slim breathed, but before he could finish the thought, Lance was on him.

Lance grabbed Slim by the throat, slamming him against the side of the vehicle, the pistol pressed hard against his temple. "You little fuck," Lance snarled, his voice low and dangerous. "You listen to me and you listen good. You pull some shit like you did out there again, you die. You question me again, you die. You hesitate, you die. You so much as breathe wrong, you fucking die. Got it?"

Slim's eyes were wide, filled with pure terror, but behind them Lance sensed something else. Hate? Perhaps. Well, that was just fine. Lance couldn't care less how Slim felt as long as he fell in line and did what he was told. He pressed the barrel of the gun harder as if he were trying to push it through the man's skull. "I asked you a question."

Slim nodded, his hands held up in surrender. "I got you, Lance. I got you."

The vehicle was rocking back and forth now as if the undead bastards were trying to flip the vehicle onto its side.

Lance's eyes flicked to the rearview mirror. Grady was

watching, a grin spreading across his face like he was enjoying the show. "You good, Grady?"

"Oh, I'm real good," Grady said, pounding his fist on the dashboard. "We got ourselves an armored fucking vehicle! That's two for Lance – he got us out of jail, and now he got us a new ride."

Lance gave Slim an almost affectionate pat on the cheek before tucking the gun back into his waistband. "Good man," he said, flashing a predatory smile. "Now get us the fuck out of here, Grady."

The armored vehicle tore out of the lot, zombies chasing after them, their twisted bodies shrinking in the rearview mirror as the Humvee sped away. Lance leaned back in his seat, a satisfied smile playing on his lips. This was his game now, and he was just getting started.

CHAPTER 19
THE PROMISE

OLIVER LEANED AGAINST THE COUNTER, his arms crossed tightly, staring at Ben, trying to find the right words. But what was he supposed to say? Should he ask Ben to leave, to go back out into the rain before he risked infecting them all? Should he ask if he was feeling hungry for brains yet, as if the man would calmly admit it? Or was he supposed to sit here and wait, listening for something crazy to come out of Ben's mouth, something that would make them all certain he was infected? And then what? Kill him in his own kitchen?

Oliver's stomach twisted at the thought. He glanced at Jurnee, who was sitting right across the table, her little hands gently patting Louie's paw as the dog rested, his breathing shallow but steady. Aaron had left the kitchen to go to the restroom and Oliver wasn't even sure the kids understood that Ben was infected. One thing was for sure, he needed to get Ben away from them, needed to find out what the man wanted him to do before the infection took full control.

Adam rushed into the kitchen, a worried look on his face. "How's he doing?" he asked, nodding toward Louie.

Zoe, standing at the sink, was scrubbing the blood from beneath her fingernails. "Resting, for now," she replied, not looking up. "How's Melissa?"

"Okay, just scared. Thank god that damn scream finally stopped." Adam wiped his forehead like he was trying to clear the memory of it away.

The scream. Oliver hadn't even noticed it had stopped, but it was true. The house had fallen silent. The distant, haunting wail that had echoed through the walls may have finally stopped but the new quiet was almost more unsettling. Maybe it was not knowing what was happening out there. Or maybe it was the fear of what came next.

"Listen, I can't stay long," Adam continued. "Melissa wanted me to check on you guys – and on Louie."

"Thanks, Adam," Oliver said, but his eyes never left Ben. The man was staring off into the distance, seemingly lost in thought. "Thanks to Ben, we got the supplies we needed from the barn. Zoe was able to patch him up best she could."

"I just hope it was enough," Zoe murmured, her voice shaking. "If the bullet did more internal damage than we realized..."

Zoe didn't finish and Oliver was thankful for that. True or not, Jurnee didn't need to hear the very real possibility Louie might... might not make it.

Adam nodded sympathetically, but his eyes flicked to Ben, narrowing slightly. "It's raining pretty hard out there now. You were lucky to make it to the barn and back when you did."

At that, Ben pushed himself up from the table with a

sudden, jerky motion. "Oliver, I... I need you to come to the basement with me."

Zoe spun around, her hands still dripping water from the sink. "The basement? Why?"

Ben dragged a hand down his face, looking more exhausted than ever. His skin was pale, and sweat glistened on his brow. "There's something I need to show him," Ben said, his voice barely above a whisper. "I had planned to show him anyway, but now... now I'm out of time."

"Out of time?" Adam frowned, stepping closer. "What do you mean, out of time?"

Oliver and Zoe shared a look, both their eyes darting to Jurnee, who was doing her best to look disinterested but was clearly listening, her small hand frozen on Louie's paw.

"This isn't a conversation for the kitchen," Zoe said quickly. "Take Adam with you. Whatever it is you want to show Oliver, I'm sure you can show Adam too."

From the doorway Aaron appeared. "Of course, I would like to go along, if that's alright?" His voice was calm but curious, his eyes flicking between the adults.

"Yes. Take him too. Jurnee and I will keep an eye on Louie."

Oliver liked that idea well enough. The more of them who went to see whatever it was Ben wanted him to see, the safer for them all.

Ben's forced smile looked almost hurt, like he knew they didn't trust him. "Of course," he said, but there was something in his eyes, a dark, resigned look that made Oliver's chest tighten. "Alright then, follow me."

They descended the carpeted stairs into the basement. At first glance, Ben's basement was nothing to be scared of. For starters, it was finished with high, tiled ceilings, painted walls, and plush carpeting. Zoe, Aaron, and Jurnee had already found the theater room and spent some time down here last night watching a Disney movie.

Gradually they made their way down the hall past the theater room. Ben moved slowly, each step labored, as if he were carrying a great weight on his back.

Oliver kept a hand on the .357 in his pocket, his eyes darting around. He'd never been past the theater room. The hallway was wide and longer than he expected, with several wood doors on either side. But as they reached the end there was something else. Something that didn't belong. The last door on the right was a heavy steel door. It stood out like a fortress gate.

Ben walked straight to it, his hand resting on the cold metal handle. He looked back at them, his face a mask of regret. "This," he said quietly, "is what I wanted to show you."

Adam frowned, stepping closer. "What's behind the door?"

Oliver felt his pulse quicken. The last time he'd faced a padlocked door in a stranger's house, the owners were keeping their undead kids locked up in the basement and feeding people to them. Zoe had nearly become their next victim.

Ben's gaze locked with Oliver's. "My armory," he said simply. "Weapons I've collected over the years. Guns, ammunition, knives – more than enough to outfit a small army."

Oliver's eyes widened. "You've got an armory down here?"

Ben nodded, his expression unreadable. "I've been collecting for decades. Not for this exactly, but... ever since I was a boy I've had a passion for weapons. My time in the military and then the money I've acquired have only fed that passion." He swallowed hard, glancing up as if he could see the rain pounding on the roof above them. "And now... now I need you to do something for me."

Oliver took a step back, feeling a cold sweat break out on his neck. "What do you mean?"

Ben's hand trembled as he pulled a string with a key from beneath his shirt. He unlocked the door and pushed it back.

Inside, the large room was lined with glass cases, each displaying dozens of rifles, handguns, boxes of ammunition, and rows of gleaming blades.

"Swords!" Aaron exhaled the word like he was witnessing Jesus descending from heaven. He hurried into the room and stood in front of the case displaying over a dozen swords, eyes wide with awe.

It was impressive, but Oliver barely noticed. His eyes were locked on Ben, watching the way the older man's chest heaved, his breath coming in ragged gasps.

"I'm infected," Ben said, the words tumbling out like stones. "I went out in the rain. I felt it on my skin." He pointed to his lip. "I know I got some in my mouth too. Now, I'm not sure how much time I have, but it's already starting."

Oliver's heart pounded in his ears. "Ben—"

"Listen to me!" Ben snapped, slamming the door shut. The sound echoed through the basement, making Aaron flinch. "You need these weapons, Oliver. You'll need them to protect the others."

"And what about you?" Adam asked, his voice low, fearful.

Ben turned to Oliver, his eyes pleading. "I need you to lock me down here. There's a storm shelter across the hall. It's stocked with food, water, and all sorts of supplies.

Maybe I can hold out until morning. But if I change... No, when I change, you need to kill me. Don't hesitate and don't let me hurt anyone."

Oliver's breath caught in his throat. He wanted to argue, to say there was another way, but he knew there wasn't and the look in Ben's eyes said the same. It was the look of a man who had already accepted his fate.

"Promise me," Ben whispered, his voice strained. "Promise me you'll do it."

Oliver couldn't find the words, so he just nodded, once, sharply.

"Good," Ben said, drawing in a breath as he changed his focus to his collection. "Now, I think you'll find you have some serious firepower on your hands."

Oliver glanced around the room. "Shotguns and pistols I understand well enough, but a lot of this stuff I wouldn't even know how to load."

Ben crossed the room to a glass case and punched in a code. "I picked a good year – 1963. That will get you into all the cases and the drawers. Now, you have your AKs, ARs, and then my personal favorite the .50 cal BMG, though admittedly I haven't shot it in several years. It will punch a hole through the engine block of a Ford F-150 and stop it dead in its tracks, but it kicks like a mule. Anyway, those will do some serious damage, but I don't have the time to teach you about them, so you'll have to teach yourself."

Ben retrieved a strange looking pistol from the case. "For in-home use, you have your tactical shotguns, .45, and 9mil, but this is my favorite close-range weapon. They call it *The Judge*." He handed the polished-chrome handgun to Oliver. "It's a revolver with five-round capacity. There's plenty of ammo in that drawer. Load it with .410 slugs for maximum damage."

"Shotgun shells?" Oliver asked.

Ben nodded. "It will sever limbs from torsos, Oliver. Believe it."

Aaron punched in the code on the sword case and removed one of the swords.

As Aaron opened the cabinet, Oliver noticed Ben stuff something behind his back. He decided not to say anything yet, but Ben was definitely hiding something. "Aaron, wait. I don't think you should mess with those," Oliver warned.

"Now hold on a second." Ben placed a hand on Oliver's shoulder as he looked at Aaron. "What made you select that sword, son? It is one of my most prized and most expensive."

"Well, of course, this is a Japanese sword favored by the samurai. It's a katana known for its high quality and cutting ability." Aaron looked up from the sword and back to the glass case.

"You see something else?" Ben asked.

Aaron nodded. "I recently read *The Book of Five Rings* by the most famous of all samurai, Miyamoto Musashi. Of course, he interests me because I love swords and Niten Ichi-ryū is a style based around the use of not one, but two swords at the same time." Aaron reached back into the glass case and retrieved a second sword. This one had the same black string-wrapped handle and black scabbard but was slightly shorter than the first.

Adam took a step back. "Aaron, I don't think that's a good idea—"

"Wait," Ben said, holding up a hand, his voice calm but curious. "Two swords at once, huh?" He took a slow step forward, eyes fixed on Aaron. "That's not something you hear about every day. Please go on, son."

"Well, a rough translation of Miyamoto Musashi's style is known as 'two heavens as one.' Of course, many styles of

Japanese swordsmanship use only the katana, but Niten Ichi-ryū utilizes two swords. This sword" – Aaron held up the shorter of the two – "is called a wakizashi and would be used to defend while counterattacking with this one." He held up the longer katana. "Of course, when used properly, the opponent has no adequate defense as they are using only one sword against an opponent with two."

"Fascinating," Ben said, wiping a hand across his sweat-slicked brow. For a moment his gaze was distant, as if sifting through old memories. "I got into swords a long time back during a deployment in Japan. I remember we had downtime waiting for orders. I wandered into this little antiques shop. They had a real katana hanging on the wall – nothing fancy, not polished like museum pieces. No special flair. Just an honest weapon built to perform."

He paused, a small smile ghosting across his lips.

"I bought it with half a month's pay. Then I paid a small fortune to have the shop ship it back to the States. I spent years learning how to use it right. Figured if you're going to own a weapon like that, you ought to respect it. I suggest you let the boy keep the swords – he knows more about their history than even I do."

Aaron lit up like Oliver had never seen. "I am... I am very pleased!" Aaron said with a laugh.

Ben smiled at Aaron. "How about this – when I'm gone, all my swords are yours. I want you to have them because I know you'll appreciate them."

Aaron glanced back at the glass case and then at the swords he was holding. "Wow! Thank you so much! Of course, this is exactly what I've always wanted!"

"Just don't take them out of their sheaths, okay?" Oliver said.

"They are called saya," Aaron corrected.

"Oh, right." Oliver was only half listening, his thoughts focused on how long they had been down here. It must have been forty to forty-five minutes since Ben was infected. He was surprised the man still had all his faculties and wasn't already talking gibberish.

As if sensing Oliver's worry, Ben's face turned grave once more. "There's more I could show you, but I'm afraid we don't have the time." Without elaborating further, Ben led them out of the room.

Back in the hallway, Ben approached another door across from the armory. This one was a wooden door that matched the others in the basement. It was solid but otherwise unremarkable. This time he pulled a set of keys from his pocket, sorting past a car key fob and house keys until he found a small brass key. He inserted it into the knob, twisted, and pushed open the door.

Cool air pushed past Oliver as if the room itself was exhaling. Oliver felt goose pimples crawling up his back.

Ben reached in and flicked a switch, revealing a big room constructed entirely of concrete, with the walls and ceiling painted stark white. The floor was the color of finished concrete. The room itself was ordinary, but what it held was amazing.

Adam whistled. "Holy moly, Ben!"

The walls on all sides were covered from floor to ceiling in metal shelves. Each shelf was stacked with canned food, dry goods, and five-gallon jugs of water. "It should come as no surprise to you that I lied when I said I didn't have enough to take in people. Truth is, I have more than enough." There was a hint of shame in Ben's voice as he turned his attention to Aaron and Adam. "Can you two excuse us for a moment? I need to talk to Oliver in private."

Adam gave Oliver a look that asked, *Are you sure?*

Oliver nodded. "I'll be okay."

Adam glanced at Ben then back to Oliver. "We'll be right outside."

Oliver and Ben stood alone among the supplies. Ben wiped his brow again. The collar of his shirt was soaked in a ring of dark sweat.

"Hold out your palm." Ben removed the key to the gun room from around his neck. Oliver did so and Ben dropped the key into his palm, the twine pooling atop it.

Oliver looped the string over his head and stuffed the key down his shirt.

Next Ben drew a handgun from the back of his waistband, revealing the secret he'd hidden there.

Oliver held up his hands. "Ben, what are you doing?"

"Calm down, Oliver." He flipped the gun around and held it by the barrel. "This is a Desert Eagle .50. Over the years I've modified the hell out of this piece. It's all customed out – eight-inch fluted barrel, enhanced trigger, titanium night sights, the list goes on. Of all my guns, this one is my favorite. Not because it is the most powerful or most expensive, but because it has been with me for a long time, and we've been through *a lot* of shit." He pushed the gun towards Oliver. "I want you to not only have it, but also to use this gun to... to kill me."

Oliver swallowed down the sick feeling creeping up the back of his throat and took the gun.

"You can shoot me here in this room. Do it tonight but not until I turn. Not until I lose my shit and start talking about eating brains." Ben pointed to the floor. "No carpet in here and there's a drain right there in the floor – easy cleanup."

"Jesus, Ben."

Ben waved a hand. "Oliver, the cancer would have

gotten me if this hadn't. Don't feel bad for me. I had a good run," the old man said with a wink. "You know what else? I was an asshole, but I got infected doing something good! And that means more to me than you'll ever know. Truth is I have plenty to regret, but getting caught in the rain, well, that's something I won't." Ben walked over to a shelf and found a roll of duct tape. "You need to tape me to the shelf." Ben eased himself down onto the floor with a grunt of aching joints. "If you don't, you risk getting attacked when you come back to check on me."

Oliver pressed his lips into a tight line and squatted down next to the man. He looked into Ben's eyes – really looked. His eyes were bloodshot. Not the kind of bloodshot you get from lack of sleep or crying but the kind that would soon leak blood. He hadn't looked this close at infected eyes since he'd inspected Sam's. Ben's were just like hers. Older, sure, and a different color, but the perforations looked the same and it took him back to that horrifying morning, to a place that still haunted his nightmares. Oliver swallowed it down, pushing the memory aside as he ripped loose a length of tape and wrapped Ben's wrists, binding him to the shelves. "How do you feel now? Are you hungry?"

Ben considered the question. "No. No, I can't say that I am. But, hey" – Ben nodded at the tape – "you're going to need to do better than that, fella."

Oliver nodded, picked up the tape again, and started wrapping his wrists over and over before going to work on the man's feet. "That will hold for sure, but tell me if it's too tight."

"It needs to be exactly what it is."

"Alright then. I'll be back in an hour. Do you need anything before I go? A drink of water?"

"No. I... I think I'm good," he said, leaning his side against the shelves.

"Okay then." Oliver turned to go.

Ben swallowed. "Oliver, wait."

"Yeah?"

"Thank you for being brave enough to knock on my door and allowing me to spend the last day or so with your family and friends. And thank you for what you did for Katie. You're a good person, Oliver, and I'm lucky to have met you."

Oliver choked down the emotion as he tried to get out the words. "Of course," he said hoarsely. "Thank you for taking us in."

Ben nodded somberly. "Go on now. I'll see you in an hour."

Oliver pulled the door shut behind him, inserted the key, and twisted it, the heavy metal mechanism clicking into place with the weight of a massive stone sealing an ancient tomb – Ben's tomb.

In the hall Oliver found Zoe waiting with Aaron and Adam; her eyes rested on him with a look of quiet sympathy. Quietly she said, "It's been fifty minutes since Ben was infected – I was worried."

Oliver wiped his eyes on his sleeve, his face flushing. "You heard all that?"

Zoe threw her arms around him. "I'm so sorry."

Adam placed a hand on his shoulder but he didn't say anything. He didn't need to.

Oliver turned away, the metallic click of the lock still ringing in his ears as they climbed the stairs. He couldn't bring himself to look back. But he knew no matter how bad he was dreading it, he'd be back in an hour. He had a promise to keep.

CHAPTER 20
CROSS THAT BRIDGE WHEN WE GET TO IT

LANCE IDLY FLIPPED through the pages of the armored vehicle's manual as Grady maneuvered the rig through the debris-choked streets of downtown River City. The vehicle rumbled over potholes and the twisted remains of abandoned cars, its reinforced tires crushing glass and metal with ease. Outside, the city looked like a war zone – charred buildings, mangled wreckage, and the occasional body left to rot where it had fallen.

"Dammit, look ahead," Grady muttered, jabbing a finger toward the windshield. The road in front of them was blocked by a barricade of burnt-out military vehicles. Smoke coiled from the remains of a tank, its turret twisted at a grotesque angle. "Looks like they tried to make a stand and lost. No way around that."

"Then find a side street," Slim snapped, glancing back through the rear window, his fingers drumming anxiously on the seat. "But whatever you do, don't stop. We've got a whole mess of those dead fucks on our ass."

Lance didn't even look up. "Says here this rig is a Lenco BearCat G4," he said, tapping the page. Its features included a V8 turbo engine, steel armor construction with frag protection, and ballistic glass panels.

"So what?" Slim's voice was a frantic hiss. His fingers gripped the seat like he was a passenger on a roller coaster, white-knuckled and bracing for the next drop.

"So it's got some pretty impressive features," Lance replied with a slow smile, enjoying the panic in Slim's eyes.

"Features?" Slim spat, his voice cracking. "Who the hell cares about features? Grady, you're slowing down! They're gonna overrun us!"

Grady's bald head gleamed with sweat as he gripped the wheel tighter. "No side streets left," he barked, glancing at the rearview mirror. "I'll have to turn around and ram through them."

Lance finally shut the manual, his gaze leveling with Grady's. "No," he said calmly. "Speed up and push through."

Grady shot him a disbelieving look. "Are you fucking nuts, man? We'll blow the engine for sure!"

"Have you not learned by now?" Lance leaned forward, his voice low and threatening. "You want out of this mess? Then do as you're told. Speed up."

Grady's jaw clenched, but he tightened his grip on the wheel and nodded. "Fine. You want to play demolition derby, I'm game." His eyes widened with manic excitement as he slammed his foot down on the accelerator.

Lance glanced back at Slim, who was scrambling to strap himself into one of the benches lining the side of the BearCat. "Better buckle up, Slim," Lance said with a smirk.

Slim fumbled with the seatbelt, his hands shaking. "You're fucking lunatics," he muttered.

The BearCat barreled forward, slamming into the barricade. The impact sent a Humvee skidding across the road, flipped an ambulance onto its roof, and crunched through several more twisted, burnt-out wrecks. The noise was deafening – metal shrieking, glass shattering, the groan of the BearCat's frame under the force.

"Shit!" Slim shouted, clutching the seatbelt like a lifeline.

"That a baby!" Grady roared, slapping the dashboard. "Like Moses parting the Red Sea!"

Lance smirked, watching the last of the wreckage fade behind them as Grady sped down the road. The zombies chasing them were now little more than specks in the rearview mirror.

"How'd you know it would work?" Slim asked, his face pale.

"Because I can fucking read. This thing is fully armored, with a built-in battering ram." Lance felt the adrenaline surge through his veins. This was the kind of chaos he thrived on. He tossed the manual onto the floor, the pages fluttering open like a broken-winged bird.

But the adrenaline rush faded quickly. Up ahead, the towering frame of the Murray Baker Bridge loomed over the river. Lance narrowed his eyes. "Slow down," he ordered, his smile giving way.

Grady eased off the gas, squinting at the bridge. "What are you thinking?"

Lance could only see the first half of the bridge. It was gridlocked – cars bumper to bumper, some overturned, others burnt out. "We push through," Lance said coolly. "The BearCat can handle it."

Grady nodded. "Damn right it can." Higher they climbed on their approach to the bridge, pushing cars aside like a plow through snow. As the opposite end came into view it was Grady who noticed it first. "Uh, boss, what the hell is that?"

Lance leaned forward, squinting into the distance. Up ahead, something massive jutted up from the bridge like a twisted monument. As they drew closer, the shape became clearer – a large Boeing passenger plane, its tail section tangled in the bridge's structure, stretched skyward at a steep angle, the fuselage torn apart like a tin can. The nose of the plane had smashed through the floor of the bridge, leaving a gaping hole that stretched across all four lanes.

"Holy shit," Slim breathed. "That's a plane?"

"Looks like it crashed straight through," Grady muttered, his hands tightening on the wheel. "No way we're getting across that."

Lance cursed under his breath, his mind racing, weighing their options. This wasn't the only bridge in River City. There were three actually, but he knew for sure the Bob Michel Bridge was closed due to construction because the guards bitched about having to go around and the time it added to their commute. There was a third bridge only about a mile south, the Cedar Street Bridge. He glanced back at Slim and Grady. "Well, boys, looks like we've got ourselves a little detour."

Grady spun the wheel, the BearCat lurching to the left as they veered off the blocked Murray Baker Bridge exit ramp and back into the twisted streets of River City. The storm clouds overhead churned with an angry, reddish hue, casting a sickly light over the city as they barreled south toward the Cedar Street Bridge.

As they sped past a strip mall, a rogue, half-deflated tube man flailed weakly outside a ruined car dealership, its remaining arm twitching like it was still trying to sell someone a great deal.

"Holy shit! Look, he's trying to flag us down!" Slim pointed to a figure standing in the middle of an intersection, one hand raised as if directing non-existent traffic, the other gripping a shopping cart.

As they drew closer, Grady slowed the BearCat and let out a hearty laugh. "Ha! You want me to stop, Slim? He looks like your type."

The figure wasn't a person at all. It was a mannequin, dressed in a tuxedo with an obnoxiously bright orange feather boa wrapped around its neck, the ends flapping wildly in the wind. The shopping cart beside it was filled to the brim with... garden gnomes.

"Fuck you, Grady." Slim slumped back in his seat and crossed his arms, then leaned forward again to address Lance. "Hey, you really think the next bridge will be clear?" His voice was high and thin, his fear palpable.

"No," Lance snapped. "It will probably be just as packed with cars, but I don't think there will be a plane sitting ass up in the middle of the bridge either. Not even we can be that unlucky. Now shut up and keep your eyes peeled."

Grady pushed the BearCat harder, the engine growling like an angry grizzly as they dodged wrecked vehicles and plowed through the occasional undead bastard that darted in their path. The windshield wipers squealed across the glass, smearing rain mixed with blood. The city felt like it was closing in around them, a graveyard of steel and shattered concrete.

As they approached the Cedar Street Bridge, Lance felt a flicker of hope. The bridge stretched out, crammed with abandoned cars, but it seemed passable.

Grady slowed, his eyes wide. "What are you thinking?"

"We push through," Lance said coolly. "This rig's got the power. We just need to be smart about it."

But as they inched closer, something caught Lance's eye. At first, he thought it was a trick of the light, perhaps something in the way the clouds cast shadows as they moved over the bridge. But then the others saw it too.

"What the fuck is that?" Grady's voice cracked, the bravado gone.

The BearCat crawled forward and Lance leaned in, squinting. The shadow came into view and he saw it then – a mass of writhing bodies fused together, a nightmarish collage of zombies blocking the middle of the span.

It was like nothing he'd ever seen before – a towering, grotesque creature made up of dozens of infected. Arms and legs protruded at odd angles, heads twisted in unnatural positions, mouths gaped in silent screams. It moved as one, a single entity dragging itself towards them from the other side, a shambling, lurching goliath.

"Turn around," Slim whispered, his voice shaking. "We can't get through that."

For once, Lance agreed. They couldn't fight this thing, not head-on. He clenched his jaw, hating the thought of retreat, but they had no choice. "Back us out, Grady. Slow and steady. We'll head south toward Bartonville and try the Highway 150 crossing."

Grady threw the BearCat into reverse, the tires screeching as they backed away from the giant monstrosity. It turned its many heads toward them, a low, guttural sound rumbling from deep within its fused chests. It began to move faster, shouldering its mass between cars, pushing them to the side and slamming them against the guardrails. The mass of bodies swayed and pulsed like a giant, diseased heart.

"Faster!" Lance barked, his cool demeanor shattered as his heart pounded in his chest. "Get us out of here!"

The BearCat swung around, its tires skidding on the wet pavement as they sped away from the bridge. Lance glanced back, watching as the monster neared the end of the bridge, its grotesque limbs reaching out like the tentacles of a sea monster.

Slim's voice was a choked gasp. "That thing… it was like they were fused together."

"I don't know what that was," Lance muttered, his mind whirling. "But we need to get out of the city, now."

Grady nodded, his face pale. He floored the gas and the BearCat responded with the now comforting roar as they sped south out of River City. Behind them, the skyline receded, replaced by the shadowed outlines of industrial buildings and vacant parking lots. They were on a straight shot through the industrial part of town only a handful of miles from the 150 bridge.

"I don't see why we need to cross at all, Lance? Why not just forget it and go west?" Slim begged.

"No. The plan is set, we're getting across this river. Trust me, it'll be worth it."

"Look, I get it. You got a plan and all, and I ain't arguing, but at least tell us how it'll be worth it?" Slim begged, clearly shaken by what he'd seen on the bridge.

Lance couldn't fault him for that. "Alright, here's the story. Before I got locked up a few years back I was doing electrical for a residential contractor. He had me installing solar power on homes all over central Illinois. I get to this place out in the middle of bumfuck Egypt – real nice place. Rich old bastard. I finish the solar job and the old guy wants to hire me for a side job, a special project wiring up his gun vault."

"He hired you to run electric in a gun safe?" Grady asked dubiously.

"Not a gun safe, a vault. It was a huge room in the basement of this mansion. I'm talking wall-to-wall shatterproof glass cabinets stacked full of guns. Rare stuff and big stuff. Enough to outfit a small army. The room itself is equipped with motion sensor lighting and the cabinets work on a key code. And that's if you can get past the steel door and a fat industrial padlock."

"Right on, I see why you want to go there, but how are we going to get in?" Grady asked.

Lance smiled. "Easy, I wired it all up including the security for the room. I also happen to know that the old man keeps the key on a string around his neck."

Slim itched at his stubbly face while Grady just nodded slowly as if contemplating.

"Look, it isn't just the guns," Lance admitted. "The house is massive, secluded, and stocked full of food."

"How could you know that?" Slim asked.

"Because I took the opportunity to poke around the basement. Back then, he had MREs and all kinds of dry goods, including five-gallon buckets of rice. I'm talking shelves upon shelves of supplies. You name it, if it has any kind of a shelf life, he had some. It's like the guy knew something like this was coming. But here's the part you won't believe. The guy had bulletproof glass installed throughout his entire house."

"Bullshit," Grady said.

"No bullshit. I didn't test it myself but the contractor told me about it. I asked why and he said the guy was paranoid about security. It's no secret old Meyer did a whole bunch of people dirty, stole their land right out from under them."

"Guys like that make me sick!" Grady snarled. "They lock us up, meanwhile the rich get richer off the backs of the poor! Well, fuck that guy. I'm with you! We'll cross that river if we have to swim across it!"

"Good! Slim, you in this? If not, speak up now. We'll get you to a car and we can part ways, no hard feelings." Of course, that wasn't true. If Slim wanted to part ways he'd be doing it with a bullet in his back. But Lance didn't want to make him feel forced. He needed Slim to want to be part of this little trio. If he tried to force Slim, the little rat-faced puke would just stab him in the back first chance he had. "Well, what do you say?"

Slim nodded. "Yeah. What the hell, I'm in. But we better hope we can cross at the 150 bridge."

"We're about to find out." Lance nodded at the sign for Bartonville, which lay just beyond the 150 bridge. The overpass came into view and Grady climbed the shoulder, making his way around abandoned cars and onto Highway 150. Lance's stomach sank at the sight – another gridlock of abandoned cars, stretching as far as the eye could see and packed in too tight to push through even with the BearCat.

"Dammit!" Grady slammed his fist against the steering wheel. "It's locked up too!"

Lance clenched his teeth and made the call. "We keep moving south. We have one option left."

"The Pekin Bridge?" Grady asked.

"That's right. It's only about five or so miles down, but it's the last bridge for... for, shit, I don't even know."

"Havana would be next," Grady said, "but, hell, that's an hour on a two-lane road in normal conditions."

Slim pulled himself between the seats. "An hour south just to come all the way back up?"

Lance didn't answer right away. He could feel the

tension thick in the air, both in the men and in the way the storm outside seemed to charge everything with a static buzz. He said finally, "If we can't cross at Pekin, we abandon the plan and head west. Now quit breathing on me and back the fuck up, Slim."

Slim nodded, seemingly satisfied, and made his way back to his seat.

The dashboard lit up with a yellow icon that read Low Fuel.

"New problem – we're running on fumes already," Grady warned. "If we don't find gas soon, we're dead in the rain."

"Then we'll find fuel," Lance said, his voice hard. "Spin around and let's keep moving."

"Right on. But we may need to park alongside a car until this rain stops, then siphon it out."

Lance glanced up at the sky. "Just go. I'll figure something out."

The BearCat roared down the road, passing a ransacked McDonald's and a burnt-out Hardee's as they entered town. The ruin that was Bartonville blurred past as they made a beeline for Pekin. The rain continued to fall as the storm clouds churned overhead and crackled with red lightning, casting a flickering, hellish light over the road.

As they approached the corner of Highway 24 and Route 9, Lance's eyes darted to the gas gauge. It was deep in the red, the needle resting on the pin. "Pull in that gas station," he ordered.

Grady veered off the highway, the BearCat skidding into a small, run-down gas station. It was a good location at the highway junction – a last stop to grab fuel after leaving Pekin and crossing the bridge. The pumps were dark, no power. Grady looked up at the sign, which read 3-WAY GAS STATION. "Three-way," he repeated with a chuckle.

"Dammit! This ain't funny," Slim shouted. "Gas pumps run on electricity! No juice! We're screwed!"

"Calm down," Lance growled, pointing to the pumps that sat protected from the rain under a large canopy.

"Like I just said, those pumps take electricity to run," Slim argued.

"No shit. I'm not interested in pumps that don't work. There're three vehicles sitting under there. Now, go inside and find some hose to siphon with."

Slim hesitated, looking back at Lance. "I need a gun."

"Slim, look under your ass," Lance pointed.

Slim looked down at the bench seat and frowned.

"Lift it, smart guy."

Slim stood, then knelt down, lifting the seat. His eyes went wide and he whistled. "Holy shit, how'd you know?"

Lance picked up the manual off the floorboard and tossed it to Slim. "Lucky guess."

Lance watched as Slim lifted a tactical shotgun, shells, and a pistol from inside the compartment. Then the little man froze and set both weapons down on the floor, grinning stupidly. "Stop the presses. What do we have here?" He lifted out an AR-15, retrieved a magazine, shoved it in the receiver, and racked the slide. "Hell yes!"

Grady pushed himself up and maneuvered between the seats.

"Where are you going?" Lance asked.

"I want a gun too," he said, lifting the seat on the opposite side and rummaging through the gear like a kid in a candy store.

Lance kept his focus on Slim. The fact he'd just armed a

murdering cannibalistic convict with a semiautomatic assault rifle wasn't lost on him. "Well, are you good now?"

"Oh, I'm real good." Slim grinned, his big ratty front teeth showing.

"Good. Go. Make fuel happen," Lance ordered.

Slim jumped out of the BearCat and made for the gas station, quickly vanishing inside.

"Flash-bangs! They got flash-bangs!" Grady announced, stuffing them into a rucksack he'd found under the seat.

"Hope he hurries the hell up," Lance muttered, turning his attention back to the gas station.

From inside they heard a sudden scream followed by a flurry of gunshots.

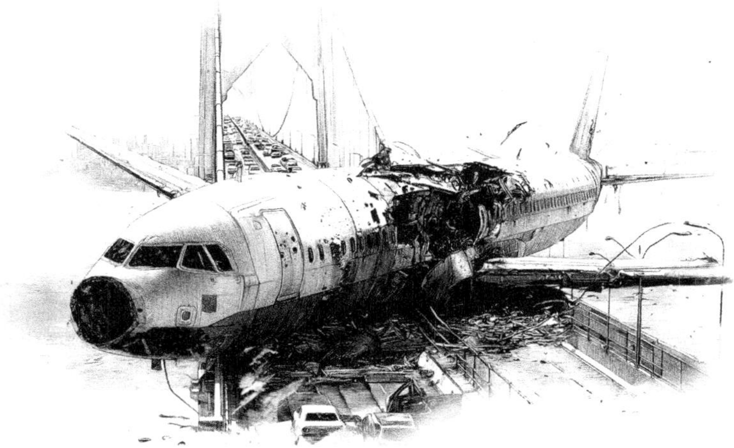

CHAPTER 21
A STRANGE RESILIENCE

THE AFTERNOON LIGHT slanted through the kitchen windows, casting long shadows across the room. The rain had picked up, hammering against the glass in a relentless downpour.

Zoe stood by the kitchen table, her gaze fixed on Louie's chest, rising and falling with shallow, labored breaths. His wound had been stitched and bandaged, but it would be hours before they knew if he would pull through. The pit bull lay still, eyes closed, a soft whine escaping his throat every now and then.

Oliver placed a hand on her shoulder, his touch gentle and warm. "How's he doing?"

Zoe sighed, brushing a stray braid behind her ear. "He's hanging in there, but it's too soon to tell. I want to move him to the front room and put him on the couch but I don't think we should do it yet. I'm worried about internal bleeding. He's lost a lot of blood."

"Thanks to you, he has a chance," Oliver said, his voice filled with gratitude. "If you hadn't stepped in..."

"If Ben hadn't gotten those supplies out in the barn,"

she corrected. Her eyes drifted to the doorway to the basement, where Ben had been locked away. "Speaking of the barn, mind telling me what you were thinking, Oliver?" The words came out sharper than she meant for them to.

But Oliver showed no surprise, nodding somberly as if he knew this was coming. Lowering his voice to a whisper he said, "I know. I fucked up, Zo, but Ben couldn't go in there. He begged me and he told me if I took care of... of the little girl, Katie, we could stay, and we could keep this place after..." He glanced at Jurnee and then Aaron. "Look, I was only—"

"Only doing what you wanted," she finished. "We're supposed to be a team, Oliver, and then you go running off and make a decision that could have gotten you killed! I don't know what to say to you to get you to stop and include me before you make decisions that can affect us all!" She was crying now and hating herself for it.

"Zo, I'm sorry," he said, reaching for her.

"If we hadn't all been out back, Louie might not have been shot. And what if he hadn't been here? What about Jurnee?"

Oliver pulled a pained face as if he'd been struck. "That's not fair."

"No? Well, I don't think what you did was fair. Louie might not make it, and Ben is infected."

"And what, that's all my fault?" Oliver crossed his arms. "I didn't know Ben was going to ask me to do that when you sent me with him to do chores and I sure as hell didn't know he was going to get rained on."

Zoe let out an exasperated sigh. "I'm not saying it's all your fault, but you have to see this could have gone differently if you'd stopped to include me before you went into that barn!"

Oliver uncrossed his arms and held his hands palms up. "Yeah, I see it and you're right. But would you have said no?"

Zoe considered the question. "This isn't about being right. This is about making decisions together. This wasn't an emergency. Katie was locked in the barn and had been since this started. I think you were afraid to stop and include me because you thought I would say no. The truth is I don't think I would have, but I wouldn't have let you do it alone. Don't you see, now you have to carry what happened in that barn with you and..."

Oliver stepped closer and took both her hands in his. "What?"

The world they had known their whole marriage, their whole lives, was ripped away, but so were all the distractions of life. No work, no studies, no phones. No more secrets, just each other. Over the past several weeks she had grown closer to Oliver than ever before. And the trust they'd built was undeniable. She couldn't bear the thought of... "There're more ways to lose you than to the infection. You don't know what the effects of doing what you did will have on you. But I don't want to lose the Oliver I love, the Oliver that's good and true... and my best friend."

"Oh, Zo, you aren't going to lose me."

"You don't know that. You don't *know*. Just please, from now on, we do this together." She just wished he understood how close he'd come and how lost she'd be without him.

"I promise. No more going rogue." He pulled her to him and wrapped his arms around her.

Zoe placed her head on his chest, listening to his heartbeat. Then she gasped and pulled back, looking him in the eyes. "Ben!"

Her eyes flipped to the microwave clock. The display read 1:45.

"It's been long enough. I promised him I would check on him in an hour or so." Oliver's jaw tightened and she could see he'd been dreading this moment, putting it off for as long as he could.

"Hey," Zoe said soothingly, "you won't be alone. I'll be right there with you."

Jurnee, who had been sitting quietly by Louie's side, looked up, her small face pale and pinched with worry. "Is Ben going to be okay too?"

Zoe forced a smile for the girl's sake. "Ben is very sick but we're going to check on him now, sweetie." But she knew the real answer to that question was no. Jurnee would never see Ben alive again.

The little girl nodded, her eyes wide as she stroked Louie's paw gently. "At least he has a doctor like you to make him all better. Will you tell him I hope he feels better?"

Zoe's heart broke and she turned away.

"We'll tell him." Oliver exchanged a look with Zoe, the weight of the unspoken task ahead hanging heavy in the air between them. "Let's go."

She composed herself and looked down at the little girl. "Jurnee, stay here and keep an eye on Louie until we get back. We don't want him to be alone, okay?" She shifted her gaze to Aaron, who'd been sitting at the other end of the table quietly reading a book from Ben's library, *The Art of War*.

"We'll make sure he isn't lonely," Jurnee said, laying her doll next to Louie. "Right, Aaron?"

Aaron crunched a mouthful of chips. "Of course," he

mumbled, pushing his bangs back from his eyes and flipping a page.

They made their way down the hall and descended the narrow staircase that led to the basement. "Hey, you think it's okay leaving Aaron alone with those swords?"

"Zo, you should have seen the way his eyes lit up when Ben gave them to him."

"I know but they're swords, Oliver – real swords."

"And he said he has swords at home. His mom allows it. Besides, I told him they had to stay in their sheaths. I mean, look, we've been living with him for weeks – Aaron's a great kid."

"Yeah," she conceded. "I know, of course he is." The air grew colder, the familiar musty smell mingling with something sharper – metallic and unpleasant. The scent reminded her of a terminal patient in the hours before death. Zoe shivered, whether from the chill or from the unease twisting in her gut, she couldn't tell.

Oliver drew an unfamiliar pistol from his waistband.

"Where did you get that?" she asked.

"Ben. He insisted I use this gun to... you know." He reached for the door, then hesitated. "Ben? Ben, can you hear me?"

He looked at Zoe. "Ready?"

She didn't know how anyone could be ready for what they were about to do, but she drew her .357 and nodded.

Oliver unlocked the door and turned the knob.

Ben was still sitting where Oliver had left him, duct-taped to the shelves.

He looked up as they approached, his face gaunt and pale. His eyes were red. Red like hay fever red but not bleeding. "Still here," Ben said with a dry chuckle. Then he eyed the guns. "You were expecting a monster? Well, I was too. Doc, you care to explain why I haven't lost my marbles yet?"

Oliver's eyes narrowed. "I half expected you to have chewed through the tape by now."

"Nope, still here," he said, eyeing Zoe. "Disappointed?" Ben's voice was teasing, but there was an edge to it.

Zoe didn't answer right away. She studied him, searching for any sign of infection – the telltale wildness in his eyes. They should be oozing blood by now. But there was nothing. He looked like hell, sure, and the smell of stale body odor and sweat was even thicker now, but he didn't look infected. At least not full blown.

"Maybe it hasn't been long enough," Oliver said, his voice low. "Or maybe you got lucky."

Ben gave a bitter laugh, coughing into his fist. "Luck? I'm the old bastard who's outlived his usefulness. Luck left me years ago."

Zoe stepped closer, but not close enough he could reach her with his teeth. She squatted down to meet his eyes. "Ben, you should be turning. You were exposed hours ago. By now, the infection should have taken over."

"You think I don't know that?" Ben's voice was harsh, but there was a flicker of something in his eyes – confusion. "I can feel it, Doc. It's in me. No doubt it's in me. But it's like... it's like something's fighting it."

"What do you mean?" Oliver asked, stepping forward.

Ben shook his head in frustration and straightened his legs with a wince. "I don't know how to explain it. It's like I can feel the parasite trying to dig in, trying to take control. But there's something pushing back, holding it at bay."

Zoe took a breath, letting instinct take over. The chaos

of the world outside faded for just a moment as her training kicked in. Assess, observe, document. This was familiar territory, and in a strange way, grounding. She slipped into nurse mode – not because she didn't care, but because it gave her something to hold on to. Something solid. "Are you hungry?" she asked, her tone calm but focused.

"No. No, I can't say that I am." His brow furrowed. "I haven't eaten a thing today – not even breakfast. Just had a cup of coffee before heading out to the barn. Normally I'd be starving by now. But then again, I don't have the appetite I used to have."

Zoe nodded, filing that away. "And what about cravings, Ben? Are you having any cravings?"

Ben thought about that longer than Zoe would have liked. "No, can't say that I am."

"Oh my god... I think I know what's happening," Oliver said, hope spilling over. "It's like in this Brad Pitt zombie movie we watched a long time back. Remember? I don't think you cared much for it being a zombie flick but you agreed to watch it because it starred Brad Pitt."

Zoe flushed vaguely, remembering the movie. Well, she didn't remember much about the movie at all but she did remember Brad Pitt was in it.

"Actually," Oliver continued, "it was a book first and the book was so much better—"

"Zombie movie, Oliver?" Zoe asked, incredulously.

"Just hear me out. In the movie Brad Pitt discovers that the virus doesn't infect people who are sick, so he injects himself with something – I don't remember what, smallpox or maybe it was the flu... doesn't matter. Point is the virus doesn't like sick people, and he walks right by the zombies!"

"That doesn't make any sense," Zoe said flatly. "This isn't a virus, it's a parasite and Ben is already infected."

"But I just thought that since Ben has cancer, maybe the cancer is somehow deterring the parasite from taking hold. I don't know, maybe—"

Zoe gasped. "The cancer! Oliver, you're a genius!"

Oliver blinked. "I am? Well, see, now that's more like it! So you think because he has cancer maybe the parasites don't like him?"

"No. Not at all." Zoe laughed.

Ben stared back and forth between them. "You two want to tell me what the hell is going on?"

Zoe's medical instincts kicked in, her mind racing through possibilities. "Ben, you said you were taking meds for your cancer. Tell me exactly what you're on."

He blinked, thrown off by the sudden shift in questioning. "Why? What difference does it make?"

"It could make all the difference," she pressed. "Please, just tell me."

Ben hesitated, then sighed. "There are so many, I can't remember all their names, but it's the usual fare, chemotherapy and immunotherapy. Of course, I did some radiation early on. Sorry I can't remember the names."

Zoe pursed her lips. "What else?"

Ben shrugged, grunted, and adjusted his position on the floor. "Anti-nausea meds and painkillers. Oh, and there's the experimental one. Pain in the ass to even get a trial. I remember I had to sign a release of liability and a bunch of other forms. They said it wasn't really designed for humans but had shown promising results in some cancer patients."

Zoe's pulse quickened. "What do you mean not designed for humans?"

"What I mean is it's not approved by the FDA because it was designed for veterinary treatment."

"For animals?" Oliver asked.

"Yeah, that's what they said, but shit, I didn't care if it was designed to kill rats. As long as it killed the cancer, I was willing to try anything."

"Ben, this is important, do you remember what it's called?" Zoe asked.

"No, but it's in my bathroom cabinet along with all the other shit that didn't work. I know it starts with an *F* and has my name in it."

Zoe holstered her .357 and made for the door. "Wait here, I'll be right back," she shouted over her shoulder as she darted for the stairs.

She raced to Ben's bathroom, opened the mirrored cabinet above the sink, and sorted through the meds, most of which she recognized. She quickly found the one that was unfamiliar and started with *F* – *Fenbendazole. Bingo!* Next she grabbed her *Parasite Field Guide* from the den and hurried back to the basement where Ben was still taped to the shelves.

"Fenbendazole," she announced as she entered the storage room.

"That's the one!" Ben said.

"Zo, what are you thinking?" Oliver asked.

Mind spinning, Zoe sat down on the edge of a shelf and cracked open the field guide, flipping to the back. "I... I have a hunch."

Ben shook his hands, rattling the shelves. "Hey, before you get into that, how about you cut me loose? I mean I still don't want to eat your face so let me get some circulation back in my hands, huh?"

Oliver shot her a look. "What do you think, Doc?" he asked. And she knew the question he was really asking was, *Do you think he's okay or faking it?* But this was unknown territory – Zoe didn't have a single example of an infected faking how badly their stomach hurt or concealing their need to eat brains. Besides, his eyes still weren't bleeding and by now they should be leaking bloody trails down his cheeks.

She nodded at Oliver. "Yeah, untape him."

As Oliver released Ben, Zoe turned her attention to the field guide's glossary of medications used to treat parasites.

"That's better," Ben said, flexing his fingers. "So, what's so special about my fenbenza whatever?"

Zoe traced her finger along the list of parasite medications in the glossary, slowing when she got to the *F*s. She gasped, her heart skipping a beat as her finger froze on the word fenbendazole. The reference next to it said page 113. Quickly she flipped to the page. "Listen to this! Fenbendazole's primary use is to treat parasitic worm infections. It's most commonly administered to dogs, cats, and livestock." She glanced up, her mind reeling. "Fenbendazole works by binding to a protein called beta tubulin present in the parasites. It interrupts the development as well as the function of microtubules. Without operative microtubules, the parasites can't absorb glucose, causing them to die."

"English, Doc!" Ben pleaded.

"Fenben is a dewormer!" Zoe shouted, standing up so quickly she almost lost her balance.

Ben nodded slowly, realization dawning in his eyes. "I've been on it for months now. You think it's killing the parasites inside me and that's why I haven't turned?"

"Of the medications you're on, I think it's the most likely explanation. The infection – this zombie parasite – it might be similar enough that the fenbendazole is acting as a suppressant."

Oliver's eyes widened. "The dewormer is stopping the infection?"

Zoe shook her head, her excitement tempered with caution as she stared into Ben's bloodshot eyes. "Not stopping it. At least not yet. You're still showing signs of infection, but it is at least slowing down the infection. Could it cure you completely? Truth is, I just don't know. It may only hold the parasite at bay. But one thing is clear, it's buying you time."

Ben stared at her, a flicker of hope breaking through his weary expression. "So what now? Should I double down? Take more and see if we can beat this thing?"

"Right now, I don't know the side effects of increasing your dosage. If overdosing you is lethal, that doesn't do us any good either. Let me read as much as I can about this drug. Ben, were you given any paperwork on this?"

Ben brightened. "Actually, yes. The doctors gave me literature on all the drugs I'm on."

"Great, that's where we start then! Let's get upstairs. I think I have a long night ahead."

Ben stood, his legs unsteady but his voice firm. "I can't go with you."

"What? Why not?" Oliver asked.

"We don't know enough yet. If I turn, I don't want to hurt any of you. I want you to lock me in here tonight."

Zoe's throat tightened. "Ben, we don't have to do that. We can monitor you closely, keep you under watch."

"No," Ben insisted, shaking his head. "If this drug isn't enough..." The old man looked to Oliver then. "You'll lock me in, and in the morning, if I'm gone – if I've turned – you do what needs to be done."

Oliver nodded solemnly. "You know I will. I gave you my word."

Silence filled the basement, heavy and suffocating. Zoe felt the sting of tears behind her eyes but blinked them back. "Alright," she said, her voice breaking. "We'll do it your way, but we're not taping you to the shelves again."

Ben gave her a small, sad smile. "Well, thank god for that. But, Doc, I'm counting on you, and you know what? Maybe there's a whole world out there counting on you and they don't even know it... Now, wouldn't that be something?"

Zoe gave a small unsure nod. Maybe Ben had a feeling, or maybe he was just telling her what she needed to hear. Either way, she felt a sudden sense of renewed purpose she hadn't felt since the church.

Ben seemed to see the drive ignite inside of her and he smiled bigger and brighter than a man being chased by death should. "Good! Now go! Lock that door, get upstairs, and figure out that medicine."

As they ascended the stairs, leaving Ben behind in the darkness, a faint whimper from Louie echoed through the stillness. Zoe froze, her gaze drifting back over her shoulder. "We're going to get through this," she whispered. The words were meant as much for herself as they were for Ben, now isolated and alone, and for Louie, still lying on the kitchen table, waging his own desperate battle.

A fierce determination began to take root within Zoe, displacing the fear that had gripped her for too long. She was done being scared – done being a victim. No longer would she stand by, powerless, as others sacrificed and died. She didn't know what was happening beyond these walls, or if there were scientists or doctors working to stop this nightmare. But one thing was certain: This war was far from over, and she would be damned if she sat idle, waiting for help that might never come.

The fenbendazole Ben had taken offered a strand of hope – a fragile thread she couldn't yet measure but was resolutely determined to follow. Whatever it took, she had to do everything within her power to find the answers, to try and somehow stop this. It was time to fight back!

CHAPTER 22
THE GAS STATION

"THE FUCK IS HE SHOOTING AT?" Lance growled, shouldering open the passenger-side door.

Grady slung the rucksack over his shoulder and lifted a tactical shotgun.

Both men booked it past the pumps towards the gas station, their prison-issued skippies echoing off the pavement as their feet slapped rhythmically.

Grady's big ass was already gasping for breath. He might have the physique of The Rock but his cardio was shit.

Beyond the canopy, a magenta sky cast the world in a surreal glow, rain streaking down like rust-tinted needles.

The two men took position on either side of the gas station's shattered glass doors.

"Slim! Talk to me!" Grady bellowed, his voice booming into the quiet.

No response. The two men exchanged wary glances.

Lance gave a curt nod, and Grady, gripping his shotgun tightly, peeked inside. He stepped through the door, shoes crunching on shards of glass.

Lance followed, stepping over a toppled display of snack cakes and sidestepping a puddle of murky water pooling near the coolers. The gas station looked like a giant had picked up the whole building, shook it, and then set it back in place. The metallic tang of blood mingled with the stench of old rot hung heavy in the air, assaulting his nostrils. His pistol was up, finger resting on the side of the trigger guard, his eyes scanning for movement.

Slim stood at the far end of the store, his back to them, motionless.

"Dammit, Slim!" Grady stomped forward, kicking potato chip bags out of the way. "When I call your name, you better—" He stopped mid-sentence, his body straightening to attention. "Well... damn."

"What is it?" Lance demanded, closing the distance.

Grady didn't respond, just stepped aside, revealing the carnage. Four zombies lay sprawled on the floor, their heads blown apart, skull fragments and viscous black blood smeared across the cracked tiles. The sight was grotesque, but it wasn't the bodies that caught Lance's attention.

"Well, well, well. What do we have here?" Lance smiled.

In front of the bodies was an ice cream chest. Inside, a woman huddled, clutching her scraped and bleeding knees. Her blond hair hung in tangled clumps, streaked with dirt. Mascara ran down her tear-streaked cheeks, and her bloodshot eyes darted wildly between the men.

She pressed her trembling hands against the chest's sliding glass door, trying in vain to keep it shut.

Grady snorted and slid the door open with ease.

"Please! Please, no!" the woman screamed, her voice raw with terror.

Grady grabbed her wrist and yanked her out of the freezer. She thrashed against him, her cries piercing the air.

"Shut her up before she draws more of those bastards in here!" Slim snapped, his voice rising at least two octaves.

"Like all the shooting you just did isn't going to bring them running!" Grady shot back, his grip tightening on the woman. He turned to her, his tone low and dangerous. "Honey, stop screaming, or I'll pop you in the mouth."

The woman stopped screaming, her eyes assessing them. "You're not like them? Not infected?"

"No, we're not like them." Grady smiled, but his smile was as ravenous as a zombie. It was a wonder the woman didn't start screaming again just seeing it.

She eyed their county orange and swallowed before continuing. "They were grabbing me, trying to eat me! I wrestled free. I'd just climbed into the freezer when I heard the gunshots."

Grady stepped close and wrapped his big arm around the small-framed woman, like a grizzly bear side-hugging a child. "Well, you're lucky we came along. Bet you're real grateful."

Lance hadn't planned for a woman – not yet, anyway – but he wouldn't deny his boys a little fun when time allowed. "We need to move. Grady, get her to the rig," Lance ordered, already moving toward the aisles. "Slim, find something to siphon gas with and I mean now!"

Slim muttered a curse and sprinted to the fountain drink machine. Slinging the AR over his shoulder, he grabbed the machine with both hands and pushed it off the counter. Wires and tubes tore free as the machine fell, soda spraying everywhere. "Bingo!" Slim shouted, snatching hold of one of the spurting hoses like a snake charmer snatching a writhing snake.

Lance spotted a red gas can under a pile of debris. He grabbed it, shoving it into Slim's arms. "Get the fuel!" The only thing telling him they needed to move and move now were his instincts, but his instincts were always right. If he'd listened to them when he'd pulled that last job, he wouldn't have landed himself in the clink to begin with. Then again maybe everything does happen for a reason. He was here now, wasn't he? Here, and a free man, but everything inside him was telling him they needed to hurry the fuck up!

"I've got the bigger gun. You siphon, and I'll cover!" Slim protested, rushing toward the door.

Lance's patience snapped. He grabbed Slim by the shoulder, jamming the barrel of his pistol against Slim's temple.

"Don't make me ask twice," Lance growled, his voice low and deadly.

Slim froze, staring at Lance. "Alright, alright! Take it!" He shoved the AR into Lance's hands, muttering under his breath.

Lance raised the rifle to his shoulder, stepped outside, and scanned the rain-soaked parking lot. "We're clear. Hurry the hell up."

Slim darted to a nearby Ford Bronco, jammed the hose into the gas tank, and gave it a long pull. Gas splattered onto the pavement before he shoved it into the red can.

"She's filling!" Slim called out, spitting gas off his lips.

A sound rose above the rain – a crunching, snapping noise, like tree limbs breaking.

Lance turned, squinting toward the hillside beyond the intersection. The trees swayed unnaturally, shadows shifting in the dim light. Then, they appeared.

First, a bloated, shirtless man stumbled out of the woods, his pale skin glistening in the slimy rain. Then came a woman in a torn red skirt, her lifeless eyes fixed dead ahead. And then behind her, a child no more than ten.

One by one, more figures emerged – five, ten, twenty. More and more came, spilling from the hillside in a surging wave.

"That's enough. We have to go!" Lance announced.

Slim yanked the hose from the fuel tank, gas sloshing over his hands as he clutched the can.

The zombies turned their heads in unison, eyes wide and hungry, and broke into a run.

"Move!" Lance shouted, firing into the advancing horde as both men made their way back to the BearCat.

Slim frantically removed the cap and inserted the spout into the fuel filler.

Lance's first shots took down the bloated man, two to the chest and one to the throat. The zombie crumpled, falling face-first into the curb.

"Hurry up, Slim!" Lance shouted, continuing to fire on the zombie horde as more of the undead crossed the intersection. The woman in the skirt went down next, then a couple kids. Zombies poured from the woods like a crowd rushing the stage at a Metallica concert. "There's too many! We got to go!"

"Almost done!" Slim said, tipping the little red can completely upside down.

At the base of the hill something emerged from within the trees. "Grady, be ready to drive!"

Then he saw it. A zombie monster like the one back in River City. But this one looked different. It had eight long multi-jointed legs. Each was made of a dozen or more human legs, all fused together in some abstract Picasso arrangement. The strange spider-like leg arrangements connected to torsos complete with arms that were twisted unnaturally into a horrific mosaic of flesh and bone. Atop the tangled torsos was a fleshy mound covered in patches of every color of hair, some long, some short. In between the blotches of hair, dozens of eyes fixed on Lance. He gasped, *Human heads. Those are human heads all stuck together.* In between the eyes were lipless mouths stretched open to reveal tongues, teeth, and gums.

"That's enough! We got to go!" Lance shouted, grabbing Slim by the collar.

Slim pulled the gas can nozzle from the tank, spilling the last bit of gas on the ground.

Tearing his eyes off the monster, Lance began firing into the crowd, dropping more zombies as they crossed the parking lot. They were about to be overwhelmed.

Pushing Slim inside, Lance jumped in behind him. "Drive, Grady – for fuck's sake, drive!"

Zombies crashed into the back of the BearCat, grabbing at the door handles and yanking wildly as they screamed and moaned.

Grady throttled the accelerator, the engine revving to life as they sped toward the bridge.

In the back, the woman's screams filled the air.

Lance pointed. "Shut her up, Slim."

Slim turned, lifted Grady's shotgun off the seat, and slammed the butt of the stock into the side of the woman's head. She collapsed in a heap and silence returned, save for the comforting growl of the engine and the now distant cries of the undead.

Lance climbed into the passenger seat, glancing into the side mirror. The zombie monster had reached the center of the intersection, its grotesque limbs pulling it forward not with the grace of a spider but with a jerky, unnatural gait like Frankenstein's monster trying out his new patchwork body for the first time.

One thing was crystal clear. The world was even more fucked than Lance could have imagined from inside his cell back at county.

Grady's eyes flicked to the rearview mirror. "What the hell are those things?"

"The question isn't what. The question is, how many are out there?" Slim said, staring out the back window.

It was more important than ever to get to someplace safe; they needed a shelter with food and guns. "Just get us across that goddammed bridge," Lance muttered, gripping the rifle tighter.

CHAPTER 23
DEWORMER

"CAREFUL, OLIVER," Zoe said, her tone sharp but tinged with worry, as she watched him lift Louie off the kitchen table.

The dog whimpered softly, his body stiff with pain as Oliver did his best to adjust his hold. "I'm being as careful as I can," he reassured her, his voice calm but firm.

"I know," she murmured, her fingers twitching as if she wanted to step in but knew better. "But he's hurting."

Oliver paused, shifting Louie's weight against his chest. The worry etched on Zoe's face made him hesitate. "Are you sure you want me to move him?"

Reluctantly, Zoe nodded. "Yeah, he can't stay on the table. That can't be comfortable, and if he tries to get up, he could fall. The couch will be better."

Gently, Oliver navigated to the front room and placed Louie on the couch. Zoe immediately knelt beside the dog, stroking his head. The whimpers subsided as Louie's breathing slowed, though the occasional wince still tugged at his frame.

While Zoe settled in next to Louie, Oliver went back to

the kitchen and sanitized the table where Louie had been lying, scrubbing it down with a determination that felt almost therapeutic, as if washing away the blood could somehow erase the horror of what had happened. Of course he knew it couldn't. Louie would still be lying on the couch, fighting for his life no matter how much elbow grease Oliver put into it.

For the next two hours, they stayed by Louie's side, Oliver reading a Stephen King novel titled *11/22/63* he'd found among Ben's bookshelves. He wasn't sure he'd like it, but the story grabbed him right away, pulling him in as King tended to do. The book had a whole lot to do with time travel and a portal to the past King called the rabbit hole. From time to time, Oliver glanced up at Zoe as she pored over Ben's cancer treatment paperwork and flipped pages in her field guide, her lips moving in soft mutters punctuated by the occasional curse. She was relentless, her eyes scanning each line with the focus of someone hunting for a lifesaving clue.

It was good to have something to take his mind off the last twenty-four hours. But as Oliver thought about King's rabbit hole, he found himself wondering, if traveling back in time was possible, what he would change. He knew one thing – he'd do his best to save those they'd lost, starting with Sam and of course Louie, but also all those in between.

After a while he put the book down, deciding he needed to get up and walk around, so he checked that the windows and doors were still locked. Then he decided he'd check in on the kids in the theater room. Aaron had a movie playing, and Oliver smiled when he realized it was *The Last Samurai*. Aaron was transfixed, his body leaning slightly forward, mimicking the intensity on the screen.

"Samurai, huh?" Oliver said lightly. "I've seen it. Not bad."

Aaron glanced at him briefly, his eyes lighting up. "The choreography is incredible. Of course, they used real sword techniques, not the fake flashy stuff."

Jurnee seemed disinterested as she and Princess worked on a puzzle she'd found on one of the shelves.

"Good to know." Oliver made a mental note to talk to him later about what movies were appropriate for six-year-olds like Jurnee.

When he finished checking in on the kids, his stomach told him it was time he returned to the kitchen. Rummaging through the cabinets and freezer, he took inventory of what he could cook. Spaghetti seemed like a safe bet. He found frozen ground beef and garlic bread, along with cans of tomato sauce and a box of pasta.

As the water began to boil and the aroma of browning beef filled the kitchen, Oliver made a fresh pot of coffee. Carrying a steaming mug, he crossed back into the den. "Zo, I hate to interrupt, but I made a pot of coffee if you want some," he said, leaning against the doorway.

Zoe looked up, her face softening for the first time in hours. "I knew there was a reason I fell in love with you."

Oliver smirked, stepping closer. "If I'd known it was this easy, I would've just bought you a coffee instead of embarrassing myself singing in front of a bar full of strangers."

Her expression turned deadpan. "Did you just call me easy?"

"What? No, I meant..." Oliver stammered, caught off guard.

Zoe cracked a smile, her signature mischievous grin lighting up her face. "I'm just messing with you. That night at karaoke was the best night of my life. It's the night I met you." Her grin deepened. "Besides, if you'd asked me out for coffee that late, I'd have assumed you were a weirdo and shot you down. I mean, no one goes for coffee at eleven o'clock at night."

Oliver laughed, shaking his head. "Point taken. Well, I better let you get back to saving the world. Meanwhile, I'll be in the kitchen enjoying a large coffee... by myself. You know, seeing how no one drinks coffee at night."

Zoe shot up from the couch, feigning indignation. "Oliver McAllister, it isn't even six yet! You better share!"

Before she could move, Oliver spun on his heel, pulling her gracefully into his arms, without spilling a drop from his mug. "Got you!"

She tilted her head up, meeting his gaze. Her brown eyes, so full of determination, now shimmered with a mix of love and exhaustion.

"I love you," he said, his voice soft but steady.

"I love you too," she replied, resting her forehead against his chest. But even as she smiled, the tension in her shoulders betrayed her.

Not letting go, he set his mug down on the end table. "Zo, it's going to be okay," he said, brushing his hand across her cheek. "You're going to figure this out."

She let out a shaky breath. "I hope so, Oliver. But..."

"But?"

She pulled back, her hands resting lightly on his chest. "This dewormer is promising, but Ben isn't exactly an ideal test subject. He's terminal. His body's already weak from cancer and the chemo. On top of that, he's on so many meds it will be hard to tell if results are truly the dewormer, another drug, or a combination of multiple drugs. And that's if I don't miscalculate the dosage of fenbendazole and kill him outright."

Oliver frowned. "So what do we do?"

"We work with what we've got," she said firmly. "Ben's the key to understanding this thing, even if it's imperfect. Every little detail we learn could save lives."

He nodded. "Okay, so what's the next step?"

"I need coffee first. Then I'll revisit the section on roundworm towers."

"Worm towers?" Oliver asked, making his way back into the kitchen.

"They're these structures roundworms form by gluing themselves together. It's how they latch onto passing beetles. I think it could be a clue to how the zombie amalgamations work."

Oliver gave the simmering spaghetti sauce a slow stir, the wooden spoon scraping against the bottom of the pot. The rich scent of garlic and tomatoes filled the kitchen, mingling with the faint, familiar bitterness of coffee. He glanced at Zoe, watching as she rubbed her temples, her brows knit in frustration.

Oliver raised an eyebrow. "You think these parasites are working the same way?" he asked, reaching for the saltshaker and tapping a few grains into the sauce.

"I don't know," Zoe admitted, taking a sip of her coffee. "But there's got to be a reason they're doing it. Parasites don't act without purpose."

Oliver hummed in response, grabbing the jar of dried basil and shaking a generous amount into the sauce. He gave it another slow stir, letting the spices blend as Zoe leaned back in her chair, exhaling sharply.

"For now," she said, stretching her arms over her head, "I need caffeine and a break. And some of that amazingness you're cooking over there. I didn't even realize how hungry I was until I walked in here."

Oliver blew on the spoon and tasted the sauce. "Not as good as yours though."

Zoe looked over her shoulder and lowered her voice. "Brown sugar."

Oliver grinned. "Seriously? In spaghetti sauce?"

"Yep. Just a little. It kills the bitterness and sweetens the sauce."

"All this time?" Oliver grinned. "That's why yours is so much better than mine?"

Zoe shrugged and gave him a wink. "I can't tell you all my secrets or you won't need me anymore."

Oliver crossed the kitchen and gave Zoe a kiss on the forehead. "That, my dear, is something you never ever need to worry about."

For a while, they sat at the table, sipping coffee, their quiet conversation meandering between the house, the others, and what lay ahead. The relaxed conversation seemed a rare comfort, even as the storm clouds outside gathered, painting the walls with shifting, eerie patterns like ripples on a dark pond.

"It's getting dark," Oliver said, glancing toward the window.

"Yeah, so maybe you don't need to keep circling the house checking that every window is locked," Zoe said, teasing gently.

He exhaled, rubbing the back of his neck. "I know it's secure, but after what happened to Louie... I can't help it."

"I get it," she said, forcing a smile. "But you've done all you can."

Oliver hesitated. "Earlier, you said Tommy shot Louie."

Zoe froze, her fingers tightening around her mug. "I know how that sounds, Oliver, but I was sure it was him."

"You saw him?" Oliver's softened his tone, careful not to

sound dismissive, but at the same time he was positive he'd killed Tommy. He'd felt the spike sink deep into the man's head, and when he'd pulled it from Tommy's lifeless body, his eyeball and retina came with it. He couldn't still be alive.

"Yes, but no. Not exactly." Her face clouded with doubt. "I saw a silhouette. It looked like Tommy. The way he stood, the way he moved."

"Zo, the gate's a hundred yards out. Are you sure it wasn't someone else?"

"I..." She trailed off, biting her lip. "I don't know."

Oliver reached for her hand. "Well, whoever it was, they can't get in. The house is secure."

Their conversation was interrupted by a small voice. "Oliver, Aaron and I are hungry," Jurnee said from the doorway, her wide eyes peeking around the frame.

Oliver smiled, pushing back from the table. "Good news, kiddo. The spaghetti's almost ready. You like spaghetti?"

"Boy, do I!" she chirped, her face lighting up.

"Where's Aaron?" Oliver asked.

"He's watching a boring movie. Something called *The Last Samers Eye*. But he promised we could watch *The Princess Bride* next!"

Zoe frowned. "*The Princess Bride*, Oliver? If I remember right, isn't there a torture scene in that movie?"

Oliver chuckled. "Let me talk to Aaron. Stir the sauce for me, okay? Dinner's almost ready."

As he headed to the movie room, he glanced back at Zoe, who was already smiling at Jurnee. Her strength and ability to hold firm for everyone else never failed to amaze him.

Oliver stepped into the theater, where Aaron was seated crosslegged in one of the movie recliners. The swords Ben had given him lay sheathed across his lap and he appeared completely engrossed in a fight scene. The flickering light from the screen danced across his face as he leaned forward, studying every movement with an intensity that only Aaron could muster.

"Hey, buddy," Oliver said, easing down into the theater chair next to Aaron's. "You're really into this one, huh?"

Aaron didn't look away, his eyes glued to the screen as Tom Cruise executed a flawless parry. "Of course, it's not just a movie. It's a study of tactics and discipline. See that move? It's historically accurate for kenjutsu."

"Yeah, looks pretty impressive," Oliver replied, leaning back and crossing his arms. "But I hear Jurnee isn't such a fan of tactical studies."

Aaron sighed and paused the movie, finally turning to face Oliver. "She said it's boring, but it's not boring. It's art."

"I get that," Oliver said, nodding. "And I'm sure it is to you. But she's six, Aaron. Her idea of a good time is more *Spy Kids* or, even better, *The Little Mermaid* and less, uh... tragic samurai death. Honestly, she's excited about *Princess Bride* but that's probably because the word princess is in the title."

Aaron frowned, his fingers fidgeting with the edge of the seat cushion. "Of course, I thought she'd like it. There's honor and fighting. Kids like that stuff."

"They do," Oliver agreed, his tone kind. "But they also like stuff that's easier to follow and doesn't have... you know, so much blood and sadness."

Aaron's shoulders slumped. "I just wanted to show her

something I like. I thought she'd think it was cool. Am I in trouble?"

Oliver softened, recognizing the vulnerability in Aaron's voice. "Hey, of course not, and I get it. You're trying to share something important to you. And that's awesome. But you've got to meet her halfway, you know? Find something you can both enjoy."

Aaron chewed on that for a moment, his eyes darting back to the frozen image on the screen. "So, maybe something like *Mulan*? It's a cartoon."

"*Mulan*! Classic choice," Oliver said, grinning. "It's got sword fights too. Plus, it's funny. I bet Jurnee will love it, and who knows? Maybe she'll start to think you're the coolest big brother ever."

Aaron raised an eyebrow. "Of course, I'm not her brother."

"No," Oliver said with a shrug. "But you're the closest thing she's got right now."

Aaron's lips twitched, almost forming a smile. "Okay. After dinner, we'll watch *Mulan* or something similar that she likes."

"Good man." Oliver clapped him on the shoulder. "I think I might even be able to scrounge up some popcorn."

Aaron tilted his head. "Deal."

Oliver pushed himself up, pausing before he left. "And for the record, your taste in movies? It's pretty badass. Just maybe save the heavy stuff for when Jurnee goes to bed, yeah?"

Aaron nodded, his focus already drifting back to the screen. "Yeah. I can do that."

"Good. And maybe I'll sneak down here after everyone goes to sleep and watch some with you."

Aaron smiled shyly. "I'd like that! Of course, I know the perfect movie for you and I to watch next!"

"Great, now how about we join the others for some spaghetti?"

Aaron nodded eagerly, a huge smile spreading across his face as he stood and slipped his swords into a sash he'd tied around his waist. "Of course, spaghetti is one of my favorites."

"Good deal," Oliver said, turning to leave.

"Wait... um, Oliver? Can I tell you something?" Aaron asked, lowering his voice as his eyes flicked to the door then back.

"Of course," he said.

"Before my mom took me out of public school and put me in special classes, kids were really mean to me. Of course, I know kids can be mean but they treated me differently. Of course, I know I'm different. I know I'm autistic and I know I'm overweight." Aaron started to rock back and forth and shake his head side to side. "They called me mean names like Ass Load Aaron and Rain Man. But a bunch of other stuff too, stuff I don't even want to say."

Oliver didn't know what to say. "I'm sorry, Aaron."

"It's okay, I just want you to know, you and Zoe have been really nice to me. Before this only my mom and dad were nice to me. After they... well, turned into zombies, I remembered the church was the only place other people had ever been nice to me, so that's why I went there." Aaron stopped rocking and pushed his bangs back out of his eyes, tucking them behind his ears. "Of course I'm glad you were there," he said with a slight smile.

Oliver forced a smile in return, though inside his heart broke for the young man. "I'm glad too, Aaron."

"Okay, can we go get that spaghetti now?" Aaron asked, adjusting his swords.

Oliver smiled again and this time it was true and good. "You bet we can. Oh, hey, are you bringing those with you?" he asked, nodding towards Aaron's swords.

Aaron froze. "Oliver, the elite samurai who carried two swords always carried at least one at all times. They would even keep their wakizashi under their pillow."

"Yeah, but even at the dinner table?"

Aaron nodded. "Of course, and given the circumstances, do you not plan to keep your pistol on your person even at the table?"

Fuck, this kid was sharp. "Fair point, kiddo. Bring your swords but prepare to debate Zoe, and for the record just know that she's way smarter than I am, so good luck."

Aaron grinned again and Oliver found himself grinning back, finding the young man's wholesome smile to be infectious.

The two made for the stairs and back to the kitchen, where the smell of spaghetti sauce filled the air.

CHAPTER 24
ROOM THIRTEEN

LANCE SAT in the passenger seat, his legs stretched out and arms crossed, gazing out at the rust-streaked rain running in rivulets down the BearCat's windshield. His mind churned with thoughts sharper than the broken cityscape beyond the bridge. Ending up in county jail had been his own damn fault – a miscalculation, a rookie mistake. But that's what you get when you're hooked up with a crew too green to stay calm when things you just can't plan for pop up. When they do, and they always do, you keep your shit together and improvise if you need to, but you never panic. You never lose control of the job.

If this apocalypse hadn't come along, he'd have been well on his way to serving his third stint in prison. And three strikes? That would have been game over for Lance.

There was no point dwelling on past mistakes. He was a free man. The world had handed him a reset button wrapped in blood and chaos. Where most people saw a nightmare, Lance saw only opportunity. If the entire world was dealing with this shit – and he was starting to think it was – then who the hell would care about a few escaped cons? There'd be no fingerprint databases, no CODIS, no APBs. Just survival, and he planned to come out on top.

Hell, they could even change their names, invent whole new lives. Nobody would know, and who'd have the time to care? The only real concerns were the zombies and what might happen if this plague hadn't reached beyond American soil.

If it was contained to the US, someone – China, Russia, maybe both – would come sniffing around like vultures over roadkill. All the more reason to get to the farmhouse and take possession of Benson Meyer's weapons stash. Armed to the teeth, they'd stand a chance no matter what or who came next.

The BearCat rumbled to a halt, jolting Lance from his thoughts.

"The fuck is this?" Lance muttered, leaning forward.

In the middle of the bridge, a cluster of vehicles blocked their path – a crunched-up mess of twisted metal, shattered glass, and burnt-out shells sat where they'd burned, in puddles of melted tires.

"Should I push through?" Grady asked, his hands tight on the wheel.

"As opposed to what? Turning around and playing tag with that horde? Or, better yet, waiting for that... that *thing* to catch up?" Lance barked. "Yeah, push the fuck through!"

"Right," Grady said, pressing his foot to the accelerator.

The BearCat groaned as it forced its way between a crumpled gray minivan and a charred Tesla. The screech of metal against metal was like nails on a chalkboard. Inside the van, a boy's tattered, blood-soaked face appeared at the window. His lifeless, bleeding eyes locked onto them, and then he started pounding the glass with frantic fists, the hollow sound echoing in their ears.

"Jesus," Grady muttered, shifting his gaze back to the road. "The rest of the bridge looks manageable."

"Good," Lance replied, his voice clipped. "Let's hope it stays that way."

They rolled off the bridge and into the city streets, where chaos had carved its signature into every corner. Downtown was a labyrinth of wrecked cars and mangled bodies. Zombies emerged from the wreckage like maggots spilling from a rotten carcass, their jerky movements frantic as they homed in on the BearCat.

"Mow 'em down. Don't stop for anything," Lance ordered.

Grady nodded, his jaw clenched. The rig surged forward, the reinforced grille smashing into the undead. Flesh and bone crumpled beneath the tires while the windshield wipers worked overtime, smearing rain and blood across the glass.

Slim, quiet for the first time in hours, sat in the back with a sick grin plastered across his face. He leaned over the unconscious woman sprawled on the floor, his nose nearly touching her hair as he inhaled deeply.

"You're a fucking creep, Slim," Grady growled, glancing in the rearview mirror.

Slim jerked back like a kid caught with his hand in the cookie jar. "What? I found her, didn't I?"

Grady's lip curled into a sneer. "Yeah, and I carried her ass to the BearCat, so she's mine." His tone dared Slim to challenge him.

"Yours?" Slim's nose wrinkled, his rat-like face twisting. "Fine. You want her, you got her. I like mine younger anyway, but I got dibs on the next one."

Lance wondered just how much younger Slim liked them. He'd heard the guy was a chomo, a child molester, and whether or not that's what had landed him in county he couldn't be sure. That was the thing about lockup – you didn't ask, and most didn't tell. But it wasn't Slim's first go either and when it came to chomos, word got around. Sometimes it was the guards themselves that would make sure it did. Anyway, all that was noise to Lance and he just plain didn't care. "Focus, assholes. We're not out of this yet."

They weaved through the debris-strewn streets, taking Broadway toward the outskirts of town. The rain fell harder, each drop a blood-tinged reminder of how fucked the world had become.

"There's a motel up ahead." Lance pointed at a neon sign, once brightly lit, now void of illumination. "Pull under the awning. We'll hole up there until the rain stops. Once it does, we'll find more fuel and head to Meyer's mansion."

Grady squinted through the rain. "What about some new threads? These prison digs are rank."

"Not a priority," Lance snapped. "We get to Meyer's, and we'll find plenty of clothes that'll fit us," he said, hooking a thumb over his shoulder to indicate himself and Slim. "But you? Well, unless you get lucky and the old man has some clothes that will stretch to fit a big-ass ogre, you're stuck with what you've got for now."

Grady grumbled but didn't argue. He steered the BearCat under the motel's covered entrance.

Inside the BearCat, the woman stirred. Her eyes fluttered open, and her voice came out hoarse. "Hey... I'm bleeding. What did you do to me? What's going on?!"

"Honey, shut up and stay calm or this time I'll bash your fucking skull in." Slim's warning came even and calm, but his tone was murder sharp.

Grady shifted the BearCat into park, the vehicle idling with a low, guttural growl. The rain hammered the metal roof of the awning, each drop sounding like the ticking of some unseen doomsday clock. Lance glanced through the windshield at the dilapidated motel. He wasn't sure if something inside moved past the window or if he was seeing things through the rain.

"We doing this?" Grady asked, gripping the wheel tightly, his knuckles white.

"We're doing this," Lance confirmed, his tone leaving no room for argument. He turned to Slim. "You stay with her." He nodded toward the bleeding woman on the floor of the BearCat. "If she tries anything, put her down."

Slim's lips curled into a sick grin. "Oh, I'll keep an eye on her."

"Not like that, you twisted bastard," Lance snapped. "You keep your hands to yourself, or I'll feed you to the dead outside. You hear me?" It wasn't because he cared about the woman or what happened to her. He just didn't want Slim fooling around with his pants down while he was supposed to be keeping an eye out. There'd be time enough for play when they were locked safely in a room.

Slim raised his hands in mock surrender. "Loud and clear, boss."

"And if you see anything, give the horn a tap."

Lance turned back to Grady. "Let's clear a couple of rooms. Maybe we'll get lucky and find something useful."

Grady grabbed the tactical shotgun from the back and chambered a round with a sharp, metallic click. "Let's do it."

The two men stepped out of the BearCat into open air. Lance moved toward the motel entrance, his AR raised, while Grady trailed behind, shotgun at the ready.

The lobby door hung slightly ajar, creaking open and shut with the wind. Lance gave it a cautious nudge with the barrel of his AK. The door swung inward, revealing a dimly lit room filled with overturned furniture, shattered glass, and streaks of dark, dried blood smeared across the walls.

"Place smells like a slaughterhouse," Grady muttered, wrinkling his nose.

Lance stepped inside, his shoes crunching on broken glass. The air was thick with the stench of decay, a nauseating mix of mold, rot, and old death. One thing was for sure, the new world smelled like ass. He motioned for Grady to move right as he went left, sweeping the room with his assault rifle. The faint sound of dripping water echoed from deeper within the building.

They reached the front desk, which had been upturned, papers and keys scattered across the floor. Lance crouched to inspect the mess. "Check behind the counter," he ordered.

Grady stepped around, peered behind the desk, and froze. "Got one."

Lance straightened. "Alive?"

"Not anymore." Grady nudged the body with the barrel of his shotgun. The corpse – a woman in a torn motel uniform – twitched, her fingers curling inward. Her bloodshot eyes snapped open, and a guttural snarl tore from her throat as she lunged upward.

Grady didn't hesitate. He fired a single blast, the shotgun roaring in the confined space. The woman's head exploded in a spray of blackened gore, splattering the wall behind her. Her body crumpled back to the floor, twitching once before going still. "What the fuck? Was she sleeping or something? Do the undead even need to sleep?"

"Christ, I don't know," Lance muttered, peering around the counter. "But so much for keeping quiet."

"I'll try and shoot quieter next time," Grady retorted, pumping the shotgun.

From somewhere deeper in the motel, a low moan echoed, growing louder.

Lance's head snapped toward the sound. "Well, if they were sleeping, I think it's safe to say you woke them up," he said through gritted teeth.

"Guess we're not the only guests," Grady replied, his grin wide and unbothered.

Lance would have preferred the careful, quiet approach but not Grady. Clearly this was the part he enjoyed. Like a bull in a china shop, Grady was the guy you send in first. He was the bulldozer, the BearCat – big and slow but capable of smashing his way through just about anything.

Grady took a hasty step toward the sound.

Lance took a cautious step back.

The moans grew closer, joined by the heavy thuds of shuffling footsteps. Shadows moved at the end of the hallway, grotesque shapes lurching into view. Three zombies ran toward them, their decayed faces contorted with hunger. One dragged a broken leg behind it, the bone jutting through the skin.

"Here we go," Lance said, raising his AR.

The first zombie reached them, its jaws snapping hungrily. Lance fired a burst from the AR; the bullets ripped through the thing's collar and throat, and finally a single round punched it through the forehead, dropping it to the floor. Grady stepped forward again, firing the shotgun at the second zombie. The blast tore through the thing's chest, black ichor spraying the walls, but it kept coming, its skeletal fingers reaching for Grady's throat.

"Persistent bastard!" Grady growled, slamming the butt of the shotgun into the zombie's head. The skull caved in with a wet crunch, and the body collapsed at his feet.

"Don't fuck around. Aim for their heads! That's the only way to stop them," Lance ordered as a third zombie lunged in, its teeth bared and arms outstretched.

Lance sidestepped, grabbing it by the back of the neck and slamming its face into the wall. The plaster cracked, and the zombie reeled back, dazed. Lance fired twice, the bullets ripping through its skull and painting the wall with gore.

"Clear?" Lance asked, his breath coming in short bursts.

Grady scanned the hallway, the shotgun at the ready. "Clear... for now."

"Good." Lance stepped over the bodies, motioning toward a door marked MANAGER'S OFFICE. "Let's check in there. Might be something useful."

They pushed the door open, revealing a small office with a desk, filing cabinets, and a set of keys hanging on the wall. Lance grabbed the keys, inspecting the tags. "Room keys."

Grady rummaged through the desk drawers, pulling out a flashlight and a nearly full bottle of whiskey. He held up the bottle with a grin. "Guess we're not leaving empty-handed," he said as if the whiskey was what they'd come for.

Lance ignored him, pocketing the keys. "Let's get back to the BearCat. We'll hole up in the rooms once we're sure the place is secure."

Grady nodded, tucking the whiskey into his waistband. "Lead the way."

They retraced their steps, stepping over the mangled bodies and out into a rainy evening. The BearCat sat waiting under the awning, its headlights cutting through the gloom. Slim was out of the rig, leaning against the vehicle; the woman was just inside, gagged and lying facedown on her belly, wrists bound behind her back with a strip of torn fabric. Her head was twisted in their direction as she glared up at Slim, her jaw tight like she had plenty to say.

"Heard the shots," Slim called as they approached. "Thought I might have to come in after you." He glanced around the parking lot nervously. "So, what's up, you find anything?"

"We've got keys," Lance said, tossing one to Grady. "Take her to room twelve. Slim and I will take thirteen. Don't wander, and don't screw this up. Clear the room before you get cozy. We don't know who or what might be holed up in there."

Grady caught the key, his grin returning. "Got it, boss."

Slim hooked a thumb over his shoulder. "Good luck – girl says she's sick. She's been spouting all kinds of weird shit. I don't know, maybe I hit her too hard back at the gas station."

"So you felt the need to bind and gag her?" Lance asked.

Slim shrugged. "Like I said, I thought I might have to come in there. Didn't want her to get away and besides, the bitch wouldn't shut up."

Grady didn't seem fazed. "I'll straighten her out." He reached in the back of the BearCat and lifted the woman as easily as a sack of potatoes. "Let's get you up, darlin' – you and I are going to have a real good time."

The woman moaned and tried to kick, but Grady slung her over his shoulder, wrapping his arm around her thighs with one arm, holding the shotgun with the other.

Lance noticed it then. The back of the woman's pants was torn, revealing a long deep scratch or cut. It had been bleeding pretty good but looked crusted over now. He almost let it go. She had been running for her life, could have got that scratch a hundred different ways, but then he remembered when they first found the girl, she'd said something that stuck in Lance's craw.

They were grabbing me, trying to eat me! I wrestled free. I'd just climbed into the freezer when I heard the gunshots.

"Grady, stop!" Lance ordered.

Grady spun back around to face him. "What's up?"

"Put her down."

Grady frowned but obeyed. He set the woman down on her feet, but he kept a hold of her wrists. "Don't try and run unless you want me to pull up and break those pretty wrists of yours."

The woman narrowed her eyes, her lips curling into a feral sneer.

"Well, what's the problem?" Grady asked.

Lance stepped forward close enough to get a good look at those eyes, eyes that were unnaturally pink.

Lance shook his head with disappointment. "What's the problem? The problem is you're both too stupid to survive this world. But luckily you have me. And I don't know about you two, but I plan to do more than simply survive. I plan to rule this motherfucker." Without a moment of further hesitation, Lance lifted the AR and shot the woman in the head.

Grady jumped and Slim backpedaled.

The back of the woman's head burst into a magnificent spray of chunky gore. She fell to the ground twitching.

"What the fuck, man!" Grady shouted, advancing towards Lance.

Lance spun, pointing the smoking muzzle of the AR at

Grady. "Don't even think about it," he said with a dead calm.

"Why? She was mine! Why did you smoke her?" Grady shouted.

"Easy, bigun, the girl was infected. I just saved your life. You should be thanking me."

"Infected?" Slim repeated. "Bullshit! And even if she was, how did you know? She wasn't trying to bite anyone!"

"Because, Slim, I already said it. I'm smarter than you. The last few weeks, were you even listening to the guards at all?"

"Those pigs!?" Slim spat at the ground.

"Right there! That's your problem. If you don't study the enemy, you can't learn what they know."

Grady took a deep breath, the red fading from his face as the bulging vein in his forehead settled back into place. "How did you know?"

Lance stepped over to the woman and pointed at her eyes – eyes that were now fixed in death. "See there, her eyes are bloodshot. That's a telltale sign she was infected."

Slim shook his head. "She'd been crying and bashed in the head – of course her eyes were bloodshot."

"No." Lance pointed. "Look. Really look! There in the corners. See the blood pooling? But that isn't all. She had a deep scratch on the back of her thigh, and you said so yourself, she was talking all kinds of crazy before you gagged her. What was she saying, Slim?"

"It was all nonsense really." Slim shrugged. "Mostly about sweets and treats and being hungry. Talked about her stomach hurting."

Lance pinched the bridge of his nose and shook his head. He really was surrounded by morons. "Exactly. She was turning. I heard the guards telling each other about when people turn, their eyes turn red and bleed, and they say their stomachs hurt and they smell sweets." Lance turned to Grady. "You would have got her in that room, took out that gag, and she would have bit you before you knew what was happening."

"Jesus H," Grady said, looking at the woman anew.

"No, but I'm the closest thing to God you got, so listen up, fuckers. If you do what I say when I say, you might not end up dead – or worse, one of them." Lance pointed at the still-twitching woman.

"I didn't even know her name," Grady said.

Lance cut him a look. "Her name? Zombie, that's the only name you need to worry about."

"I call her dead meat." Slim snorted.

"Yeah, well, she'd have been a fun ride. Hey, once we get settled at your new place we need to make a run, raid some houses. Find us all some girls. It's been a long time," Grady said.

Slim grinned. "I like the way you think."

Lance lowered his AR and gave the surrounding area a cursory glance, but he saw no sign of movement out there beyond the canopy. "All that shit will come in time but right now we need to be smart. For you guys, that just means doing what I tell you, when I tell you. Can you do that?"

"Ain't that what we been doing?" Slim asked.

Lance just stared at him.

"I mean, yeah, course we can," Slim said. "Right, Grady?"

Grady glanced down at the girl then back up at Lance. "Since it's back to just the three of us, I might as well bunk with you guys," Grady said, but the shaky tone told Lance all he needed to hear. The big man was scared to bunk alone. *Good,* he thought. That's exactly what he wanted. *Stay scared and look to me for safety.*

Lance pointed towards the room. "C'mon, let's get some rest while this rain blows over. We have a big day tomorrow."

Both men nodded, their faces hardening as they lifted their gear and headed toward room thirteen.

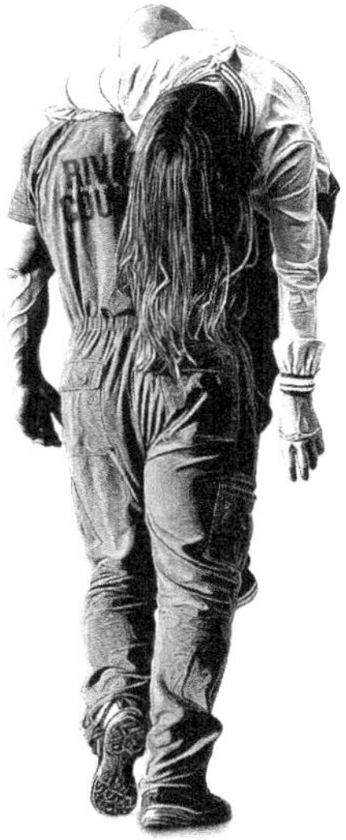

CHAPTER 25
UNRAVELING THE THREAD

IT WAS LATE, and the house had settled into an uneasy quiet. Zoe sat in the den, hunched over the *Parasite Field Guide*, her mind racing. Louie rested on the couch next to her, his breathing shallow but steady. He was holding on. She glanced at him occasionally, drawing some small measure of comfort from his resilience, but her thoughts were consumed by the puzzle in front of her.

Ben's condition remained unchanged – his severely bloodshot eyes the only visible sign of infection. That gave her hope, though she knew the situation was a ticking time bomb.

She had some tough decisions to make. Should she simply increase his dosage of fenbendazole or try to get her hands on another dewormer meant for human consumption, like albendazole? Of course, there were other medications for specific parasites, but albendazole was the most commonly used with the widest spectrum of impact.

But therein lay another problem. Even if she had albendazole, she couldn't simply give it to Ben in conjunction with the fenbendazole. Not without risk, anyway. Both drugs were metabolized in the liver and taking both would likely do serious damage. So to even try alben, she would have to pull him off the fenben. Then what if it didn't work and he turned completely? But what if it did? Another option was to simply increase his current dosage of the fenben, but again the risk of liver damage was still very real. Ben would probably say, "Who cares, Doc? I'm a dead man walking either way."

Oliver's voice broke her concentration. "Still at it?" he asked from the doorway, his hands in his pockets, a soft smile playing on his lips.

She gave a tired laugh. "Oh you know, just trying to decide whether or not to destroy Ben's liver."

Oliver raised an eyebrow, stepping into the room. "Isn't that kind of an important organ?"

"Very," she replied dryly, closing the book for a moment.

He gestured toward her lap. "Think the answer's in that thing?"

"Doubt it," she admitted, sighing.

"Then come to bed?" he asked, his voice warm.

She hesitated. The thought of collapsing into bed was tempting, but the work gnawed at her and she wasn't ready to throw in the towel – not yet. "Just let me finish this section. I'll be right behind you."

"I know what that means – you'll be at it for hours." He sighed in resignation. "It's okay, I know this is important and besides, I've got a promise to keep to Aaron anyway. Jurnee fell asleep, so it's just me and him for some action flick bonding time."

"Have fun. I'm going to make a quick trip upstairs and check in on Melissa and Adam one more time, just to make sure they're okay and don't need anything."

"Okay, Doc, have fun with your studies," Oliver teased. "Meanwhile Aaron and I will be watching Keanu Reeves pretend to be a samurai."

"Thought it was Tom Cruise?"

Oliver waved a hand. "Totally different movie."

"Oh, and hey, that reminds me. Baby Jonathan needs diapers, baby formula, and other supplies."

"I'm not sure how Keanu Reeves reminded you about baby supplies, since the guy doesn't even have a baby."

"You're stupid," Zoe said, chuckling. "We'll have to go on a supply run soon. Plus, I want to go to a pharmacy and try and find some of the dewormers listed in the field guide."

"Sure, make me a list and I'll talk to Adam about heading out tomorrow morning," Oliver offered.

Zoe's smile fell away, and she stiffened. "Hold on. You think you're just going to decide that? Your track record for going out there isn't the best."

"Wait, what? I went on one supply run and Tommy ambushed me! How is that my fault?"

"I'm not saying it is but before that you went to the neighbors' house when I didn't want you to and ran a nail through your foot, got rained on, and were nearly killed. I still don't know how you lucked out and didn't get infected. Then there was the trip with Tommy, and then earlier today the barn."

Oliver opened his mouth to argue but caught himself. She could see the frustration boiling under the surface, but he clamped it down.

"Look, I love you," Zoe said, her voice softening. "But I know what I'm looking for. You don't. It makes more sense for me to go with Adam. You can stay here with Jurnee. She needs stability. Can you imagine the freak-out she would have if we both left her? And could you blame her? She's already lost too much."

"You think I'm letting you go out there without me?" Oliver asked, his hurt visible in the set of his jaw.

"I'm a big girl," she replied, trying to stay calm. "I can handle it."

The two stared at each other, the silence thick with tension. Finally, Oliver exhaled and rubbed his face. "Fine. But I hate it."

"I know," Zoe said, reaching for his hand. "Thank you. We need these things. Besides, you can't have all the fun."

"That's what you think it is out there? Fun? I'll be sick to my stomach until you get back here, so you better make this a quick run."

"Hey, I get it! I've been there, remember? But look at it this way, Adam has done lots of supply runs and he knows what he's doing."

Oliver knelt down next to the leather chair. "God, I hope so. I want to know exactly which stores you're going to and in what order. Then I want a schedule we all agree on, and if you don't make it back by a specific time, I come running. First light. Straight there and back."

"Straight there and back," she promised. "Can we kiss now?" she said, gripping a fistful of his shirt and pulling him towards her.

"I'm serious, Zo!"

"Mmm hmm, me too." She pulled harder, pressing her lips into his.

Later, when the house was asleep, she ventured downstairs to the theater room. Oliver had his reclining theater seat on full tilt and was snoring softly. Jurnee must have woken at some point because she was now curled up in the recliner sleeping. Aaron, however, was still wide awake.

"You going to sleep down here?" Zoe asked.

"Of course, this is the only place to watch movies. Is it alright if I stay here?" Aaron asked.

"Sure. But this guy is going to bed." She smiled, giving Oliver a shake. "Come on, Oli. I need your help with Jurnee and Louie."

"I'm awake," he said groggily. He scooped Jurnee into his arms, her head already lolling against his shoulder. They made their way up from the basement and paused in the den. Louie was still on the couch, exactly where they'd left him. He didn't lift his head or wag his tail, but his chest rose and fell in slow, shallow breaths.

Zoe stepped close, brushing her fingers gently through the fur on his head. "Please, hang in there, Lou," she whispered. "We love you so much."

"Hey, babe. You sure you don't want me to come back down and get him?"

"No. I think it's best we don't move him if we don't have to."

Oliver adjusted Jurnee and gave Zoe a soft nod. Together, they climbed the stairs in silence, the weight of the day pressing down, but softened by the quiet comfort of still being together.

Zoe climbed into bed, and closed her eyes, her head throbbing from the endless spiral of questions no amount of thought would seem to answer: Increase Ben's dosage of fenbendazole or wait and try and find a human dewormer like albendazole? Then risk switching him? With her mind refusing to rest, how was she supposed to sleep?

She opened her eyes and massaged her temples, willing the answers to come. When they didn't, she changed her focus to the amalgamation. She switched on the lamp and flipped to a familiar section in the field guide – *Pristionchus pacificus*, better known as roundworms.

Her eyes scanned the text to pick up where she'd left off this morning.

"The worms create towers by secreting a waxy chemical called *nematoil*, which acts as a binding agent, allowing them to essentially glue themselves together. The towers, composed of thousands of worms, wave as one, hoping to latch on to a passing beetle."

She skimmed ahead, her pulse quickening. Poking the towers with wires or submerging them in water hadn't dislodged them. But then came the breakthrough. Zoe's breath caught as she read the final experiment. The scientists *had* discovered a way to dissolve the towers entirely!

They used… a chemical that she'd never fucking heard of. "Dammit!" she muttered aloud.

Oliver moaned and turned onto his side and Jurnee kicked off her blanket.

Another dead end. If only she could pull out her phone and google the word – how was she supposed to get the answer now? It could be a drug or a poison of some kind, probably something highly toxic and not readily available or she'd have heard of it. And, of course, the zombie amalgamations weren't roundworms, but could the same principle still apply? If she threw – her finger hovered again over the unfamiliar word – *surfactants* on the amalgamation, would it break into pieces, just like the roundworm towers had for the scientists?

Of course, none of that mattered – she didn't even know what a surfactant was, let alone how to acquire any.

CHAPTER 26
FLAMING SAUSAGE

THE MORNING SUNLIGHT spilled into the grimy motel room, illuminating peeling wallpaper and a carpet stained with cigarette burns. Lance stood by the window, peering out at the parking lot. The rain had passed, leaving rust-colored puddles that reflected the wrecked grocery store sign across the street. He released the magazine on his pistol, checked the rounds, shoved the magazine back in place, and tucked the gun into his waistband. Today, they'd make real progress, and Lance was anxious to get on the road.

He gave the queen bed opposite his own a kick. "Wake the fuck up, boys."

Behind him, Grady groaned, rolling onto his side like a boulder shifting downstream. "I'm moving, I'm moving," he muttered, swinging his tree-trunk legs over the edge of the bed. His bald head gleamed in the light, and his bloodshot eyes squinted as though daylight was a personal insult. "What's the damn rush? I drank that whole fifth last night and my head's throbbing like a bass drum."

"I don't give a shit if your head is throbbing like my cock

after four years in the clink – get your asses up! The rush is we're running on fumes and the rain has passed," Lance snapped, jerking the curtain back into place.

Grady moaned again, stuffing his two meat muffin paws into his eyes and rubbing vigorously before shoving a fist down his underwear and scratching.

Slim, already strapping down the Velcro of his skippies, shot Grady a sly grin. "Between your hangover breath and the smell of this place, I don't know which is worse – but probably your breath. Either way, I can't wait to get the hell out of here."

Grady snarled, hurling a pillow at Slim, who ducked it with a laugh. Lance spun, the room crackling with his authority. "Knock it off, both of you. Ten minutes. Meet me in the rig."

The BearCat sat in the motel parking lot like a dragon dozing after a battle, its black surface covered in scrapes and scratches. Lance ran his hand over the cool metal, silently thanking the beast for getting them this far. He climbed inside, the door closing with a satisfying thud that echoed with authority.

Ten minutes later, Grady slid into the driver's seat, still groggy but functional. Slim sprawled out in the back, his rat-like face staring out the side window.

"Any idea where we're finding gas?" Grady asked, twisting the ignition. The engine growled to life, a sound Lance had come to find comforting.

"Just head out of town. We'll check the next abandoned car we come across, get what we can, then hit the next one," Lance said. "There's a Casey's gas station in Groveland. If we can access the holding tanks, we might actually be able to fill this big beast up. Now get this thing moving and keep your eyes peeled. We don't need another zombie ambush."

The BearCat rolled out of the lot, its tires crunching over gravel and broken glass. Lance scanned the horizon, his sharp eyes catching every detail: the empty roads, the scattered wrecks, the occasional running corpse.

They stopped at the first car they saw, a black Cadillac half in the ditch. Slim went to work with the siphon but was only able to pull a couple quarts.

The next was a Ford Ranger completely out of gas. After that it was hit and miss, but they never found much.

When they finally reached the gas station it came into view like a mirage, its rusted pumps sitting beneath a sagging canopy. The store itself was no more than a burnt-out husk. Lance signaled for Grady to slow. "Cut the engine. Coast in quiet."

As they rolled to a stop, Slim hopped out first, his gas can in hand. He scanned the area with twitchy paranoia. "Looks clear," he said, his voice low but uncertain.

"It always looks clear," Lance muttered, stepping out and motioning for Grady to cover the rear. He held his AR-15 steady, his finger brushing the trigger guard. "Slim, get your hose. We have you covered. Let's make this quick."

Slim darted toward the holding tanks in the center of the parking lot with his siphon hose coiled over a shoulder, a crowbar in one hand and his gas can in the other. Grady pumped his shotgun and moved to the edge of the canopy, his massive frame ready to block any threat.

The first sound came from inside the station: a faint scuffling, then a low, guttural groan.

Lance froze, signaling Grady to hold position. "Slim!" he hissed. "Hurry it up!"

"I'm trying, but the inner lid is stuck," Slim whined, heaving with all he had.

The groan grew louder. Lance turned the AR toward

the busted-out glass doors of the station, their frames twisted and smeared with blood and grime. A face appeared in the doorway – a woman, her jaw unhinged, her eyes glowing with rage. Behind her, more shadows moved, pressing toward the door like a rising tide.

"Fuck!" Grady barked, lifting his shotgun.

The door frame burst apart, and three zombies stumbled out in a hungry run, their bloodied hands reaching. Lance fired, the crack of the AR echoing in the empty lot. The first zombie's head snapped back, its body crumpling. Grady took aim at the next one, his shotgun roaring as the creature's head exploded in a spray of gore.

Slim finally got the fuel tank lid loose, fumbled with the hose, and took several long pulls. "C'mon! C'mon! Work!" He glanced back. "Keep them off me!" he yelled, his voice frantic.

More zombies poured out of the station, and even more from the neighborhood across the street, their numbers swelling, summoned by the noise. Lance shot another, its head bursting like a rotten pumpkin. "Grady, left!" he shouted, spinning to fire at a runner closing in from the side. *Clack, clack, clack, clack.* As fast as he could pull the trigger.

Slim spun, his cheeks puffing out as he ripped the hose from his mouth and spit a mouthful of gas into the face of a man who only had one arm and a hole in his chest big enough to see through. In the same smooth motion he shoved the now flowing hose into the can and sat it down before backpedaling away from the gas-soaked zombie.

Slim dug into his pocket, producing a Zippo. The crazy bastard smiled as he flicked the lid open and snapped his fingers against the flint wheel, flame erupting like a magician producing a rabbit from his hat. "Fuck you!" he shouted, tossing the lighter.

The zombie burst into flames.

"Slim, what the shit!" Lance shouted, seeing the inevitable events to come like two trains on a collision course.

Slim saw it a nanosecond later. The flaming zombie staggered forward toward the open hole – the hole leading to an underground tank of explosive fuel!

The only thing Lance could do was shoot the burning bastard and so he did. But the zombie didn't fall back as he'd hoped it would; instead it stumbled forward.

Slim's eyes went wide. He snatched the gas can and ran.

To Lance's right, Grady pivoted, his shotgun barking again, but one of the zombies managed to grab his arm. The big man roared, smashing the creature's head against the side of the BearCat until it caved in.

Slim scrambled back, the gas can sloshing in his hands. "I got it! Let's go!!"

The flaming zombie collapsed, falling atop the tank's open lid.

"Go, go, go!" Lance ordered, covering their retreat. He fired two more shots before diving into the BearCat. Grady slammed the door shut behind him, panting like a bull.

Lance stared out the window, his eyes on the burning zombie. For whatever reason, the tank didn't ignite.

Grady stomped on the gas.

Lance let out a breath. "Jesus, that was too—"

The gas station's underground tank erupted in a blinding flash of orange and white. The rig lurched forward, the rear wheels coming off the ground as the force of the explosion hit the BearCat. They might have screamed like scared little girls, but it wouldn't have mattered. The deafening explosion consumed all sound.

Flames surrounded the BearCat and for a moment Lance thought they were going to flip ass over front.

Finally, he heard Slim's panicked scream. "Oh god, please! Please god!"

The wheels settled back down, and they pulled out free of the flames. Around them debris rained down and clanked off the BearCat.

Once clear of the chaos, Grady pulled over and climbed out from behind the wheel, making his way to the back.

"What the hell are you doing?" Lance asked.

"I'm killing this stupid little puke! That's the last time I let him nearly get me killed! You hear me, you little shit-stain? I'm going to twist you into a fucking knot and bounce you off the pavement! I'm going to—"

Grady froze.

Lance raised an eyebrow.

Slim pulled the hammer back on the Glock. "Think again, Grady, you overgrown toddler. I'll blow your brains all over that windshield and have lunch afterward. That's how much I don't give a single solitary fuck about your life."

Grady narrowed his eyes, a big, crooked vein bulging out the side of his forehead. "Big talk when you got the drop, but what about when you don't?"

Why couldn't these two realize the amazing gift they'd been given? All three of them were lifers and now they were free, for Christ's sake. They'd been dealt not a new hand, but a whole new deck. Lance knew what needed to be done. He knew what the coming weeks and months would require. "Both of you, stop. We aren't each other's enemies. And, Slim, that was so fucking dumb, but I know you weren't thinking it was going to go down like that. Now, I need you to stop pointing that gun at your partner. And goddammit, Grady, get behind that wheel and get me to my farmhouse."

To his surprise both men obeyed without question.

Slim nodded and lowered the gun.

Grady's skin color returned to its normal shade of red and he climbed back behind the wheel, shaking his head. "Never been so close to getting my ass eaten before."

"Really? Even after the last seven years in the pen?" Slim grinned.

Grady's face went slack and silent, the cab quiet enough to hear a heartbeat.

Then Grady began to laugh, and it was the deepest belly laugh Lance had ever heard. They all laughed then – and they couldn't stop. Between breaths and with tears streaming down his face, Grady pointed at Slim. "You should have seen the look on your face after that flaming dead sausage fell over the hole and the whole place went up! *Please, oh god, please god!*" he mimicked. And they all laughed harder.

The BearCat turned onto Unsicker Road and the men settled back down. The road to Meyer's farm was eerily quiet, the only sound the hum of the engine and Slim sliding rounds into magazines as he reloaded all their weapons. When they reached the edge of the property, Lance signaled for Grady to stop.

"There it is," Lance said, pointing to the sprawling farmhouse nestled between a small wood and empty fields. "Pull off in those woods, out of view." The sight of the house made his heart race – not from fear, but from anticipation. Finally, their prize in the flesh.

As they watched, the front gate opened, and a white van with a carpenter's union decal on the side and large letters that read BAUSER CONSTRUCTION pulled out of the driveway. Lance leaned forward, narrowing his eyes. "What the hell? Who's leaving?"

Grady frowned. "Shit, someone got here before us? Do we follow?"

Slim chimed in, his voice tinged with greed, "What if the house is empty now? We could take it, no problem. Surprise whoever that is when they get back."

Lance considered the options, his mind racing. Follow the van and see where it led? Or stay and secure the house, dealing with whoever might still be inside?

"Decisions, boys," he muttered, his fingers tapping against the grip of his pistol. This was their moment. No matter how he decided to play it, this house was going to be his.

CHAPTER 27
WHEN IT ALL GOES HORRIBLY WRONG

THE MORNING SUN crept over the horizon, casting long, golden beams across the farmhouse porch. Zoe adjusted her backpack, tugging her jacket tighter against the crisp air. Despite the sunshine, every instinct told her to stay, to turn back to Oliver and Jurnee. But she couldn't. Only she knew the medications they were looking for. She had to go.

Zoe chewed at the corner of her lip, a nervous habit she'd picked up on test days back in school. "Maybe I should run down and check on Ben?"

"Well, he was sleeping like a log when I peeked in earlier. No sense waking him," Oliver reassured her.

"Okay," she sighed. "But check on him again in a half hour, okay?"

"Zo, I got this – just promise me you'll be safe out there. Two stops, that's it. Then straight back here," Oliver said, his expression etched with concern.

"I promise, again... for the tenth time." Zoe smiled, rocking up onto the balls of her feet to kiss him. "Hey, I might have figured out something last night. I'm not sure what it means yet, but I'll explain everything when we get back."

"Well, that's cryptic. Is it about the parasite?"

Zoe smirked. "Yeah, sort of. More about the amalgamation."

Oliver's face was a mask of worry. "Well, I can't wait to hear about it, so hurry the hell up and get back here safe, okay?"

Adam slapped Oliver on the shoulder. "Don't you worry, partner. I don't want to be out there any longer than we have to. And, Oliver, I really appreciate you trusting me to keep Zoe safe. I won't let her out of my sight."

"Hey, when Jurnee wakes up, tell her the baby needs things and that I'll be right back." Zoe instinctively glanced at the cloudless sky before stepping down off the front porch.

As she climbed into the van, her heart started to pound. She was leaving the farmhouse, with its brick walls and relative safety. This would be her first time away from Oliver, Jurnee, and Louie since all this started. Unless you counted those minutes in Minnie's basement. Zoe pushed those thoughts away and took a calming breath. She could do this. She had to do this.

The farmhouse faded into the distance as the beat-up work van made its way toward Libbyton. Inside, the air was heavy with anticipation. The quiet hum of the engine was the only sound as Zoe kept her eyes fixed on the road ahead, scanning for movement.

Adam broke the silence, his hands gripping the steering wheel like it might fly away. "Have you been into town since... you know... all this started?"

"No," Zoe said, her voice steady but taut. "This will be my first time."

"I think you're in for a surprise," Adam muttered, his jaw tight. "How was the old man this morning?"

"He's worse. I could tell the drugs are fighting the parasites and I can tell Ben is fighting too, but he's already weak from the cancer and I just don't know how much fight the guy's got left." Her voice was grim. She wanted to sound hopeful, but the truth was she wasn't. Not for Ben.

"Still the fact he hasn't completely turned is progress," Adam said, sounding far more hopeful than she had.

Zoe forced a smile. "You're right, it is progress. When we get back I'm going to increase his dosage of fenbendazole."

"That safe?"

"No, but it is clearly having an effect and I don't want to risk pulling him off it to try something else, so instead I'll increase it slowly and then monitor him closely."

The van passed an overturned school bus, its windows smashed, with streaks of red trailing down the yellow paint. Zoe's stomach tightened at the sight. A child's handprint, smeared in dried blood, stained the rear window like a haunting signature. It was no larger than Jurnee's.

"Jesus," Adam murmured, his knuckles whitening.

The outskirts of Libbyton came into view, and with it, a landscape of ruin. Homes that had once been modest and neat were now charred skeletons of wood and brick. Cars sat abandoned in chaotic positions, their doors hanging open as if their occupants had fled mid-drive. The occasional zombie darted toward them from between the wreckage, their hollow moans carried by the wind. Sometimes they'd even make it to the van, smashing themselves into the side.

Taking the van had been a conscious decision. Ben had a truck in the garage, and they had a truck as well, but as

Adam explained, when you are moving through a town heavy with zombies, a van is better. "Trucks invite the undead to climb aboard," he'd said, and she remembered how the undead had climbed into their truck when they'd been forced to flee the farmhouse with Linda and Howard.

"I know seeing them run at us like that is scary, but I don't worry as much about the zombies as I do the infected," Adam said.

"What do you mean?"

"Well, it's just that zombies aren't tricky, but an infected – they can plan, set a trap, fire a gun."

Zoe felt suddenly terrified. "You've had that happen? They've set traps?"

"Well, not exactly, but I have had one try and ram the van with his car. And on one supply run with Jesse, someone shot at us. We never saw who because we hightailed it out of there, but I suspect it must have been an infected."

"Jesus," she said, her mind still on Linda and Howard. "What about people who aren't infected. People like us? Do you think we'll see any?"

"It's possible. But I think if they see us first, they'll likely hide. But you can't blame them – it's hard to know who to trust when you got people like Tommy out here who'd rather shoot first and ask questions later."

Tommy, she thought, and pushed those memories away. The horror of the present was bad enough without digging up old ghosts. She swallowed hard, the enormity of the devastation around her sinking in. "This isn't just chaos," she whispered. "This is annihilation."

Adam nodded grimly. "I told you. It's unimaginable until you see it for yourself. No one was ready for this. Not really."

The van rolled to a stop outside a small strip mall. The sign for Dollar Days hung crookedly above shattered glass doors, its once-cheerful brightly lit lettering now dark and cracked. Zoe adjusted the straps on her backpack and glanced at Adam.

"Hopefully we can get everything you'll need for baby Jonathan here," she said. "They should have it all – baby supplies, diapers, formula, anything else we can find."

After hearing of Melissa's concerns about breastfeeding, formula was high on Zoe's list. She remembered that some two-thirds of mothers are unable to breastfeed for the duration needed by their infant. Therefore, statistically, formula was likely to become a need, and regardless, she'd rather have it and not need it.

"Got it," Adam replied, slipping his shotgun strap over his shoulder and pulling a crowbar from behind the seat. He glanced at her and must have noticed the look. "Once we shoot, they'll all come running. This way" – he held up the crowbar – "if we run into only one or two, I can take them out without making too much noise."

Zoe nodded. "Right," she said, holstering her .357 and lifting a steel pipe.

Adam raised an eyebrow. "Good choice but if swinging needs to happen, let me go first, okay?"

She narrowed her eyes. "Because I'm a girl?"

"No. Because Oliver will kill me if I let anything happen to you. I gave my word, Zoe. So please, I'm not saying you can't bash some zombie skulls, just let me keep my promise, okay?"

In truth, she hoped there would be no bashing of skulls. In fact, she hoped they could get in and out quickly and undetected. "Yeah, of course. Ready?"

They approached the store cautiously, careful to walk

quietly. Inside, the air was heavy with the stench of rot. The shelves were in disarray, many of them picked clean. Near the check-out area, Zoe found several large bags, those cloth kind you can opt to buy rather than using plastic or paper. She grabbed two for herself and handed two more to Adam, wrinkling her nose at the smell of the place. "Look." She pointed Adam toward the baby aisle. "Hurry, let's grab what we can," she whispered.

The two worked quickly, stuffing diapers, formula, and baby wipes into their bags. Zoe found a breast pump and a stash of pacifiers and bottles tucked behind a display of coloring books. She added them to her pack, her fingers trembling slightly.

"Hey, you see that bassinet?" Adam asked, his voice low.

"Yeah," Zoe said, feeling a sense of urgency to get the hell out of there.

"I'll drop this stuff in the van and come back for it," Adam said.

As they stepped back outside, a distant moan echoed through the parking lot. Both froze, their eyes scanning the area.

"I don't see it," Adam said.

"Well, I sure as hell hear it," Zoe countered.

"Stay in the van and lock it. I'll hurry," Adam said, vanishing back into the store.

Zoe climbed in the van and spent the next three minutes scanning the parking lot and checking the mirrors.

Finally, Adam appeared, hugging a large box with a picture of a white bassinet on it.

"Hurry," Zoe hissed, reaching from the passenger's seat and pushing open the driver's door.

"I got it." He smiled, jumping back in and closing the

door. "We did good! Look at all this stuff! Melissa is going to be so happy."

They drove deeper into town, the skeletal remains of Libbyton closing in around them. Burnt-out cars lined the streets, their blackened frames like tombstones marking the apocalypse. In the distance, a plume of smoke twisted into the sky, a grim reminder that chaos wasn't confined to the past.

Despite the gloomy atmosphere outside, the mood in the van was happy. They really had done good, and Adam was right, Melissa would be thrilled when she saw all the stuff they'd managed to score for the baby. She supposed newborn supplies hadn't been in high demand as the end of days unfolded.

Adam was on cloud nine, laughing and talking about all the stuff he'd score on his next supply run. He'd get little Jonathan one of those bouncy swings you hang in a doorway and then a walker and maybe a racecar bed too. He was having so much fun Zoe didn't have the heart to tell him he was probably six to nine months away from needing a walker and longer than that for a racecar bed. Adam's excitement was so infectious, Zoe found her spirits running just as high. And so she listened and laughed along as Adam talked about the future. A future with no mention of zombies or fear, never mind that it was the reality. In this moment it wasn't the focus and that felt damn good.

This rare moment lasted until they reached Walgreens and Zoe's heart sank back into the rank pit of reality. The parking lot was a maze of abandoned, burnt, and wrecked cars. Rotting corpses lay in twisted ruin throughout the lot, their heads broken and brains missing.

A white Toyota 4Runner sat wedged halfway inside the storefront, having smashed right through the wall. Next to the wrecked car the bifold automatic doors were twisted open.

"This is going to be bad," Adam muttered, parking the van.

On the opposite end of the lot a silver Mercedes turned in and stopped a good distance away.

"You see that?" Zoe pointed, trying to get a better look. "That's got to be a person, right? I mean a real person."

Adam pinched his nose and rubbed his lips. "Maybe. Maybe not. Remember what I said, Zoe. There's people out here like us. Then there's the infected, and then there's the Tommys."

"The Tommys?" She felt her stomach tighten at the name and all the horrors that came with it.

"People who would kill us without a second thought."

The car backed up and sped away.

"Well, there you go. Definitely not an infected. They don't give up. And probably not a Tommy either. Likely whoever that was is just as scared of us as we are of them. But you see my point? Even if they mean well, the risk of contact is just too high."

Zoe let that sink in. How were they ever going to rebuild the world if they couldn't even trust each other enough to make contact? "This world is so fucked," she whispered.

"Yeah. But it could be worse."

"Worse?"

"We aren't alone. We all have each other and that's something, right?"

Zoe pressed her lips into a tight line and nodded. "Yeah, you're right. It could be worse."

"Hey, I don't want to freak you out but there's a chance that car is carrying a Tommy after all. He or she could be with a larger group and going back for reinforcements."

"Shit. They could come back." Zoe turned in the direction the Mercedes had gone.

Adam nodded. "Yeah, and honestly, I don't like the look of this place. But if we are still doing this, let's be quick about it?"

"Are you sure we shouldn't leave and come back later?" Zoe asked, feeling her chest getting tighter by the moment.

"We could, but we're here and it isn't going to be any better next time. Who knows – it might be worse."

"And I really do need to find something to help Ben," Zoe replied. "But listen, if you want to stay out here and keep watch, I can do this. I promise I'll be quick. In and out in five minutes tops." She lifted the latch to the van door. It opened with a creak so loud it seemed to echo across the parking lot.

"Have you lost your mind? No way I'm letting you go in there alone."

Zoe gave a nervous nod. "Okay then." Truth was she was glad he insisted on coming along. She didn't want to go in there alone.

They entered cautiously as a breeze blew through the store, rattling fifty-percent-off signs. The shelves were in better shape than at Dollar Days, though most of the aisles had been looted. Zoe didn't care about that and headed straight for the pharmacy counter, her steps quick but careful.

"Cover me," she said, glancing back at Adam.

He nodded, his crowbar at the ready.

Zoe climbed over the counter, her boots landing with a dull thud on the tiled floor. Her heart hammered in her chest, each beat reverberating like a drum in the suffocating silence. Searching desperately, her eyes darted over the shelves. She couldn't shake this feeling of an invisible clock counting down and, though she didn't know how much time she had before it hit zero, she worried that when it did things were going to go very badly.

The metal racks were all but barren. A few bottles or packages remained, but most of the unwanted medication had been shoved out of place or scattered across the floor. The empty spaces didn't care about Zoe's invisible countdown, seeming only to mock her urgency.

Before the apocalypse and subsequent ransacking of the pharmacy, the drugs had been arranged alphabetically. Zoe found the *A*'s easy enough. "Come on, come on," she whispered under her breath, her fingers trembling as they skimmed the remaining bottles. She must have skimmed past a dozen different drugs starting with *A*, none of them the dewormer she was looking for. She scanned the floor too, but the mess of scattered pills, empty bottles, and stomped boxes made finding albendazole like searching for a needle in a haystack. But she couldn't give up – too much depended on this. She returned to the *A*'s.

"Zoe!" Adam whispered from the other side of the counter. "Anything?"

"Just a moment longer," she answered. She expected most of the good stuff to have been looted long ago by others just as desperate as she was, but they hadn't been looking for dewormers. It had to be here somewhere!

Her pulse quickened when her eyes landed on a group of dusty bottles knocked over and shoved toward the back. She yanked one free, her hands shaking as she read the label: A<small>LBENDAZOLE</small>. Relief surged through her veins like a jolt of electricity. It wasn't much – just a few bottles – but it was something. She shoved them into her pack, her movements frantic.

Still, she couldn't stop. Not yet. She felt the invisible clock press in – every second felt like a countdown to disaster. She scanned the shelves again, hastily grabbing anything that looked remotely useful – painkillers, antibiotics, antiseptics – her mind racing as she tried to prioritize. She'd like to search the shelves for other dewormers but she knew she didn't have time. Was this enough? Would it even work?

She turned back to Adam, clutching the strap of her pack tightly as she tossed it over her shoulder. "Okay," she whispered, her voice urgent. "I've got what I need. Let's get back—"

A sudden crash interrupted her, followed by a guttural snarl, and in Zoe's mind the invisible clock hit zero.

"Shit," Adam hissed, raising his crowbar.

Zoe scrambled over the counter.

A zombie bolted out of the vitamin aisle, its head tilted unnaturally to the side, one arm hanging uselessly. Its cloudy eyes locked onto Adam, and it let out a screech that sent chills down Zoe's spine.

More moans followed, and Zoe's heart dropped into the pit of her stomach. They weren't alone. "Back to the van!" she yelled, raising her steel pipe.

Adam swung the crowbar, cracking the zombie's skull with a sickening thud.

Another one lunged from the shadows, a woman with dead eyes and long brown hair. Her hands clawed for Zoe. She swung and the pipe connected, cracking the zombie's head open. The zombie woman spun; the thwack of steel on bone reverberated through Zoe's hands, echoing across the store as the zombie fell back. It lay sprawled out on the floor, the side of its head caved in and bleeding.

They moved quickly, but the noise had drawn more of the undead. She could hear their excited moans as their feet slapped against the tile floor. Zoe's own breath came ragged and panicked. Then they appeared, their grotesque forms illuminated by the rising sun spilling through the front windows.

"Go! Go!" Zoe shouted, tossing the pipe to fire her .357 at anything that moved.

Adam dropped the crowbar and fired the shotgun. Over and over, he fired, clearing a path toward the door.

Hope filled Zoe. They were right there! They were going to make it! But as they neared the exit, one of the zombies grabbed Adam's arm, its teeth sinking into his hand.

Adam screamed, shoving the creature away and smashing its head with the butt of the shotgun. Blood streamed from the back of his hand, and the color drained from his face.

"Adam!" Zoe yelled, grabbing his shoulder.

"I'm fine," he said through gritted teeth, but the fear in his eyes betrayed him. "Let's move!"

They stumbled out of the store, the horde chasing close behind. Zoe fired a few more shots, but it was clear they were outnumbered.

"Get in the van!" Adam barked, shoving her toward the vehicle.

They barely managed to slam the doors shut as the zombies reached them, their bloodied hands clawing at the windows.

A woman reared back and slammed her head into the side window, and Zoe was sure she was coming through. A dull thud reverberated through the van but somehow the window held.

Adam floored the gas, the van lurching forward and leaving the horde behind.

Inside the van, the air was thick with tension. The laughter they had shared earlier now seemed so far away, like some distant memory of happier times. That was the horror of this new world – everything could change on a dime.

Zoe glanced at Adam, her chest heaving. "Let me see," she said, her voice trembling.

Adam hesitated before showing her his hand. The bite was deep, the pad of his palm torn open, the flesh around it already reddening.

Zoe's stomach churned. "We'll figure this out," she said, though her voice wavered.

Adam didn't reply, his eyes fixed on the road ahead. Suddenly he jerked the wheel and pulled off to the side of the road. He climbed out of his seat, into the back of the van, and started rummaging through the bins until he found what he was looking for.

"What are you doing?" she asked.

"Take this and cut my hand off," he said desperately.

Zoe's eyes went wide. Adam was holding a small DeWalt cordless saw with a round, toothy blade. "Adam, we can't cut off your hand."

"You can! You have to! Zoe, I don't want to die. I don't want to leave Melissa and the baby alone in this world! Please, hurry. It's a circular saw – all you have to do is line up this line with my wrist, pull the trigger, and push," he said and set his jaw.

"Adam, I'm not saying I can't do it. I'm saying I don't think it will work. The parasite was moving through your bloodstream seconds after you were bitten." Zoe swallowed dryly. "If I cut your hand off it won't stop anything."

Adam collapsed onto the floor of the van like he'd just been struck. "So, I'm fucked. But... you can't be sure, right? I mean if there's even a slight chance." He grabbed the saw and gritted his teeth.

"Adam, wait! What are you doing?!"

Tears streaked down the man's cheeks as he pressed the saw blade against his wrist. "What I have to do!"

CHAPTER 28
WAKEY WAKEY, EGGS AND BAKEY

THE KITCHEN WAS alive with the smell of bacon frying and coffee brewing. Oliver moved between the stove and the counter, flipping pancakes with practiced ease. He glanced at Melissa, who sat at the table nursing a cup of coffee, baby Jonathan on one shoulder sleeping, and her hair down over the other, still damp from a shower. It was the first time she'd ventured downstairs since they'd arrived at the farmhouse.

"That smells amazing," Melissa said, her voice warm but tired.

"Thanks," Oliver replied, sliding a pancake onto the growing stack. "Figured we could all use something good to start the day."

Melissa offered a small smile but it didn't hide the stress they were both feeling with Adam and Zoe out there. "It's been a while since I've sat at a table like this. Thank you for... for letting us be here." She pulled a sip of coffee, set the mug down, and pushed a blue lock of hair back behind her ear.

"You don't have to thank me," Oliver said, giving her a reassuring look. "We're all in this together."

Aaron leaned against the counter, watching Oliver cook. "You sure you're not a chef? This is way better than my mom's pancakes. Of course, she always used the sugar-free syrup crap."

Oliver chuckled. "Well, don't give me too much credit. Pancakes and bacon are about my limit. Now sit down before Jurnee shows up and eats your share."

Aaron smirked and leaned forward. "Of course, if pancakes were currency in medieval times, you'd be the king of breakfast. But bacon? That's dragon treasure for sure. They'd hoard it like gold." He mimed guarding his plate, crouching over it like a dragon with its hoard. "No one's getting mine."

On cue, Jurnee darted into the kitchen, her face lighting up when she saw the food. "Wakey wakey, eggs and bakey! And pancakes!" she cheered, grabbing a plate and sliding into the seat next to Melissa. She sat up on her knees and made a googly face at the baby, then stuck her tongue out. Melissa laughed but little Jonathan seemed not to notice. "What about Louie? Is he hungry too?"

Oliver pressed his lips into a tight line. "No, kiddo. I don't think he's ready to eat just yet."

Louie lay curled up in the den, his eyes half closed but alert. Normally he would be up, sitting obediently at Oliver's feet. Not begging for food but waiting for his own breakfast. The fact his eyes were open at all brought a small measure of hope he might somehow survive the bullet wound.

After breakfast, Melissa went upstairs to give the baby a bath, leaving Oliver to clean up while Aaron helped Jurnee clear the table. But the little girl had other ideas.

"I'm going to check on Louie," Jurnee announced, skipping out of the kitchen before anyone could protest.

Oliver turned, fixing Jurnee with a serious gaze. "Alright, but promise me you won't touch him. He's hurt and needs to rest, okay?"

"I won't," she called over her shoulder.

Aaron glanced at Oliver, who was rinsing dishes in the sink. "Want me to keep an eye on her?"

Oliver waved him off. "She's fine. Louie's been her shadow. Maybe it will do him good to hear her voice."

Jurnee tiptoed through the den. She paused at Louie and whispered, "Hi, Louie. I hope you feel better soon. I miss playing and Princess misses you too. I got to go now, but I'll come back after I check on Mr. Ben." Her gaze darted toward the basement door.

Louie didn't move, other than the slow rising and falling of his chest.

Jurnee reached the door and looked back over her shoulder, her small hand hovering over the knob before she turned it and slipped inside.

The stairs creaked under her weight as she descended into the dimly lit basement. She paused at the bottom, her heart thudding in her chest. "Mr. Ben? It's me," she whispered, quickly finding the hall light switch and flipping it on. Light filled the hall and pushed all the bad things hiding in the dark back to... well, back to wherever bad things go when the lights are on. Mustering her courage, Jurnee walked down the hall past the theater room, the furthest she'd ever gone. "Mr. Ben?" she called again.

From further down the hall Ben's voice answered, low and gravelly. "Jurnee, sweetheart, is that you?"

Jurnee blew out a breath and smiled. As she made her way to the door she nodded, even though he couldn't see her. "Yeah, it's me. Are you okay?"

"I'm better now that you're here," Ben said, his voice different, not like his usual grumpiness. "You always bring such a... well, freshness with you. Like sunshine."

Jurnee giggled. "That's silly. Sunshine doesn't have a smell."

"Oh, but you do," Ben said softly. "So young. So warm. So alive. You know, I think you're the only one who truly understands how hard this is for me. Locked away like a monster..."

"You're not a monster, Mr. Ben," she said earnestly. "You're just sick. That's all."

"Such a sweet girl," Ben murmured. "But I'm all better now. I can't stay in here forever. I need to get out. I need... help. Can you do that for me?"

Jurnee hesitated, glancing back up the stairs. "Oliver has the key. I could ask him."

"No, no," Ben said quickly, his voice sharper. "Don't bother Oliver. He's a busy man. There's another key. It's in my nightstand, upstairs. Just bring it to me, and we'll surprise him together. Oh, and hey, I have some special cupcakes in here. They're the Hostess kind with the creamy inside. They're sweet... just like you."

She bit her lip. If Mr. Ben said it was time to come out, he would know best. He was a grown-up, and even older than everyone else. Plus, she really wanted one of those cupcakes. "Weeelll, okay. I'll be right back."

"Good girl! Sweet girl!" he called through the door. "But don't tell. Remember, this is our secret. I want it to be a surprise. Besides, I only have two cupcakes, one for me and one for you."

One cupcake just for her. "Okay!" she shouted through the door. She ran back down the hall and darted up the stairs, crossing the den and slipping into Ben's room. She opened the nightstand drawer and found the key hidden beneath a crumpled handkerchief. She clutched it tightly in her fist and hurried back to the basement.

At the bottom of the stairs, she hesitated again. "I've got the key, Mr. Ben," she whispered.

"Good girl," Ben replied. His voice was excited and she was excited too – after all, she was about to eat a cupcake!

"Okay, now slip the key in the keyhole and unlock the door, sweetheart."

Boy, he sure was ready to come out. She sure wouldn't want to be locked in there all by herself either. Jurnee slid the key into the lock and turned it. The metallic *click* echoed through the basement. But before she could open the door, footsteps thundered down the stairs.

"Jurnee!" Aaron's voice was sharp. "What are you doing down here by yourself?"

She spun around, the key slipping from her hand. "Nothing!"

Aaron's eyes narrowed, and he grabbed her arm gently but firmly. "Come on. You're not supposed to be back here alone."

"But—" she started, glancing back at the door.

"No buts, Jurnee," Aaron said, his voice firm but kind. "Let's go."

He led her back to the theater room, his grip steady as he ushered her inside. "Stay here and pick out a movie for us," he said, his tone softening. "I'll find Oliver."

Jurnee nodded, her lower lip trembling. She curled up

in one of the oversized chairs, hugging her knees to her chest as Aaron started for the door. Now she wasn't going to get the cupcake Ben promised her, but even worse she might be in big trouble. She hoped Oliver wouldn't be mad. But Ben was all better. And she had only been doing what a grownup asked.

Wouldn't Oliver want her to let him out? No. She knew that wasn't right. Her innerstinks knew better. That's what her mom told her she needed to always listen to, her innerstinks. And hers were telling her she should have asked Oliver first no matter how bad she wanted that cupcake. But it wasn't really that. She hadn't even known about the cupcakes before. She just wanted to see Ben again.

As Aaron's footsteps faded, she hugged herself tighter and started to cry.

Oliver turned from the sink, dish towel in hand, and peered toward the living room. "What's the matter, boy?" he called gently, draping the towel over the back of a chair. "You need to go outside?"

Louie let out another low whimper.

Oliver sighed and crossed the kitchen. He knew he'd have to be careful carrying Louie out. Glancing toward the back door, he said, "Alright. Let me get this open first."

He unlocked the door and had just started to swing it wide when, from out front, a sharp crash of metal on metal split the air like a gunshot.

His heart kicked into overdrive.

He spun, instincts flaring, and rushed to the front of the house.

"What the fuck?"

A black vehicle displaying white lettering that read RIVER CITY SWAT had smashed through the front gate, its armored frame gleaming in the sunlight as it raced up the driveway, skidding to a stop in front of the steps. Three figures wearing bright orange jumpsuits climbed out, their silhouettes menacing as they brandished weapons.

"Open up!" a man about Oliver's stature bellowed, his voice carrying across the yard and echoing off the fence. "We don't want to break your pretty little house, but we will if we have to. You hear me, old man? You've got thirty seconds before we knock that door off its hinges. One! Two! Three!"

Oliver's stomach twisted. His mind raced as he pulled the Desert Eagle .50 from its holster, checked the magazine, and shoved it back in. He turned, searching – there in the den next to the sofa was The Judge, the other hand-cannon Ben had given him. Currently The Judge was loaded with five .410 rounds. He darted toward the basement door, throwing it open. "Aaron! Jurnee!" he called, his voice echoing.

No answer.

The pounding on the front door grew louder. "We know you're in there, old man!" the man shouted. "Come out, or we're coming in! Nine! Ten! Eleven!"

Oliver ran down the stairs, his heart pounding. He checked the theater room and found Aaron standing near the door, his sword at the ready.

"Jurnee is down here," Aaron said quickly. "She's safe. I was coming up but ran back down when I heard the crash!"

Oliver nodded, gripping The Judge tighter. "Good man, stay here. Hide. Keep quiet and don't come out until I say."

"What about you?" Aaron asked, his eyes wide.

"I'll handle it," Oliver said, his voice steady despite the fear coursing through him.

He turned back toward the stairs, ready to face whatever nightmare was waiting at the top.

From the darkness behind him, beyond the theater room, a door creaked. Oliver glanced back down the hall. "Ben?"

No answer.

Upstairs, someone shouted through the door again. "You got ten seconds!"

PART THREE
THE NEXUS OF DESTINY

At the crossroads of fate and choice, we often find ourselves in a delicate balance. How curious then, that we all converge here, in this place, at this very moment, where every decision carries with it the weight of destiny.

BEN MEYER

CHAPTER 29
ECHOES

TOMMY'S CONSCIOUSNESS floated in a sea of torment, buried beneath layers of writhing flesh and malformed bones. His body, once his own, was now twisted into something monstrous and grotesque. The amalgamation had grown since the day the endless scream began. How many hours or days it had taken her to cast him, and the undead who answered her call, into a towering abomination, well, Tommy couldn't say. Because somewhere in those seemingly endless hours, he had lost himself both physically and mentally. For Tommy, time felt like an elastic band – it stretched out an unknown distance only to snap back and now here he was, a bloated form, oozing and shifting as he, or they, or it, lumbered through the forest.

All he knew for sure was that he'd been returned from timeless madness back to the here and now, the haze clearing from his mind like a heavy fog burning off in the morning sun. He was moving now, but Tommy wasn't directing his movement. She had given him back his consciousness, but he was still a prisoner, locked inside a grotesque cathedral of twisted flesh.

So, too, could he feel his body – or what was left of it – at the core of the monstrosity. His head was still his, still recognizable in a horrifying way, perched at the forefront of the creature's elongated neck. He knew this because he could see himself somehow. But how? Then he realized he was seeing through another human's eye, one that was attached to one of many arms. At that very moment it was looking back at his own face. But it was no longer a lone, single face. A chorus of other faces had fused into his misshapen skull, their mouths forming a jagged line along the sides of his cheeks and jaw. Some gaped open in eternal screams, others snarled with jagged, broken teeth, and a few twitched as though trying to form words they'd never be able to speak. Their glassy, lifeless eyes stared in all directions – an unholy collage of expressions twisted into his own visage.

Tommy's mouth – his original mouth – was currently forced open in a ghastly grin that never closed, stretched unnaturally wide as if mocking the humanity he had lost. He could feel the muscles in his jaw straining, locked in a permanent rictus. Drool and viscous fluid dripped from his own lips, mingling with the honey-thick secretions oozing from the other mouths fused into his face.

He hated the parasite for what it had done to him. But there was something worse than the physical horror.

He could feel them. The others.

Their thoughts weren't coherent, not like his. They were fragments, fleeting bursts of emotion and instinct. Hunger. Fear. Rage. Desperation. Each mind was like a faint whisper in the back of his own, a primal static hiss that never went silent. And though they didn't speak, he could sense their agony. Every fused body, every face and limb – were they trapped just like he was? No, not like him. He was still fucking alive, wasn't he? These others were zombies, undead bastards, but not him. *I am still alive.* Was this how it worked for all the alpha parasites? They kept their prime host alive for some unholy reason?

It didn't matter. Fact was, Tommy was in a living hell, a prison of flesh threatening him with claustrophobic madness. Insanity was pressing in at the periphery of his mind, but so were his mortal memories. He would not – could not – give in to this! He could not lose himself, not yet. And so he clung to those fragments, pulling on memories, reeling them in like a kite on a string. These belonged to him, not the goddamned parasite! Him! Instinctively, he knew this was the only way to stay anchored to whatever was left of himself. He concentrated on the rage and the vengeance. At first he wasn't sure what he was trying to remember, but as he pulled, the kite drew closer and a name emerged.

Oliver.

The name, lost in previous hours, now burned like a beacon in a forest of black. Images of the man flashed before him: that smug grin, the satisfaction on his face as he swung the axe, the sickening thud as the blade sunk into Tommy's skull. He remembered the pain too. *You left me for dead, Oliver!*

Tommy's thoughts twisted, boiling with fury. *This is all Oliver's fault!* He hadn't just lost his life – he'd lost his humanity. His body, his voice, his very identity had been stripped away, reduced to nothing more than a tool for the parasite.

But not entirely.

It seemed true enough, the parasite attached to Tommy's brain controlled the monster's body, including its massive limbs as it crashed through the underbrush with its own mysterious and no doubt horrifying purpose. But Tommy felt something else. The only way he could describe it to himself was an echo. As if he were back in the caves of Afghanistan, machine-gun fire thundering all around him. In between the bursts, his own angry shouts were thrown back at him as if the cave walls themselves had become just as angry as he was. Except here, inside the monster, he wasn't hearing the echo, he was feeling it reverberate through him like the machine-gun fire back in the cave.

The angrier Tommy became the more he could feel his mood influencing the monster, and the monster was becoming enraged.

I'm still here. You haven't taken everything... not everything.

He pushed his rage against the beast, testing the limits of his influence. At first, the monster faltered, its massive limbs pausing mid-swing as if confused. But then it resumed its march, the parasite's hunger driving it forward. Still, Tommy had felt it – the faintest reaction, the echo. The parasite was responding to his emotions and Tommy had plenty of those.

I can steer it. If I focus, I can use it.

He latched onto that thought, feeding it with his rage.

The amalgamation moved through the forest, its grotesque form pushing down saplings and scattering wildlife. As Tommy experimented, he realized he could see through dozens of eyes – some still whole, others warped and bulbous, their pupils dilated into inky voids. His view was a fractured kaleidoscope of perspectives, overlapping and distorted. The world spun in vertigo but soon he balanced it, realizing he could control which eyes he chose to look through. But there was one thing he had no influence over. One thing he couldn't control. One uninterruptible constant – the hunger.

The parasite's need to feed was relentless, gnawing at every nerve, every muscle. But Tommy's hatred burned just as bright. There was no reason he and the parasite couldn't both have what they wanted.

This would be the real test.

The monster controlling him, or rather that *was* him, was heading east toward Unsicker Road and from there, who knew. But the farmhouse was north. Neither was far, but if Tommy were to have his vengeance they had to change course.

If you won't let me die, at least give me this one thing! Again, he pushed with all his rage, channeling it, and with it, shaping the creature's instincts toward a singular goal. *Now stop and turn to our left!*

The monster stomped forward, one step. *Come on, you son of a bitch!* Another step and a sapling bowed and snapped. Another step. *So much food is waiting for you right over there!*

Tommy's hope sank like a lead weight, but then abruptly, the monster stopped. For a long moment it stood perfectly still like a deer frozen in place just before getting spooked.

That's it! Turn! Turn damn you!

The monster twisted its massive frame to the north. *Yes. That's it!* Tommy wasn't sure if he actually smiled but it sure as shit felt like he did.

With renewed vigor the monster lumbered forward. Finally the farmhouse fence line came into view as the monster crashed through the last of the trees. The high fence surrounding the property was stained with rusty streaks from yesterday's rain. The fence and its sturdy cedar boards were a futile barrier against Tommy's mass.

Through the creature's many eyes, Tommy saw movement and through its many ears he heard their voices drifting faintly on the wind. His rage surged, and the parasite responded, its misshapen body vibrating with a guttural growl.

At the forefront of Tommy's mind, the memory of Oliver blazed like a hot brand sizzling into his brain. The smug face, the arrogance – it was all Tommy needed to focus the parasite's fury.

The amalgamation reached the fence, its grotesque limbs clawing at the wood. Tommy's mouth moved, his jaw stretching wider as a voice – his voice, twisted and unholy – emerged from the creature's many mouths.

"Olllivvverrr," Tommy growled, the sound distorted, layered with the moans and wails of the other faces fused into his body.

The parasite roared, its hunger intertwining with Tommy's vengeance, shaking the skeletal remains of autumn leaves that clung desperately to the barren branches of the surrounding trees. One massive arm – formed from countless others – gripped the top of the privacy fence, pulling the wood with the screeching groan of nails losing their fight for purchase.

Beyond the fence, Tommy saw a large black vehicle parked in the driveway. Men in orange prison uniforms stood on both sides of the front door. Their sweet smell was heavy on the breeze. Something like adrenaline coursed through him. The parasite was excited.

For a moment, time seemed to freeze. The creature's many eyes locked onto the farmhouse, its jagged maw splitting into a grotesque semblance of a grin.

Tommy forced a single thought, no more than a whisper in his mind. *Let us in.* The amalgamation's twisted mouths answered. "Lllettt... usss... innn."

The monster lunged at the fence, its immense weight slamming into the wood with a crunching crash. Dog-eared cedar panels flexed inward until they snapped like toothpicks and fell onto the lawn. The parasite's hunger burned hotter, driving the creature forward, but Tommy's thoughts were clear, sharp, focused.

This ends today. You're mine. You're all mine.

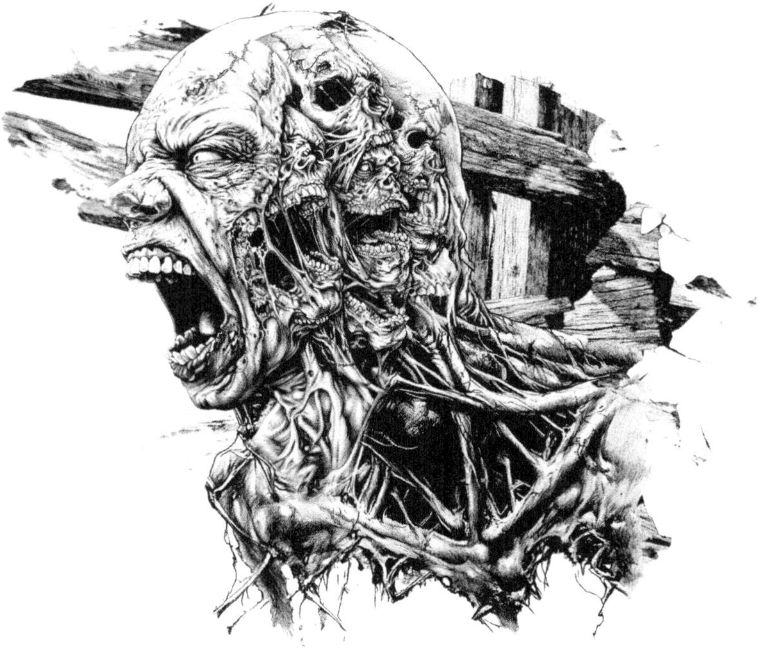

CHAPTER 30
INSIDE THE LION'S DEN

LANCE FIRED another burst from his AR-15, each shot slamming into the towering monstrosity barreling across the lawn. The creature – a grotesque fusion of bodies, limbs, and screaming mouths – seemed to absorb the bullets like they were nothing.

It roared, a guttural sound that shook the air and sent a chill down Lance's spine.

"Boss, this thing's not going down!" Slim shouted, his voice high-pitched with panic as he emptied his pistol.

"It's still coming!" Grady yelled from behind the Bear-Cat, his shotgun barking another blast into the creature's chest.

"Keep shooting!" Lance demanded, his voice cutting through the chaos. "Aim for the heads! Slow it down!"

The amalgamation crossed the yard in seconds, its massive form tearing up grass as it half pulled, half dragged itself forward.

Lance gritted his teeth, his mind racing. They needed cover – and fast. They could jump back in the BearCat and make a break for the road, but Lance wasn't willing to give up the prize that easily. The home was brick, with bulletproof windows. If they could just get the old man to open the fucking door, maybe the house could keep this thing out.

"Grady, on me!" Lance shouted.

Grady hesitated, his eyes darting between the monster and the farmhouse.

"Now, goddammit!" Lance roared, slapping the hood of the BearCat for emphasis.

Grady bolted from his cover, his skippies slipping on the wet concrete as he sprinted onto the front porch.

Lance pounded on the farmhouse door with the butt of his rifle. "Open up!" he bellowed. "Last chance or so help me, I'm driving my rig through your front door, old man!"

The door stayed shut, silence greeting him from the other side. The monster's guttural growls grew louder, closer.

"Fuck you! Have it your way then!" Lance yelled, his voice full of fury and desperation.

The door finally cracked open, and a man stood just inside, a chrome hand cannon clutched tightly in his grip. This wasn't Old Man Meyer. This guy was younger, midthirties, with sharp eyes that darted from Lance to the chaos outside.

Lance didn't wait for an invitation. He shoved the door wide open, forcing the man back. "Move! We're coming in!" he snapped, motioning for Grady and Slim to follow.

"Who the hell are you?" the man demanded, his voice tight with anger.

"Shut the door and lock it," Lance ordered, his rifle pointing at the man. "That thing out there is coming for all of us."

The man hesitated, his face fixed with fear.

"Now!" Lance barked, his tone leaving no room for argument.

The man slammed the door shut and threw the deadbolt, his face pale. "Another amalgamation. If that thing wants in, the door won't hold it – not for long."

"You sure about that?" Lance growled, stepping further into the house.

The man nodded. "I've seen what they can do. I've watched them rip through walls like it was nothing."

"Oh, yeah. Well, we better get ready then. All those guns still down in the basement?" Lance asked.

"How do you know about that?" the man asked.

"Not your concern. Now listen up because I think you're confused. My name is Lance. These are my associates, Grady and Slim."

Grady grinned his best evil grin and Slim gave a curt nod.

"Now, what's your name?"

The man looked from one to the other, seeming to eye their orange jumpsuits. "Name's Oliver – this is my place now."

"Well, Oliver," Lance said, his voice cold and menacing, "you're gonna listen, and you're gonna listen good. This house isn't yours anymore. It's mine. You do what I say, when I say it, or you and everyone else here dies. Got it?"

The red-haired man just stared at him, looking less frightened and more angry than Lance would have liked. "And if we somehow survive that thing, what then? You just let me and mine leave?"

Lance took a step towards Oliver. This guy was brave enough, but Lance knew from the comment 'me and mine' he had a lot to lose. That was good. That was control.

"Oh, you still don't get it. Look at me – at us." Lance

hooked a thumb over his shoulder. "You can see where we came from, right?" He didn't wait for an answer. "That's right, we were incarcerated for a very long time – and for very serious crimes, I might add." Lance took another step closer. Oliver was tall and well built, and he had a sort of rugged look about him. This wasn't from the last few weeks either. Lance was sure of that. No, this came with time. He could tell from the man's callused hands, Oliver was a physical guy who likely did some form of manual work for a living.

This man was dangerous. And the best way to control a dangerous man was through fear. Fear for himself or, when that didn't work, fear for his loved ones.

"Yes, that's right. I see that little mouse spinning the wheels of that tiny brain of yours. Each one of us have done some very bad things – horrible things." Lance focused his gaze into his best murder-sharp glare. "So when I say to you that if you dare ask me one more fucking question I will blow your brains all over the fucking wall, you better damn well believe I'll do it. And if I ask you a question and you don't answer or I think for one second you're lying to me, same thing – brains all over the fucking wall. You have loved ones here."

"I—"

"It isn't a question, Oliver. Brains all over the fucking wall!"

Outside, the creature screamed and the walking collection of body parts came into view through the sidelight window. There was a loud boom and the house shook.

Lance didn't flinch. "We understand each other, Oliver?" he asked, keeping the AR trained on him.

Oliver nodded.

Lance knew the power of even the smallest amount of

trust and though he had none for this Oliver prick, the situation dictated that he make the man feel like he did. He needed the illusion of trust because he needed cooperation, and he needed it fast. "Good. Now, I am going to be real reasonable given that zombie shitshow outside and let you keep those pistols. But so help me, if you point that thing at me or my boys, you die. Got it?"

Oliver nodded again.

"Good. Grady, Slim, with me." His eyes scanned the room. "You" – he pointed at Oliver – "let's go." He'd keep Oliver in front, where he could see those hands, never at his back.

Grady gave the man a toothy grin as he pumped his shotgun. "You heard the boss – move out."

The group moved quickly, Lance taking the lead as they headed toward the basement door. He opened it without hesitation, the creak of the hinges echoing in the tense silence.

"You two, down first," Lance ordered, motioning to Grady and Slim. "You next, Oliver. I'll cover the rear."

The basement was cool and dimly lit, the faint smell of gun oil and damp concrete hanging in the air. At the far end of the hall on the right, the steel vault door loomed, just as Lance remembered it.

"Let me guess, you have the key on a string around your neck?" Lance asked, his voice low but sharp.

Oliver nodded, reached beneath the collar of his shirt, and produced a key.

Slim snatched hold of the key and yanked. The string snapped. Grinning, Slim approached the heavy steel door and inserted the key in the padlock.

Lance looked at Oliver. "How many others in the house? Before you answer, know I am going to search this place top to bottom and if I find out you lied, remember... brains all over the wall."

"A woman upstairs just gave birth to a child a few days back. There's also a little girl, Jurnee, and another kid, Aaron."

Lance locked eyes with Oliver, as if he were staring into the man's soul. Odd that he would say a woman and not his wife or girlfriend, unless the woman wasn't his woman. So another man then, the one driving the van away from here this morning. The one Oliver wasn't telling him about. When this situation with the zombie monster was over, this guy was as good as dead. Lance didn't see no need for a woman with a new baby either and he sure as hell wasn't interested in kids being around. "And that's it? No one else?" Lance asked, narrowing his eyes.

Above them, the house shook.

"Just my dog, Louie. But he's hurt – recovering from a gunshot wound."

As Slim toggled open the padlock, Grady nodded to a darkened doorway across the hall. "What's in there?"

"That's where Ben kept his supplies. Tons of dried goods, toilet paper, all kinds of shit," Oliver answered, a strange look of confusion on his face.

Grady moved toward the door and peeked inside.

Slim fidgeted with the lock.

Lance didn't like this. Something was off. He looked at Oliver again. "What's wrong with you?"

Grady reached in and swiped a hand down the wall, looking for a light switch.

"Nothing I... I just thought that door was shut."

A soft moan filled the hall.

"What the hell is that?" Grady muttered, stepping back from the room.

"Grady, move!" Lance warned, but it was too late. Before anyone could react, a figure lunged from the shadows – a pale, bloodshot man with a skeletal frame and red-rimmed eyes. Benson.

At the last second, the big man sidestepped.

Benson stumbled forward from the shadows, missing Grady.

Slim spun. "Shit!" he shouted, falling back into the door as the infected man latched onto his arm, his teeth sinking deep into the flesh. Slim screamed, thrashing violently as blood sprayed across the concrete floor.

"Get it off me!" Slim shrieked, his voice raw with terror.

Grady fired his shotgun, the blast echoing in the confined space. The shot hit Benson square in the chest, sending him falling backwards into the storage room, but the damage was done.

Lance's ears were ringing. The hall was heavy with the smell of human stink and gunpowder.

"Boss, he's bitten!" Grady yelled, his face pale as a sun-bleached fence post.

Slim was screaming now.

"Get inside the vault!" Lance ordered, his voice ice-cold. "We're not leaving without that firepower."

Slim clutched his arm, his breaths ragged and panicked. "What the fuck, Lance? I'm done for!"

"Not yet, you're not," Lance snapped. But he knew it was bad – Slim was squirting blood everywhere. Above them, the house shook again and this time a ceiling tile fell at the other end of the hall. "Go! Go! Go!" he shouted. They needed those guns and they needed them now! "If we don't get armed none of us survive this!"

Slim and Grady pushed into the gun room with Lance on their heels. Oliver, that prick, had lied to him about who was in the house and now he was going to keep his promise and blow that bastard's brains all over the walls. It was that very moment, just as Lance was crossing the threshold, he realized he'd made a very stupid mistake.

In the chaos he'd lost track of Oliver.

Lance spun back in time to hear the heavy door slam. He grabbed at the handle and jerked but it was too late. On the opposite side the padlock clicked into place. "No! You motherfucker!" he shouted and beat his fist against the door.

Closing his eyes, Lance took a deep, calming breath. Finally, he opened them and in an even voice called through the door, "Oliver! You can't lock us in here. We have all the firepower. That thing gets inside and you, that woman upstairs, her baby, those kids – all dead. You hear me? Can you live with that? All your loved ones dead, and all because you decided to be a hero."

Above them, the sound of the monster smashing against the house grew louder, the walls trembling with each impact.

Lance was outwardly calm but inside he fumed, more mad at his own stupidity than anything or anyone else. "It's coming in, Oliver. Now listen to me. You made a mistake. I can forgive one mistake. Open that door right now and we defeat this thing together." Lance glanced back at Grady and tipped his head to the side, lowering his voice. "Over there, the .50 cal. This guy won't let us out, we'll blast the fucking door off the hinges, and when I'm done with that zombie monster, I'm going to make that dickhole watch as I kill everyone in this fucking house."

"Lance! Please, my arm!" Slim cried as he wrapped a piece of torn material from his sleeve around his wrist.

Lance walked over to the bleeding man, who had now sunk down to the floor, his knees pulled up to his chest, hand squeezing his bloody wrist. "You know why we're locked in this fucking room right now? Because you getting bit like a dumbass distracted me. Now, once again it's up to me to figure out how to get us out of this!" He knelt down and picked up the pistol Slim had been using, ejected the magazine, inserted a full one, and racked the slide.

"What the fuck, Lance?! Don't you get it? I'm bitten! I'm fucked, man! I'm gonna turn into one of those things!" Slim's voice cracked, and he started to sob. "One of those goddamned things!"

"No. No, you're not," Lance replied, his tone calm, almost indifferent, like he was stating a fact.

Grady lifted a .50 cal off the holders and glanced back, giving Lance a sharp side-eye. The big man pressed his lips into a tight line and turned his attention back to the gun.

"But I'm bit, man!" Slim cried, his desperation clawing at the edges of his voice.

Lance studied him for a long moment, his eyes flat and calculating. He didn't feel anything for Slim but then he didn't feel anything for anyone, never had. Sometimes that was a gift, but more often it was a curse. Despite their differences along the way, Slim had followed orders and turned out to be damn loyal.

Finally, Lance spoke, his words sincere and honest. "You're wrong. You're not turning into one of those things. Trust me. I won't let that happen."

"But Lance! How? How can you stop it from—"

Lance lifted the pistol and pulled the trigger.

CHAPTER 31
A FRACTION OF A CHANCE

THE BUZZ of the saw filled the van, the metallic whine slicing through Zoe's nerves like a serrated blade. Her heart lurched as she saw Adam preparing to press the blade against his wrist, his face a grim mask of desperation.

"Adam, no!" she screamed, lunging forward.

Her hands slapped against his arms, forcing the saw away before he could press it into his flesh. The blade skipped against the metal floor with a jarring screech as it clattered to a stop.

Zoe grabbed the tool and flung it aside, her chest heaving as she stared at him. "What the hell do you think you're doing?"

"I have to do this!" he shouted, his voice trembling. Tears streaked his dirt-smudged cheeks. "It's my only chance, Zoe! I can't – won't – turn into one of those things!"

"It's not your only chance!" Zoe yelled back, her voice sharp with desperation. "Albendazole is your only chance."

Adam froze, her words piercing through the storm of panic in his mind. His hands dropped to his sides, shaking.

"Albendazole?" he echoed, his tone tinged with both hope and disbelief. "You think that could actually stop this?"

"It's all we've got," she said, her voice softening but no less urgent. She reached into her bag, fumbling for one of the bottles she'd grabbed from the Walgreens pharmacy. Her hands trembled as she unscrewed the cap, the pills rattling inside. "I don't know if it will work. But if you cut off your hand, it won't stop the parasite. It's already in your bloodstream, Adam. Besides, we aren't prepared for an amputation! I can't treat you for that here and you might bleed to death before I get you back to the farmhouse."

He stared at her, the desperation in his eyes giving way to a flicker of hope. "Okay, how much do I take?"

Zoe swallowed hard, her mind racing. She'd read the standard dosage on the bottle, but this wasn't a standard case. "The typical dose for Albendazole is 400 milligrams twice a day, but that's for routine parasitic infections," she said, her voice low and steady as if she were talking to herself. "This parasite is... something else entirely."

She looked at Adam, her chest tight. "I'm going to give you more than the usual dose. It might be risky – your liver is going to hate me – but we don't have time to play it safe." What she didn't tell him was that he would likely get diarrhea, lose his appetite and vomit, break out in a rash, or potentially, if she kept giving him this much, he could get insomnia or even become confused. None of that was worth mentioning because none of that mattered. Nothing was worse than the alternative that was sure to happen if he didn't take it.

Adam nodded, his jaw tightening. "Give it to me. I don't care what it does to me as long as it gives me a shot."

Zoe measured out 800 milligrams – double the normal

dose – and handed him the pills. "Take these. All of them. And let's pray it's enough."

He took the pills from her, his hands trembling as he swallowed them dry.

Zoe watched his throat move, the pills disappearing into his body. She felt a pang of guilt – this was a gamble, and she knew it. But she couldn't let him see her doubt.

"Now what?" Adam asked, his voice hoarse.

"Now we wait," Zoe said, her voice barely above a whisper. Her eyes darted to the wound on his hand, the teeth marks a stark reminder of the ticking clock.

The van felt impossibly small, the air heavy with tension. Outside, the groans of the undead reached them faintly, a chilling reminder of the chaos just beyond their metal sanctuary. Zoe sat back against the wall, her hands shaking as she clutched the pill bottle. Glancing back at Adam's still-bleeding hand, she pulled herself together. Ripping off one of the straps from a Walgreens bag, she said, "Here, let me see that hand." She wrapped the strap around his hand as best she could and cinched it tight. "We need to clean that proper when we get back."

Adam's breathing was ragged, his face pale. "If this doesn't work," he said, breaking the silence, "promise me you'll take care of Melissa and the baby."

"It will work," Zoe snapped, refusing to entertain the possibility of failure. But when she met his eyes, her voice softened. "I promise, Adam. If it comes to that, I'll do everything I can for them. So will Oliver. You know we will."

Adam nodded, his shoulders sagging with relief. "Thank you."

She didn't deserve that. She'd taken too damn long at the Walgreens and now Adam was bitten. All this was her fault. "I better drive, okay? That way you can rest and let the medicine start to take effect. When we get back, I want you to eat. You need to get some food in there. I don't want you puking up the meds. You have to hold them down, no matter what."

Adam agreed and lay back in the passenger seat, closing his eyes.

The drive back to the farmhouse was silent, broken only by the occasional groan of the undead as they passed through the wreckage of Libbyton. Zoe kept glancing at Adam, watching for any sign of change. His face was a sickly shade of gray and sweat beaded on his forehead, but he was still alert. It wasn't until they were almost back and Adam opened his eyes and stretched that she noticed both his sclera were so severely bloodshot it was as though the blood vessels had burst, completely shading the whites of his eyes a deep red.

As she turned the van onto Unsicker Road, Zoe carefully asked, "How do you feel?"

"Hungry. Hungry and tired. My stomach hurts too," Adam replied, rubbing at his eyes. "And my eyes burn."

Zoe knew this didn't mean the medicine wasn't working or wouldn't work. The problem was the parasite turned humans into brain-craving maniacs within thirty to forty minutes of being infected, while the dewormer might take a few hours to begin to work.

"Why? Do I look sick?" Adam asked, his visage changing to worry.

Zoe wasn't going to lie to him. "Yes. Pull the visor down and look at your eyes."

Adam flipped the visor down and peered into the mirror. "Fuck! The medicine isn't working! Fuck!"

"Adam, I know this is scary, but I need you to trust me, okay? This isn't over. The parasite is moving faster than the medicine but that doesn't mean it isn't working. It's just taking time is all."

"Time! I don't have time. I can feel it, Zoe! I can smell it! Jesus, I can smell it!"

Zoe pulled off onto the gravel shoulder next to an empty field. She was completely aware her hand was only inches from her .357. The last thing she wanted was to shoot Adam.

Adam twisted towards her. "Why are we stopping?"

"Adam, I need you to trust me."

"You already said that!" he snapped.

"I want to zip-tie your hands," she said.

"What? You want to tie me up?" Adam's face contorted, deep rows of horizontal creases stacked on his forehead.

"You don't want to hurt me, and I don't want to give up on you. If you let me bind your hands, then we can safely wait this out until the medication kicks in." She looked Adam in the eyes steady and firm, but inside, she was unraveling.

She'd said a lot of things to patients over the years – things meant to soothe, to reassure. But this? This was different. This was something she was trained never to say. Medical professionals don't make promises.

She'd learned that lesson early, during her first rotation in the ER. A young girl, no older than seven, had come in after a car crash, her tiny body broken in ways that shouldn't have been possible. Zoe had knelt beside her, held her hand, and wanted – desperately wanted – to say 'You're going to be okay.'

But she hadn't. Because she couldn't. Because the worst thing you could do was give someone false hope. Instead, she found other words of comfort, but in the end words of comfort weren't enough.

Now, staring at Adam, watching the war rage behind his bloodshot eyes, she broke that rule. "I promise, Adam," she whispered, her voice steady even as her chest tightened. "It's going to be okay."

Adam's eyes darted around, wild and made wilder by his blood-red sclera. "How can you know that?"

"Because I just do! Trust me, please. The medicine is going to work. I know it is."

Adam nodded. "Okay, Zoe, I trust you. Do it! Hurry. I'm having a very strong desire to... God, you smell so freaking good – so damn sweet!" As soon as the words left his mouth, Adam's eyes welled up. "I... I'm sorry... I didn't mean... gah!" He squeezed his eyes shut, fighting back tears – but when they came, they came in blood-red trickles.

"It's okay, Adam." But this was anything but okay. At Adam's familiar words, Zoe's stomach turned. Time was everything and she wasted none as she climbed out from behind the driver's seat and retrieved a handful of zip ties from one of the tool baskets. Above the passenger door was a grab handle – or what Oliver always referred to as an 'oh my god' handle because Zoe always grabbed hold of it when she thought he was driving too fast. "Hold your hands up here."

Adam did so and she quickly zip-tied his hands to the oh my god handle. "Okay, let's get you back."

"Zoe, when we get back, Melissa can't see me like this... Not like this. Put me in the basement with Ben until... until I—"

"Until the medicine kicks in," she interjected, glancing over at the new father.

Adam pressed his lips into a tight line and nodded, tears spilling down his cheeks in a full stream now... Bloody tears.

The rest of the way back to the farmhouse, Adam leaned against the passenger door, his eyes closed.

Finally they turned onto Unsicker Road, the tree line next to the farmhouse coming into view. As the van descended a small hill, Zoe's stomach dropped along with the van. Even before she could see it, she knew almost instinctually something was wrong.

At first, it was just an unease prickling up her spine – a warning deep in her gut that told her something wasn't right. But as she approached the turn into the driveway, the house came fully into view and the details sharpened, one by one, each more wrong than the last.

The front gate hung crooked, one side dangling off its hinges like a broken jaw, the other side twisted wrongly, as if in a contortionist pose.

Her eyes flicked to the house. And then she saw it.

A shifting, writhing mass loomed in the farmhouse doorway, a nightmare of tangled limbs and melted faces slamming itself against the door frame, trying to force its way inside.

Zoe sucked in a breath, ice spreading through her veins.

"Oh my god," she whispered.

Beside her, Adam stirred, his nose twitching as he sniffed the air, a habit that wasn't his own, not before the parasite. His posture stiffened, his fingers curling into fists as he pushed himself upright.

"What the hell is that?" His voice was low, almost a growl.

Zoe barely heard him. She couldn't look away.

Then, another detail slammed into focus.

A black armored police vehicle sat at an angle in the driveway, massive and imposing, its doors flung open as if someone had abandoned it in a hurry. From their position Zoe could barely make out the words River City SWAT.

Zoe's chest tightened. Who the hell had brought that here? And more importantly, where were they now?

Adam let out a sharp breath, then jerked forward in his seat, his entire body tensing. "Melissa and the baby," he rasped. "We have to get inside!"

Zoe's heart was in her throat. "How? How are we going to get past that?!"

"We won't. Pull around to the barn. To get there, you'll have to drive around to a side road at the northern end of the property. That little concrete bridge back the other way. You'll see it. It crosses over to a dirt road between the field and the fence that leads to the barn."

Zoe's mind scrambled to understand what was happening as she backed out and back onto Unsicker Road. As she switched from reverse to drive, a zombie slammed into the driver's side door. She screamed and stepped on the gas. As she glanced at the side mirror, she saw more zombies running through the gate toward the amalgamation.

Zoe turned onto the smaller bridge and crossed, finally reaching the barn and parking along the side. "Stay here. You're in no shape to fight."

"Like hell I'm staying here," Adam shot back. "I'm not leaving Melissa and the baby in there alone."

"Adam, if you can't control it, you could cause more harm than good."

"I'll fight it. I'll stay in control," Adam insisted, jerking his hands against the zip ties, his breathing shallow and ragged. "Melissa... and the baby... they need me," he murmured, his voice trembling with anguish.

Zoe saw it then – the flicker of the man he was, fighting valiantly against the monster clawing its way to the surface.

His eyes flicked to a pair of pliers in the console. "There in the console, cut me loose. C'mon! It's an amalgamation, Zoe! Let me help you stop it!"

"We can't stop it, Adam! We need surfactants and I don't know what the fuck that even is!" All she could hope to do was find the others and get them out before that thing got in.

"Surfactants? I know what those are. I learned about them when Jesse and I took a class to get our food handlers' certificate for our coffee shop. The Department of... of Public Health requires it for... sanitation... cleanliness!" Adam winced and let out a guttural moan. "Cut me loose, Zoe! Please! I'll show you. Surfactants are active ingredients like... Guah!" he shouted, squeezing his eyes shut. "Sodium sulfate! Please! Hurry!"

There wasn't time to argue. Zoe picked up the pliers and reached across him. Her braids brushed his face, her ear only inches away from his mouth.

"Ohhh, sweet, sweet." He inhaled a deep breath through his nose.

Zoe froze and then withdrew.

"What?" He frowned, as if that hadn't just happened. "Come on! Cut me loose!"

"I'm sorry, Adam. I'll be back as soon as I can."

"No! Zoe, don't leave me here! I need to get inside! I need to eat! I need to *eat*!" he shouted, jerking against the zip ties so hard the van rocked from side to side.

Zoe gasped and slipped out of the van.

Leaving him like this felt like betrayal. But bringing him along was too great a risk. Closing the door behind her, she clenched her fists as she stepped away, willing herself to focus on the greater danger at hand.

She could hear Adam's muffled cries and groans as she

moved along the fence, sticking to the shadows. When she came to the point where the fence met the barn she climbed over the fence. From the opposite side of the house the amalgamation roared. The sounds of wood splintering and brick breaking free of mortar filled the air. She could imagine its massive limbs smashing through the front door and the wall that held it.

She reached the back door, which was oddly ajar, and slipped inside. Through the kitchen and across the den she saw it, an arm – no, several arms twisted and glued into one thick limb. It had punched out the bulletproof sidelights alongside the front door. The glass was intact, but the whole frame had been shoved free and pushed inside. Now a collage of twisted hands gripped the door frame as the monster leaned back with all its weight and pulled. It was only a matter of time before the whole door came apart.

She flashed back to the church and the amalgamation that had almost claimed them all and here she was again, watching another monster hell-bent on getting in.

Beneath the arm a zombie was wedging its way inside.

Zoe didn't hesitate – she ran forward through the den, lifting the .357, and fired at the undead.

The zombie, a teenager in life, took the bullet in the face, his head bursting like a ripe tomato in the sun.

The amalgamation stopped fighting with the door. A head lowered and stared right at her with a single unblinking eye.

Zoe sucked in a sharp breath and her heart stopped cold. The face was awful and deformed, with a collage of other faces and portions of skulls pressed into the main one. But the main face – the one looking at her – was unmistakably familiar.

"Zzzoooeee!" the voice called to her, ragged and strained.

"Tommy," she breathed in disbelief.

The monster laughed, hissed, or cried – or maybe all those things at once. All its mouths quivered as if suddenly struck with uncontrollable shivers. A string of pink drool hung from the main mouth – Tommy's mouth – and it spoke again, all its mouths moving as one. "Yyyyooouuu aaarrre mmmiiinnne!" It was a grotesque symphony of sounds, its words dripping with malice as they echoed from a dozen sets of vocal cords.

Zoe pointed the gun at Tommy's face.

The Tommy monster jerked its head back as she fired and missed, vanishing back beyond the door. With a newfound vigor it went back to work yanking and pulling.

"Oliver?" Zoe called out, her voice hushed but urgent.

No response.

She glanced up the stairs then toward the basement door, which was slightly ajar. Weighing the odds, she bet on the basement and the gun room as the most likely place he and whoever owned that police vehicle outside would be.

As she moved towards the basement stairs, the front wall groaned and cracked in protest before the door, frame and all, exploded outward, wood splinters flying like shrapnel. It was as if a tornado had just sucked the front door right off the house. The amalgamation pressed its massive body through the opening, its grotesque limbs dragging through shattered glass and debris.

Zoe backpedaled toward the basement, the floor trembling beneath her feet.

The monster straightened, twelve feet tall if it were an inch, shoving the foyer's chandelier upward until it smashed into the ceiling, only to rain back down, crystal shards scattering across the floor.

Zoe froze, her breath catching as the Tommy monster loomed above her, its many faces and eyes writhing in a grotesque symphony of suffering. But it was *his* face – Tommy's face – that stopped her heart. His original face, twisted yet unmistakable, was staring right at her.

What ran her blood cold wasn't the deformity or the monstrous amalgamation – it was the look in his remaining eye, the one Oliver hadn't taken. It burned with hatred, raw and unrelenting, directed solely at her.

He's still in there, she realized, horror tightening around her chest like a vise. *Still alive.*

As if reading her thoughts, Tommy's mouth – *his* mouth – stretched into a grotesque, jagged smile.

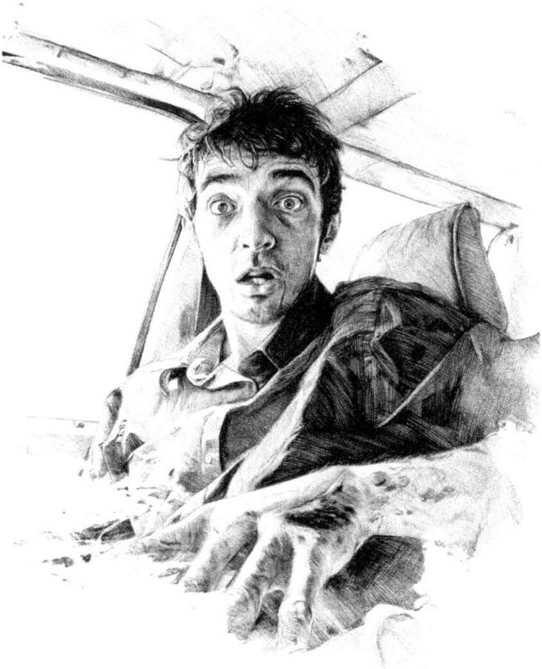

CHAPTER 32
AT THE END OF THE HALL

THE HEAVY METAL door slammed shut, the sound reverberating down the basement hallway. Oliver scrambled to secure the padlock. He wasn't sure how long the gun room would hold the three men, especially with all that firepower locked inside. But one thing was certain: Lance was a maniac. Despite his shouts through the door, claiming Oliver had made a forgivable mistake, he knew there was no scenario in which Lance would let him live. Especially not after locking the three men inside.

He didn't know how they knew about this place, the guns, or the key around his neck, but somehow they had.

Beneath Lance's ever-increasing shouts to let them out, the little rat-faced one they called Slim was screaming something awful, while upstairs the house shook and something cracked, like a tree just after someone shouts 'Timber!' Melissa and the baby were up there and he prayed the thing wouldn't go up the stairs. *Hide, Melissa! Hide!* he begged internally. And where were Aaron and Jurnee? The theater room – he hoped, but hope wasn't enough. He had to be sure.

Oliver flinched from his thoughts as a gunshot rang out from inside the gun room. Slim went quiet. It didn't take much deduction for Oliver to figure out what had just happened. These were bad men – the worst men.

He glanced over at the storage room, quickly crossing the hall and peering into the darkness. "Ben?" he called. He couldn't see the old man and even though he knew Ben was now dead, that didn't mean he was what Zoe had coined dead-dead. In fact, Oliver was sure he could feel the old man staring at him from somewhere in the darkness.

The house shook above him.

"No time." Pulling the door shut, he decided finding out Ben's state wasn't his biggest problem. Why couldn't Ben have bitten the one Lance called Grady? That guy had the physique of a Chicago Bears linebacker. Still, at least Ben had gotten one of them. He just prayed that the room held the other two.

Another crash from upstairs. It sounded like the whole entryway of the house had given way. Oliver's ears rang from the deafening roar of the zombie monster. The monster was louder now. It had to be inside! The house trembled with each crash as Oliver imagined the amalgamation smashing its massive body against the walls of the foyer. Then he heard a gunshot. *Melissa doesn't have a gun.* Someone shouted, "Oliver!"

"Zoe!" he shouted, running past the theater room, taking the stairs two at a time. When he reached the top, his heart stopped. Zoe stood in the doorway of the den, her back to him, her gun raised toward the monstrosity filling the front entryway. Louie sat up wearily behind her, growling weakly.

The monster loomed, a grotesque mass of limbs and faces, its many mouths quivering and muttering incomprehensible words. Its head – a hideous patchwork of fused skulls – turned toward Zoe, its single intact eye locking onto her.

"Mmmiiinnne..." it growled, its voice stretched and distorted.

Oliver couldn't believe what he was seeing. "What in the actual fuck!" It was... Tommy! Somehow it was Tommy! Oliver didn't think. He raised The Judge and fired, the blast tearing into one of the monster's secondary faces. The creature reeled, roaring in pain, but the damage only seemed to enrage it.

"Get downstairs!" he yelled, firing again as he cut into the kitchen then circled around to the den from the other side.

More zombies filled the hole where the front door used to be, each one scrambling to be the first.

He grabbed Louie, cradling the dog. "Go for the stairs!" he shouted, running back into the kitchen and around.

Zoe was there, at the basement door. "It's Tommy!" she shouted over the chaos, her voice trembling. "That thing is Tommy!"

"I know!" he shouted as the monster lunged, its massive arm smashing into the wall and sending splinters flying. Zoe fired once more, then turned and ran down the stairs.

Oliver followed, his heart pounding.

The basement was dimly lit, the air thick with tension. The hallway itself was wide, at least four feet, each side lined with photos of a younger Benson Meyer and his family. The ceiling was tiled and only about eight feet high. Could that thing get down here?

In Oliver's arms, Louie whined. His expression told Oliver he wished he could do more. This dog had saved him and Zoe more times than he cared to count. "It's okay, pal.

You're a good boy." He hurried into the theater room. "Aaron! Jurnee!"

The silhouette of a tiny head with bouncy afro puffs peeked up from behind a row of theater chairs, the distinct shape reminding Oliver of Minnie Mouse ears. His chest ached with relief. Then, another head popped up beside her – this one taller, with the handle of his long sword jutting up like Excalibur from the stone.

"Aaron! Jurnee! Thank god! Both of you get in that bathroom, close the door, and lock it! Stay there until I tell you to come out."

"What's happening!" Jurnee cried out.

From the top of the basement stairs, Oliver heard something. Something guttural and wrong. "Jurnee! Eyes closed!"

Jurnee slammed her eyes shut. "I don't know why you think this is less scary, Oliver! But now I can't even see what's going to get me!"

"Take her, Aaron! Just hide and don't come out!" Oliver said, his voice more stern than normal.

Aaron adjusted the short sword on his hip and took Jurnee by the hand. "It's okay, Jurnee. I've got you." The boy glanced back. "But Oliver, maybe I should come—"

"Aaron, no time. Hide. Please! Just do it!"

Aaron nodded, opened the bathroom door, and ushered Jurnee inside.

"Louie too!" Jurnee called.

"Right." Oliver pushed Louie into Aaron's arms. "Don't come out! Not until I come back!"

"But Oliver, I... I can help!" Aaron tried again.

"I know you can. And that's what I need you to do. Please, keep them safe, Aaron!" He closed the bathroom door and ran back to the hallway.

Lance's and Grady's muffled shouts echoed from the gun room at the far end of the hallway. "Open this door, asshole!" Lance bellowed, followed by the sound of gunfire as they tried to shoot their way out.

"Zoe, where's Adam?" Oliver asked as he flipped open the cylinder on The Judge, reached in his pocket, and pulled out two more .410 cartridges to replace the two he'd spent upstairs. One after the other, he shoved them into the cylinder and flipped it closed with a snap of his wrist. He still had another gun, Ben's Desert Eagle, holstered on his hip. But he planned on spending all five rounds of The Judge first. He pulled back the hammer.

"He's in the van," she said, her voice tight with emotion. "He was bitten. I tied him up."

Emotions swelled inside him like an ocean's surge, but there was no time to fully feel them. At the top of the stairs, bodies slammed into the basement door, followed by the unmistakable sound of splintering wood. The Tommy monster was destroying the wall around the basement door, forcing its way down onto the stairs. Its massive body shook the house with each movement.

"I'm out of ammo," Zoe said, her voice trembling.

"I have five rounds in this thing," he said, holding up The Judge. "Here take this." He handed her Ben's Desert Eagle.

The moans of the undead echoed down the stairs, filling the basement hall.

"This isn't going to be enough," Zoe said, glancing at the steel door.

"Sounds like you're fucked, Oliver," Lance shouted. "Unless you open the door."

Zoe looked at him and whispered, "Who's in there?"

"Bad guys. Convicts."

"Convicts?" Zoe repeated but there was no time to explain. They were coming.

Zombies poured down the stairs, their guttural moans electric with excitement.

Oliver slowed down his normally panicked firing and forced himself to take a breath and focus. He fired at the first zombie to find its feet. But these guns were new to him and the first round from The Judge pulled to the left, removing the arm of the vile creature at the elbow. He fired again, obliterating the upper half of its head. The zombie collapsed as another came on. Oliver fired again. This time the shot went low, tearing a chunk the size of a bowling ball out of the torso of a plump middle-aged woman, spilling her innards into the hallway. When she didn't stop, Zoe fired the Desert Eagle. The gun bucked in her hands as the woman's head exploded like a ripe melon. "Oh my god!" Zoe shouted, neither of them expecting the Desert Eagle to do what it had.

"Keep shooting!" Oliver shouted, leveling The Judge at a hunched figure struggling to its feet. Its frame was draped in what had once been a business suit but now hung in tatters like seaweed clinging to driftwood. Its skin was gray and sloughing off in blackened chunks, with patches of skull showing, like it had been underwater for days. But worst of all, its lower jaw was missing entirely, leaving its tongue to loll uselessly against its chest like a dead slug.

Oliver squeezed the trigger, and The Judge roared. The slug tore through the zombie's tongue and upper mouth, shattering molars and blowing out the back of its skull like a ruptured melon. The force sent its head spinning backward while the body staggered forward – one final step on reflex – before crumpling like a puppet with its strings cut.

Zoe fired five more rounds from the hand cannon into the horde, killing three more of the undead.

Oliver fired into another woman as she leapt off the stairs. She looked young and fit. His shot went low, opening up her bowels. Unfazed, the young woman stomped barefoot across her own guts, slipping and falling. Her eyes were stretched cartoonishly wide with excitement. Oliver fired once more, The Judge clicking with the damming sound of an empty gun.

"I'm out!" Oliver announced.

Zoe fired, her shot removing the side of the girl's face, finally stopping the zombie.

But the dead were still coming, their bloodshot eyes locked on the living, and up above, the Tommy monster was trying relentlessly to get his massive bulk past the doorway and onto the stairs, like a wolf trying to get at a rabbit hiding deep in its burrow.

Oliver crouched near Zoe, The Judge empty, the click of the last dry fire still echoing in his ears, as if whispering *you're so fucked*, over and over. Zoe's Desert Eagle, too, was spent. She held her wrist in one hand, no doubt strained from the recoil.

The hallway filled with the groans and moans of the descending horde as they squeezed past Tommy. The stairway was now a mass of writhing, undead forms, their bloated bodies tumbling one over the other, an avalanche of undead.

From inside the gun room Lance was shouting, "You're out of bullets! Open up, Oliver! We can still salvage this!"

Zoe's face was pale, her chest heaving. "You're going to have to open the door to the gun room, Oliver," she whispered.

Oliver glanced at the door. Though the padlock was

locked, the key was still inserted. He only needed to turn it. "Zo, if I let them out, they're going to kill us!"

"But if you don't, *they're* going to kill us!" she cried, her eyes fixed on the opposite end of the hallway and the monsters piling up. She stood and stumbled backward, her eyes wide with terror as the zombies began to rise from their tangled knot, their grotesque feet slipping in the bodily muck as they tried to find their balance. Desperately, they both pressed their backs into the cold, unforgiving wall. *End of the line*, Oliver thought, but maybe not.

Their best bet now was to charge forward. If they hurried they could get to the theater room and take cover with Jurnee and Aaron. Maybe they could barricade the door. It wasn't much of a plan but it might give them time, if they moved right now, before the room was blocked off by the undead. "Come on! Get up, Zo!" he shouted, taking her hand.

"What are you doing?!" Zoe shouted.

"We have to run toward them before we're cut off from the theater room!" Oliver started to pull her forward but froze before he made it two steps. At the other end of the hallway a shape appeared between them and the horde. It was the unmistakable silhouette of a familiar boy.

CHAPTER 33
THE PROMISE

JURNEE SAT on the bathroom floor, Louie's big head resting in her lap, her fingers gently scratching behind his ears. His stubby tail wiggled, which had to be good, but she could tell he was still hurting. He was supposed to protect them, but now she felt like she needed to keep him safe.

Aaron sat rocking back and forth against the bathtub with one of his swords resting across his lap. He hadn't said much since Oliver made them hide in here. Every time a loud noise came from outside – gunfire, growling, something crashing – he would grip the handle a little tighter.

She watched him carefully. His face didn't look scared. It looked… like he was thinking really hard.

"Aaron?" she whispered.

His eyes flicked up. "Of course, we should try and stay quiet."

"I know." She glanced at the door, then back at him. "You wanna go out there?"

Aaron looked down at his sword. "Of course I do."

The walls shook and the light above the sink flickered.

Jurnee's stomach felt funny. She didn't like the idea of

him leaving. But she was worried about Oliver and Zoe, and Aaron said he was a Samers Eye, which she knew meant he was a sword guy. She remembered in the last Samers Eye there was a guy Aaron called Tom Cruise but she didn't think that was right because no one in the movie called him Tom. He was a Samers Eye and he had swords like Aaron's and he fought *lots* of bad guys. But what if Aaron went out there and got hurt?

"Oliver told us to stay," she reminded him.

Aaron's fingers curled around the handle of his sword, tight, like when she held on to the edge of a pool so she wouldn't sink.

"Of course he did. But the gunfire stopped, and I heard them yell that they were out of bullets." He looked at her now, his voice quiet but sure. "Maybe I should go check on them?"

Jurnee pressed her lips together. She wasn't dumb. She knew monsters were out there.

She reached down and grabbed Louie's big paw, squeezing it gently. "So if you go, what happens to me and Louie?"

Aaron hesitated. "Of course, you stay here and keep Louie safe."

She thought about that. Louie needed her, and she had to protect Princess too.

"If I go, will you be scared?" Aaron asked.

"I'm really brave too, you know. I'm not a baby. I can stay by myself."

Aaron frowned. "Of course, I didn't say you were a baby."

"You didn't have to." Grown-ups always thought she was too little and too scared, but she was brave too. She had saved Oliver once and even tried to fix his back when he almost went into the rain. She told Louie to save Zoe, and he listened. She was brave.

But... she was also really scared for Aaron to go.

Outside a grown-up shouted something mean, but she couldn't understand the words. The house shook, another crash of breaking wood making her jump. Louie whined.

"It's okay, Louie." She squeezed his paw again, then let go and sat up straighter. "I'll be okay, Aaron."

Aaron rocked back and forth for a moment, then finally nodded. "Okay."

Jurnee swallowed. She didn't know what to call the feeling, but it was the same one she got when she missed her mom too much – like something heavy was sitting on her chest. But she wasn't going to cry.

Aaron stood up, adjusting his swords. He turned to the door but then stopped.

"Jurnee..."

"Yeah?"

"You sure you'll be okay?"

She nodded, giving him a small smile. "I'll be okay. Just promise you'll hurry back."

Aaron hesitated. Then, slowly, he smiled. It was a little smile but it made her smile back even though she still wanted to cry. "Of course. I promise."

He pulled open the door and stepped out.

Jurnee set Princess down beside Louie and scooted closer to the door, pressing her ear against the wood.

For a second, there was nothing.

Then—

"Aaron, no! Go back!"

Her tummy felt like it flipped over, like when she swung too high on the swings. She grabbed Louie's paw again and squeezed it tight.

CHAPTER 34
THE DEADLY DANCE

"AARON, NO! GO BACK!" Oliver shouted, motioning wildly as he hurried forward, but the boy was too far down the hall – too close to the undead.

Aaron turned and glanced over at them, hesitating, like he was waiting for them to say something else, completely unaware of the chaos at his back. If he would just look to the right, he'd see zombies piling up at the base of the stairs, scrambling to their feet! Couldn't he hear them?! "Aaron, behind you! Run!"

Aaron's face was innocent, like he'd no idea what was about to happen. No idea he was about to be pulled down by a dozen reaching hands, devoured by the horde, and there was nothing Oliver could do about it.

Aaron nodded to Oliver as if he were nodding to a passerby on the sidewalk.

Hey, Oliver!
Oh, hey there, Aaron. How are you doing?
Oh, I'm good. Boy, it sure is a pretty day!
Indeed it is. Hey, you know there's a horde of zombies to

your right and you're about three seconds from being eaten to death, right?

Huh, you don't say?

After the friendly nod, Aaron did turn to the right. Several zombies, having now found their feet, screeched with glee and reached for their prize.

This is when Aaron should have shit himself and run towards Oliver and Zoe. That's what any normal teenage boy would do... But not Aaron.

The single second stretched out as Oliver's whole world went into slow motion, but no matter how slow the second passed it wouldn't be enough time. The distance from himself to the opposite end of the hallway might as well have been the distance to the sun. He simply couldn't save the young man from the inevitability of what was about to happen, and in that single second Aaron's horrific future played out in camera flashes through Oliver's mind.

Flash – Aaron turns to face the horde.

Flash – his eyes go wide.

Flash – they pull him down onto the floor.

Flash – teeth sink into the boy's face and neck.

Flash! Flash! Flash!

Wait... What is that? A different flash. Not one in his mind's eye playing out the horrors to come, but an actual flash of light reflected off something in Aaron's hands as his body turned to face the horde. The swords Ben had given him – one long and gleaming, the other short and deadly – were held at his sides.

And then... Aaron moved.

His steps were careful, his expression calm, almost serene.

The first zombie – a grotesque man with exposed ribs and no lower jaw – swiped a hand toward him. Aaron twisted, pulling his head to the side. The zombie's hooked fingers missed his face only barely as the long sword swept through the air, slicing cleanly through its neck. The thing's head toppled to the ground with a wet thud, and the body crumpled.

Zoe gasped beside Oliver, her voice trembling. "Oh my god..."

More and more zombies were standing now, screeching through bared teeth with delight as they lunged, all desperate to be the first.

The second zombie came at Aaron from the side – a woman in a tattered nightgown, her skeletal frame jerking awkwardly. Aaron spun, the short sword in his left hand flashing upward to bury itself in the creature's temple. He pulled the blade free with a fluid motion, already pivoting to meet the next attacker.

Oliver couldn't look away. It was like watching a deadly dance, every movement precise and purposeful. Aaron wasn't just swinging wildly – he was calculating, anticipating. His feet moved with the grace of a samurai, his body fluid and balanced. Each step seemed to guide his blades into perfect arcs of destruction.

"Is that... is that really Aaron?" Oliver muttered, his voice barely audible.

Zoe clutched his arm, her eyes wide with awe. "I've never seen anything like it."

A zombie wearing the remnants of a military uniform leaped off the third step and charged, its cloudy eyes locked on Aaron. Its movements were faster than the others, more deliberate. But Aaron didn't falter. He stepped aside at the last moment, his short sword darting out to sever the tendons at the back of the creature's knees. As it collapsed, his long blade swept down, cleaving its head in two.

A hulking brute of a zombie – a man who must have been six-and-a-half feet tall in life – bounded down the stairs, slipping in the blood and falling onto his ass on the steps, but he was right back up, lunging in with his thick arms. Aaron met it head-on, his long sword flashing in a downward arc that severed the creature's left arm at the shoulder. The big man roared, his remaining arm swinging wildly. Aaron ducked, stepping inside its reach, and drove his short sword up beneath its chin. The blade pierced through the top of its skull, and the giant fell backward, lifeless.

At the top of the stairs the house shook and wood crunched.

More zombies came and in the seconds that followed Aaron became a blur of flashing metal and the hallway became a battlefield, the floor slick with gore, the air thick with the coppery stench of blood. Zombies continued to pile off the stairs, surrounding Aaron, but the young man was relentless, his blades cutting through the undead with surgical efficiency.

Oliver felt his breath catch in his throat. This young man must have spent countless hours practicing alone in his bedroom. The overweight boy with autism, who struggled to fit in. Ass Load Aaron, they'd called him, along with a dozen other horrible names. If only they could see him now as he moved with the grace of a dancer and precision that defied belief. Now, he stood like a warrior out of legend, a living, breathing force of nature.

"Aaron, behind you!" Zoe shouted as a zombie lunged from a darkened corner of the hallway.

Aaron didn't turn. Instead, his short sword flicked backward, impaling the creature without so much as a glance.

He spun, pulling the blade free, and decapitated another zombie in the same motion.

Oliver could only watch, his heart pounding. Less than thirty seconds had passed and Aaron had killed dozens. "He's... incredible," he whispered.

Zoe nodded, her voice thick with emotion. "He's saving us."

The horde began to thin, the once-overwhelming flood reduced to stragglers. Aaron's movements never slowed and his blades never faltered as they cut down the remaining zombies with ruthless efficiency. One by one, they fell, their lifeless bodies piling up in the hallway.

Finally, the last zombie – a child with a gaping hole where its stomach had been – bolted forward. Aaron stepped toward it, crossing his arms at the wrist in front of himself, reaching. When both blades met the undead boy's throat, Aaron pulled, uncrossing his arms. The blades made a *shwang* sound as they slid across each other and sheared through the zombie's neck like a pair of oversized scissors. Like so many others, the creature's head rolled to the floor.

The hallway fell still, save for the chunks of ceiling tile, drywall, and wood scraps raining down onto the stairwell. It sounded like a dozen axe men were up there felling trees.

Aaron stood amidst the carnage, his chest heaving, his swords dripping with black viscous blood. For a moment, he didn't move, his eyes fixed on the bodies at his feet.

Oliver took a cautious step forward. "Aaron..." he began, his voice trembling.

Aaron turned to him, his face calm but his eyes burning with an intensity that sent a chill down Oliver's spine. "You guys okay?" he asked simply, his voice steady.

Zoe stepped beside Oliver, her hand over her mouth. "You... you were amazing, Aaron." Her voice was barely above a whisper or maybe Oliver's hearing was just screwed up from all the gunfire.

Aaron didn't respond. He held the blades down at his sides and turned toward the stairs. "Of course, we're not done yet. More are coming," he said, his voice carrying the weight of someone far older than his years. Calmly but carefully he walked toward the stairs, stepping over and in between the fallen, swords at the ready, leaving Oliver and Zoe staring after him, stunned.

Above them the Tommy monster cried out like a pack of wolves set to pounce, its moans reverberating down the stairs.

Oliver found his voice. "Aaron! Wait, the next thing that comes down those stairs isn't going to be a zombie. It's one of those monsters. But... but it's also... Tommy."

Aaron halted and glanced back. "Tommy is one of those things." It wasn't a question, just a statement. Perhaps it was Aaron's way of making sense of what he'd just been told.

Suddenly the snapping and crunching of wood and drywall ceased and everything went quiet like the house had just taken a breath and held it. Then one of the monster's congealed legs came into view as it lowered itself down and onto the stairs. The step flexed and creaked in protest as it took all the monster's weight.

"It made it through the door!" Oliver said, stating the obvious. But obvious or not, it was coming down the fucking stairs and they had no way to stop it and nowhere to go.

The Tommy monster screamed with rage. *No, not rage*, Oliver thought. *Excitement*. Tommy was excited. He knew it had them trapped. Again, it stomped down, the next step mimicking the first as it let out a tortured creak. Then another stair, then the next. Its grotesque conglomeration of mismatched legs came into full view.

From up above and still out of sight, the sound of lumberjacks at work returned, filling the basement. More drywall rained down in chunks, like a heavy snowfall. Oliver could hear Tommy's grotesque body raking the walls, gripping and ripping everything apart as it shouldered its way down the staircase.

"We can't fight that thing with no ammo!" Oliver shouted.

Inside the gun room came more shots and then the sound of someone kicking the door. "You're so fucking dead when I get out of this room!" Lance shouted.

Oliver turned to the door. "You were right, Zo. I have to open the door. We need those guns!"

"No, wait!" Zoe said, her eyes igniting in some realization only she understood. "Maybe not! I think I know what it is! What Adam meant! The coffee shop! The health department! I know what a surfactant is!"

"What are you saying?" Oliver asked, frowning as he turned to find her hand on the doorknob of the supply room.

Oliver's eyes went wide. "Zoe, wait!" he shouted, lunging for her. But before he could get to her the door swung in and Ben leapt out from the darkness.

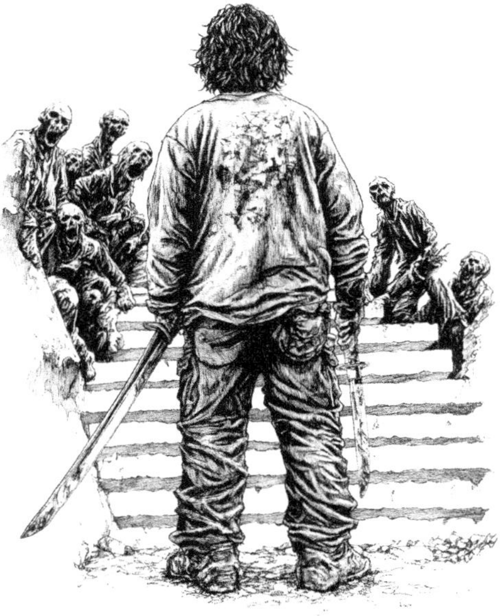

CHAPTER 35
DISSOLUTION AND DESPERATION

ZOE HIT THE FLOOR HARD, her breath rushing from her lungs as Ben's snarling face loomed above her. His bloodshot eyes were wild, lips peeled back to reveal blood-coated teeth. The stench of his coppery breath filled her nostrils as he snapped at her, missing her face by inches.

"Zoe!" Oliver roared, his voice cutting through the chaos.

Ben lunged again, but before his teeth could sink in, Oliver's shoe connected with Ben's head. The impact snapped Ben's head back. Oliver grabbed him by the collar, yanking him off of her.

Ben snarled, his movements feral and relentless as he clawed at Oliver.

"Get into the supply room!" Oliver shouted, struggling to hold Ben back.

Zoe scrambled to her feet, heart pounding. She wouldn't leave him. She grabbed the empty Desert Eagle lying on the floor and swung it with all her strength, the handgun connecting with Ben's temple with a loud crack of bone. He collapsed in a heap, twitching but no longer moving.

"Go! Hide!" Oliver barked, already stepping back toward Aaron.

Zoe didn't hesitate and ran into the supply room. Her mind raced as she scanned the shelves. She wasn't hiding – she was searching.

Zoe had read the passage on roundworm amalgamations from the *Parasite Field Guide* so many times she'd set it to memory and now in this most dire of moments it played through her mind like a recording.

The scientists tried prodding the tower with a metal wire, and the tower didn't fall apart. Next they stuck the towers in water, but the worms remained bonded and began to swim in a single cohesive mass. But then the team had an idea. Because the nematoil was a waxy molecule formed from fat, perhaps surfactants would have an effect. Adam said he had to take a class on food handling, sanitation, cleanliness – sodium sulfate. There! The familiar blue bottles beckoned like beacons in the black of night. She wrapped her hand around one bottle of the Dawn dish soap, spun it around, and read the ingredients: water, sodium lauryl sulfate, sodium laureth sulfate. "Yes!" she screamed. Surfactants were detergents!

"Please work," she whispered, grabbing two bottles and rushing back to the hallway.

When she returned, Aaron was standing firm in the hallway, his swords still dripping with blood as the Tommy monster descended the last of the stairs. The creature filled the opening to the stairwell from floor to ceiling, its grotesque limbs ending in multiple sets of twisted hands. Some of the Tommy thing's hands pressed against both walls; others gripped the corners of the wall where the stairwell ended.

"Run, Aaron!" Oliver shouted, but Aaron didn't budge.

The basement hall filled with a single name that sounded like it had come from vocal cords that had been dragged across concrete. "Olllivvverrr."

Aaron stood firm, gripping his swords tightly, his feet planted with the precision of a seasoned warrior. As the monster lunged, Aaron moved with startling speed, sidestepping its massive limb and slicing his long sword across the sinewy arm. The blade bit deep, severing one of the grotesque amalgamated fingers. The creature howled, ichor spraying across the walls.

Undeterred, Aaron pressed forward, slashing his short sword in a swift arc that tore through one of the monster's smaller faces, which appeared grafted onto its torso. The face split open, a grotesque scream echoing as it retreated into the writhing mass. Aaron's movements were sharp and deliberate, each strike aimed with purpose.

But the Tommy monster was relentless too. Its massive arm swung down like a wrecking ball, and though Aaron raised his swords to block, the force was overwhelming. The impact sent him flying backward, his blades spinning from his grip as he crashed through the doorway and vanished into the theater room.

"Aaron!" Zoe shouted.

The Tommy monster must have felt like it was squeezing itself through a garden hose. For a second Zoe thought it might actually get stuck. Then, as if in a claustrophobic fit, it shouldered itself into the walls and swung its appendages wildly, bashing its conjoined arms into the wall of the gun room over and over until finally... a loud pop of fracturing concrete echoed through the basement hall.

A giant crack spread down the wall ahead of the monster toward Zoe and the steel door where the two men on the other side still struggled to get free.

Tommy swung again, slamming his tangle of fused arms into the now broken wall.

Zoe saw Oliver's eyes go wide as the concrete wall caved inward into the gun room. "Oh, that's not good!" Oliver shouted.

Through the cloud of dust and falling rubble, two figures in orange jumpsuits emerged, coughing and covered in concrete dust. One was about Oliver's size, dark-haired and wiry, while the other was a good six inches taller and built like a damn tank, muscles straining beneath his torn shirt. Both wore expressions twisted with fury. Worse, they were both armed – and they were staring directly at Oliver.

"You locked us in, you son of a bitch!" the average-sized guy growled, leveling his rifle at Oliver.

Matching up the voice, Zoe knew that one had to be the Lance guy.

"Shit! Lance?! Turn around, bro!" the giant man shouted as he pulled on Lance's shoulder.

Oliver pointed past them, toward the Tommy monster now moving down the hall again. The thing was still in an awkward low crouch as it pushed its way deeper, but nonetheless it was moving and they had nowhere to go.

"Fuck me! It's one of those things we saw on the bridge! Shoot it, Grady!" Lance barked, raising his AR-15 and firing a burst into the creature's torso as he backed towards Oliver and Zoe.

Grady followed suit, pumping and firing the shotgun as he backpedaled.

Zoe threw her hands over her ears as bullets tore through the Tommy monster, but it barely flinched. The bullets seemed to have little effect, the bullet holes closing after only seconds. Even the long slashes from Aaron's swords had seemed to glue themselves shut.

Zoe knew it must be the waxy molecule filling the holes and gashes like icing over a cake.

The bullets did seem to piss it off though, because now its massive limbs moved with horrifying urgency, and its many mouths let out a cacophony of screeches and growls.

"Shoot it in the head! The main one!" Oliver shouted.

As if the Tommy monster heard the command, it raised its thick arms to shield its face.

"We need an egress window! Every modern basement should have one!" Lance shouted between firing at the monster.

"There's a window but it's in the theater room on the opposite side of that thing!" Oliver answered.

Zoe pushed past Oliver, clutching the bottles of dish soap. "Stop shooting," she shouted as loud as she could. "Back! Everyone, back!"

"What the hell are you doing?" Lance demanded, his voice dripping with disdain.

"The answer to stopping this thing isn't bullets! Let me through!"

"Zoe! Wait!" Oliver shouted, terror in his voice.

"This is the only way!" Zoe shouted, pulling up the cap on both bottles as she started forward to face Tommy.

The Tommy monster's eye widened as Zoe came within its grasp. "Zzzoooeee!" he squealed with sick excitement. He swung a long patchwork of arms.

Zoe ducked, feeling the rush of wind above her head. The arms struck the wall on the supply room side, caving in the drywall with a loud pop.

Zoe jolted up, pointed the bottles of soap, and squeezed.

Thick blue liquid streamed from the bottles onto the monster's advancing form.

"I don't see how giving this thing a bath is going to help!" the bigger man shouted.

"It'll work," Zoe rasped. "It has to work!"

The Tommy monster roared, swiping another massive arm at Zoe. This time she jumped back, barely dodging the limb, which swooped into the gun room and shattered a wall of glass gun cases.

"Zoe, for god sakes, get back!" Oliver shouted, grabbing her arm and pulling her away.

"Get that bitch out of the way or she gets shot along with that fucking thing," Lance ordered.

Zoe held her breath begging, *Please, god! Please!* At first, nothing happened. The monster continued to advance, backing them to the end of the hallway with nowhere left to go except into the supply room.

"Not enough!" Zoe shouted. "Get more soap!"

"Soap?! Fuck that!" Lance fired the AR. "Shoot it, Grady," he shouted.

But they didn't know what she knew – what the scientists in the field guide had learned. *Please*, she begged again, hoping with all her soul the detergent would somehow work on this thing the same as it had on the roundworm amalgamations.

Lance's gun clicked empty.

Oliver looked at her, his eyes full of trust. "C'mon!" he shouted, hurrying into the supply room.

Boom! Boom! Boom! "We're running out of space here!" Grady shouted.

Zoe grabbed more Dawn, but as she prepared her bottles Oliver went for one of the giant jugs of Tide laundry soap. Using a pair of scissors from the shelf he stabbed into the top and cut out a large hole in the plastic.

Without words they nodded to each other and ran back into the hall.

"Stand aside!" Oliver shouted.

Zoe rushed in and squeezed her bottles again.

Tommy's eye found her, and she could see him in there, alive and desperate.

With Tommy focused on her, Oliver rushed forward and chucked his container into the monster's face as if he were emptying a pail of slop.

Blue liquid Tide dripped from its grotesque limbs – limbs still horrifyingly intact.

"Zo, it isn't doing anything!" Oliver shouted, as he pulled her back towards the supply room.

Lance returned from the gun vault with a full magazine and a box of shotgun shells, tossing the box to Grady. "Of course it isn't doing anything, you stupid fucks. Grady, stand your ground! On my count! Put everything you have into the main head!"

Lance tried to shove the magazine into the receiver but fumbled it onto the floor.

The monster's many faces contorted in rage and it stomped forward.

They couldn't back up any further.

Zoe could feel Tommy's single eye fixed on her as he reached one long appendage made of many arms. Zoe tried to bolt for the supply room but was too late. Several icy cold hands grabbed her by the arm, squeezing her like a vise.

"MMMIIINNNE!" Tommy hissed.

Oliver threw himself onto the amalgamated arms, as if he was climbing a tree, wrapping himself around the tree branch to pull himself up. "Let go of her, you bastard!"

Once on top of the arms, Oliver drove his elbow down over and over. "Let her go, Tommy! She was never yours! You hear me?! She was never YOURS!"

Bones snapped under Oliver's strikes, but Tommy still wouldn't let go. He lifted her up in front of himself towards his amalgamated mouths.

"Shoot!" Lance ordered.

Oliver cried out, "No! You'll hit Zoe!"

But Zoe knew Lance didn't care about them. She fought, pulling at the dead fingers and trying to kick, but it was no use.

Grady aimed the shotgun. "I got him!"

But before Grady fired, a low hiss filled the air like someone letting the air out of a car tire.

"What's happening?" someone shouted – Grady, or maybe Lance. Zoe wasn't sure, too busy screaming and fighting to get free.

Through the hiss, Zoe heard a roar. At first she thought it must have been Tommy. But then she heard the words that followed. "She was never going to be with you, Tommy! You hear me, you sick fuck? Now, let! Her! Go!"

Oliver roared again and what followed was a great wet ripping sound. Tommy's arms faltered. The hands squeezing Zoe's arm lost their grip as the whole mash of appendages broke loose from the creature.

Zoe dropped to the floor, quickly turning in time to see Oliver standing at the opposite end of the amalgamation of arms, his chest heaving. He looked at her, still bear hugging the group of torn appendages in his arms. He let them fall and what followed was a domino effect as the waxy substance binding Tommy's amalgamated form began to dissolve. Flesh and bone separated with sickening squelches, revealing thin, translucent tentacles emerging from the cracks, writhing and latching onto nearby limbs in a futile attempt by the parasite to hold itself together.

The Tommy monster roared in agony, its remaining eye still fixed on Zoe with pure hatred. It tried to lunge forward again, its massive body quivering as its legs began to separate.

"It's working!" Oliver shouted.

"More soap!" Lance cried out as he vanished into the supply room, returning seconds later with another jug of laundry detergent.

Zoe watched as Lance knifed open the jug and Oliver grabbed it, chucking it at the creature, the blue liquid mixing with the ichor oozing from its melting form. The parasite's tentacles flailed wildly, trying to repair the damage, but it was too late.

"Get more soap!" Grady yelled.

"Negative! That was it!" Lance said.

But Zoe knew it didn't matter. They'd won!

The monster staggered, its limbs falling away one by one. Its original head – the twisted visage of Tommy – remained intact, glaring at Zoe with a mix of rage and desperation. She could see in that remaining eye, Tommy the person wasn't ready to give up.

The Tommy monster's left legs finally gave out and collapsed altogether, sending it into an awkward sideways fall into the hallway wall, before falling forward toward her.

Then like a wounded grizzly it swiped out with its one remaining arm for a final desperate attack.

Zoe backpedaled, slamming herself against the back wall.

The monster's arm missed her but found someone else.

The amalgamation snatched hold of the bodybuilder, yanking him in close, like a child about to touch a hot stove might be yanked close by their parents. But Grady wasn't being yanked away from the hot stove – he was being yanked into it.

Grady screamed, his shotgun falling from his hands. "Help me, Lance!"

Lance stepped back and lifted his AR but there was no help for Grady. It all happened so fast. The mouth that Zoe knew to be Tommy's one true mouth in his whole visage of Picasso cubism–style patchwork sank its jagged teeth into Grady's throat, ripping out the man's Adam's apple in a single awful tear.

Blood sprayed across the hallway as Grady's scream turned into voiceless gurgles.

"Grady!" Lance shouted, finally firing the AR. Round after round punched into the creature's rapidly disintegrating body, but it didn't matter. All Lance was doing now was making ear-splitting noise. Finally the AR clicked empty and Lance tossed it to the ground.

Zoe pulled her palms off her ears and with a final, earth-shaking roar, the Tommy monster collapsed, its remaining mass falling into a heap of gooey flesh and broken bones. In the center of it all Tommy's single eye lay amongst a writhing knot of parasitic tentacles.

Oliver grabbed Zoe by the shoulders and pulled her to him. "You did it, Zo! It worked! It actually fucking worked!" He hugged her and kissed her. And all she could think was that he'd just saved her life, again. He'd faced Tommy in the hallway back at the church and now he'd faced him as this thing of nightmares.

She kissed him and she never wanted to stop kissing him.

When his lips finally pulled away from hers, she opened her eyes and gasped. "No!"

CHAPTER 36
BETRAYAL AND REDEMPTION

THE BARREL of Grady's shotgun pressed against Oliver's temple, the hot steel biting into his skin. Time seemed to freeze, the air thick with tension. Zoe's sharp intake of breath was the only sound in the hall aside from the faint sucking from the soap-slicked tendrils as they wriggled in their death throes.

"Lance," Oliver began, his voice steady despite the adrenaline surging through him. "You don't have to do this."

Lance's lips curled into a sneer. "Oh, but I do. You think what happened here changes anything? You think, what, we're going to hold hands and sing kumbaya? You locked us up! I've been locked up, Oliver. But I'll tell you this, no man will ever lock me up again and live to tell. I'll never go back to a cage. Now I want the house, the supplies... everything."

"We'll leave. You can have it all, just let us go!" Zoe begged, taking a step forward.

"Stay where you are!" Lance snapped, jerking the gun toward her briefly before returning it to Oliver's head.

With his eyes, Oliver begged her to stand down. If something happened to Zoe, he'd never forgive himself.

Mind racing, he searched for a solution, but he came up empty. His body was tense, ready to spring at the slightest opening, but he could feel Lance wasn't bluffing. At any moment they would both be dead.

The air between them went quiet and Oliver could feel the man was thinking.

Carefully Oliver said, "You don't want to kill everyone. You're not a kid killer." Although in truth, Oliver had no idea what Lance was. "Let us go. You can have it all. We'll take the van and we're gone. Please? Just let us leave."

Thoughtfully, Lance said, "Okay. You want to live. Maybe there's one way you all get to live." His eyes locked on Zoe. He poked the gun barrel harder against Oliver's temple. "This guy, the kids, and the bitch with the baby take the van and get lost. But you" – he smiled at Zoe – "you stay here with me."

Zoe's face was a visage of horror. "I'd never be with you!"

"Hey, no need to be rude. Just say you don't like the idea. That's fine by me. I can always find another girl. But choose your words wisely. Because saying no to me means you all die. You, the kids, the baby – and that's all on you. Your choice. So I'll ask again and for the last time, what's it going to be? Do I pull the trigger?"

Tears streaked down Zoe's face, her hands shook, and Oliver could see she was searching but coming up empty. Just as she opened her mouth to say something, perhaps that she would stay, Oliver caught movement from the corner of his eye – Adam, stepping off the last stair. He couldn't sneak through unnoticed. There was too much debris he'd have to climb over.

Instead, Adam didn't make any attempt at stealth as he

navigated forward through the tangled carnage of the gut-slicked hallway.

"Don't shoot!" Adam called, his voice strained and hands raised high. "I'm not here to fight. I don't even have a weapon!"

Lance spun, using Oliver as a shield while aiming the gun at Adam. "Stop right there. One more step and you become part of the mess you're standing in!"

Adam froze, his red-streaked eyes locking on Lance's. "You don't need to do this," he said, his tone calm but firm. "We can all walk away."

"Walk away?" Lance laughed darkly. "Who the fuck are you?"

"Adam, I... I live here."

"Really? Because judging by the looks of your face, you don't plan to walk away from shit. You look like you're here to feed."

Oliver's eyes flicked to Adam – observing the bloody strap wrapped around his hand, the sweat-soaked collar of his T-shirt, and the brown crust dried in the corners of eyes rimmed with exhaustion. He didn't just look bad. He looked barely alive.

"Just please put down the gun and we can work this out." Adam lowered his hands just a little and took a cautious step forward.

Oliver could feel Lance's patience slipping as he jammed the barrel hard back against his head. "You think this is some kind of negotiation? One more step, and I shoot."

Adam froze, his chest heaving as he struggled to control himself. Oliver saw the way his hands trembled, the way his jaw clenched as though fighting back some deep, primal urge.

"Lance," Oliver said, trying to keep his voice steady, "you've got the gun, but if you kill us, what then? You'll be alone with a woman who will hate you for this. Then what? What happens when another one of those things shows up? Are you gonna fight it alone?"

Lance barked out another laugh. "Oh, I see, you think I need you? Why? You've already shown me how to kill these things."

"You're insane," Zoe spat, her voice filled with hate.

Lance's face hardened, his finger tightening on the trigger. Oliver's world narrowed. Time slowed, his racing heart pounding loud enough to drown out everything around him. This was it. The end.

Regret rushed in like a tide, an overwhelming flood of unfinished promises and missed chances. He thought of Zoe, the way she never stopped fighting, her determination like a blazing fire in the darkness. He thought of Jurnee and the loss she'd already endured and how brave she'd been through it all. He thought of Aaron, the innocent boy who wielded his swords like a warrior from some ancient time. And then Melissa and her baby – so small, so vulnerable. They were all depending on him, and here he was, powerless to protect them.

The edges of his vision blurred. Not from fear – no, he wasn't afraid to die – but from the ache of leaving them. Of not knowing if they'd make it. A desperate thought clawed its way to the surface: *I should have done more... been more.*

"Don't! Don't, please!"

He closed his eyes, bracing for the end.

The moment hung in the air, a fragile thread stretched to its breaking point.

"We're done here." Then, Lance squeezed the trigger.

But nothing happened, not even a click.

Lance's eyes flicked to the gun, his moment of confusion costing him.

Seizing the opportunity, Oliver slammed his shoulder into Lance, knocking the weapon from his hand.

The two men hit the floor hard, sliding across the soapy mess. Oliver grunted as Lance punched Oliver in the kidney, the larger man scrambling to regain the upper hand.

Oliver reared his head back and headbutted Lance in the mouth, splitting the man's bottom lip.

"Let him go!" Zoe shouted as she jumped on Lance's back. He threw an elbow back, cracking Zoe in the ribs and throwing her off of him.

Lance pinned Oliver down, his hands closing around his throat. The edges of Oliver's vision blurred, his airways constricting as he felt around for something, anything to use as a weapon.

As his vision narrowed in, a shadow loomed over them.

Adam.

Without hesitation, Adam grabbed a heavy-framed picture that had fallen off the wall and brought it crashing down onto Lance's back. The force sent Lance sprawling, freeing Oliver.

Lance rolled onto his side, coughing and cursing. He reached for his side and brandished a knife. "You son of a—"

Adam dove on top of him.

Oliver blinked, trying to get his vision to clear as the two men grappled, slipping and sliding in the mix of soap and blood. Both trying to gain leverage and control the knife.

Adam got ahold of Lance's wrist and slammed it into the floor, the knife flying out of reach and vanishing into the muck.

Lance managed to land a punch, his fist connecting

with Adam's jaw. But Adam barely flinched, his desperation outweighing the pain.

With a guttural shout, Adam grabbed a piece of fallen ceiling tile track and drove the jagged metal into Lance's shoulder.

Lance screamed, blood spurting from the wound as he thrashed beneath Adam.

"You're a dead man!" Lance spat.

But Adam didn't stop. "This is for Melissa," he growled, his voice trembling with emotion, as he twisted the metal and then ripped it from the man's shoulder.

Lance screamed. "Ah! Dead! You're fucking dead! I'm going—"

This time, with the metal track clenched in his fist, Adam reared back and swung, plunging half the length of jagged metal deep into the side of Lance's head. Blood sprayed across the hallway as Lance's body went limp, his eyes staring lifelessly at the ceiling.

A momentary quiet settled over the carnage.

Oliver was sitting up, his vision returning as he gasped for breath and rubbed his bruised throat.

Adam stood over Lance's body, his chest heaving. He turned to face Oliver and Zoe, his red-streaked eyes glistening with tears.

"I've never killed another living person before," he stammered. "But he was going to kill you, Melissa, and Jonathan. I couldn't let that happen."

Zoe stepped forward cautiously, her hands trembling as she reached out to him. "Adam," she said softly, "are you... are you okay?"

Adam nodded, though his expression was far from certain. "I think so," he said, his voice breaking. "A few minutes after you left me in the van the hunger started to fade. I was able to chew through the zip tie enough to twist my hands until it snapped."

Oliver glanced down at Adam's wrists. They were bruised and cut.

"I don't... Well, I barely feel the hunger at all anymore." Adam turned to Oliver. "I got bit back at the Walgreens, but Zoe gave me some medicine and... it's working."

Oliver stared at him, a mix of relief and disbelief washing over him. "You're sure? You really are okay?"

Adam nodded again, his gaze dropping to Ben's lifeless body only a few feet away. "I'm still me. I'm just sorry it didn't work out for Ben."

Zoe gave Adam a hug, her relief spilling out in tears. "Thank god," she whispered.

Pushing himself to his feet, Oliver stood on shaky legs. He could already feel his right eye swelling shut as he put his arm around Zoe and kissed her on the side of her head. He looked up at Adam extending his hand. When the taller man took it, he pulled him into an embrace. "Fuck, I owe you one."

Adam shook his head. "No, sir. You don't owe me a damn thing. Jesus, Oliver, we're family now. You and Zoe have saved Melissa and I and our baby – shit, I don't even know how many times. But you can bet on this. Long as I still breathe, I got your back."

Oliver felt his own eyes welling up but he held it in, pressed his lips into a tight line, and nodded. Knowing that someone in this world had their back, really and truly meant more to him than anything. Maybe someone up above had their back too. "Hold on a second," he said, picking up the shotgun Lance had pressed to his head and tried to shoot him with.

He pumped the gun. An unspent shotgun shell ejected. "So it wasn't empty."

"Jammed?" Adam asked.

Oliver twisted the gun and smiled. "No. The safety is on."

"You're shitting me?" Adam laughed.

"No. It must have gotten pushed in when Grady dropped it." Oliver didn't know whether to laugh along or puke. Either he'd gotten damn lucky or someone up there really was watching out for him. *Was that you, Ben?* he wondered as he scanned the floor and retrieved Ben's Desert Eagle and knelt next to the man. "Ben," he said in a whisper as if he were checking to see if he were awake.

Zoe and Adam knelt down on either side of him.

"I know I promised that if you turned I would shoot you with this gun and, well, things didn't exactly work out that way. I just want you to know the only person you hurt deserved it and even though I didn't shoot you with this, Zoe" – he glanced over at her – "well, she used it alright, and I think you'd find some humor in that."

Zoe smiled a little then and even through the sadness it was beautiful.

"Anyway, I will get you buried out back next to Katie." He placed the Desert Eagle on the old man's chest. "It's a hell of a gun, Ben, and I'll make sure it stays with you." A tear leaked a trail down Oliver's quickly swelling cheek and he felt Adam and Zoe's hands on his back. He swallowed down the lump as a voice called from down the hall, "Guys."

Oliver stood and turned to find Aaron at the other end of the hallway, a long blood-slicked sword in one hand, the other rubbing the top of his head. He looked over the carnage of the collapsed ceiling tiles, dead bodies, and the destroyed Tommy monster. "Has anyone seen my other sword?"

Adam pushed his palms out toward Aaron. "Stay over there, bud. It's too dangerous. You might slip and fall on that thing."

Oliver and Zoe looked at each other and without exchanging a word she smiled at him. Oliver returned her smile with a soft chuckle that drove a wince of pain through his ribs.

Adam looked from one to the other. "What? Why's that funny? Look at this place. It's dangerous."

Oliver put a hand on Adam's shoulder. "I think the kid can handle it."

CHAPTER 37
HOPE

WITH EVERYONE ACCOUNTED for and safely upstairs except for Oliver, who was bagging body parts in the hall, Zoe crouched in the storage room, her flashlight beam scanning a bottom shelf stacked with supplies. Her eyes landed on a two-gallon plastic bucket half-filled with rice. "This should work," she mumbled as she dumped the contents into a tote, wiped the bucket clean, and inspected it for cracks. Satisfied, she turned toward the grotesque mass in the hallway.

The parasite – a translucent, waxy creature reminiscent of a giant maggot with tentacles – lay motionless among the wreckage of the basement hall. Around it the appendages spooled this way and that like a pile of tangled extension cords. Zoe pulled on rubber gloves and grabbed a pair of grilling tongs, ignoring Oliver's skeptical look.

"You're really keeping that thing?" he asked, dropping a goo-covered foot into the garbage bag.

"We have to," she said, lifting the parasite into the bucket and feeling the weight of the thing for the first time. It was much larger than the parasites she'd preserved before, and now she found herself hoping a two-gallon bucket would be enough. Its slippery body coiled as she worked it into the bucket. "This is the first specimen we've seen from an amalgamation. It could help us better understand its life cycle, and that might ultimately tell us what to expect. For example, how long these things can live, how big they can get, or even what might come next. Jesus, Oliver, who knows what secrets this thing might teach us."

Zoe paused then, noticing what was at the end of one of its many tentacles.

"What's wrong?" Oliver asked.

Zoe swallowed and lifted the thick cord. From the end dangled a single eyeball. Its retina was intertwined into the end of the tentacle, reminding her of micro braids attached to natural hair.

"Tommy's eye," she said queasily, flipping it into the bucket along with the final translucent cord.

Oliver grimaced. "Well, that's unsettling." Then he shot her an ornery grin.

"What?"

Oliver leaned over the bucket. "Hey, Tommy, you dick. You see this?" He flipped the eyeball the bird. "Fuck you."

"Really." Zoe laughed, shaking her head.

"Yeah, really. I freaking hate that guy. We should pack it in gasoline and light it on fire."

"Nope, it's research." She lifted the bucket and carried it into the supply room with Oliver on her heels.

"Did Ben have any isopropyl alcohol?" she asked, more to herself as she scanned the shelves.

"Hey, what about this?" Oliver grabbed a bottle of Tennessee's Finest from a shelf and held it up.

"Moonshine?" she chortled.

"Says here it's 120 proof and alcohol is alcohol, right?"

"I don't think so, but I don't have a better idea." She shrugged. "Let's just use a little and dilute it with a bottle of water. I don't want the alcohol to degrade the specimen." She poured a splash of the moonshine over the parasite as Oliver emptied two full bottles of water into the bucket, Tommy's eyeball vanishing into the now cloudy liquid.

In the dim light, Zoe snapped the lid into place and Oliver sealed the bucket with duct tape.

"There," she said, placing the bucket on a low shelf. "It'll stay preserved down here until I can get the equipment I need to study it."

Oliver shook his head. "If it grows legs, I'm not taking the blame."

Zoe smiled, giving the bucket a final pat. "Funny, but this thing is dead-dead. Alright, now back to cleaning."

Aaron appeared at the bottom of the stairs. "Adam needs you, Oliver. Some help with the door. Of course, I can stay down here and clean. I still need to find my other sword anyway."

"Okay, there's plenty more cleaning gear in the supply room. I got all the big stuff," he said, tying up the garbage bag.

By morning, sun streamed through the window of the farmhouse, its golden light illuminating the chaos of the night before. Zoe stood at the kitchen sink. Even though she'd been wearing rubber cleaning gloves when she'd handled the parasite, she couldn't help feeling the need to repeatedly wash her hands. The cool water was a stark contrast to the warmth of the sunlight on her face. The house was quiet – not eerily so, but settled into a kind of tentative peace that made her chest ache with gratitude. How close they'd come to losing everything – to losing each other – wasn't lost on her.

Behind her, she could hear the soft murmur of voices. Oliver was somewhere near the front door; the electric buzz of a cordless drill hummed as he screwed a piece of plywood over the shattered frame while muttering something about his poor carpentry skills. They had secured it enough for the night but were now making it stronger and more functional.

Zoe was grateful, too, that for the first time since Tommy shot him, Louie was up and walking. He was still limping but determined to follow Oliver like a shadow, his nub of a tail wagging faintly.

Zoe dried her hands on a towel and turned to peer through the doorway and survey the living room, den, and front entryway. The place was still a disaster – upturned furniture, shattered glass, and smears of blood on the walls and floor. Though most of the night had been spent with the heavy lifting of removing body parts, she didn't even want to think about the amount of work ahead of them. The stench of death still lingered, but the house felt alive again, as if it were breathing with them, and that gave her the strength to smile. Somehow, they were all alive.

Melissa sat on the couch, the baby nestled in her arms. When it had all gone down, she'd taken little Jonathan and hid in an upstairs closet. She looked tired, but there was a serene strength in her eyes as she hummed softly to the infant. Jurnee sat beside her, waving a stuffed animal in front of the baby's face, making exaggerated noises in an attempt to make him smile.

Aaron emerged from the basement, dragging a mop behind him, his long sword strapped across his back. He was covered from head to toe in coveralls, and wearing rubber gloves and a medical mask. His blond hair was damp with sweat, and his expression was unusually serious. "Of course, I got the bulk of the zombie goo off the floor," he announced, his voice tinged with both pride and precision. "But as I was pushing some of the... well, the guts and chunks into a pile, I... I think I broke the mop."

Oliver poked his head around the corner, a smirk tugging at his bruised face. "Kid, I think you broke the whole basement."

Aaron frowned slightly, considering. "Of course, the basement is still standing although the ceiling and walls are severely damaged. Technically, the monster did that." He paused, then added, "But yes, the mop is completely broken."

Zoe hid a smile, watching the exchange. "It's fine, Aaron. You've done enough cleaning for today. You must be exhausted and starving."

Aaron glanced at her, his tone direct but thoughtful. "Of course, food sounds amazing. But the floor still needs a lot of work. Perhaps some shovels, containers, and a shop vac would be beneficial. Of course, even after that it will take several more passes." He hesitated, his hand brushing the hilt of his sword. "Also... I still haven't found my other sword?"

Oliver laughed softly, shaking his head. "You saved our asses with those swords, Aaron. We'll find it, I promise."

Aaron's lips quirked upward in a brief, shy smile. "Of course. Thank you."

"Come sit down," Melissa called softly to Zoe, shifting to make room on the couch. "You were on your feet all night."

"In a minute," Zoe replied, her gaze drifting to the

dining table where Adam was stacking boards they'd salvaged from the barn. She'd been watching him closely, her medical instincts on high alert. His red-streaked eyes had cleared to a dull pink, and his movements were steady. He caught her staring and raised an eyebrow.

"I'm fine," he said, a small smile tugging at the corners of his mouth. "You can stop hovering."

"I'm not hovering," Zoe shot back, crossing her arms. "I'm observing."

Adam chuckled, the sound low and warm. "If you say so, Doc." He picked up a board and turned to Oliver. "I cut this one to thirty-six inches like you wanted. Where do you want it?"

"Right. That one goes across the top of the door to reinforce the plywood," Oliver replied, wiping sweat from his brow.

"And these other two?"

"Those just put anywhere that keeps zombies out." He smiled. "Although, once word gets out that we have a bona fide samurai warrior in our midst, they'd be wise to stay well clear of here."

Aaron shot him a shy smile and snorted. "Of course, you know the undead don't communicate that way, Oliver. Despite how badly they were defeated, they will still come." He frowned then, his face becoming serious. "This is why it's so important I find my second sword."

"Despite how badly they were defeated," Adam repeated with a laugh. "Alright, Aaron!"

The rest of the day passed in a blur of work. They reinforced the entryway, took turns napping, vacuumed and mopped blood from the floors, and dragged broken furniture out back. By late afternoon, the house was beginning to resemble a home again, albeit a battered one.

As the sun dipped below the horizon, casting the fields in shades of orange and gold, they gathered around the dining table for a meal. It was a simple spread – canned stew and veggies with homemade bread – but it felt like a feast.

The baby cooed happily in Melissa's lap as they all chatted about the events the day before. When baby Jonathan spit up, Jurnee pretended to gag at the sight, making everyone laugh. Aaron, having finally found his short sword stuck in the ceiling of the theater room, scooped spoonfuls of stew into his overstuffed cheeks like a chipmunk gathering food for the long winter.

Zoe watched them all, her chest tightening with emotion. They'd survived. Against all odds, they'd made it through another night. Well, most of them had. There was a void in the home without Ben but she knew he'd be happy they were still here – that they had survived another attack. And though the road ahead was uncertain, she dared to feel hopeful for tomorrow. Zoe had proved her theory about the waxy molecule. Detergent was the amalgamation's kryptonite. She'd also learned common dewormers were effective. Adam seemed to be winning the battle. And although much more observation was needed, Zoe was hopeful. Preliminarily, it seemed that if an infected could be treated quickly, before the parasite had time to take root, perhaps there was a chance for humanity after all.

After dinner, as the others cleaned up from the meal, Zoe stepped onto the back porch. The air was crisp, carrying the faint scent of hay and earth. Oliver joined her a moment later, leaning against the railing with a tired smile.

"We did good today," he said, his voice low.

Zoe nodded, her gaze on the horizon. "Yeah. We did."

He was quiet for a moment, then said, "Figuring out

that thing about the soap and facing what Tommy had become head-on the way you did was, well... you were incredible."

She turned to him, her eyes softening. "You were pretty damn incredible yourself. But there was a moment I thought for sure we..." She couldn't finish. Something about giving voice to her worst fear seemed like a bad idea.

He reached for her hand, his fingers warm against hers. "We made it. Together."

She squeezed his hand, a smile tugging at her lips. "Yeah. Together."

Behind them, the door creaked open, and Jurnee poked her head out. "Hey, are you guys gonna kiss or what? Because it's gross, and Aaron says he's claiming the last cookie."

Oliver laughed, pulling Zoe close. "Tell him the last cookie's mine. And yes, we're gonna kiss. Deal with it."

Zoe rolled her eyes but couldn't help laughing as Jurnee groaned and disappeared back inside. Suddenly, the world didn't feel so heavy. Maybe they could get past the point of surviving and actually live.

Oliver pulled her into him and kissed her.

Somewhere in the background a tiny voice said, "Eeewww."

Zoe pulled away and she and Oliver chuckled.

"Look out there, Zo." Oliver pointed across the field. Strange-looking clouds were rolling in.

"Come on, we better get inside," she said, leading him back into the kitchen.

A few minutes later, Oliver shouted, "You guys, come quick!"

Zoe and the others gathered around the French doors and stared out into the backyard.

"I knew those clouds looked weird," Oliver said.

"If by weird you mean normal, yeah. Yeah they do." Adam smiled.

From the sky a cold clear rain fell. Within a few moments the rain turned to sleet and the sleet to snow. Fat puffy white flakes melted as they touched down. They all watched as if this were the first snow they'd ever seen. Soon it began to stick, covering the grass and patio.

"It's white," Aaron whispered as if to state the obvious any louder might make it somehow less real. "Do you think this means the red rains are over?"

"Does this mean I can go out there and make a snowman?" Jurnee asked excitedly.

"Now hold on, I don't know what this means," Zoe answered, her face unable to contain the smile, cautious as it was. "We don't know if it's safe or not, but it isn't red."

"It isn't red," Adam repeated.

Jurnee let out an exaggerated sigh. "So, no snowman?"

Oliver gave Jurnee a pat on the back. "Sorry, kiddo, no snowman. But maybe someday soon."

Those words, 'maybe someday soon,' promised a future in which playing in the snow was possible. Over the last few weeks talking about anything other than surviving tomorrow had seemed so far away. But now, as Zoe looked at the others, she could see, despite their exhaustion, hope filled their expressions.

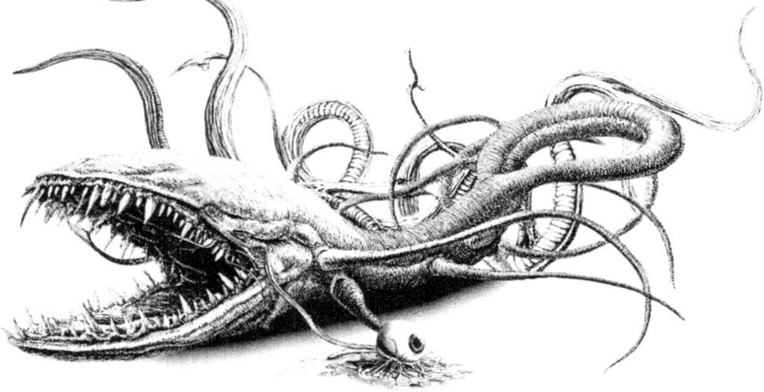

EPILOGUE – THE LETTER

OLIVER BACKED the BearCat up to the garage and shoved the shifter into park but he didn't get out. Instead, he sat there, still processing the events of the day.

Adam, seeming to read his mind, asked the very question Oliver sat pondering. "How do you think Zoe's going to take the news?"

Oliver blew out a breath. "Honestly, I don't know." And he didn't, but he feared what she might want to do.

Since the home invasion, several weeks had passed without incident and through the use of lots of soap, bleach, and a shop vac, the house no longer smelled of decomposing guts.

Outside, late November brought with it a foot of snow, blanketing the blood-soaked landscape in bright white. Zombies still roamed the area and they'd seen three different amalgamations, thankfully all from a safe distance. Yet despite the presence of the undead, the gray clouds and white snow felt somehow cleansing. The red rains seemed to have passed and he'd take that as a win.

The past few weeks, Oliver had learned a lot about

taking care of horses, chickens, and cows. Frankly, it was exhausting and he was thankful he had Adam – thankful, too, that Adam was showing no signs of having been infected. Even his eyes had cleared up.

Despite how hard this new life was, Oliver felt he had a lot to be thankful for, like this armored car Lance and his boys had left behind, which was proving fantastic for supply runs. He was thankful for the several sets of full-armor SWAT gear they'd found under the seats, along with more handguns and assault rifles.

They had a fortified home, plenty of supplies, and each other. All in all, things were going as well as they could be. But – as Oliver was learning, there always was a but – he sensed an ever-growing restlessness in Zoe. Thanks to her parasite research they knew things – things that others probably didn't. Things perhaps even their government didn't – assuming there was some semblance of a government out there somewhere.

But that was only part of her restlessness. Often in the late hours he and Zoe had talked about old friends and family. Oliver still had his sister, Sarah, out in California, if she hadn't turned or been... Jesus, he hated to think about that. And Zoe had her parents in Indianapolis. Though she'd admitted they were likely gone. It was her childhood friend, Alexis, also living just one state over in Indiana, that she talked about most. Up until the apocalypse, Zoe had talked to Alexis at least once a day since they were kids.

He knew what he had to tell Zoe wouldn't be easy.

He and Adam had just returned from a special supply run. Special because this time they had driven the fifteen minutes back to Mackinaw – back to the burnt-out ruins of his old home. The idea was to leave a note there so anyone who knew them from before would know how to find them if they came looking. Zoe reasoned that if friends or family somehow made it there, they would know the couple hadn't burned up along with the house, that they were still very much alive and, most importantly, where they could be found.

Oliver knew above all else, the single person Zoe was most worried about and hoped to hear from was Alexis.

The problem Oliver faced now was that he'd been too late. In their mailbox he'd found a note in a plain white envelope simply labeled Zoe. Hastily, he had opened and read the note, quickly learning Alexis had already been to the house.

Now, Oliver sat in the BearCat, reflecting and trying to predict how Zoe was going to react once she'd read the letter. Adam reached over and placed a hand on Oliver's shoulder and squeezed. "You know, no matter how long we sit out here, this isn't going to get any easier."

"I know," Oliver admitted.

"Hey, won't she be happy to find out her friend is still alive and that she made it all the way here? And, c'mon, chances are if she could do that she'll make it all the way."

Oliver nodded. "Yeah, probably so. But that won't take the sting out of the fact that we missed her. And honestly, after she reads this, I'm pretty sure I know what she is going to want to do."

Adam nodded thoughtfully. "Yeah, I can see that. Well, let's just talk about it as a group. I mean, Jesus, there's a lot to digest in that letter."

"Yeah, you're right. I just feel bad, you know. Not just about missing Alexis but Zoe hasn't been herself the last few days. I think she's got the flu or something and now this."

"The flu? You hadn't said anything. She okay?"

"Yeah, just trouble keeping food down. Stomach bug, I think."

Adam winced. "Could you not say 'stomach' and 'bug' in the same sentence, bro?"

Oliver smiled. "Sorry. Poor choice of words. We better get this shit unloaded before they start to wonder if something is wrong."

Inside, Zoe embraced him with a tight hug. "I can't stand it when you go out there."

"Well, I can't stand it when you go out there either," Oliver shot back with a smirk. "Hey, you don't look so good. You still feeling sick?"

Zoe nodded. "Yep, but it will pass soon. I just have to wait it out."

"Okay, you're the doctor," he said, smiling. "Hey, there's something I need to tell you."

"Really? Me too, come to the kitchen."

They made their way into the kitchen where Jurnee, Aaron, Melissa, and the baby were all gathered as if they were waiting. "Well, hey gang, what's up?" Oliver asked. "You guys are looking at me like I just walked into an intervention or something."

Adam looked at the group, then at Oliver. "Yeah, they are definitely all looking at you." He pecked Melissa on the cheek and baby Jonathan on the forehead before grabbing a chair and sitting down, then proceeded to stare at Oliver with a disapproving look.

"Now, why are you looking at me like that?" Oliver asked.

"I have no idea what you did wrong, but I want to be on the right side of this thing," Adam said, grinning.

"Okay, okay." Zoe held up her hands. "He didn't do anything."

"Well, that isn't exactly true." Melissa giggled.

Zoe turned and laughed. "Melissa!"

"Well!"

Oliver was confused. "What the hell is happening?"

"Okay, well, Melissa already knows but she's the only one."

Adam looked at Melissa with the same expression Oliver was giving Zoe.

"You better sit down," Zoe said, gesturing to the chair next to hers.

Oliver pulled out the chair and dropped into it. "Somebody tell me what the hell is going on?"

"I'm late," Zoe blurted.

"For what?" Oliver asked.

"I'm *late!*" Zoe repeated with more emphasis.

Oliver's frown deepened and he shook his head. "Zoe, late for..." His eyes widened.

Zoe smiled and nodded.

"But... how can that be?"

Melissa laughed. "Oh, you damn well know how."

Oliver felt his heart jump into his throat and pound in his ears. "Are you... are you sure?"

"I was already pretty sure. I mean, I'm never late and I've been puking every morning, craving weird stuff too. Remember a couple days back when I went on the supply run? Well, I picked up a pregnancy test. I'm sure, Oliver. I'm sure I'm pregnant!"

Oliver smiled so hard he thought his face was going to break. He stood up from the chair. "Pregnant!"

Zoe stood too, laughing as she threw her arms around him.

Oliver picked her up and spun her in a circle, then kissed her over and over. "We're pregnant!"

Jurnee laughed hysterically. "I'm going to have a baby stepsister!"

Melissa and Adam applauded, and Aaron grinned.

Oliver looked at Adam, a question in his eyes. Adam seemed to understand and agree. This wasn't the moment to share the note with Zoe, but as he stuffed the letter deep into his pocket he promised himself he would break the news the moment the time was right.

Many decisions had to be made, but not now. This moment was Zoe's moment, his moment, and their moment. He was already a dad to Jurnee and would be as long as she needed him to be. But now he was going to have a child of his own. Zoe was pregnant. In the back of his mind, a deeper worry took root. They had been pregnant once before and they had lost the baby. Neither was sure they would have another chance at childbirth, especially without medical intervention. Yet here they were.

With the news of the pregnancy came the need to celebrate. The group settled, and the men went to work cooking dinner for the ladies. They laughed and ate until they were stuffed. It was a good meal and a good day.

Adam snapped his fingers thoughtfully. "You know, we never did the cigar thing when little Jonathan was born."

"You're right!" Oliver announced. "Next supply run, we have to get cigars! Two to smoke now in celebration of Jonathan's birth and two for when we have ours!"

"You're smoking those things outside!" Melissa warned.

"Sure, sure," Oliver said, waving a hand.

"Of course, hun," Adam agreed and the two of them smiled at each other like kids up to no good.

"Oh hey, you had something you wanted to tell me?" Zoe asked as she started to clear the table.

Oliver intercepted her, taking the plates from her hands. "Um, no. None of that! You sit, I'll clear the table."

Melissa laughed. "Girl, take it while you can get it. Once the baby comes you're going to be exhausted all the time."

"So, what did you want to tell me?" Zoe asked.

Oliver's face became serious. "It's more what I need to show you."

Zoe's smile slipped. "So, show me."

He reached into his pocket and took out the folded envelope, passing it to Zoe.

She read her name and her face lit with recognition. "Alexis!" She collapsed into the chair, pulled the note free, unfolded it, and began to read aloud.

> Zoe,
>
> If you're reading this, then you're not dead. We spent the night in your driveway hoping you would show up. I even searched the neighbors' houses just in case you guys stayed close. I prayed and prayed you would pull up any second. I wanted to stay longer, I really did, but the group I'm traveling with are in a hurry to get going. I have so much to tell you. So much has happened. Mostly though, I'm scared, Zoe. Some of these guys are... I don't know. Most of them are okay, but the others, they really give me the creeps. There were thirty-three of us when we set off but the rains and the... the zombies. I'm the only girl left in the group. God, I wish you were here. Somehow, I know you're out there and not in the ashes of your house. I mean, I

feel it, you know? If you were gone, really gone, I'd feel that too. I'm sure I would. I miss you so bad, Zo.

If you are reading this note, we're heading west to Cheyenne Mountain Space Force Station near Colorado Springs. We got word that there's a huge underground bunker there – lots of supplies too. Most of the military was wiped out from the rains and the zombies, but those left are building a whole new community there. They've put out a call to anyone still left alive to come and help start over! Strength in numbers. 'Together we can figure out how to beat this.' That's what they said, and that's something, right? That's hope!

Please, Zoe, if you're reading this, come find me! Your bestie forever, Alexis

By the time Zoe had finished the letter she was crying. Carefully, she folded the note and held it to her chest. She looked across all the faces.

Oliver pressed his lips into a tight line. He knew before she spoke what came next.

Zoe's eyes searched the others' with frantic desperation. "I have to go find her. But... will you all come with me?"

Oliver's heart sank. Here in this place they were safe. Safe-ish anyway. This was his *Mountain Man* mansion on the hills of Halifax. Maybe it wasn't exactly like ole Gus's place, but it was theirs and they'd fought and nearly died for it. Now she was asking him to leave it behind. And Oliver knew, too, that he would leave it behind. Because not only was Zoe his safe place, she was his home. Even if he could talk her out of it, tell her it's a bad idea to travel halfway across the country pregnant, that it was too dangerous for Jurnee, she might listen but she would be utterly miserable. Besides, Zoe had something to give the world. Maybe others had figured out part of it, or maybe all of it, but what if they hadn't? If there really was a community forming in Colorado, how many could be saved if they knew about the effect common detergent had on the amalgamations? Or that treating the parasite was possible if done quickly? How could he be so selfish as to keep that knowledge only among themselves?

Oliver was already nodding before he spoke. "Of course, Zo. Of course I'm in, but Adam, if you guys want to stay here, I get it. I mean with the new baby and the risk of travel... And hey, there's plenty of supplies to divide between us. We don't even need half really. I mean some of the guns and some food..." He realized Adam and Melissa were both smiling. "What? What's funny?"

"We're a family, Oliver. You're like the big brother I never wanted." There was a glimmer of humor in Adam's tone, but it was tempered by the weight of all they'd endured. But then he added, his tone firm, "Of course we're going. This isn't just about surviving anymore – it's about finding a place where Jonathan grows up with more than fear."

Melissa smiled at him, cradling the baby close. "We want to see this through together. There's hope in a real community. And we'd rather face the risk with you than stay here alone."

Adam's grin returned. "Besides, this place still smells questionable."

"You guys, are you sure? This is a really dangerous ask," Zoe said.

"We have a freaking armored SWAT car! If we're going, we have the best vehicle for the trip! I mean unless old Ben has a plane stashed around here and one of you can fly it?" Adam waved away the idea. "Seriously, you guys. A community? A place where we can feel safe and have each other's backs? I mean, I don't know about you guys but I don't want to fight another horde or one of those zombie monsters again, especially not on our own. Not if we don't have to. Yes, the trip will be dangerous, but the reward is worth the risk – for all of us!"

Zoe started crying again.

Oliver didn't understand. "What? What's wrong?"

She slapped his chest. "I'm just happy!"

Adam grinned. "And pregnant, bro. They do that all the time. You'll get used to it."

"So, that's it. We're really doing this?" Oliver asked.

Adam looked at Melissa and she smiled, nodding enthusiastically.

Adam stretched his hand out to the center of the table, palm down. "We're doing it!"

Melissa, with the baby on one shoulder, reached in and squeezed Adam's hand. "We're doing it!"

Aaron and the others followed suit, placing one hand atop the others.

Jurnee crossed her arms. "Hey, wait a minute, will there be other kids there to play with?"

"I would imagine so," Oliver said.

Jurnee nodded approvingly, then glanced over at Louie, who lay quietly on a blanket Zoe had placed near the back door so he could look outside. "And will there be other dogs for Louie to meet?"

Louie's ears perked up and he lifted his head.

"I don't know, but if there's a lot of people, some are likely to have pets too," Zoe said.

Jurnee smiled and stood up in her chair, stretching her tiny arm out. She had to practically crawl onto the table to reach. Finally, she placed her little hand on the pile and shouted, with a sharp nod of finality, "We're in!"

Oliver smiled, his heart full in a way he hadn't expected. As he looked at the faces around the table – tired but hopeful, scared but smiling – he realized leaving this place behind wouldn't be as hard as he'd once thought.

The farmhouse had been their refuge, their fortress against the chaos. But it wasn't home. Home was here, in the laughter that defied the darkness, in the bonds forged through survival and trust. Home was the shared promise that, no matter how uncertain the future, they would face it together.

And that hope – that fragile, resilient hope – was worth every risk.

THE PARASITE FIELD GUIDE

UNREAD APPENDIX ENTRY, PAGE 613

Ethanol Exposure and Larval Longevity in *C. Elegans*
Excerpted from Parasite Biochemistry Quarterly, Vol. 67, 2023
Harwick & Alvanos

A RECENT SCIENTIFIC study examining the life cycle of helminth-class parasites revealed an unexpected relationship between ethanol exposure and longevity in dormant larval stages. When exposed to trace amounts of ethanol – concentrations as low as 0.05 percent in aqueous environments – certain roundworm models demonstrated a significant increase in viability, remaining active or viable well beyond expected decay cycles.

In repeated trials, helminth larvae suspended in low-ethanol solutions not only resisted cellular breakdown, but in some cases displayed accelerated regenerative behavior when introduced to host tissue cultures. Though the mechanism remains unclear, researchers theorize the ethanol may act as a biochemical stabilizer, delaying apoptosis or enabling the parasite to remain in a semi-dormant, yet viable state for extended periods.

This recent study has raised interest in the aging research

community, as approximately half of all genes in helminth models share functional counterparts in humans. While the implications for human longevity remain purely speculative, the potential for ethanol-modulated metabolic pathways is being closely examined.

Further studies are underway to explore these effects in related species.

ACKNOWLEDGMENTS

Book three of the *Wrack and Ruin* series is complete, and what a wild, gut-splattered ride it's been.

With every book, I feel like I'm becoming a stronger writer—but I'm no closer to planning anything in advance. I still begin each story with a blank page and a half-baked idea, trusting that my characters will figure it out before I do and show me the way. I've learned to embrace that chaos, that cliff-leap moment where I throw logic out the window and follow the spark. When it works, it's magic. When it doesn't... well, that's what the backspace key is for.

This time around, Zoe and Oliver took me into deeper waters. I researched parasites, veterinary surgical procedures, chemical reactions, and parasite-induced zombie behavior—just your typical Tuesday night at the keyboard. I packed their story full of tension, heart, and just enough scientific plausibility to make it scary.

And to make it all work seamlessly, I relied on the brilliant Kristen Tate and her team at The Blue Garret. Kristen, thank you for being my go-to sounding board, my editor, my science checker, and my friend. Eight books together—and counting. There is no one I'd rather be doing this with.

Thank you to my early readers—JC, Mandy, Kamy, Dexter, Audrey, and LaRae—who read fast, read smart, and give me the notes I need (and the encouragement I don't always know I do). You're the best kind of co-conspirators.

To my readers—thank you for coming along on this

apocalypse with me. You leave reviews, you recommend these books, and you make it all possible.

And to my wife: thank you for loving me through deadlines and dinner conversations about brain-munching and shotgun blast physics. You are the reason I can do this. And Mom... you never got to read these books, but your love of story still walks with me every time I open a new document. I miss you.

And if you're wondering whether there will be a Book 4...

For Zoe, Oliver, and the others, the road ahead is long and fraught with peril.

Hope is out there but so are the ever-evolving undead.

And trust me... the last place you want to be is...

Adrift Among the Dead.

Oh yes, my friends—we've still got a hell of a lot of story to tell.

—Otto Schafer

ABOUT THE AUTHOR

Otto Schafer grew up exploring the small historic town in central Illinois featured in his award-winning *God Stones* series. If you visit Petersburg, Illinois, you may find locations familiar from his stories. You may even discover, as Otto did, that history has left behind cleverly hidden traces of magic, whispered secrets, and untold treasures.

Otto and his loving wife reside in a quiet log cabin tucked deep in the woods. When he's not writing, he's likely running imaginary supply raids, cataloging worst-case survival scenarios, or binge-watching zombie flicks under the guise of "research."

Currently, Otto is working on the next installment of his popular zombie apocalypse series, *Wrack and Ruin*, continuing to captivate readers with gripping tension, layered characters, and chillingly plausible horrors.

Check out my website: www.ottoschafer.com
Connect with me on social:
Instagram – www.instagram.com/ottoschaferwriter
Facebook – www.facebook.com/ottoschaferauthor
TikTok – www.tiktok.com/@ottoschaferauthor

ALSO BY OTTO SCHAFER

A history hidden from the world. A truth long sought, but better left unfound. Will two teenagers survive the magical secrets they unearth?

Oak Island, Nova Scotia. Breanne Moore blames herself for her mother's tragic death. So when her archaeologist father is invited on an exciting new dig, she's determined to tag along and keep him safe. But as the mystery leads them closer to the island's secret, Breanne's dreams are filled with visions of a strange boy she's never met... and a world of flaming carnage.

Petersburg, Illinois. Sixteen-year-old Garrett Turek is the unofficial leader of his fellow outcasts. Grappling with a volatile relationship with his stepfather, he avoids his home life by helping an eccentric accountant restore a historic Victorian house. But when he and his crew stumble upon a crusty journal in the basement, Garrett uncovers a dead president's key to a secret world-saving society.

As Breanne and her dad seek clues to a treasure hidden deep beneath the surface, they trigger a dangerous magic that should have stayed dormant forever. And when Garrett closes in on the truth, he'll question everything he thought he knew and find trust in a girl from far away as they prepare to battle a dangerous foe.

Can the two would-be heroes fulfill a powerful prophecy and save the planet from destruction?

The Secret Journal is the first book in the sensational God Stones YA contemporary fantasy series. If you like unusual pairings, well-researched historical backgrounds, and heated suspense, then you'll love Otto Schafer's coming-of-age adventure.

Destiny awaits those brave enough to turn the page!

Click here to check it out: God Stones (5 book series) Kindle Edition (amazon.com)

Printed in Great Britain
by Amazon